Sergio Olguín was born in Buenos Aires in 1967. His first work of fiction, *Lanús*, was published in 2002. It was followed by a number of successful novels, including *Oscura monótona sangre* (*Dark Monotonous Blood*), which won the Tusquets Prize in 2009. His books have been translated into German, French and Italian. *The Fragility of Bodies* is his first novel to be translated into English, and is the first in a crime series of three novels featuring journalist Veronica Rosenthal. Sergio Olguin is also a scriptwriter and has been the editor of a number of cultural publications.

THE FRAGILITY OF BODIES

Sergio Olguín

Translated by Miranda France

BITTER LEMON PRESS
LONDON

BITTER LEMON PRESS

First published in the United Kingdom in 2019 by
Bitter Lemon Press, 47 Wilmington Square, London WC1X 0ET

www.bitterlemonpress.com

First published in Spanish as *La fragilidad de los cuerpos*
by Tusquets Editores Argentina, Buenos Aires, 2012

Bitter Lemon Press gratefully acknowledges the financial
assistance of the Arts Council of England

Work published within the framework of "Sur" Translation Support Program
of the Ministry of Foreign Affairs and Worship of the Argentine Republic

Obra editada en el marco del Programa "Sur" de Apoyo a las Traducciones
del Ministerio de Relaciones Exteriores y Culto de la República Argentina

A CIP record for this book is available from the British Library

ISBN 978–1–912242–191
eBook ISBN 978-1-912242-207

Typeset by Tetragon, London
Printed and bound by CPI Group (UK) Ltd, Croydon, CR0 4YY

Supported using public funding by
ARTS COUNCIL
ENGLAND
LOTTERY FUNDED

To Gabriela Franco, Natalia Méndez and Pablo Robledo

The complete truth about someone or something can only be told in a novel.

STEPHEN VIZINCZEY,
THE MAN WITH THE MAGIC TOUCH

[...] structural weaknesses in all fields, considerable fundamental disadvantages: technical and economic backwardness, a society dominated by a minority of exploiters and wastrels, the fragility of bodies, the instability of a rough sensibility, the primitivism of logic as an instrument, the rule of an ideology that preaches scorn for the world and that science is profane. All these traits continue to prevail throughout the entire period that we are considering and, nevertheless, it is a time of awakening, of boom, of progress.

JACQUES LE GOFF,
LE MOYEN AGE

If you want a lover
I'll do anything you ask me to
And if you want another kind of love
I'll wear a mask for you
If you want a partner, take my hand, or
If you want to strike me down in anger
Here I stand
I'm your man.

LEONARD COHEN,
'I'M YOUR MAN'

Contents

Prologue

The building was at least eighty years old. Once it had been the Hotel Arizona, but Alfredo Carranza didn't know that, nor would he have cared. For him it was the place where he went to see the psychologist the company had arranged for him. He didn't know that the building at 1000 Calle Talcahuano provided space not only to psychologists and doctors but also to lawyers, small businesses and prostitutes offering a discreet service from rented apartments. For that reason, the number of casual visitors every day was considerable and security on the door was correspondingly lax, despite the presence of two employees in reception.

Carranza knew exactly where he was going. He had taken the number 39 bus from Constitución to a stop on Marcelo T de Alvear, just as he had twice a week for the last three months. As he turned onto Talcahuano he felt a cold wind hit him full in the face. It was one of those autumn evenings when you start to feel winter in the air, pricking your face. Carranza wore brown chinos, a checked shirt beneath a cream-coloured pullover and on top of everything a raincoat which was arguably too light for such a cold day. A storm was brewing. Flashes of lightning lit up the sky and any minute the downpour would be unleashed.

Carranza walked with his hands in his pockets, his head down, his gaze lost among the broken paving stones and dog shit. In the last few weeks he had familiarized himself pretty well with the building. He had noted the indifference with which visitors were greeted and been heartened by it. He couldn't have coped with anyone catching his eye between the entrance and the therapist's consulting room.

When had his plan for that day begun to take shape? Perhaps it was on the afternoon when he came out of his appointment with no stomach for the street, people, buses, the journey home, his family and his wife's quizzical gaze. She was always trying to read in his expression if the therapy was working.

Carranza crossed the street, keeping a tight hold on the paper that he carried in his left pocket. It was a lined sheet of notepaper which he had taken from his eldest son's folder. He had written on it while locked in the bathroom, before leaving home, in that uneven handwriting that he had never managed to improve, not since primary school. He had folded it four times and stored it carefully in his coat pocket.

Nobody but me is to blame for this.

A few yards before reaching the building, he bumped into someone, a young man who got annoyed and told him to look where he was going. The man looked ready for a fight, but he had to resign himself to continuing on his way, because Carranza apologized without even looking up.

I can't go on any more. I killed them. All four of them.

Carranza entered the building and, as usual, nobody paid him any attention. The receptionist, short, dark-skinned, with a cheerful face, would later not remember having seen him at all, and – if it hadn't been for the security camera at the entrance, the only one in the building – it would have been difficult to ascertain exactly when he came in. The people who took the elevator with him wouldn't remember him either, nor would the lady who, on the fifth floor, was about to get in and asked Carranza if he was going down to the lobby. Nobody saw him enter, or go up in the elevator, or get out on the top floor.

I thought that I could live with this. I thought that I could live with the deaths of the first three. But not with the child's.

There was nobody on the roof. The lowering sky was lit up by periodic lightning and a few drops of rain began to fall. He walked to the edge of the terrace, which was contained by a low wall, not much higher than his waist. Leaning against the wet concrete, he looked down. He saw the cars waiting at a red light and people hurrying along the sidewalk. Some umbrellas moved from one side of the street to the other, like balls in an electronic game.

I knew that day that I would kill him. That it would fall to me. We all knew it. All the way round I was waiting to come across them. At that moment I wanted to kill them. Both of them. Just for being there, for wanting to ruin my life.

There was no time for anything else. It was all decided. He had thought about it a lot and, although he would have done everything in his power to avoid this, there was no other way out of the hell he was living in, the deep pit into which he had fallen years ago.

But when they appeared I didn't want to kill them any more. I wanted everything to be different. I wanted to go back to Sandra and the kids. But I killed him, I killed the little one. I want to say that I'm so sorry, say it to everyone, to his family. Sandra, forgive me. Look after Dani and Mati. Forgive me. I just can't bear it any more.

With difficulty he climbed onto the wall, which the rain had made slippery. He stood up straight, like an Olympic swimmer about to dive. It was simple. All he had to do was step forward and jump. But his legs wouldn't obey him, he couldn't bring himself to take the step. The body rebelled against the mind's plan. Carranza had imagined

13

that something like this might happen, so he reached into the right pocket of his raincoat and took out the pistol he'd brought with him. Then his hand accomplished what his legs had refused to do. He shot himself in the temple and his body fell like a rock, ricocheted off the top floor overhang and finally slammed onto the sidewalk. There were screams of panic, confused movements around the body, the sound of a police siren approaching, another siren, more distant, from an ambulance. And all of it beneath a rain that kept coming harder, crueller and more desolate.

1   *Editorial Meeting*

I

One good reason to pursue a career in magazine journalism is that you don't need to get up early. Sure, every now and then you have to cover some event in the morning, and there are also journalists who work for news agencies or websites on the early shift, but the majority start work after 2 p.m. This was not the main reason Verónica Rosenthal embraced the career when she was barely out of her teens, but it had certainly played a part in her choice.

"Whores and journalists get up late," she would explain sleepily to any friend who called before ten o'clock in the morning.

In fact, it was rare for Verónica to sleep until midday, but it did take her a while to get going. That morning was a case in point. With her eyes half-closed she got into the shower and let the hot water run over her body like the slow caress of a virile lover. She spent less time on the morning shower now that she had cut her hair to shoulder-length – sacrificing the chestnut mane that she used to comb carefully under the water so as not to look like the Lion King's girlfriend. When she finished she wrapped her short hair rather unnecessarily in a towel and looked for a tampon in the cupboard that contained a mad array of perfumes, talcum powders, hair dyes that she had never used and never would, half-finished deodorants, boxes of panty liners, an electric hair remover that didn't work and even an ultrasonic nebulizer that her sister Leticia had lent her and which should have been returned a year ago. There was only one tampon left in the box, plus the one she reckoned was in her bag. She'd stop by the pharmacy on the way to work.

Verónica put on mismatched underwear: multicoloured pants she should never have bought, let alone worn, and an aquamarine bra which was at least more comfortable than the ones she usually wore. She didn't look at herself in the bedroom mirror. Avoiding her reflection was increasingly becoming a habit since she had turned thirty and her body had made its own adjustments to the new decade. She kept promising herself to go to the gym or take up running in Parque Centenario or visit a plastic surgeon, but never got round to any of these, chiefly because she realized that men were much less critical of her than she expected them to be. A pair of tight jeans, a push-up bra or a new bikini easily satisfied them; they didn't seem to notice all the details that worried her. Perhaps this farce could continue for a few more years.

She urgently needed coffee.

She didn't feel well, not because she had her period but because she was still a bit hung-over from the night before. Her friends had come over and stayed until the early hours, drinking every last bottle of wine, smoking all the cigarettes and all the available weed. Verónica contemplated with dismay the disastrous scene in the living room. Her friends had shown some solidarity by collecting all the plates, but there were still coffee cups, glasses, overflowing ashtrays, CDs separated from their cases, books taken from the shelves and strewn about. And presumably they thought they had left her apartment tidy because they had washed up a few plates and thrown away what remained of the quickly improvised supper.

Verónica shook her head as though denying the reality of her living room and went to the kitchen to make a coffee.

Two heaped spoons of Bonafide Fluminense went in the Volturno. She waited for the boiled water to reach the top part of the coffee pot, then poured it into the big cup her sister Daniela had given her. She added a dash of skimmed milk but no sugar. As she drank the coffee she began to feel better. All the same, she took a strong aspirin with a glass of tap water. She decided to tidy up the living room before getting dressed.

II

It had rained all night and the bad weather looked set to continue. She didn't like umbrellas, so Verónica went out into the rain in a black raincoat, a waterproof version of the coat she usually wore on these cold days at the end of autumn. The thought of walking to the number 39 bus stop, then walking three more blocks in the rain at the other end was unappealing. Much better to go to the pharmacy around the corner then take a taxi to the door of *Nuestro Tiempo*.

She had eaten nothing with the coffee and having an empty stomach made her feel nauseous. She didn't want to arrive at work in that state, so she asked the taxi driver to take her to Masamadre, a small wholefoods restaurant three blocks from the newsroom. Any other day she would have gone to Cantina Rondinella or got a takeaway from McDonald's to eat in the kitchen at the magazine, but she felt a pressure to eat healthy food when she had her period.

By the time Verónica arrived at the newsroom it was about two o'clock. *Nuestro Tiempo* was on the third floor of an office block that had been completed two years ago and still had the new and soulless feel of a place where nobody lives.

The magazine had relocated there soon after the building opened and occupied two whole floors: the third for editorial and the second for administration and the publicity, circulation and IT departments. The journalists sat in clusters distributed along the whole length of the third floor, together with designers, photographers and digital retouchers, each division grouped in small cubicles according to their job.

The first person any visitor to *Nuestro Tiempo* saw was Adela, the receptionist, a woman close to retirement age, unlike the majority of people who worked at the magazine, who tended to be under forty. Verónica greeted her with a kiss and Adela handed her an envelope: an invitation to an opening at the Museum of Latin American Art. She should find out if any of the girls were going. She'd get bored on her own.

Verónica sat at a long table with the other members of the Society section: her editor Patricia Beltrán, three other writers and an intern. Everyone, apart from Patricia, was already sitting at a computer when she arrived.

"Where's Patricia?" she asked, putting her coat on a hanger and rearranging her wet hair.

"Don't you have an umbrella?" Roberto Giménez, one of the section writers, looked at her with the expression of someone puzzling over a hieroglyph.

"Don't like them. And Fallaci?" she asked again.

"She's in a meeting with Goicochea and someone else. Remember we've got the editorial meeting in twenty minutes?"

No. She hadn't remembered. She was good at denial: she loathed editorial meetings because they went on for so long and achieved so little. Each writer proposed ideas for an article and discussed or fine-tuned them with Patricia while the others checked their phones, made doodles or stared woefully through the glass wall, as though appealing to a colleague from some other section to come and rescue them. Given that nobody contributed anything to the others' pitches, Verónica thought that it would make more sense for them to meet alone with the editor rather than collectively lose an hour locked in a room. Worse, since none of them had ever had much time to consider their ideas before the meeting (because some pieces had already been finished the day before, because a new article might now be under way, because the best ideas always strike when least expected, because the best content for a current affairs publication was precisely what was happening at that moment), the majority of pitches were just a formality, ideas that would never come to fruition. Some came up week in, week out (the rise in car ownership, the excessive medication of hyperactive kids, the exotic pets of the rich and famous), but nobody ever wrote them, or even acknowledged that these ideas had been on the table thousands of times before. Patricia would put on a face that said this was either an interesting idea or a shit one (depending on her mood that day), then move on to the next item. At the end, Patricia would dish out articles she had thought of herself or which had been sent down from management (Verónica had the impression that executive meetings were much more productive than editorial ones), or she would end up accepting suggestions at some other point in the working day.

Verónica had twenty minutes before the meeting. Usually five were enough to assemble a list of possible articles that would pass muster with her boss. That day, however, she was clean out of inspiration. Perhaps because she had delivered a big piece the day before on a scam run by the medication mafia operating in public hospitals in Buenos Aires. They were using Plan Remediar (the Ministry of Health system which provided free medication to patients) to record deliveries of drugs that never actually made it to the patient.

19

For example, the doctor would prescribe two boxes of an antibiotic. When the patient went to the hospital pharmacy, they would give him or her only one box, claiming that there were no more left. The patient would leave, and the pharmacist would record two units as having been delivered. It wasn't that they had stolen the other box. It had never arrived at the pharmacy because the laboratory hadn't sent it, although it had invoiced for it. Verónica had uncovered the doctors–pharmacists–laboratories nexus without much effort (nobody involved had tried very hard to conceal their part in the crime), and her feature was going to press that night, in the new edition of *Nuestro Tiempo*.

She opened a blank document and typed: *Growing number of vehicles in the city and rest of the country. What can be done about streets and roads collapsing under the sheer weight of cars?* And she stared at the computer screen as if this document itself might suggest an article. That was when Giménez spoke up:

"Ha, this guy had the right idea. Listen up," he said to the others, but none of them looked away from their screens or phones.

Verónica did look up, in fact, but her colleague didn't notice, because he was reading from the screen.

"A railway employee killed himself by jumping from the roof of a building at 1000 Talcahuano. He fell onto the road and the traffic on Talcahuano was disrupted for more than an hour. Isn't that brilliant? Instead of throwing himself under a train to screw over his co-workers, the guy decides to piss off the bus and taxi drivers."

"I bet he killed himself for love," ventured Verónica, looking back at her barely begun document. "The girlfriend or the lover probably lived in that building or the one opposite and he was trying to get her attention. They're all like that."

"All men?" asked Bárbara McDonnell, the journalist who sat opposite her, while typing frenetically.

"Let's just say all suicidal psychopaths," Verónica clarified, not wanting to embark on one of those men-versus-women polemics that Bárbara seemed to relish.

"You're wrong," said Giménez. "This report says the guy left a letter that said he was sorry for the crimes he had committed. Apparently he was a serial killer or something."

A murderer-suicide. A criminal with a guilty conscience. It didn't sound bad. There might not be much for a journalist to get her teeth into, but all the same, the story had potential. Crime wasn't Verónica's speciality, but she had always been drawn to lurid stories. She dreamed of writing a feature on a murderous cannibal or an Umbanda priestess who took the blood of virgin girls.

"Where did you read the thing about the railwayman?"

"It's on the Télam wire."

Verónica read the news agency story and saw a possible article. *Tiempo Nuevo*'s crime correspondent had left a month ago for a national newspaper, so crime stories were now distributed haphazardly among the other journalists. She had a hunch that Giménez would want to write about the suicide himself, and thought she'd sound him out.

"How come there are never articles on suicides?"

"To avoid the copycat effect. Apparently when details are published about how someone committed suicide, it sparks a trend and a load of morons go off to do the same thing. Until recently *La Nación* wouldn't even print the words 'he committed suicide'. You had to put 'he took his own life'."

"What a bunch of idiots. So, are you thinking of pitching a piece on this guy? The wire story is quite skimpy."

"No. Deaths are tiring."

"I might do something, then. Even if only to write 'he committed suicide'."

That was Giménez out of the way. She read the story again. What was it in these twenty lines that particularly caught her eye? Perhaps it was the fragment of the letter they had reproduced. It was addressed neither to his family nor to a judge and yet it asked forgiveness for his crimes, specifically for the death of a child. So was the letter a confession, or an explanation?

Patricia Beltrán came out of Management with the newsroom secretary. She went over to where the journalists sat and asked them to go to the meeting room. Verónica quickly typed up a summary of the wire story and printed the page along with her other article suggestion. With any luck, she wouldn't have to do that piece on the exponential growth of car ownership in Argentina.

III

Verónica came out of the editorial meeting with a headache and took an aspirin from the packet she kept in her desk drawer. Patricia had listened to the pitches and handed out articles. She wanted Verónica to write a piece on the rising popularity of home births.

"My grandmother gave birth to my mother in the middle of a field," said Patricia. "I thought that humanity had advanced since then, but it seems that some rich girls want to go back to the dark ages."

Verónica didn't dislike the idea, although the subject of motherhood was uninteresting to her. It was something that might happen to her one day, in a few centuries. But the thought of giving birth in her bedroom with the help of a midwife horrified her as much as it did her editor.

She had already agreed to hunt down some prospective New Age mothers when Patricia looked at her page of notes and said:

"Hmm, not a single crime story. Anyone got anything?"

Since nobody else replied, Verónica spoke up.

"A railway worker committed suicide last night."

"We don't cover suicides unless it's someone famous."

"The man left a note saying that he was killing himself because he couldn't live with the guilt of having committed murders."

"So he was an unconvicted murderer? Who had he killed?"

"That seems to be the case. Télam hasn't got much yet, but apparently there was a child among his victims."

"Right, now you're talking. If you can find out more this could be a double-page spread."

"Shall I go with the guilt-ridden suicide, or the stupid expectant mothers?"

"Start with the suicide."

First she needed to get hold of the letter so that she could examine it. It shouldn't be difficult to get a copy. Lawyers and judges were generous with journalists, so long as it wasn't a sensitive case, and even then they were often willing to share evidence, witness statements or whatever. Any time a judge or lawyer put up objections, Verónica brandished her surname: Rosenthal. When she introduced herself this way it was rare for a member of the judiciary not to ask:

"Any connection with Aarón Rosenthal?"

And she, with a carefully calibrated tone of resignation, would admit:

"His youngest daughter."

Often they had been students of her father, or they had had dealings with the Rosenthal firm in connection with some lawsuit, or there would be some other link of which she was unaware and which she did not wish to know about.

The agency story named Pablo Romanín as the judge in the case. She already knew him from some other trial. He was in his late fifties, sported a fake tan and looked more like a yuppie than a judge. Nevertheless, he seemed to take his work seriously. She looked up Dr Romanín's mobile number and called him. The irascible tone with which he answered changed entirely when she told him who she was.

"My wife always buys *Nuestro Tiempo*. How's the magazine going? You see it everywhere."

"It's going pretty well. Doctor, I'm calling you about a case that was heard in your court. The one concerning the railway worker who killed himself by jumping from a building on Calle Talcahuano."

"Ah yes, a colleague of yours from Télam came to see me this morning."

"Right, they put out a wire story. I'd love to get a look at the letter."

"No problem. I'll ask someone to email it to you. You'll get it last thing today or first thing tomorrow."

"Is anything known about the crimes referred to in the letter?"

"We're just looking into that at the moment. Why don't you call me tomorrow? I'm sure I'll have more news then."

"If you don't mind, I'd rather come by your office, just to make sure I'm getting the full picture."

The judge sent his regards to her father before ending the conversation. Until she got hold of the letter and a little more information from the judge, Verónica didn't have much to do. She stayed on in the newsroom for a couple of hours, sending emails, and later on had a meeting with a journalist from the Politics section, who was considering investigating further links between the Ministry of Health and the medication scam in public hospitals. Verónica didn't tell him that she had already checked out all the possible ramifications of the case and not found anything. She gave him the telephone numbers and email addresses of the sources which he thought could be useful to him and which she had already dismissed as unhelpful. An experienced journalist would have realized that, if Verónica had found anything worth pursuing, she would be writing a piece about it herself. But the Politics editor – who was also a deputy editor – was too young for his position and very wet behind the ears. What he lacked in pretension, he made up for with arrogance. Verónica couldn't stand him, for professional reasons as well as personal ones.

It was six o'clock in the evening by the time she had finished with everything. Outside it was dark and the rain was relentless. She called a radio taxi. She wanted to see the building from which the suicidal man had jumped.

IV

Twenty-four hours after Alfredo Carranza had fallen into the void, there was no evidence of the event at 1000 Calle Talcahuano. It was as though the rain had washed away all traces of his death, for the neighbours' peace of mind. Verónica studied the building's facade from the opposite sidewalk and thought it particularly grim. A good building to jump from, she thought. The front door was open, which was quite unusual in Buenos Aires.

Verónica crossed the road and entered the old luxury hotel, now converted into offices and apartments for professionals. There were two people in the lobby: an older man who seemed to be monitoring those who came in without intercepting any of them, and a young receptionist who was talking on the phone. Verónica approached the girl and waited until she had stopped speaking.

"Sorry to bother you – have you got a minute?"

She explained that she was a journalist and that she was trying to find out more about the person who had jumped from the roof the previous evening. Like most people in such circumstances, the girl was happy to talk to the press. But unfortunately she didn't know very much. She said that nobody in the building seemed particularly upset. The girl wanted to talk, to provide some helpful detail. She told Verónica that she hadn't seen the body – she wasn't brave enough – but the doorman had. He was the other person working in reception but, apart from a horror-movie description of the body dashed onto the sidewalk, he had nothing useful to contribute. Verónica asked if she could go onto the roof and was told that she couldn't, that the police had cordoned off the area.

By the time Verónica left the building the rain had stopped. She had learned nothing useful about Carranza. She felt as though she were at the start of something but was moving more by instinct than in response to any particular lead. She didn't even have a copy of the letter. At this stage, it was better to be patient and wait until the next day, when she would meet Judge Romanín.

Her mouth was dry. She wanted a drink. She was close to Milion, but didn't relish the thought of running into some of the regulars (including an ex, suitors of various ages and marital statuses and acquaintances whose status varied, depending on what they were drinking and who they hoped to seduce that night). And if she went to one of the night-clubs in El Bajo, like La Cigale or Dadá, she'd be pestered by those creeps who jump on any girl who happens to be alone. She decided to walk down Avenida Córdoba as far as Calle Florida and go to Claridge. At least nobody would bother her there. She liked the bar in Claridge because you always saw little old ladies having tea alongside provincial businessmen pouring alcohol down their throats as a coping mechanism for life in the capital. Anyone at Claridge under the age of forty could be taken for a child. And she was still a long way off forty. She was barely into her thirties and still had the best part of a decade to enjoy feeling like a child at Claridge.

She sat on one of the stools at the empty bar.

"A double Jim Beam with ice."

An argument in favour of drinking alone was not having to defend her preference for bourbon over Scotch, and especially not having to endure the look of disgust on her friends' faces when she gave her order. They, meanwhile, would be asking for a Sex on the Beach or a second-rate mojito made with mint, or any other cocktail which they could preface with the word 'frozen'. The disadvantage was the lack of a friend to chat to while she sipped her drink and gazed at the many different kinds of bottle that lined the shelves against the back of the bar. She called Paula. Her friend answered, then immediately started shouting at someone else.

"Juanfra didn't want to have a bath," she explained. "But it's fine. He's in the bath now. Think hard before you decide to have children."

"It's not in my immediate plans."

"One can never be sure with you. What news of the Bengali Sailor?"

Verónica stirred the ice cubes in her bourbon with one finger. Her friends had a habit of not naming men in conversation unless the relationship had become formal. So long as they were lovers, occasional boyfriends or guys who they liked but who didn't give them the time of day, they were given a nickname based on some absurdly exaggerated characteristic. A redhead might be called Fire Lord, a doctor Dr House, a premature ejaculator Mr Speedy and a rock musician Charly García, even if he looked nothing like that Argentine icon. The Bengali Sailor (whose name came from a song by Los Abuelos de la Nada) was in fact quite a successful architect who had a really impressive yacht that he had taken her out on as far as the Uruguayan coast. Every time they had had sex it had been on board the boat, which had led her friends to draw all kinds of conclusions about his needs, limitations, fetishes and fantasies. It was true that her relationship with the Bengali Sailor (who for a short time had been known as Sandokan after Salgari's fictional pirate but who was better suited to the epithet Paula had given him) had turned into something habitual for Verónica. At one point they had seen each other most weeks. But for a month now he hadn't called, emailed or texted. She had left a message on his phone and sent him an email. But nothing.

"He's shipwrecked. He drowned before reaching Carmelo."

"So, are you upset?"

She stirred the ice cubes in her glass again, then dried her finger on a paper napkin. She would have liked to smoke a cigarette, but it was forbidden in the bar. Verónica hated not being able to smoke in bars.

"I liked the boat, for sure. But if the best he can do is send the odd email or make an occasional phone call, it's his loss. The guy can't commit."

She liked talking to her friends, especially to Paula. It wasn't the first time she had gone to a bar and called one of them up. Their conversation might be interrupted if the friend in question had to stop to pay a taxi driver or help a child with some task or attend to an inconvenient boss.

They chatted for half an hour. By then the glass was empty. Verónica thought of asking for another Jim Beam but decided to go home instead, to see if the suicide note had come through. She really needed to buy a phone that would allow her to check emails wherever she was.

V

By the time she set off for the Palace of Justice at Tribunales the next morning, Verónica had already read the railwayman's letter – sent to her in the early hours by an assistant of Judge Romanín – several times. The letter had been typed up and saved as a Word file. She would need to get a look at the original, Verónica thought, to see the man's handwriting and to study the marks on the paper, see if there were any emphasized words, if his hand had shaken on writing a particular phrase or if his writing had any other particular characteristics.

Basically the letter was a confession. Carranza said that he had killed four people, one of them a child. He asked for forgiveness from his family and from the victims. He seemed to linger most on the death of the child, as though the other deaths were less important, or this death had broken something. A pact with accomplices? Were the other deaths in some sense natural, and the child's a murder that defied logic? What kind of logic, then?

She reached the Tribunales law courts early. It was an area of Buenos Aires she knew well: she had gone to high school at Instituto Libre de Segunda Enseñanza, almost opposite the Palace of Justice, and her father's law practice had been on Tucumán since before she was born; it was a solemn-looking office which she had sometimes visited with her mother and sisters before or after going to the cinema. She knew every bar in the area, every bus stop, every bookshop, every stall in the book market in the Plaza Lavalle, every tree in that square. She would never have claimed she was brought up in Tribunales, but she had certainly spent many of the days of her childhood and adolescence in and around its buildings.

By contrast, the Palace of Justice was still a mystery to her, even though she had often needed to go there in search of information. In the past it had been the place where her father waged epic battles, like a prince in his enemy's castle. At least that was how she had imagined it, especially when her father disappeared for weeks, physically or mentally. At those times, even when he was at home, he was like a kind of ghost who spoke on the phone or received guests in the library. Every now and then he would return to normal life, smiling and triumphant. She couldn't remember ever seeing him defeated. All the city's lawyers converged in that building full of stairs and doors leading nowhere, an example of a kind of demented architecture rarely seen in Buenos Aires. Now she too was climbing the marble stairs towards the office of Judge Romanín, and every corridor filled with lawyers and clients revived that sense of mystery she had felt as a child about the castle in which she sometimes lost her father.

After various twists and turns she arrived at Romanín's criminal courtroom. The judge had not yet arrived, but five minutes later he appeared. He apologized for the delay, gave some instructions to his staff and asked for two coffees. He ushered her into his office. For all the efforts he made to stay young, Romanín was an older man now, not far off retirement. Verónica didn't know exactly how he was connected to her father, but from the way he spoke, she gathered that there was some affection between them. He even knew that her mother had died five years ago.

"Did you receive a copy of the dead man's letter?"

"Yes, thank you, Doctor, I got it this morning."

"The man clearly wanted to commit suicide. He shot himself in the temple, then fell from the roof."

"There's no possibility he was coerced into going to the building's edge and shot there?"

"No. The expert evidence all points to him holding the gun in his right hand. There were also traces of gunshot residue. There's nothing to suggest he had any enemies."

"In the letter he talks about four murders. Is anything known about those?"

The judge sprawled in his chair and smiled at her.

"If you're asking because you believe the deceased was murdered, I'm afraid I have to disappoint you."

He searched among the files on his desk, taking off his glasses to see better close-up. He read something in an incomprehensible whisper, put the folder down, put his glasses back on and continued:

"The poor man hadn't killed anyone. Bah, *sensu stricto* he had, but no judge would ever have convicted him, even though he was under arrest for a few hours. Carranza was a train driver on the Sarmiento railway. And he ran over four people. On different occasions, over a period of three years."

"You mean the four deaths he refers to in his letter were the result of train accidents?"

"Suicides, misadventure. Accidents – yes. I have the worksheets here provided by Trenes de Buenos Aires, the concession holder, where the four fatal incidents are recorded."

"Is one a child?"

"Exactly. Yes, a *nomen nescio*, a John Doe. It was never possible to identify the body, and nobody came forward to claim it."

They both fell silent. Verónica tried to fit this new information into the scenario she had been mentally building.

"So Carranza killed himself because he ran over four people in separate accidents."

"Apparently the engine drivers get quite traumatized. In fact, here's an interesting detail for you: that man fell from the building where he used to see his psychologist. He had been sent for therapy by the company. We spoke to the psychotherapist and, even allowing for patient confidentiality, he told us everything we needed to know: Carranza had been shaken by the accidents, and perhaps that sparked a suicidal tendency that was already there."

"I can see it must be a terrifying experience to run someone over with a train, but would that actually lead you to take your own life?"

"Look, Verónica, we judge the facts. And very often the intentions. But, to be frank with you, we know very little about the real reasons that lead people to become criminals, to kill or to commit suicide. That's the job of psychologists and people like you – journalists."

"Journalists," Verónica repeated. "Once upon a time, poets were the ones who knew most about the heart's secrets. Things have come to a pretty pass if we're relying on psychologists and journalists now."

She asked if she could see the original letter. The judge found it in his folder and passed it to her. A shiver ran down her spine. On this page, torn from an exercise book, in this uneven handwriting, the dead man ceased to be an abstract entity and became a real person. Death was in these written words much more than it was in a corpse.

She handed him back the letter and had stood up to say goodbye when a doubt occurred to her.

"Just one other thing: has all this information been corroborated by the family?"

"We've spoken to his wife. In cases like this the family is

very stricken. She told us that she had imagined something like this could happen and that she couldn't forgive herself for not having done more to prevent it. You see, guilt is like an oil stain transferred from one body to the next: someone jumps in front of a train – for whatever reason – triggering guilt in the driver that in turn leads him to suicide, which then makes a loved one feel guilty for not taking enough precautions. And I'm sure that she did take them, that the driver did what he could with the train, that the first suicide should have given life another chance. What can one say?…I don't want to get maudlin."

If anyone had asked Verónica which streets she walked down in the half hour following her interview with Romanín, she would have struggled to reconstruct the route. Her mind was completely focussed on the new information the judge had given her. Somehow, though, she had ended up in a bar on Avenida de Mayo, where she was now reading the suicide note yet again. There were so many loose ends in the confession that it was impossible to be satisfied with Romanín's explanation. Judges – as she had once said during an argument with her father (a few years ago now, when they still argued about such things) – don't want to deliver justice but to close cases. If the clues and evidence pointed to the guilt or innocence of the accused, they acted accordingly. They never dwelt on or worried about the deeper causes, about the motives that underlay what was self-evident. That was why, as Verónica told her father, she preferred being a journalist: she crossed the line at which the judges stopped. The conscience of a magistrate – she had declared passionately, mindful of her father's growing anger – is happy with the most superficial forms of justice.

And Romanín struck Verónica as one of those judges who are happy with little. A guy shoots himself and jumps from a rooftop. Suicide. Case closed. Bring out the next one.

Carranza had committed suicide, no doubt about that. He had killed four people while driving his train. He was getting therapy for the trauma those accidents had caused him. Going on what the letter said, he had been able to deal with the first three deaths, those of the adults, but not the last, the child's. And that was the point where the letter started to reveal more than what was written.

I knew that day that I would kill him. How could Carranza have known that he was going to run the child down? Or was this simply a way of expressing himself? A kind of premonition?

That it would fall to me. To him and not to someone else? Would it fall to him by chance, or for some reason? What was that reason, if there was one?

We all knew it. The change from singular to plural struck Verónica as the clearest sign that this was more than a simple suicide. And that plural implied various people. Who? If they all knew, it was not a premonition but a foregone conclusion. And if they had known that this would happen, why had they not tried to prevent it?

All the way round I was waiting to come across them. Another troubling plural. He had run over a child who was not alone. How had the other one escaped injury? Or had someone pushed the child under the train? If so, then there was a criminal involved who was not the driver. Did Carranza know him? Had there been some sort of arrangement between them?

At that moment I wanted to kill them. Both of them. Just for being there, for wanting to ruin my life. But when they appeared I didn't want to kill them any more. That abrupt change in mood reminded Verónica of something that had happened recently: she had never run over anyone, but a little while ago a motorcyclist had crossed in front of the car her sister Leticia had lent her. Her first reaction had been terror at the thought of crashing into someone but afterwards, after frantically applying the brakes to avoid an accident, she had felt a dreadful desire to run over that idiot in the helmet, who was still progressing down Avenida Córdoba without a care in the world. Perhaps that was what had happened to Carranza. He felt like killing because he had experienced the terror of being in a position to kill.

There were too many doubts to resolve alone. She called her editor. She would see her at the magazine anyway, but this was something that couldn't wait until the afternoon. Besides, she knew that Patricia didn't mind being called at any time if it was about work.

"I'm literally as lost as the characters in *Lost*," she replied when Patricia asked her how the investigation was going.

"So – have crimes been committed here, or not?"

"Judge Romanín says not. Carranza ran over four people in separate accidents. Three men and a boy."

"I figured as much yesterday when you suggested the piece."

It annoyed her that her editor should be a step ahead of the rest of them, the journalistic pack.

"Why didn't you say anything, then?"

"Because figuring something isn't the same as knowing it. A basic principle, not much taught in journalism schools."

"Something in that letter doesn't add up – lots of things don't. There's something fishy about it, Pato. I don't know what, but there's definitely something going on."

"So I won't cross off the piece for this week?"

"Cross it off for this week, definitely, but I'm going to keep investigating. I need to find a way in."

"Have you worked out what to do next?"

"I need to find out more about the people who died. And speak to someone from Trenes de Buenos Aires."

"Over what period of time did he run over the four people?"

"Three years."

"If I ran over someone in my car I'd never drive again."

"A person has to work."

"An employee kills four people in three years and the company lets him keep working in that capacity? It'd be good to find out if there are other train drivers in the same situation. How many deaths are there a year? What's the protocol when a driver runs over someone?"

"I don't think that's the kind of information the PR person at TBA is going to give me."

"You mean the spokesperson. That kind of company has a spokesperson, just like ministries."

"Is a spokesperson any more likely to be helpful?"

"No. But first you should try to resolve the doubts you have about the letter. Start with the driver's family. Try to speak to someone close to him, and perhaps they'll suggest a way into the company."

Patricia always knew which way a journalist should go. Where others were myopic – or completely blind – she saw clearly. It was a quality that inspired both admiration and irritation in Verónica, because she couldn't help feeling that she would have reached the same conclusion five minutes later. But Pato always got there first. Like a good chess player, she thought one or several moves ahead.

Verónica called Judge Romanín on his mobile phone, apologizing for bothering him again.

"Do you happen to know where Carranza's wake is?"

"It's already finished. He must be on his way to the cemetery in Avellaneda by now. They were going to bury him at midday."

She paid for the coffee, went outside and hailed a taxi. With any luck she could get to the funeral before the mourners dispersed.

VI

Unfortunately, she didn't know where in Avellaneda the cemetery was. Her knowledge of that area was limited to the home grounds of Independiente and Racing, the train station, the street leading to the soccer grounds, Calle Alsina and Avenida Mitre. It seemed like a bad idea to arrive at the cemetery in a taxi from the capital: it would attract too much attention. So she asked the taxi driver to take her as far as 500 Avenida Mitre (wherever that was – she hoped it existed).

On the way she called her sister Daniela. They had arranged to have lunch together, but it was going to be impossible to get there on time. She felt a little guilty cancelling it, because she very often had to call off arrangements with her sisters. It was bad luck that something came up every time they were due to meet. They thought she was making excuses. Verónica didn't want to believe that this was symptomatic of some phobia brought on by family life.

Soon after they had crossed the Pueyrredón bridge and were on Avenida Belgrano, Verónica spotted a minicab company and asked the taxi driver to drop her there. It would be better to continue the journey in a local cab.

This second driver took her right to the information office, inside the cemetery itself. There she found out that Carranza's interment must already be under way, a few hundred yards away. She asked the driver to wait for her and set off alone to find the plot where she had been told the mourners would be. The previous days' rain had left puddles on the path and there was a smell of damp earth. If she disregarded the tombs around her, she felt as though she were walking through a muddy field.

In the distance she saw a sizeable group of people standing in the place to which she had been directed. She walked towards them without hurrying. There must have been about thirty people, perhaps more. She had never been good at calculating the number of people present at any event. Verónica stood at the back of the group, hoping to seem like a member of the funeral party, not a busybody. Her arrival had coincided with the moment the coffin was lowered into the grave. The mourners pressed forward to throw handfuls of earth onto the coffin. The sound of loud sobbing helped her to pick out the people who must be Carranza's wife and children: the three of them clinging together as a single body, as though wrapped in a magnetic cape that prevented anyone else from joining the embrace or consoling them. There was also a woman who walked up to the grave, threw in a handful of dirt and stood staring into it as though waiting for something to happen, for reality to change and for the dead man to emerge from the grave. Someone approached the woman, gently took her by the shoulders and led her away. To one side of the grave was a group of unaccompanied men: they must be Carranza's fellow workers. She counted them, to be sure of the number: nine. They looked serious, neither crying nor consoling each other. Verónica wished that she had been present when the cortège arrived, to see which of his colleagues had carried the coffin from the hearse to the grave. She tried to make out gestures, anything to help her deduce which of the men was a greater friend of Carranza's than the others. But there was nothing. They were a block, distinct from the rest of the mourners, a separate group within the funeral party. For a moment it seemed to her that one of them stood out from the rest. She kept watching him, but she didn't see anything more to back up her hunch.

The burial ceremony was over. The people returned to their cars. The co-workers made for the exit. Verónica was thinking of going up to talk to them when she heard an older man say to the elderly lady who was with him:

"Did you give your condolences to the sister?"

"To whom?" asked the woman, louder. She must be a little deaf.

"To Carina, Alfredo's sister."

The old couple walked towards the woman who had stood longer than usual beside the grave. Verónica followed them.

Both of them greeted the woman, who must have been about forty-five. She thanked them, looking dazed, and the couple moved to one side. Verónica walked up to the woman then and gave her a kiss, as though she too had been a friend of the dead man. The woman must have been greeted in similar fashion by many people she didn't know that day.

"Carina, forgive me for bothering you at such an awful time."

"Were you a friend of Alfredo?"

"No, I'm a journalist. I don't want to intrude, but I wondered if I could talk to you about your brother at some point."

The woman gave her a sullen look. A man started walking towards them.

"My brother committed suicide. There's nothing else to say."

The man took Carina gently by the arm and told her that he would walk her to the car, which was parked about fifty yards away. Carina let herself be led. Verónica kept pace with them both.

"Your brother suffered a great deal. And the company he worked for did nothing for him."

"They paid for a psychiatrist or something," said Carina, without looking at her.

"I believe that the company is responsible for what happened to your brother." She took the woman's hand and placed her business card in it. "Here's my number. Please call me."

Carina nodded briefly, either in agreement or as a way of asking her to go away, which Verónica did immediately. She doubted that Carina would call, but if she did not do so in the next few days, she would think of another way to find her.

VII

The weekend was uneventful. On Friday night she went to Bar Martataka, knowing that some of her friends would be there. By the time she arrived, Alma, Marian, The Other Verónica and Pili, sometimes known as Spanish Pili, were already there. Absent were Paula – who had to look after her son – and some girls who were variously on holiday, in relationships or sitting at home depressed, eating chocolate and binge-watching box sets.

She was in need of her friends and their debauchery, of their light-hearted, boastful and mercilessly cynical conversation about the rest of humanity, especially the men who passed through their lives or paraded themselves in the bar that night. A few tables away was a group of men she knew. In fact, in terms of age and profession, this coterie was quite similar to theirs. It included the odd journalist, a writer supporting himself with workshops, a psychologist and a philosophy teacher. What with various comings and goings, and trips outside to smoke, by around 11 p.m. half the girls' group had moved over to the boys' table, and vice versa. Verónica had ended up on the same table as the writer who lived off his workshops. He was telling her she ought to write fiction.

"Whenever I read your pieces I notice how well written they are. You've got such a good style – I think you should write novels or short stories. Don't you agree?"

"Well, such a forthright observation doesn't leave me much room to think about it."

"Seriously. You're very good. And hot. You're very hot. Let's make a deal," the writer continued. "I give you a grant to come to my workshop and you —"

"And I what?"

"You dedicate your first novel to me."

This game of cat and mouse went on for a while. Verónica found the writer amusing, but she hadn't yet put him to the test. For some time now, whenever she was in two minds whether or not to go to bed with a guy, she tried an experiment (if she was sure, she didn't make him undergo any kind of intellectual assessment, needless to say). The test consisted in seeing if they had anything in common: the same taste, the same knowledge about something, the same passion for something trivial. On such flimsy evidence was she willing to persuade herself of a man's virtues. For example, if she said, "Navigating is necessary," the man should know that this was a line from the poem by Fernando Pessoa and reply, "Living is not necessary." It was like a password, a more interesting way to admit someone into her life. Once, in Spain, driving through Murcia with a Spanish colleague, she saw a road sign that said JAEN 70 KILOMETRES and murmured to herself: "Andaluces of Jaén" and the journalist immediately recognized the line from Miguel Hernández, and in the same tone, continued "haughty olive growers". She fell in love with him on the spot. And now the writer who lived off his workshops was working hard to get her out of that bar and take her somewhere else. At that moment "Friday Night, Saturday Morning", the Nouvelle Vague version, was playing in the bar. She would make it easy for him. When the chorus started, she made him stop talking and said, translating the words of the song into Spanish:

"I go out on Friday night and I come home on Saturday morning."

"Are you inviting me to spend the night with you?"

No, no, no. There had been so many possibilities for him: he could have followed the lyrics in English and realized that she was translating them. He could have recognized the band and said, "so you like Nouvelle Vague." She would even have accepted him expressing a preference for the original version by The Specials. The writer took none of these options. And nothing he said from that moment on earned him a single point. Verónica ended up going home in a taxi with Marian and Spanish Pili.

VIII

On Sunday night Carina called her. It was a short conversation. She suggested they meet on Monday morning at her home, in Crucecita, which Verónica understood to be a district of Avellaneda.

She arrived at the house on Calle General Lemos a little before eleven o'clock and asked the taxi driver to wait for her. The house was typical of those in Greater Buenos Aires: it had a ground floor that could be used as a workshop or some other business, with living space above it. Carina invited her to come upstairs and led her into a sitting room that must not have changed for twenty years, although doubtless it had become increasingly cluttered over time, with photos, souvenirs, the odd cuddly toy and some trophies which Verónica found herself studying.

"Tae kwon do," said Carina, seeing her interest. "My son is an associated member."

"How old is your son?"

"Fifteen."

They sat down in armchairs separated by a glass coffee table. Carina was not just visibly tense, she seemed subdued, too. It was hard to tell whether that was because of her brother's death or if a lack of vitality was part of her personality. Verónica explained why she wanted to talk about her brother. She told Carina that she had read his letter and that she believed his suicide was a consequence of the situations and pressures suffered by drivers in his profession. That her brother should have been protected by the company, that they should not have let him be exposed to so many accidents.

"Alfredo was in a really bad way after the first one," said Carina. "He used to be a cheerful guy, he liked to have a laugh. But after he ran over that man who had thrown himself in front of the train, he changed completely."

"Was that not long after he had started working on the Sarmiento line?"

"He'd been a driver for just over a year. Before that he was in the Roca division, but in the workshops."

"And after that first accident he didn't think of going back to the workshops, or something similar?"

"He said that drivers earned more money than non-specialist mechanics like him. He had a family to support."

"I imagine that with each successive accident his morale got worse."

"The company assigned him a psychologist. They treated him as though he were mad when what he felt was an unending sadness."

"Has anyone from the company been in touch with the family?"

"I think somebody contacted my sister-in-law. But what could they say when they were the ones who had forced him to keep driving those trains?"

"According to the letter, it was after the fourth accident, when he hit the child, that he hit rock bottom."

"Well, what would you expect? He never spoke about it, but my husband and I saw him that night. We went to the hospital with my sister-in-law, because he had been taken there in a state of shock. He was completely out of it, poor guy."

"He had anticipated the possibility of the accident with the boy – do you know why?"

"No, but my sister-in-law told me that he had been very anxious towards the end of his life."

"As if he knew what was going to happen."

"Alfredo had really lost his way by then. Not even his friends from the railway could reassure him. Much less that doctor they sent him to."

"Did he have good friends at the Sarmiento railway?"

"He had a lot of friends from work, but only one he was close to, I think. Hang on a minute."

She went over to a small table in a corner of the room and returned with a framed photograph. It showed a group of men, before or after a soccer match. They were all wearing shorts, posing with the goalposts visible in the background. Some smiled. Carranza looked seriously at the camera.

"Here he is with the other drivers. This one" – she pointed at one of the men – "is his friend, Lucio."

"He was at the funeral, wasn't he?" Verónica said, taking the photo from her.

"I think they all were."

Studying the picture, Verónica felt something strange. Months later she would identify this as a premonition of all the things that were going to happen to her. But at that moment this slight shiver came merely as confirmation that her instincts in the cemetery had been correct: she had identified the right person.

"Do you have a telephone number for his friend?"

Carina got up to fetch a notebook that was lying on the stereo. Verónica traced with a finger the face of the friend in the photograph.

"What did you say his name was?"

"Lucio. Lucio Valrossa."

"Lucio," she whispered, not knowing that it was a name she was to repeat so many times, and in so many different ways.

Carina passed her the telephone number. They spoke for a little while longer, then Verónica left the grieving woman alone with her brother's shadow.

2 *Two Brave Boys*

I

His name was Cristian, but people called him Peque, or El Peque, and two months ago he had turned ten. They called him that because he had been very little – *pequeño* in Spanish – when he joined the gang of friends, so little, in fact, that he could not now remember who had given him the nickname. It was his street name, coined by the boys who used to gather on the corner of Zelarrayán and Cañada de Gómez, but now he was El Peque to everyone, apart from his mother, who still called him by the name with which he had been baptized. Even his two younger brothers called him El Peque, and he didn't turn around if someone other than his mother said "Cristian". So when he went to join the Spring Breezes neighbourhood club and they asked for his name, he said "El Peque".

"Your full name," said the woman in charge of filling out forms.

"Cristian Arrúa, El Peque," he said, and that was how he was registered at the club.

El Peque had learned to play soccer with the boys from his block and honed his art in the school of hard kicks. He had learned to duck and dive, dodging the assaults on his knees and ankles. He knew that he was good at not flinching, and he learned how to hit back, too. In time, he became the one using his strength to dominate in the streets and squares. He had been on the receiving end of a lot of rough treatment and was ready to return all of it. To kids of any size. El Peque could kick, and hard.

At ten years old he already knew that he would never be a skilful midfielder or a dazzling goalkeeper; but he also knew that he could be an unbeatable defender, a leader who could protect his teammates when the game turned dirty and violent. He had learned to dodge kicks and to dole out punches when the occasion called for it. All the boys in the neighbourhood wanted him on their team.

Every so often they played in a park in Ramos Mejía against boys from other neighbourhoods. Getting to the park meant walking twenty blocks and sometimes they had to wait an hour to play a game, but it was worth it. There were actual goalposts and the field was much bigger than what could be recreated on the streets of his barrio, or the Plaza de Santa Cruz. Once, on the biggest field, they had played eleven-a-side, just like professional soccer players.

It was in the park in Ramos Mejía that El Peque first met Rivero. The guy was watching them play and came up to him at the end of a game. He congratulated him and told him that he reminded him of another player, who must have been from a different time, because El Peque didn't recognize the name. Rivero told him that he managed the junior teams at Spring Breezes, a youth soccer club that was nearby, in Lugano itself. He said that he would love El Peque to come and play for the club. That he should go along with his parents the following Thursday at six o'clock.

"What did that guy want?" Dientes asked him. His nickname was actually Dientes de Rata – "Rat's Teeth" – but for more than a year he had been beating up anyone who called him that, so now the boys from the barrio had shortened it to "Teeth".

"He wants to take me to play for a club, Spring Breezes."

"And who's ever heard of them? They're not even in the D league."

"I still want to go."

"Go then, dickhead."

"But he said I have to go with my folks. My dad's God knows where. And my mum will throw a fit if I ask her to take me to the club."

"Where is it?"

El Peque showed him the card that Rivero had given him.

"Ah, I know that street. It's really close. I'll take you. I'll tell them you're an orphan and I'm your older brother."

Dientes was two years older than El Peque and exactly the same height. El Peque thought that sounded like a great idea, too.

II

Dientes and Peque lived in the same building. It was a tenement house, in fact, shared by four families: there was Dientes' family – his mother was the landlady – and El Peque's, as well as an older lady with her daughter and eleven-year-old granddaughter, and a single man. El Peque's mother had two rooms and shared the bathroom with the other two families, whereas Dientes' family had a bathroom to themselves. And a real kitchen, unlike El Peque's, which was incorporated into the main room. The house, which was on two floors, also had two internal courtyards and two roof terraces. The smaller of these terraces was Dientes and El Peque's favourite place.

The boys had one thing in common: neither of them knew much about their fathers. El Peque's lived in Corrientes and they hadn't seen him since moving to Buenos Aires. Dientes' father had died a few years ago. El Peque had heard from some gossipy neighbour or another that Dientes' father had been riddled with bullets by a gang of men who hated him. Why they hated him and had killed him he didn't know, and he had never felt able to ask his friend.

Dientes remembered perfectly the day, seven years previously, when El Peque had arrived at the house with his mother, who was pregnant with one baby and holding another. He also had two siblings, but they were older. One had already left home, while his fifteen-year-old sister never acknowledged his presence unless it was to shove him, shout at him or pull his hair. His grandmother also lived with them, but she was always ill. Sometimes they had visits from his older brother, his godfathers and some uncles who lived far away. Nobody ever visited El Peque's family, though.

At home they didn't call him Dientes, but Kevin, which was his real name. His mother rented out rooms, while El Peque's was a cleaner. They both went to the same school in the afternoons. In the mornings Dientes' sister was supposed to look after them, but in fact the one making sure that nothing disastrous happened to them was Dientes' mother.

After lunch, the five of them set off for school, which was ten blocks away: El Peque and his siblings, Dientes, and Dientes' sister, who went to the high school on the same block. The teenager went with them because her mother insisted on it, but as soon as they had rounded the first corner she crossed the road so that she didn't have to walk with them. After school they came home without Dientes' sister, who walked back with her friends. The four children took their time on the return journey. Sometimes they played soccer or stopped to watch some older children play a game, or they swapped cards or simply took a circuitous route to make the walk home longer. The one thing El Peque couldn't do was let his brothers out of his sight. If they got too far away, he and Dientes yelled at them to stay close, delivering a sharp rap to the head when they came back within reach. They often preferred to take the little ones home, leave them there and go out to the plaza on Avenida Castañares.

III

There was something that Dientes and El Peque wanted: money. A bit of cash. Enough to buy a Coke whenever they wanted one, or cookies, or chewing gum or a hot dog. Not designer sneakers, or mobile phones or a bike. They would have been happy with very little. But neither mother gave them any money. El Peque's, because she didn't have enough to live on; Dientes', because she was scared that he would use the money to buy drugs and get addicted. Every so often Dientes got a few coins off her or a two-peso note, but not much more.

"We need to do a hit," Dientes said to El Peque in a low voice.

"A hit? Who do we need to hit?" asked El Peque, so loudly that he irritated his friend.

"A hit," said Dientes, suddenly adopting the voice of his teacher, "is a big job where we make lots of dough."

"Like that's going to happen."

"I've got a biiiiiig plan."

Dientes and El Peque had a job washing the car of a neighbour, a childless widower who lived two blocks away. This man had a hardware store on Avenida Zelarrayán and got them to wash his car every Saturday morning. He paid them two pesos each. To make it easier for the boys to get around the car, the store owner would bring it out onto the sidewalk and connect a hose to a tap that was inside the garage.

"Inside the garage there is a box, this big" – Dientes opened his arms as wide as they would go – "full of cables. The side gate, the one into the garden, is never locked."

"And what do we want with a box full of cables?"

"The cables, dickhead, have got copper in them. We strip them and sell them to El Pardo, who buys metal. Reckon on fifty pesos each."

The reason the store owner didn't bother locking the garden gate was because on the other side was an untethered German Shepherd which barked at everyone who walked past the house. Whenever Dientes and El Peque washed the car, the dog was around and would come up to them and sniff them; otherwise it left them alone.

"All we have to do is go there, grab the cables and come out as if nothing had happened."

They decided to go the following morning, a Tuesday. At that time the owner of the car, dog and cables would be at his shop.

They met, as they almost always did, in the larger of their building's two internal courtyards. Dientes said simply, "Let's go" and off they went, under the weak June sun. El Peque hung back a little, as though Dientes alone knew the route to the store owner's house.

When they arrived, they stopped outside the gate that led to the garden. Beyond it lay the dog, on a mat in front of the door to the house. On the left and also very close to the mat was the other door, the one to the garage, which the store owner never locked. The dog barely looked up when the two boys came to the gate. Dientes opened it without taking his eyes off the dog. The animal stood up and watched them.

Somebody had told Dientes that if a dog wagged its tail it was because it was happy. The dog was wagging its tail, so he repeated the only words that had crossed his lips in the last few minutes.

"Let's go."

They walked slowly towards the garage. The dog merely watched them. It had stopped wagging its tail. That seemed like a bad sign to Dientes, but he decided not to say anything about it. He went straight to the garage door and opened it as casually as if he had spent his life opening it, as if his entire purpose in life was to open garage doors. He felt the dog's gaze on his shoulders. Without moving, he looked around for the box. It was in the same place that he had seen it the previous Saturday.

"Help me lift it," he said to El Peque.

The box wasn't heavy, but it was too square and too big for one person to carry alone. It was only when they had lifted the box, one on each side, that they became aware of the dog. First they heard it and then they saw it. It was at the gate, blocking their exit from the garden. It was barking while cocking its head towards them, as though pointing at them. Its black snout seemed to grow until it was all they could see.

They stopped moving. Dientes let go of the box and El Peque, who had been clinging to it, lost his footing and almost fell onto the cables. Then Dientes took something from his trouser pocket, showed it to the dog and threw it to the other end of the garage, as far away from them as from the animal. The dog raced towards it, picked up whatever Dientes had thrown and started chewing it. The boys seized their chance to make for the door, but El Peque was not yet out of it when the dog was back again and bit his leg. This time he was the one who dropped the box. He started to scream. Dientes grabbed a hose that was lying on the floor and used it to strike the dog's back, forcing the animal to let go of El Peque and retreat into the garage. They got out and closed the door, leaving the dog – which had started barking again and was hurling itself against the door, trying to break it down – shut inside.

"It hurts," moaned El Peque.

"Run, you faggot, or they'll catch us."

They didn't run but went as quickly as they could with all four hands occupied in carrying the box and El Peque limping. Blood was running down his leg.

"What did you throw it?" El Peque asked.

"A bit of salami sandwich," said Dientes, adding bitterly, "I was going to eat that later."

Once they were home, they made straight for the smaller roof terrace, which was above the back bedrooms and which nobody ever visited, apart from them. Dientes went to his house and came back a few minutes later carrying a half-full bottle of red wine, another of alcohol and a dishcloth.

"What's that for?"

"I'm going to clean your wound."

He uncorked the wine, opened the alcohol and poured some onto the dishcloth. The bottle of wine he passed to El Peque.

"I don't drink wine."

"You have to drink some, so that it doesn't hurt. Have one gulp." El Peque lifted the bottle and took a long sip. He put on a disgusted face.

"Don't be gay. Have a bit more."

He did as he was told and if he didn't spit out the wine it was because at that moment Dientes placed the dishcloth on the place where the dog had bitten him and El Peque had to swallow quickly so as to scream better.

"Ow, blow on it, it's burning."

53

Dientes wiped his leg with the cloth again until the wound was clean, and only then did he blow on it to calm El Peque down and get him to stop screaming. He took a few plasters from his pocket and applied two of them, trying to cover the fang marks left by the dog.

"What if the dog was rabid? Look at the bruise it's given me."

"It's not going to be rabid, is it."

El Peque grasped his friend's arm, like a man on his deathbed about to pronounce his last words.

"Dientes, promise me something: that dog is a dead dog."

"I promise. But first let's sort out the copper."

They spent the rest of the week, each with a knife, peeling the cables to reveal the copper. The work had to be done with great care, because it was easy for the knife to slip and cut a finger. As they stripped more cables they honed their skill, and the last ones were ready in just a few minutes.

"Piece of cake."

The terrace was full of stripped cables, but the resulting copper was a small portion of what they had lugged back from the garage. That Saturday they didn't go to wash the car. They didn't even dare walk in front of the store owner's house, for fear that the dog was loose and might launch itself at them. It didn't occur to them that the owner might link their absence to the loss of the box with the cables or with the dog's incarceration in the garage. That day, instead, they went to see El Pardo, the scrap dealer who bought any kind of metal. El Pardo asked no questions about the source of the copper – it wasn't his job to ask. He merely inspected it and weighed it on his scales: just under four pounds.

"Eighteen pesos," he decreed.

"We were thinking of more like a hundred," El Peque said to him.

"And I was thinking of marrying Angelina Jolie."

"But isn't it seven pesos a pound?" insisted Dientes, who was good at maths. "You should be giving us at least twenty-seven pesos."

"That's the price if you bring me more than twenty pounds, and if the copper is top quality, not surplus. Eighteen, or you can take it away again."

The boys took the money. El Pardo paid them with two five-peso notes and four of two, so that they could split it between them. The first thing they did was go to the corner store to buy a litre-and-a-half bottle of Coca-Cola. Next they went to the plaza to see if they could join in a game. El Peque's leg wasn't hurting any more.

The following week they turned their attention to the dog. Dientes had got hold of some meatballs, to which he had added reckless quantities of rat poison. The meatballs had fallen apart a bit, but they didn't think that that would bother the dog.

"This is what my mum did with Adriana's dog."

Dientes and El Peque went to the store owner's house. There was the dog, lying by the door, just like last time. He looked at them as though he didn't remember what had happened before. Dientes took out the meatballs and threw them towards the dog, which sniffed and then ate them one after the other. They stayed to watch the dog's demise, but the animal continued as normal. After finishing the last meatball he lay back down on the doormat, watching them with an indifferent expression. The boys waited for twenty minutes, half an hour, and there was no change. They went away disappointed. They had expected to see the dog have a seizure and keel over with its four stiffened paws pointing at the sky. But nothing like that happened. The following day they walked past the store owner's house and the dog was not lying on the doormat. They made the same trip a week later and didn't see it then, either. They never saw it again. By then, the eighteen pesos they had made from the cables were only a memory and they no longer had the option of earning two pesos by washing the store owner's car. Lounging on the roof terrace, with no enthusiasm for games, they let the Sunday afternoon go by.

"We need to get hold of more cables to sell," said Dientes.

"What we need to get hold of is money," El Peque said, not knowing that in a few days he was going to get his hands on a sum that in that moment he couldn't even dream of.

3   *Iron Man*

I

The first time Lucio saw Verónica was in the bar at the Plaza Once train station, on the Sarmiento line. Lucio had arrived half an hour before; he had dropped in at the offices of TBA and together with one of the railway spokespeople, a certain Ignacio Álvarez Carrizo, continued to the bar. A few days earlier, Álvarez Carrizo had brought him very quickly up to speed on the concession company's plans, its history, its social engagement and its constant development. The spokesman slapped his back and reminded Lucio again that the honour of the old Sarmiento railway was in his hands – or at least in his words. His tone was cheerful and good-natured, but Lucio couldn't help noticing a certain underlying menace. As a colleague had already observed, they had chosen Lucio because he knew his stuff, he spoke well and wasn't going to go shooting his mouth off like some others. Besides, he was the only one who had known these trains all his life.

Verónica arrived punctually and he recognized her as soon as she entered the bar: she looked nothing like the women who would usually come somewhere like this. She didn't seem surprised or intimidated by the place. Lucio watched as she looked around the room, trying to spot them. Álvarez Carrizo made some friendly gesture and she came forward, with a sure step and a half-smile. She was wearing glasses, woollen gloves and a black raincoat that made her look very tall. Her hair, which she wore short, was chestnut with blonde tones. She looked to him like a psychologist, or an architect.

He knew that she was a journalist, though. She worked on a weekly magazine called *Nuestro Tiempo*, which Lucio had sometimes seen on the news stands but never bought. She wanted to write a piece about Buenos Aires trains. And who better to talk about the company, Álvarez Carrizo had said, than Lucio himself: a veteran who had joined the company nearly twenty years ago as second assistant. A son and grandson of railwaymen.

They stood up as Verónica approached their table. She spoke first to Álvarez Carrizo.

"Ignacio?"

"Verónica. I told you it wouldn't be difficult to recognize us. Let me introduce you to Lucio Valrossa. I promise you, by the time you've finished the interview you'll have enough for a book."

Lucio awkwardly stuck out his hand, but she greeted him with a kiss on the cheek. They sat down. Álvarez Carrizo seemed as nervous and uncomfortable as he was. She didn't seem nervous at all.

II

Verónica's meeting with Lucio and Álvarez Carrizo took place a week after she had met Carina, Carranza's sister. Her first instinct then had been to call Lucio Valrossa, the dead man's friend. It was the most obvious thing to do. He could tell her about Carranza, the accidents, what was happening in the rail company. The number Carina had given her was for a landline, not a mobile. When she dialled it, a woman had answered. Verónica had immediately hung up, as though she had been caught out. She couldn't understand why she had reacted in that way. She should simply have asked to speak to him. Perhaps he was at work. The woman would have given her his mobile number or told her what time she could find him at home. But Verónica had hung up, like a teenager calling a boy at his house.

Since she wasn't a teenager any more – and certainly not calling a boy – she had better buck up her ideas if she wanted to make any headway with the piece. Carranza's friend might be a good source, but couldn't be the only one. She needed to find others, try other avenues. She would have preferred to be meeting Carranza's friend with a bit more research under her belt. Just in case the guy turned out to have something to do with the deaths, or got frightened and decided not to tell her anything. Yes, ideally Valrossa would have been better handled further down the line.

What she needed were statistics, concrete data on the deaths. Since Patricia could do without her for the close of their section, Verónica took the opportunity to spend all of Thursday making enquiries. She called the Ministry of Transport, the body responsible for overseeing public transport, and the City Transport Department. All of them seemed to be playing a strange game of ping-pong. They were short on statistics but long on compelling reasons why she should call another office. When some bureaucrat did come up with official data, Verónica did not need to dig very deep to realize that the numbers were more clumsy than clever. Only one gave her an interesting piece of information: he said that the trains were fitted with a camera, in the driver's cabin, which recorded journeys and therefore any accidents – but this official could not tell her how a copy of these recordings might be obtained. She also tried two foundations dedicated to traffic accidents and was surprised by their lack of interest in trains. They only cared about train accidents when cars were also involved. She made a note to herself to investigate, some time in the future, what these foundations were hiding. Neither the federal nor the metropolitan police had any idea what she was talking about. People who die under trains? Well, we all have to die of something. If there was no crime, they weren't getting involved.

Finally she realized that she needed inside information from someone employed by the company. Someone who worked in admin and wasn't too loyal. Either that or an ex-worker.

The quickest solution was also the one she would rather have avoided: calling Federico. If she was clear about one thing, it was that you should never mix business with pleasure: keep work and sex separate and, as far as possible, emotions and family far away from both. That rule foundered when Federico was involved, though. With him, every one of those components got mixed up in a sticky mess. It was fatal to mix. That was the advice she always gave herself at the start of a drinking session. But she always ended up mixing. There were various reasons why she should never have had sex with Federico: they had known each other for a decade, when Federico had started working at her father's law firm; in those years he had been like a brother to her and a son to her father, who trusted him blindly to the point of making him a junior partner in the company. Aarón Rosenthal would have given his right arm for one of his daughters to marry Federico. And, of the three Rosenthal sisters, she was the only one who was single. She shouldn't have fucked Fede, but she had. And now she avoided crossing paths with him: she met her father outside the office, stayed away from family get-togethers (to which Federico was always invited, as much on her sisters' say-so as her father's) and ran in the opposite direction any time he popped up with an invitation to something. This time, however, Federico was the very person she needed to turn to. His voice on the other end of the line was rich with that falsely professional tone she knew and always found amusing. But, not having time to make any observation about that, she got straight to the point:

"I'm writing a piece and I need your help."

"The Rosenthal Studio is at your disposal. Which judge do you want put behind bars?"

"None, not right now. I'm writing a piece on the Sarmiento Railway Company."

"Ex."

"Ex what?"

"The ex-Sarmiento Railway Company. That's been defunct for a long time. The Sarmiento line is run by Trenes de Buenos Aires now."

"The ex-Sarmiento Railway Company, then. I need someone to get me some administrative information. Company statistics, accident protocols, stuff like that. And since I can't go and ask for it at the offices of TBA, I thought an ex-employee would be ideal."

"An ex."

"An ex-employee, a disgruntled worker. The kind of person who brings a lawsuit. There must be loads of cases."

"Hundreds. Open, closed, however you like them."

"I want an employee who'll talk."

"An ex."

"Yes, an ex. Can you see if you can find one?"

"Exes are my speciality. I imagine this is urgent? I'll call you in a few hours."

While Federico made his own investigations, Verónica asked a colleague from the Politics section for a contact in the railway workers' union. When he asked her what she needed to find out, she was deliberately ambiguous. She didn't like to reveal too much about an article to a fellow journalist. But it turned out that he was asking because the union body and the railway line delegates were separate organizations with different political allegiances.

"Do you want a big cheese from the Fraternity, or a delegate from the rank and file?"

"I think a delegate from the Sarmiento would suit me fine."

He gave her the details of a Trotskyite militant employed in the Sarmiento workshops who opposed the political line espoused by the Fraternity. Verónica called him and the delegate agreed to meet her the next day in a bar close to Moreno Station, at the other end of the railway line, twenty-five miles from Buenos Aires.

Mid-afternoon, Federico called her. He had what she needed.

"Francisco López. He worked in Accounts. They fired him, alleging that he had stolen a computer monitor, but he won the suit against TBA and they had to pay him compensation."

Verónica called López and they arranged to meet two days later at a bar in Almagro, where he worked on the till. He told her to come between four and five o'clock in the afternoon, when the bar was less busy.

The next day she set off to meet the unionist. She decided to make the journey by train, partly to avoid a tussle with Accounts over the cost of a taxi to Moreno, and partly because she wanted to know more about the territory she was investigating. Fortunately, she was making the journey out to Greater Buenos Aires at midday, which meant she got a seat. At rush hour it would have been a struggle even to get on. Verónica was not all that used to travelling by train and had never been on the Western Railway. From Plaza

Miserere to the first stop, in Caballito, she felt an unease verging on fear. The compartment moved much more than she had expected. After that she relaxed, or got used to it, and the train's rhythmic clatter could have sent her to sleep for the rest of the journey if she had not been alert to everything that was happening around her: from the mother wrangling four children who must all have been under four, to the endless procession of hawkers who came by offering sweets, folders or wallets in the colours of some soccer club, MP3 compilations on CD, the latest movies on DVD and even a set of brushes and combs that she was quite tempted to buy.

She spent almost an hour talking to the unionist and struggled to direct the conversation towards what she wanted to know. He was more interested in denouncing the low salaries and union-bashing by the management than anything else. He knew about Carranza's suicide, but it was hard to steer him away from spouting joint statements that sounded like written communiqués. What Verónica found most useful was his criticism of the company's lack of support, which was limited to sending employees to a state psychologist. He confirmed that drivers were made to return to work before they had fully recovered, and told her that it was impossible to drive a train without clocking up at least one fatal accident. If Verónica had been looking to write a critical article on the current state of railways in Buenos Aires, she would have come away with plenty of material. She could write such a piece now for the next edition of the magazine. Carranza's death could not simply be the consequence of labour or management problems, though. There was definitely more to it, but the unionist was not about to help her find out what. When she asked him about the child Carranza had run over, and the confusing allusion to this in his letter, she noticed a very slight change in the unionist's manner, as when a dog responds to a faraway noise.

"I don't know about that specific case, but anyone can be the victim of a train accident, old or young. And somebody about to commit suicide doubtless doesn't express himself clearly."

Things didn't go much better with the ex-employee. She found López behind the till at his workplace, a seedy joint that would at any minute be ravaged by the winds of modernity and reborn as a heritage bar, falsely rustic, with that patina of antiquity demanded by current tastes. López came out from behind the bar and sat down with Verónica at a table looking onto the street. It was early enough that all the other tables were empty. Verónica took out her notebook. She rarely taped interviews, unless she needed a record of what had been said or wanted her subject to experience a real sense of being interviewed. When she was questioning a source, she took notes and sometimes simply relied on her memory, which seemed, for the moment, to be quite good. The tape recorder intimidated interviewees, but taking notes necessarily meant losing eye contact with the person she was talking to, something she didn't like.

"They steal everything. They over-invoice, there's a trade in items stolen from other train companies. And because I didn't want to get involved in their corrupt little game, they threw me out, saying that I was the one who stole. Bastards."

López had information about illegal financial transactions, trains repaired with substandard materials, a black market in stolen items, and other shady dealings. But when Verónica tried to find out more about the drivers and people killed by trains, López replied with some platitude about the lives lost, then continued with more examples of bad management.

"Tell me something, López, do all the trains have a camera installed in the driver's cabin?"

"Yes, of course, the security camera."

"So all accidents are recorded, right?"

"Absolutely. Whenever there's an accident, the first thing the company does is take away the camera. For the insurance – right? The insurance company uses it to prove negligence on the part of the person who got knocked down, so they don't have to pay anything out. They didn't want to pay me anything, either, but I won my case."

"Is it possible to get hold of those recordings?"

"They're kept under lock and key. Or the insurance company keeps them. But there are people in your line of work who buy recordings to show on TV programmes. If you want to buy them, you'll have to speak to one of the reprobates who work on the legal team. Or with someone from the insurance company."

III

Sex and sources. It was an unbreakable ethical principle for Verónica that she would pay for neither. Perhaps when she was old, she'd pay some gigolo to sleep with her but, as far as journalistic sources were concerned, she was keeping herself pure. Even if that meant not getting her hands on a video that could open up the investigation.

But why make so much of this when what she needed to do was call Lucio Valrossa? Something was putting her off and she tried to find a logical explanation for her feelings. She was worried that, if Valrossa had advance warning of what she was investigating, he might go on the defensive and hide important information from her. She had to find another way to reach him.

After meeting López that afternoon, she went to the Plaza Miserere station instead of returning to the newsroom. She had a very vague hope of catching Valrossa getting off a train or about to get into the driver's cabin. The chance of that happening might be one in a thousand, but still she felt compelled to do it. Even if she did see him, she hadn't thought about what she would do next, what excuse she would use to approach him.

At that time of day Once was crammed with people. The terminal floor vibrated with commuters hurrying towards the platforms. That constant buzz of human activity reminded her of bees flying around a hive. She walked towards the turnstiles and looked into the TBA offices, then went from the ticket offices to the fast-food joints, but there was no sign of Valrossa. What if she had forgotten what he looked like? That was impossible. His every feature was imprinted on her mind. She knew that when she saw him again she would feel the same unquiet that had come over her at the funeral and then again when she saw him in the photograph at Carina's house.

After spending two hours walking pointlessly from one end of the terminal to the other, she decided to go.

Back at home on her computer, she looked up Lucio Valrossa's name on Google. She thought he might be on Facebook. She herself had an account, but used it only to snoop on other people. In fact, what she found on Google was better than a Facebook page. At first there was nothing. Then she ran a search without quotation marks – with very little hope of turning up anything on the the driver – and, to her surprise, found something. On a fan site dedicated to the Sarmiento line trains (that there were fanatics of any railway, including a badly run one, didn't surprise her: she had seen other extreme cases of devotion) she found a blog post titled "Farewell to a legend". It was an obituary for Carlos

Valrossa. It said that Carlos had worked on the Sarmiento line for forty years, that he was the son of a railwayman and the father of one too, because his son Lucio was following in the family tradition of driving the trains that ran between the stations of Once and Moreno.

Verónica saw now what she had to do. She started by getting the contact details of spokespeople for the TBA company. The following morning she called one of them, a certain Álvarez Carrizo, who sounded like an old lecher. So she put on one of her voices – that of a slightly stupid girl who's eager to learn – which, according to her friend Paula, she had suspiciously down pat.

"The thing is, Señor Álvarez Carrizo —"

"Please, call me Ignacio. Let's not be formal."

"The thing is, Ignacio, I'm planning to write about the history of the old Sarmiento railway and the future prospects of the company."

"But wouldn't you prefer to write about the Mitre line? The route is much more interesting. And the people who use it are more…how shall I put this…more photogenic."

"I'm interested in the Sarmiento because it used to be the Western Railway. Argentina's first railway."

"That's true."

"I'd love to get all the information I can from you, both historical and current."

"You can count on it."

"I'd also love to interview someone who's very familiar with the trains."

"That could be one of our engineers."

"No. What I'm after is a driver. When I looked on the internet I found out that there's a driver on the Sarmiento who's the son and grandson of railwaymen."

"Really? You know more about my company than I do."

They both laughed.

"Far from it, Ignacio – it was just something I happened to stumble across. Perhaps that man doesn't work for you any more. But don't you think it's lovely to think of three generations of a family working for the same company?"

"Yes indeed. Do you have his name? If he's one of our employees, I'll get hold of him for your article. You can count on it."

IV

Lucio was nervous, uncomfortable and annoyed with Álvarez Carrizo. He felt as though he were being shown off like a trained seal. Worse still, the journalist didn't seem that impressed. Every remark from Álvarez Carrizo – who wanted to be actively involved in the interview – elicited a condescending smile. The spokesman provided figures, trotted out set phrases from the publicity brochure, told barefaced lies about the state of the trains and the plans for investment. Every now and then he let Lucio speak. Verónica asked him about the railwaymen in his family.

"My grandfather and father were drivers. My grandfather drove the steam train that crossed Patagonia and my father also began by driving steam trains. He was the first person to drive a diesel locomotive. He worked on the Sarmiento line until he retired in 1993."

"Did you always want to be a driver like your dad and your grandfather?"

"No, I didn't want to be like them. Well, maybe when I was a child, but not afterwards. As a boy I liked going out with my father and taking charge of the controls. But as I got older I thought that I could be something else. Something…I don't know…professional."

Álvarez Carrizo seemed to feel compelled to offer some wisdom on this point.

"Blood will out, as they say."

"What did you want to be?"

"A civil engineer. I went to university the same year I started in the Sarmiento workshops."

"You worked and studied at the same time."

"Yes, but I gave up in the second year. And here I did the training to be a driver, which I didn't need because I already knew how to drive. I ended up staying."

The conversation, which Verónica recorded on a gadget about half the size of a mobile phone, lasted fifty minutes. Álvarez Carrizo, like a child with a toy, quickly lost interest in the stories about trains and drummed his fingers on the table or gazed off into the distance, now and then returning his attention to them with a fake smile.

"Thank you so much, Lucio," Verónica said, switching off the recording device.

Álvarez Carrizo suddenly became animated again, showing the same enthusiasm he had at the start.

"I told you that Lucio would give you enough for a book."

"All the same, if you and the company don't have any objection, I'd like to accompany Lucio on a journey."

"Go with him in the driver's cabin?" asked Álvarez Carrizo, and she nodded. "No, I'm afraid that's not possible. It's against the regulations."

"But didn't Lucio learn to drive while accompanying his father?"

"Those were other times. The train belonged to the state, there were no rules."

Verónica smiled at Álvarez Carrizo. Lucio felt that she would never direct a smile like that at a man like him.

"Ignacio, you are the voice and the eyes of this company. It's up to you whether or not I can go in the cabin. Or are you going to tell me that I have to speak to one of those stuffy old directors that TBA presumably has?"

Either the smile or the words were enough finally to persuade Álvarez Carrizo to authorize her to travel in the cabin.

V

It was cold, in a way that stung the lips and which the energy of the hurrying crowd did nothing to assuage. Their second meeting took place in the central hall of the station and, once again, he got there first. Verónica arrived in an overcoat, her face half hidden in a garish coloured scarf. She lowered it, gave him a kiss on the cheek by way of greeting, and Lucio felt her warm lips barely graze his frozen features.

They went through the turnstiles, the ticket collectors eyeing them curiously. Everyone knew that Lucio was taking a female journalist with him in the driver's compartment. For days he had been the butt of their jokes, especially when he'd told them that the journalist was hot. That detail was invented, because he had been so nervous the first time they met that he hadn't dared look at her body. It was true, though, that he had thought her very pretty. A cold and distant beauty.

They came to the first compartment and climbed into the cabin. In the metal box where tools were kept some joker had left him a condom. Lucio quickly closed the box before she saw anything. Verónica stood to one side and leaned against the window, a position that allowed her to watch as he handled the controls. Lucio didn't much like that – he would have preferred to be the one watching her. To make things worse, there were still a few minutes before they would get the order to leave.

70

"A few years ago," he told her, "I used to work with freight trains. I liked that more. Freight trains have real locomotives. Not these little rooms."

"Like those engines you see in the movies. Black, belching smoke."

"Well no, not as old as that. When I was a boy I liked seeing the trains my old man used to drive. They called them 'sows'. They had a Fiat engine and they were quite frightening. They looked as though they had giant heads, like the one in *The War of the Worlds*. A kind of galactic warrior with barred windows that looked like eyes and a metal jaw."

A voice came over the loudspeaker announcing that the train at platform two was ready to depart. A few seconds later the train embarked on its westward journey. Lucio felt her watching his hands. It had to be on a day when he felt clumsy.

Even so, he preferred chatting with her here to in the station bar, without the annoying presence of Álvarez Carrizo and doing, at the end of the day, what he knew how to do best: drive trains. After a bit he admitted to her that he didn't want his children to work on the railways.

"The eldest is seven. I've never brought him into the cabin and I wouldn't think of bringing either of them. I don't want them to work here when they're older."

"You'd prefer them to study."

"Of course."

"To be civil engineers."

"Whatever they want. I just don't want them to drive trains."

What he was telling Verónica was something he didn't usually talk about to friends. Perhaps because they took it for granted that Lucio's sons would study for a career, that they would forge a much more promising future for themselves than a job on the railways. And if he ever did mention that he didn't want his children to be railwaymen, they would all understand and wouldn't ask him the question Verónica was asking now.

"Why?"

"Because I don't."

"Aha. I suspect that's the short answer. Now give me the longer one."

He took a few seconds to reply.

"Promise me you won't put it in the article? Álvarez will haul me over the coals."

"I promise."

"Because the job is shit."

They had arrived at Villa Luro. The sun was shining right into the cabin and the morning's cold had dissipated. Verónica had unbuttoned her overcoat and Lucio would have liked to look and see if she was as hot as he had told his colleagues she was. But he didn't dare, like when as a boy he noticed a woman's cleavage in the bus: his eyes would become heavy, and he'd feel that he couldn't move them in that direction. He kept concentrating on the sleepers between the tracks and on the controls.

"You don't earn much money, you work rotating shifts, plus terrible things happen that no amount of money could make up for."

"What sort of things?" she asked, and Lucio felt her watching him more intently.

Just as he could tell if some mechanism in the train was failing from signs that nobody else would notice, the journalist must have spotted in his last remark something juicy for her article. He shouldn't have said anything.

"Things. I'd rather not talk about it."

Her gaze fell away, and instead she looked out at the landscape. The city disappeared for a few seconds: there was an absence of buildings or houses, creating the false sensation of having arrived in the country. The only thing to see was abandoned rolling stock, and this space between Haedo and Morón looked like a graveyard for trains.

"You see?" said Lucio, pointing at the carriages which lay broken and rusting at the side of the tracks. Those are the sows I was telling you about a minute ago. When I was a boy people called them lobsters. I got to drive a few in the 1990s. Then the camels came along and now we even have pumas. They didn't give this train an animal's name. She's a little old Toyota. Still, gets the job done."

He looked at Verónica, hoping for a journalist's approval of his description of the Sarmiento carriages, but her gaze was fixed on the city which was slowly beginning to reappear before them. Then she asked him something surprising:

"Did you know that we have the same surname?"

Now he looked at her incredulously.

"Seriously?"

"You're called Valrossa and I'm Rosenthal. Mine is a Jewish surname and yours is Italian, but they mean the same thing: valley of roses."

"Valley of roses."

"Life isn't a valley of roses."

"No."

"Come on, Lucio."

Finally he dared to look at her. Not at her body but at her face, that pale face, accentuated by chestnut hair, with delicate lips and green eyes that weren't about to release their prey. How old must she be? Twenty-eight, twenty-nine? Why wouldn't she smile at him the way she had kept smiling during that meeting in the bar?

"'Come on, Lucio' what?"

"Tell me about the suicides. About the people who throw themselves under trains. Because the terrible things that happen are suicides, aren't they?"

VI

Morón was behind them. The train was emptying out as they approached Moreno. Inside the cabin, Lucio and Verónica were locked in a sordid, subterranean fight no less dogged than the ones you see taking place on top of train carriages in westerns. Verónica was asking him to reveal something he never spoke about, not with his wife, his friends, not even people he worked with. When something like that happened, nobody ever asked him about it. A merciful silence always covered it and now Verónica wanted to stick her fingers not in the wounds, because there were no wounds, but right into his brain. He had managed – and it had been a struggle – not to go crazy, and now she was messing with his head and once again he felt that fear of madness.

"There are thefts, too, and car accidents."

"But suicides are the worst."

"They aren't always suicides."

"Murders, then?"

"No, I'm not saying that. Accidents. People come along, they don't see a train approaching, they walk on the line, they cross the tracks without looking. And there's no time to do anything."

"It's impossible to brake, or to warn them."

"Some never know what happened. Others realize half a second before. They try to get off the track, to jump out of the way, they put their hand up as if to stop the train."

"Have you had a lot of accidents?"

"Me? Five accidents and six deaths. Someone I work with has had fifteen."

"It must be hard to go back to driving a train after you've run someone over."

"Impossible, more like."

"But you do go back, just like your friend who had fifteen."

"A lot of the ticket inspectors are drivers who couldn't face driving a train again. I keep going back because it's the only thing I know how to do and I've got a wife and two kids to support."

"You could become a ticket inspector too."

"Or I could shoot myself. The possibilities are endless."

"Do you think the deaths could be avoided?"

"What can I say? That you shouldn't cross when the barrier is down, that you shouldn't walk on the line, that if you're going to commit suicide you should take pills or jump from the tenth floor? I don't know. Excuse my language, but I couldn't give a shit about their prevention policy. Nobody can take away the fact that I've killed six people."

"You didn't kill them. They threw themselves under your train."

"Do you know what it feels like? First a sharp blow, like a shot, then, after that shot, you're aware of the body bursting, of terrified screams which you can't cover with the horn, and which you can still hear even after the body has been destroyed. You feel the bones cracking under your feet."

"But it's not your responsibility."

"Sometimes you see them quite a long time before, or you realize that the guy on the edge of the platform is going to jump when the train passes. You sound the horn, you apply the emergency brake, even though you know that that noise like a shot is coming and that sound of bones breaking under your cabin. Where does responsibility, or whether or not you did the right thing, come into that? Two years ago some skinny guy, about twenty years old, was standing in the middle of the tracks, on a stretch where the train moves at top speed. I saw him and managed to brake, I sounded the horn but he didn't move. To start with I didn't realize I had started shouting, I was screaming, 'Get out of the way, idiot!' For a second I saw his face. It was as though he were asking my forgiveness for what he was doing. He wasn't afraid. He saw my terrified face. The last thing he saw was me, shouting desperately at him."

"What do you do when there's an accident like that?"

"Nothing. You're aware of a few people screaming in the first compartment. People come, the police, railway workers, an ambulance. That particular time I got out of the train and before they took me away in the ambulance I saw the guy's torn clothes and parts of his body all over the place."

"That boy wanted to die. It was a suicide. He could have taken pills or jumped from the tenth floor, like you said. The train was an instrument."

"Nothing personal."

"Exactly."

"You still feel that you've killed someone. Afterwards you're always thinking that it could happen again on the next journey. And sometimes it does."

They were close to Moreno now, and for a time neither of them spoke. Verónica decided to put her cards on the table.

"That's what happened to Carranza, isn't it?"

Lucio let go of the controls and turned his body to look at her straight on. He didn't just look at her with his eyes, though, but with his whole body. Like the male of any species seconds before confronting an enemy. There was a challenging violence in his eyes. Verónica held his gaze, calmly, coldly.

"What do you know about Carranza?"

"That he killed himself because he could no longer live with the deaths on the tracks. That he was your friend. That he felt that you were his only friend."

"Who told you that?"

"Carina, his sister."

Lucio turned back to the cabin controls and looked into the distance.

"What do you know about Carranza's accidents?" Verónica asked him.

"I don't want to talk about it."

"I tried to get hold of videos of those accidents, but I couldn't."

"Why do you want to see the videos? The deaths are all the same."

"I wanted to see what happened with the child Carranza went over."

Lucio said nothing. He was concentrating on the tracks, which seemed to undulate in front of the train.

"Was there anybody else on the line?"

They had arrived at the last station. Lucio gently brought the train to a halt. Verónica watched the people getting off. The compartments emptied.

"Not all of them are suicides and not all of them are accidents. Some of them are playing," Lucio said as they climbed down from the driver's cabin, breaking the silence of the last few minutes.

"What do you mean?"

"When do you have to publish the article?"

"I don't have a deadline. I can be flexible."

"If you can wait a week, I'll show you something you may find interesting."

Why had he done it? During the last year, every time he had
to drive a night train on the first Thursday of the month,
he knew that there would be a moment of hell. Much as he
dreaded that day coming round he couldn't ask to change
shift, and neither could anyone else scheduled to drive that
night, but everyone knew what was going to happen and
accepted it as their fate. For that reason he had been very
happy to learn that he was being transferred to the morning
shift. And when he asked a co-worker to swap shifts so that he
could drive the night train, nobody could bring himself to ask
the reason why. Inviting Verónica to accompany him meant
that, alongside the dread of that terrible moment, there
was the excitement of seeing her again, a sensation he had
never experienced before. Because that was definitely what
he wanted: to be with her again. It was absurd, but there was
no getting away from it. That week, instead of the nightmares
filled with the sound of breaking bones, the insomnia was
back. He thought about Verónica all the time. He had only
seen her twice, she was only a journalist researching a piece,
and yet she had insinuated herself into his life.

It was obvious that she was after a good story, that she
wanted him to reveal all those things which he hid even from
himself. Those fears that assaulted him in bed while he slept,
or on the night train when he became seized by a conviction
that the worst was about to happen. Six deaths: four men and
two women. A vagrant he never even saw, perhaps because he
was stretched out on the line. Two girls who were walking on
the tracks on a December afternoon. He did see those ones
from a long way off; he had sounded the horn and applied
the emergency brakes. A guy who jumped from a railway
crossing like someone plunging into a river. Another who

had taken a slow, interminable step forward, as though he wanted to delay contact with the train for as long as possible but was nevertheless absolutely determined that this contact take place. And the skinny guy whose expression seemed to be one of apology for making Lucio end his life. Six deaths, six murders. Because didn't the police treat them as though they were guilty? On three occasions they had taken him to a police station and kept him there all night. The company's lawyer had even had to go and get him out. Then again, perhaps that was better than ending up in hospital in a state of shock. Or having to endure the attention of the company psychologist, who wanted to cure with aspirin the cancer that eats at a person's very core. The cancer of having seen, of remembering images, sounds, and also the silence, the scene that disappears behind a white mantle, like the one blind people speak of seeing.

Forty-eight hours. That was how long the psychologist gave him to rest before carrying out further observation. Sometimes he prescribed two more days off, but Lucio did everything possible to be sent back to work. He couldn't stand to be alone in the house while his wife and children were at school (she teaching, the oldest in primary school and the youngest in kindergarten). No television or radio could drown out the noises in his head. So he would kill time in a bar. Drink a glass of wine mid-morning, read the sports pages of some newspaper. Talk about politics or soccer with inebriated strangers. Anything to take his mind away from the railway.

On more than one occasion they had offered to transfer him to a different section. To the warehouse, ticket inspection, maintenance, moves many of his colleagues had made since he began driving trains. Once somebody in management told him that, if he had been ten years older, he could have applied for early retirement. After all, railway workers retire at fifty-five. It qualified as "insalubrious work", like working in a mine five hundred yards below ground.

In this case the insalubrious element was the burden of deaths borne by each of them. Borne by him. The deaths and the possible deaths. The fear that that very day somebody would decide to throw himself under the train or be idiotic enough not to realize that ten thousand tons of metal were about to roll over him. Six was the number darkly inscribed on his heart, but seven was the one that awakened his worst fears.

And yet he always went back to driving trains. More than a vocation, it was his fate, his doom. The best way for him to endure it was with silence, a conscious attempt to forget everything. Then Verónica had turned up, confronting him with everything that had been locked up inside him. What other deeply buried feelings of which he himself was ignorant was she prepared to unearth?

VIII

A week. That was how long Verónica had to wait. What was it that Lucio was going to show her? What was he involved in? The week seemed endless and full of expectation; the days had no purpose other than to delay their meeting. Were these feelings a sign that she was reaching some crucial point in her investigation? She wasn't naive enough to kid herself that that was the case. Lucio attracted her in a way that was not purely sexual but owed something to intrigue too. It was the kind of arousal that Oedipus must have felt in front of the Sphinx, knowing that if he could not answer her question he would die. When she had asked him about Carranza and Lucio had turned to face her, she had seen in his eyes a defiance that made her shiver inside. He gave off a violence that she found disturbing but also attractive. She had found it hard to hold her nerve.

What was it about Lucio that attracted her? Those shadows that covered him like a veil? The possibility of manipulating him, of extracting from him the information that she needed?

What was she willing to do? Or rather, what would she not do? What threshold would she not be prepared to cross with Lucio?

It was a week characterized by questions like these and by a desire that seemed to feed more on uncertainty than on anything that had happened so far. At the end of the day, Lucio was a source – nothing more. A reliable source who seemed honest, a little remiss when it came to giving her the information she needed but someone she felt she could manage: she could get what she needed from him. However, when she imagined herself getting to this point, the one at which Lucio would yield the information she needed for her article, she couldn't help thinking that writing the piece was less important than drawing aside the veil to find out what those eyes charged with violence were hiding. Reveal the truth, or die trying.

During those days she had received emails and phone calls from the man her friends called the Bengali Sailor. Verónica neither answered nor returned the calls. He seemed as irrelevant to her now as the memory of a card game played on a Sunday afternoon. Something done to fend off boredom and forgotten as soon as it is over.

Verónica also said nothing during that week to Patricia Beltrán about her investigation into the trains. She went to the *Nuestro Tiempo* newsroom every afternoon and wrapped up some articles for that week's deadline, but she kept quiet about what she was doing. She didn't want Patricia to get involved. Or for her editor to outsmart her and prove that she was wrong. That she wasn't behaving like the professional journalist she ought to be.

IX

She had been told to go straight to the first compartment of "Plate Number Six" – the train which left at 21.50 from platform 3 – and to wait for Lucio there. The fewer people who saw her with him the better, and the last trains of the day were not monitored by supervisors, nor were there any railway workers loitering on the platforms.

This time she had been the first to arrive and had sat in the seat closest to the driver's cabin. She was wearing a black ski jacket, jeans and sneakers, clothes befitting someone who might at any moment have to make a quick getaway. Her outfit made her look younger, like someone of twenty-six or -seven.

"Are you going to tell me what to expect?" Verónica asked after Lucio had started the engine and the train had begun to snake out of the station and away from the Plaza Once station.

"You asked me about the terrible things that happen in this job. You're going to see one."

"When?"

"That I don't know. It could be any time between here and Castelar, or on the return journey."

They didn't speak again until they reached Flores. For that first part of the route they had watched the rails illuminated by the train's headlight, which pierced the dense darkness of the night as though it were advancing through a tunnel or under the ground.

At Flores, he asked her if she had been a journalist for a long time. Verónica told him that she had started more than ten years ago. That she had been writing for *Nuestro Tiempo* for three of these years. Lucio wanted to know how old she was. Thirty. He felt confident asking these questions, while she seemed very nervous. Lucio no longer saw her as a journalist leading the conversation, but as a girl who was being taken on a train towards something which she must imagine to be very sinister and all the more alarming because it was unknown. He asked her if she was married. She said that she wasn't. If she had a boyfriend. Again, no. Regaining the role of questioner, Verónica wanted to know what being a father of two meant to him. Obligations, he replied. Obligations and a great love, very different from the love you might feel for a partner or for your parents; a sense of never being alone. How long had he been married? Eight years: he had married at her age. 'Perhaps you'll get married this year too,' he said. 'I don't think so,' said Verónica.

They reached Castelar without incident and, as they began the journey back to Plaza Once, the demeanour of both had changed. Lucio had become more tense because he knew that what was about to happen was coming ever closer. Verónica could not conceal a slight irritation, as if she had been deceived, brought this far just to be interrogated about her private life, an unfamiliar experience for her and rather annoying. Then Lucio remembered something that they had talked about last time, a half answer he had given which he now wanted to complete.

"When you see someone walk onto the tracks, you can't take your eyes off them. I always tell myself that the next time I'll close my eyes, because I don't want to see the moment of impact, but I can't. The suicidal person locks onto your eyes and won't let go."

They travelled on in silence until, with not far to go until they arrived at Caballito, Lucio said, more to himself than for her benefit:

"There they are."

X

In an instant Lucio applied the emergency brake and sounded a continuous blast on the horn. At first, she saw nothing. The train's light did not extend as far as whatever it was Lucio was seeing or thought he saw. Then suddenly, as though materializing out of the dark, two boys appeared, about ten or twelve years old. They were standing on the line looking right at the train. Everything that happened next took a couple of seconds – perhaps less. Verónica realized that they were about to run into these two small boys, that they were going to crush them even though the brake had been applied. The train continued implacably towards them. She wanted to close her eyes, but terror prevented her. The image of those two boys grew until it covered the night. One boy seemed to lose his nerve then and threw himself to one side of the track. Immediately the other boy did the same, towards the other side. The train came to a stop a few yards later.

"Bastards," said Lucio, a visceral hatred in his voice. There was some shouting from the compartments in response to the emergency stop. In a little more than a minute Lucio had the train moving again.

"What just happened?" asked Verónica, in a voice that seemed to belong to someone else.

"The same thing that happens on the first Thursday of every month. They're boys from the shanty town, from some slum or I don't know what shithole. Someone I work with ran over one of these kids a year ago."

Verónica was dumbstruck. She couldn't move. What she had seen had turned her into a pillar of salt. Lucio – who in all this time had not lifted his gaze from the tracks – turned to look at her and asked if she was all right. She said that she was, but she had started to shake and couldn't help crying.

"I couldn't take my eyes off them either," she said, in a barely audible voice.

He took her hand and she squeezed his. She felt her own nails digging into the palm of Lucio's hand. The train stopped in the station at Caballito and, before pulling away, with the compartment doors still open, Lucio left the controls, turned to Verónica and kissed her. It was a clumsy kiss to which her first response was to bite his lips while desperately seeking his mouth. As if she wanted to get right inside him, take refuge in his mouth. Verónica was a frightened animal looking for shelter. She felt fragile against his solid body, which was pushing her against the wall of the cabin. Lucio's hands under her sweater were not caressing but squeezing her. They kissed until there was an aftertaste of blood. Then Lucio let her go and started up the train again.

4   *El Peque versus Cholito*

I

El Peque had completely recovered from the dog's attack by the first time they went to Spring Breezes. They had to walk about fifteen blocks to get there. Dientes had said that he knew the way, but more than once they got lost and had to ask for directions.

Spring Breezes was a neighbourhood club like any other: its name emblazoned on a peeling facade, a function room with tables where a handful of pensioners played dominoes, a concrete five-a-side soccer pitch, an office, changing rooms and not much else.

There were some boys kicking a ball around. And there was Rivero. He was wearing a blue Adidas tracksuit. When he saw El Peque, he beckoned to him to come over. Dientes went with him.

"Have you come with your parents?"

"My old man doesn't live with us, and my mum works until late."

El Peque had decided to tell the truth. At worst he would have to persuade his mother to go and talk to Rivero sometime, like when she had to go and meet the teacher.

"And who are you?" Rivero asked Dientes.

"I look after him."

"Ah, OK. You were there playing in the park the other day, right?"

Rivero was bald, or almost. He had a few strands of hair which he combed across his head in an effort to conceal the bald patch. His hands were hairy, like a monkey's. A bald monkey. He wasn't fat, but not thin either. He was the world's thinnest fat man, or vice versa. His eyes shone as though they were wet. His expression, however, was as dry as a cardboard box left out in the sun.

"I remember, you were playing on the right wing."

He spoke in a loud voice, like you would imagine a soccer coach might speak. He spoke as though he were giving orders. He could be a coach, a policeman or the kind of father who demands old-fashioned courtesy.

"How old are you?"

Dientes distrusted adult males. They had killed his father. Any adult could be a murderer. He looked at all of them and thought that they could be to blame for leaving him fatherless.

"We're already full in that division, but if you want to stay…"

Dientes didn't say either yes or no. He went to one side of the room and sat there, watching how El Peque submitted to the coach's orders.

Rivero told El Peque that boys were expected to come with their parents the first time, but that for him he was going to make an exception. He sent him to the office, where an old woman made him fill out a form with his details. When he came back to the pitch, the coach got him to practise with the other boys. They did a few exercises which El Peque found boring and finally played a twenty-minute game. They agreed to see each other the following Thursday.

"I have to come back on Thursday," El Peque told Dientes.

"Well, then memorize the route, because I'm not coming with you."

If El Peque had envisaged a club where shirts, shorts and boots would all be provided, he was wrong. Spring Breezes was a club befitting the neighbourhood in which it found itself. The boys played in whatever clothes they were wearing. At most, they might all agree to try and wear a red T-shirt or a white one. Later he found out that they were planning a raffle to raise money to buy a set of shirts. That the older boys had done this and that there was already a club kit for the senior divisions: violet with a yellow diagonal stripe from right to left. At least there was a leather soccer ball in better condition than the one they usually used in the plaza, or in the street.

They trained twice a week and played in between. Breezes wasn't registered in any championship or league, so it didn't compete in official games with other teams, but every now and then friendlies were organized with other clubs in the area. The boys travelled in a beat-up school bus driven by an old man who either was, or had been, or appeared to be drunk.

Rivero wasn't a friendly coach, or even a nice one. He gave a few directions and raised his voice when something was done badly, but nothing made him passionate. In fact he often seemed distracted, or tired, or uninterested. It was hard to imagine him saying that "his boys" meant the world to him, for the simple reason that he didn't seem to feel that this group of headstrong young soccer players belonged to him. He was different with El Peque, though, or at least he swore at him less and every so often he would say, "That's right, Peque, that's the way." And El Peque was far from being the best. He wasn't very skilful, but he was a plucky defender. He attacked every ball and wasn't afraid of kicks. Receiving them or giving them.

When they had finished that day's activity, they would all chip in for a litre-and-a-half bottle of Pepsi in the club bar. It was difficult for El Peque to get hold of the cash, and for that reason he sometimes didn't even have one coin to put towards the communal purchase. Even then, Rafael, who worked behind the bar, was charging them half what was written on the price list.

Rafael was young, bearded and scrawny, with a permanently vacant expression, but he was kind to the boys. Once he said to El Peque and another of the boys:

"I'm not going to be able to sell these sandwiches now and it seems a shame to throw them out. Why don't you two take them?"

So he gave them three salami and cheese rolls. And he always had something to give them – to El Peque and the other boys. A sandwich, a plate of breadsticks or peanuts, potato chips – a bit on the soggy side perhaps, but still potato chips.

One day, when nobody else was there, he surprised El Peque by saying:

"I know you. You live in that house on Cañada de Gómez and Salvador."

"Yes," said El Peque, somewhat warily.

"I thought I'd seen you. I mean, this was when I was younger. I used to live there."

"I don't remember."

"Children never notice grown-ups."

"Now there are two women living there with a girl, and in the other room is a man on his own, as well as us and the landlady."

El Peque got back to his house at around eight o'clock, by which time his mother was already home and cooking dinner. She didn't mind him going to the club, so long as he did his homework. El Peque lied about this all the time, telling her that he had already done it, but generally he did get it done the next morning, albeit hurriedly.

Rivero also asked him about his mother, his father and if he had contact with him. El Peque didn't much like talking about that kind of thing. However, he told him that he had seen photos of his father – in reality he had only seen one, which his mother kept in a box in the dresser, beneath some folded sheets. She was in the photo with his father and him as a baby, in a plaza in Corrientes.

In a short time Rivero found out about his mother's work, where they lived, his younger siblings, his neighbours and that photo of his father. And about Rivero, El Peque knew simply that he was the head coach at Spring Breezes, that they spoke respectfully to him in the club and that sometimes he would join a table with some card players who drank wine and smoked.

One day they had finished a bit later than usual. Rivero told him to stay back because he wanted to speak to him. The other children dispersed quickly, hurried on their way by the late hour and the cold. El Peque put on his coat and sat waiting on the cement step that served as Breezes' humble rostrum. Rivero came over, smoking, and stood in front of him.

"Peque, you're a brave boy. You play on the front foot. I like that in a player. Not like those faggots who take a dive at the first kick or think they're Maradona because they play a one-two."

El Peque couldn't help thinking – despite these words of praise – that he was about to be thrown out of the club. Not because he was bad, but because he couldn't pay the membership fee or because he rarely contributed anything towards the Pepsi.

"I know you've got money problems, right?"

"My mother works in a lot of houses so that my little brothers can go to school and eat."

"But you'd like to have a bit of pocket money, wouldn't you? Every lad wants to have a bit of cash. And the older they get, the more they want."

El Peque didn't answer. Rivero took it for granted that they were in agreement on this point.

"So I have a proposal for you. Look, I don't make this offer to everyone. Only a select few. Ever since I saw you in the park I've been thinking that you could be one of them. So I'm going to propose a deal that will make you some good money. To avoid misunderstandings, I'll tell you straight off that this isn't for cissies. I don't mix with faggots. What I'm about to offer you is only for really tough boys. It's not for anyone."

El Peque was putting all his attention into understanding each word as it was spoken, but so far none of it was clear to him.

"What I'm proposing here is that you take part in a competition. A competition between two brave boys. There are some games that aren't shown on TV and which people like to watch, to place bets on, who knows. Like cockfights. Have you ever seen cockerels fighting each other on TV? Well, this is something similar. I've got friends who love placing bets on which guy is braver. It's easy. Two boys stand on the railway track and wait for the train to get closer. When they think it's close, they jump to the side and that's it. Nobody makes them do anything. You can see the train coming from three blocks away, and if you decide you don't want to stay on the track you jump off, job done. Don't tell me that isn't easy. It's easy as pie, especially for a kid like you."

"You want me to go and stand on a train track and wait for the train to come?"

"That's about the size of it. Obviously I'll take you to the place where the competition is going to happen. I'll drive you there and take you home afterwards. It's you against another boy. I'm sure you know him. It's Cholito."

El Peque had seen him once or twice. He played with the under-twelves at Breezes.

"I'll take you both. We wait for the train to come. Whenever you feel like it, you jump to one side and off you go with your money. That's the best thing about it. You get twenty pesos just for showing up. Twenty. Even better, I pay you before you get on the track. And if you manage to stay on longer than Cholito you get – listen to this – one hundred pesos. A hundred smackers just for you, to buy whatever you want, to spend on all the things you like. Have you ever seen a one-hundred-peso bill? You can walk away with one in less than ten minutes. What do you think?"

Twenty pesos. A hundred pesos. When in his life would he be able to make a sum like that?

"Are you up for it?"

"Yes, yes."

"You know what? I always knew that you were going to say yes. You're as tough as they come. You're going to go far in soccer. In fact, if you carry on like this, next year I'll take you to try out for Boca or River."

Twenty pesos. A hundred pesos.

"One other thing. People can be idiots. So I'm going to ask you, I'd almost say I'm going to insist, that you do not tell anyone. Because the likelihood is that if they find out they won't let you take part and then you can wave goodbye to the money. You'll never see another peso."

As he was leaving, El Peque ran into Rafael, who shot him a questioning look. El Peque said a quick hello and ran back to his barrio, head spinning. He couldn't tell anyone. Not even Dientes.

III

He didn't have many options to choose from. He put on his newest sneakers, which were not different in any way from the oldest ones. He would have liked to have a padded jacket. He thought that something like that could be useful in case the train got too close. With a good padded jacket he could wait until the train touched him then fire off it, like a cannonball. Or more like a soccer ball, bouncing off the engine and then falling onto the road or landing in the branches of a tree or some electricity cables. But he would have to make do with his usual jacket, which was warm enough but as thin as the coat on a skinny dog. Underneath that he put on the thick sweater he usually kept for special occasions. After all, tonight was a special occasion.

Lies and promises. He told his mother that the Breezes team was going to play a game at River's home ground and that he had a lift there and back. His mother wasn't sure about letting him go. He was going to get back very late. She didn't like him being out and about at night. He told her that the club's coaching staff were very good and that if he played the game they would take him to try out for the Boca youth academy. He promised to do his homework early and that he wouldn't hang about in the street when they brought him back that night.

Rivero picked him up on the corner of Zelarrayán and Gordillo. In fact they were already waiting for him halfway down the block. He climbed into the back seat already occupied by Cholito, who gave him a frosty look and didn't even say hello. Rivero was driving, and in the passenger seat was a man who didn't introduce himself but said to him, "Here comes our champion." That man – who had a black leather jacket like the kind bikers wear – spent the whole trip talking on the phone. From what El Peque could understand, he was telling everyone he spoke to that they were on their way.

After going up and down hundreds of streets and avenues which El Peque had never seen before, they arrived at a railway crossing. They drove across the tracks and parked a few yards further on. When they got out of the car and were standing on the sidewalk, El Peque saw that Cholito was wearing a padded jacket. Rivero gave each of them twenty pesos. El Peque put the money in his good trouser pocket.

There were various parked cars around with people inside them. Some people got out and walked towards the barriers, which were still raised. Then there were other cars – between five and ten – parked on the other side of the tracks. The man who had come in their car kept talking on his phone. "Five minutes," he said loudly, as though announcing the start of a show.

"This is Peque, and you already know Cholito," Rivero said, addressing the rest of the men and then, looking at the boys, he added: "All right boys, we're expecting the best of you."

The other man crossed over to the other side of the tracks. He had a notebook in which he was jotting down what the others said to him. El Peque heard each of the men say one of their names: "Peque" or "Cholito".

Rivero, still in his role as coach, was giving last-minute directions.

"Boys, you have to stand right beside each other. You can't step backwards. Whenever you think the time's right, jump to the side of the track that you're standing on. Take up your positions. Peque, take half a step back. That's it. Stay right there. May the bravest one win."

However hard he looked, El Peque could see nothing in front of him. Nor could he hear a train in the distance or anything that sounded like it. Out of the corner of his eye he noticed that the men standing on the sidelines had retreated and he could no longer make them out.

"You should jump quickly," Cholito told him.

"So should you."

"Do you know Negro Mauro?"

"No."

"He waited for ages and when he jumped the train hit him. Moron lost an arm."

"What a moron."

"So jump quickly."

He wanted to scare him. There was no doubt that he wanted to scare him. El Peque saw a light that was coming closer but that was still very far away. So should he jump now?

The light began to grow. Slowly, it was getting bigger.

Twenty pesos. He had twenty pesos in his pocket. That was already fantastic. He should jump.

The light was coming towards him. It couldn't be very far away now. Beside him, Cholito was like a statue.

A hundred pesos.

A padded jacket, some new sneakers. What can you buy with a hundred pesos?

It wasn't a light. It was a shining ball getting bigger all the time. A giant ball rolling towards them, making a terrifying noise.

"Jump, dickhead, what are you waiting for?"

A hundred pesos. He was waiting for a hundred pesos.

It was like when the hardman from the other team came at you studs up. You had to calculate exactly the right moment to move your legs to avoid getting gouged by the son of a bitch.

It seemed to him that the train was howling. There was a terrible screech that frightened him in a way the light had not.

"Fuck's sake," shouted Cholito, and that was the last thing El Peque heard him say. Because Cholito threw himself to one side while he stayed in position.

Then he jumped.

The hardman on the other team arrives too late and you escape with the ball towards the goal.

It was like scoring a goal.

The train kept bellowing like an injured dinosaur.

A hundred pesos.

In the darkness he could make out Rivero gesturing at him to run towards the shadows. He ran. They got him into the car. Inside, Rivero was exultant. As he was driving he kept turning back to look at El Peque, shouting, "You won, you champion, you won!"

They drove around for a bit before arriving at the street corner where Cholito and the other guy were waiting. They got in. Cholito sat in the back and, as on the outward journey, said nothing. The guy gave El Peque a hundred-peso bill and asked for the twenty back.

They dropped him three blocks from his house. He hadn't put the money in his pocket, but still held it tight in his hand. As he ran home he thought about the surprise he was going to give Dientes. He was so happy that he felt like crying.

5   *The Others*

I

They had both arrived in the building on the same day. Marcelo started work on the first of March and Verónica moved in then too, on a day of suffocating heat. In truth, Marcelo had moved in the day before, with his wife, into a small apartment on the ninth floor, which served as the doorman's living quarters. At seven o'clock the next morning he came out to wash the sidewalk and an hour later Verónica arrived in a removals van from which a couple of men began to unload furniture and packing boxes. Verónica introduced herself and Marcelo mentioned that it was his first day. She smiled at him.

"Then today is the first day of our new lives," said Verónica, beaming.

It was more than five years now since that first encounter, and Verónica had marked every intervening anniversary by giving Marcelo a bottle of Rutini wine which he opened that same night to drink with his wife. He didn't give her anything because doormen aren't expected to give presents to the occupants of the buildings where they work, but he was always ready to help with any repair that needed to be made in Verónica's apartment.

Perhaps there is no such thing as coincidence; perhaps there is a world of secretly magical encounters. If so, their arrival on the same day at that building on Calle Lerma had joined Marcelo and Verónica's lives in a special way. At least he liked to think that, and he treated her differently to all the other neighbours. Obviously he liked her – a lot. Verónica was a pretty girl, tall and with short chestnut hair which put him in mind of a North American actress, a nice ass that made up for her small tits, a sweet voice and a captivating smile. She lived on her own, and he still indulged a fantasy of getting her into bed. But he didn't want to make a false move. He wasn't prepared to lose this job that it had been so hard to get, not least because he had lost his last job as the caretaker of a building for holding on to the service charge money too long, among other trivialities. He had been sacked without any compensation and would never have worked in his profession again if it had not been for his contacts in the building managers' union, who had wiped his record clean and had even arranged this job for him. Besides, when he had arrived it had just been his wife and him, but two years ago his first child had been born and he couldn't really play the romantic hero with the female residents like he had in previous jobs. He was thirty-five years old and had a family to look after. All the same, he still let his mind wander whenever Verónica called him to carry out some electrical or plumbing work in her apartment.

In those five years, Verónica had become a part of his life. He had been wise enough not to talk about this with his wife, although every now and then, when they were commenting on the neighbours' various comings and goings, they would talk about the girl in 2A. And if Marcelo knew secrets about all the building's inhabitants, none of their lives interested him as much as Verónica's. In five years he had found out a lot of things about her. She was the youngest of three sisters, the only one still single and childless. The other two visited her apartment every now and then with their children. A less frequent visitor was her father, who had given her the apartment. Well, actually she had inherited it from her mother, who had died a few months before she moved in. Her father had just helped her with some of the costs.

In contrast to the other neighbours, whose lives were more or less structured around schedules and visitors, Verónica's routine was always changing. He had seen her go out very early, to the gym; he had known her to work from home for a few years or go travelling in Europe for three months. Sometimes she filled the apartment with friends, but then weeks or months could pass without anyone visiting her, not even her sisters and nephews and nieces. She was always coming home at different times – when she came home at all, because days could go by without her returning to the apartment. That was unusual, though, and when it happened Marcelo felt particularly anxious and tempted to call the mobile number which she had once given him.

Perhaps for that reason, the best time he could remember was when Verónica had been in a steady relationship. For a year she had gone out with a boy who sometimes stayed in her apartment but never moved in altogether. Not even during that time did Verónica stop calling Marcelo to fix problems in her home. The guy was clearly useless. He edited books or something, according to Verónica. Marcelo wasn't jealous (not all that jealous, anyway). All he had ever hoped for was a brief sexual encounter, and that could happen whether or not she was engaged, married or single, as she so often was. Before and after that boyfriend the men had come and gone with some regularity. None of them lasted long. And, in contrast to her unpredictable routine, Verónica's men resembled one another to an astonishing degree. They were guys between thirty and forty, dressed like those men he had occasionally seen on television in the audience of fashion shows, polite and gentlemanly. Perhaps a bit shy or stuck-up. Or both. Most of them wore glasses. Marcelo had no idea whether they were good-looking or not.

Since she had been working at the magazine, Verónica had developed some routines. On working days she usually left home at about midday and didn't come back before 9 p.m. That afternoon she was wearing long boots and a coat that hardly allowed him to imagine her tight jeans or the shape of her body underneath it. Another reason to hate cold winter days. Verónica was dressed and made up a little more formally than usual. Marcelo was standing at the door when she went out and asked her:

"Got an important meeting?"

"Lunch with my father. Not the best date in the world, but not the worst, either."

Marcelo handed her an envelope containing the telephone bill, which had arrived a few minutes earlier, and she hurried out.

I'm your best date, he thought as he watched her walk away. Then he carried on sorting the other neighbours' bills.

II

Since his wife had died, Aarón felt that some link with his daughters had broken. It wasn't that he loved them less, or that he wasn't interested in their future, or that he didn't value their company, but he couldn't honestly have said that the death had brought them closer together. In fact, the opposite seemed to be true. His wife had always been the family's catalyst, the one who resolved conflicts, who received any kind of news, who communicated, healed, protected, cautioned, restricted, influenced. Her illness had been long and exhausting for all of them. During those months there had been a few disagreements with his daughters, but he could no longer count on his wife to resolve them. When she died, alongside the pain he had felt a certain liberation, not only from living around illness but also from the bond that tied him to his daughters. Since then they had seen each other and met up on certain occasions – they never missed a birthday or a Rosh Hashanah – but something had been lost forever and now it seemed too difficult to get it back.

It was true that Aarón found it hard to maintain an easy relationship with Verónica, perhaps because, as the single one with no children, there were no tales of little ones' antics to break awkward silences. She visited him once or twice a month, or they went out to lunch at a restaurant of his choosing. There wasn't much personal news they could share and, to avoid fights, they steered clear of politics.

He didn't mind that his daughter was a journalist, but he would have preferred her to take up law as he had done, and his father before him. None of his three daughters had continued the family tradition. The eldest was a clinician, the middle one an educational psychologist and Verónica had a degree in communications. With no husband and those qualifications she wasn't going to get very far, unless she worked in television. But she had decided that her thing was print journalism. He respected the decision and felt proud every time a colleague mentioned seeing her byline in a newspaper or magazine. However, he had always thought that, of the three daughters, she was the one who had the greatest chance of succeeding in law. She had always been good at making an argument and was quick to defend any hard-luck case she came across in life, be it a pet or a friend. She hated injustice and never chose silence over action. She would have been an excellent lawyer. Like him, like her grandfather. If she had been male, he had no doubt that his third child would have been the one to continue the law firm which was so respected and feared in the Palace of Justice.

"Did you know that Alfonsín used to eat here?" he asked as his daughter (ten minutes late, as usual) settled into her seat opposite him, arranging the napkin over her lap.

"Yes, Dad, you told me all the other times that we've come here."

"I like my dining companions to be well informed. So I'm going to tell you again."

But it was only a joke. He didn't continue with the story that she already knew – that in this restaurant, Pedemonte, on Avenida de Mayo, her father had often lunched with Raúl Alfonsín, the President of the Republic. In the 1980s her father's law firm had been close to the government and it still maintained links with the Radicals and with other parties, although he had never been an activist except, for several decades now, at the Buenos Aires Bar Association.

Aarón ordered a sirloin steak, medium rare, with a tomato and carrot salad, a half-bottle of Chateau Vieux and a sparkling water. Verónica opted for grilled Patagonian toothfish with a green salad and still water. Neither of them ate dessert. He asked for a herbal tea and she a black coffee, no sugar.

"What are you up to at the magazine?"

"I'm at the start of an investigation that I think is going to be really important. It's for a piece looking into the dark side of the railways."

"About the privatization of the branch lines? We've got a Metrovías case on at the firm."

"No, nothing to do with contracts. It's about suicides, people who throw themselves under trains."

"Ah, very dark."

"Yes, but with some interesting twists in the tale."

"I don't know how you don't get depressed working on this sort of stuff."

"I do get depressed, but I hide it."

"How about your boss – do you get on well with him?"

"With her. My boss is a woman."

"But the magazine's editor is a man."

"Yes, but I don't answer to him. Luckily. In his office, which is pretty big, there's only room for him and his ego."

They left the restaurant quickly, not because they were keen to get the lunch over with but because neither could wait any longer for a cigarette. Both of them lit up in the door of the restaurant.

"I don't like you smoking, darling, it's not good."

"I, on the other hand, love you smoking. It makes you look like Charles Boyer in an old movie. Bye, Dad, I'm off to the magazine."

She gave him a noisy kiss, then headed off in the opposite direction from the way he was going.

III

It wasn't that Patricia hated her work, she was just tired of journalism. She hid the fact under a display of scepticism about the career she had chosen twenty years earlier. Perhaps her mistake had been to marry her work and never apply for a separation. She, who had been divorced twice, who had managed to have children with two husbands, who had slipped off so many bonds, had never been able to step away from journalism. She no longer felt the same excitement that she used to, years ago, when she saw her name at the head of an article: Patricia Beltrán. Her colleagues used to call her 'La Beltraneja', an allusion to the nickname mockingly given to the medieval infanta Juana of Castile because she

103

was presumed to be the illegitimate child of the nobleman Beltrán de La Cueva. Patricia, who had never been unfaithful but had always known how to break off relations the day before disaster struck, lived a kind of double life. Everyone thought of her as a brilliant journalist whose work her colleagues remembered (the general public tends to have shorter memories). But the truth was that she was no longer truly a journalist. She took refuge in editing the work of her team and scarcely wrote any articles herself. She thought up the headlines, scheduled pieces, counted characters and improved badly written articles. She was like a priest who has lost faith in God and now goes through the motions at Mass, repeating what comes easily after so many years as an officiant. That was Patricia: a journalistic atheist. Her weekly Mass was editing the Society section in *Nuestro Tiempo*. The magazine had been launched in the mid-1990s under the title *Última Decada*. In the year 2000 it had needed a new name.

Her years of experience allowed Patricia to carry out her work with a certain professional dignity. Nobody ever reproached her for her cynicism or weariness. She had put together an excellent team: four outstanding writers, an intelligent intern and contributors chosen with her unerring instinct for picking out reliable colleagues. Society was one of the magazine's longest and most important sections. She got on well with the back-room team who managed the publication and, since she had no interest in joining them, they treated her with respect and gratitude.

If there was one thing that did still have the power to move her, it was witnessing other people's passion. When she saw a journalist who could still get fired up about the job, Patricia couldn't help feeling a special emotion and a desire to protect them. That was particularly the case with Verónica. If it weren't for the fact that, at Verónica's age, she had been in a relationship and pregnant with her first child, you could say that she had been the same when she was thirty. She had watched Verónica grow as a journalist, from the time she started as an intern on the magazine of which Patricia was already editor. She had seen something different in the young reporter and a few years later she had had no hesitation in taking Verónica with her to her next job. Of her staff writers she was the best, and the only one without ambitions to become an editor or deputy editor. Verónica, like Patricia light years ago, wanted to be on the street investigating, meeting people, finding explanations for problems, naming and shaming those responsible for them. She was meticulous, obsessive, clear-eyed and a very good writer. Patricia trusted her, and that is always the best thing an editor can say about one of her journalists. Plus she had an instinct. A sixth sense. Where someone else saw ordinary behaviour, Verónica might uncover some hair-raising back-story. When she had said that she was going to write about a suicidal railwayman, Patricia had expected to get a nice crime story with some heart-wrenching anecdote. She didn't imagine that there could be much else to say. However, early that morning she had received an email from Verónica that read:

Dear Pato,

When I was a little girl I used to get frightened on the ghost train in Italpark. Now I'm starting to see that the real horror stories are on the normal, everyday trains. I've got some good leads and if all goes to plan I think we can pull a nice big rabbit out of the hat. A terrifying rabbit, in fact. Tomorrow I'll tell you everything.

That afternoon Patricia watched Verónica walk through reception and into the newsroom. She said hello to the colleagues who were already there and walked on towards Patricia, smiling.

"You're smiling like the cat that got the cream…"

"I prefer the Cheshire cat. I'm exhausted. I've just had lunch with my esteemed father and I ate too much. I need a siesta urgently."

"Did he take you to Hermann again?"

"No, we went to Pedemonte."

She hung up her coat and perched her shapely rear on the desk. Looking at her, Patricia couldn't help thinking that she would give anything to be thirty again. Although she had never had a body like Verónica's. Or perhaps she had. Who isn't beautiful when they're young? And the chances were that Verónica didn't even know it. If somebody had told Patricia at twenty-five (let alone twenty) that someone of thirty was young she would have burst out laughing. She'd have done the same, for that matter, if someone had told her at thirty that she was young.

"Pato, start lining up the cover for me, because I've got a big fat story for you."

"The suicidal railwayman with criminal tendencies is really that big a deal?"

"I can assure you it is."

How must Verónica see her? As an older woman, no doubt, even though she was only twenty years older. A colleague who had run the gamut of the leading newsrooms of Buenos Aires and who had chosen where and with whom to work. Who had reached all life's milestones – marriage, children, separation – twice over. She must see her as a historic monument.

"There are actually two articles. Or rather, two subjects that I want to cover in the article. The theme is death."

"Trains and death. I'm beginning to get it."

"Let's say that the railwayman's suicide was the trigger. I went down that road, but what I found was a guy haunted by the ghosts of the people he's run over. You wouldn't believe how many suicides there are on the line. Anyway, the number isn't important. Figures are never that useful."

"What do you mean 'not useful'? Figures are essential. We're journalists."

"Yes, but stories are what stay with the reader. And there are some terrible tales. The men who run over people suffer dreadful guilt. Some of them go mad. In some cases the company takes them off driving duties, but most of them carry on as before. All of them are, or should be, getting psychiatric treatment for the rest of their lives."

"It certainly seems to meet the legal definition of 'insalubrious work'."

"Do you know of any other job where you wind up in a psychiatric hospital?"

"Darling, I've worked on the Politics section of several newspapers."

"These people go off their rockers for a long, long time."

"Blood and madness. I'm liking it, but I'm not seeing a cover story. I see a headline on the cover, certainly, but not the lead piece."

Patricia would be the first to admit that she enjoyed pulling apart her writers' proposals. At the end of the day, she might say, she was paid for good stories and not for being kind to journalists who didn't know how to come up with a winning idea. It was because she admired Verónica that she took particular pleasure in being hypercritical of her ideas. It was also true that she delighted in seeing her protégée double down on an idea and talk her out of her doubts, and she relished her role as devil's advocate. So far, Verónica had brought her a good idea for a piece, but there must be something more. She wouldn't settle merely for a good idea.

"There are children. Not exactly suicidal children, but almost. Kids who stand on the tracks and compete to see who can last the longest before jumping off to one side. Imagine it. The train is bearing down on them and they don't move a muscle, holding out to the last minute."

"This is really happening?"

"I saw it last night with my own eyes. Between Caballito and Flores. On the Sarmiento line. Two boys of about ten. I was in the driver's cabin."

"What were you doing there?"

"A source had told me that it might happen, and he took me along with him. And it did happen."

"What a macabre game."

"You know what I think? That those boys weren't just messing about – someone is making them do it. If I could find something on that side of things we're looking at a criminal case. And you know how this kind of thing works. If there's betting, there are powerful people implicated, there's impunity. The same old thing as always, except that in this case it could lead to the deaths of children."

Verónica was managing to draw her in, turning her into an atheist who doubted. What if God in fact existed? What if journalism was a worthwhile endeavour after all?

"OK, let's get ourselves organized. There are two articles here. First, one about work insecurity with some highly dramatic content: suicides and the train drivers who are left traumatized by them. End of story. Cover line. Pretty pictures of dismembered bodies, or grisly illustration by Sapo González. Second, a piece on a potentially criminal instance of child abuse. It's not going to be easy to find more than what you've already seen, but it has to be found all the same. Start with the suicides and take as long as you need for the other piece. Without abusing my generosity, of course."

"OK. I'm on it. I can't do anything for this week's deadline, anyway."

"I thought as much."

"I'm not staying late tonight."

"You all go off and leave me then, as usual."

"I'm meeting Paula at eight o'clock for a drink."

"Tell her that she promised to send me Katherine Mansfield's *Collected Stories* and they never arrived."

"I'll tell her, before we get too drunk."

IV

I need to speak to you urgently. And get drunk. Are you free? Paula had received the text message at eleven o'clock in the morning, four and a half hours after her day had begun: first she had taken her son to school, then she had gone to kick up a fuss at a branch of Movistar because they wouldn't let her increase her calling credit; she had gone to a bank to pay in a cheque for a freelance job and finally she had gone to the offices of the publishing house where she worked as the press officer, counterphobic assistant to the general manager, general assistant to anyone who needed a hand and part-time carer for Luz, the office dog. The message had Verónica's name on it, but she would have known who it was from just by reading it. Verónica was the only person Paula knew who always put complete words in her texts, who used full stops and accents and whose only act of grammatical rebellion was to permit herself not to start questions with the inverted question mark used in Spanish. Paula checked her diary for that night: the people in relationships would be with their partners, her single friends were suffering from various phobias and the only passable divorcee was out of the country. Her ex was going to pick their son up from school.

So she had a free night. *OK 8pm in Martataka*, she replied, and didn't think of her friend again until she was heading towards Palermo Hollywood, where the bar was.

From Congreso she took a taxi, an expensive option, but she didn't feel like getting a bus and much less like walking to the underground station. If Verónica was so eager to see her it must be because she had, or was about to have, man problems. It wouldn't be the first time that they had disguised themselves as entomologists in order to dissect the brain and sex of a male specimen. Sometimes the specimen was provided by herself or Verónica, and sometimes by one of the other women they met at Martataka or at private views and other events in the intellectual world. The women were journalists, editors, press officers and the odd psychologist who had attached herself to the group. But when push came to shove, these conversations usually became two-handers and the larger groups were reserved for gossip and entertainment.

She had known Verónica since the days when her friend wrote reviews and book commentaries for a magazine at the Public Bar Association. Later she found out that her father had got her the job so that she could take her first steps in journalism while still studying communications. The publication's editor, thanks to her father – and Verónica never tired of saying that this was the only time in her career that he had helped her – had invented just for her a page devoted to book reviews. As a student, she couldn't believe that publishers gave away books for free. Paula had already been working in publicity at the time and had forwarded a few press copies to this virtual adolescent. And in those ten or eleven years a lot of things had happened. Paula had married, had a child and separated. Her friend, meanwhile, had grown into a respected journalist. During that time Paula had seen her falling for, suffering and cursing the various men who came her way. She had seen her break off a six-year relationship with a friend from secondary school; she had been a witness to Verónica's most promiscuous phase, a time when she might date two different men in one weekend (or three, if it was a long weekend). That chapter, which Verónica herself referred to as 'sampling the goods', had not been as much fun as her journalist friend liked to remember. Paula had seen her unhappy, suffering from panic attacks and having therapy four times a week. Her mother's illness had marked a change in the way Verónica related to men, and to the rest of her life, too. That change became more entrenched with her mother's death. Simply put, she had grown up. And although there was the odd encounter which took place in the middle of the night, or on a trip, or in some unexpected place, Verónica had lasted more than a year with Anibal, the editor of *Exlibris*. She had been at her most settled during that relationship. Ever since it had ended, almost two years ago, she had seemed to be drifting here and there. "The wrong man, at the wrong time", one or another of the friends would decide. Whenever Verónica had a love-related problem she turned to Paula for advice. Verónica, like the other girls in the group, seemed to see her as a spiritual guide – perhaps motherhood and a stint in lawful matrimony had given her an aura of wisdom.

Paula saw her from the taxi. Verónica was standing outside the door of Martataka, braving the cold along with many others who had come out to smoke. Her left arm was crossed over her body, while she held the cigarette in her right hand. She glanced around her, as though looking for someone. From the way she squinted, Paula suspected that her friend was a little short-sighted, that those glasses she wore were part of her look but inadequate compensation for her myopia. When she saw her, Verónica threw the cigarette away.

"Let's go inside. I'm freezing to death out here."

They sat at the back, at a table that still bore witness to its previous occupants. Paula cleared it, sweeping the peanut shells on to the floor. The waitress took a long time to come. A young man walked over from the bar. He was the owner of a bookshop who often organized literary events and he knew both of them – Paula a little better than Verónica. They greeted one another but, since neither woman invited him to sit down with them, he returned to the bar. There were so many people that the waitress practically had to climb into their laps to clean the table and take their order. They asked for a margarita and a caipiroska. The waitress may have been slow, but the drinks came quickly. They talked about this and that. As a general rule, the serious conversation only started after the first round of tequila and vodka.

"I'm writing a piece for the magazine, and it's doing my head in. It started as a crime report on a railway worker who committed suicide, then it segued into an article about people who kill themselves by jumping under trains and then that opened up a new line of investigation into some fucked-up story about kids who play chicken on the tracks."

"It sounds like a dark piece."

"But I didn't call to ask you for editing advice. That pleasure falls to Pato, who gets harder to please by the day. She thinks she's some big-shot journalist, like Oriana Fallaci."

"I warned you about her a long time ago. I've known her since she was married to that loser Salvador Lutz."

"Aaanyway, that's not the issue here. One of my sources is a driver on the Sarmiento line. He's called Lucio Valrossa. Valrossa, Rosenthal: Valley of Roses – get it?"

"No, you've lost me. How old is this driver?"

"Thirty-eight."

"Physical shape?"

"Good verging on great."

"Marital status?"

"Married."

"Now I understand the problem."

"You see?"

"Girl, you never learn."

"It's my target market. Married men with children."

"Have you slept with him?"

"Not yet."

"Yet."

"Last night he let me travel in the driver's cabin while he was operating the train. At one point he showed me something terrible."

"He dropped his trousers?"

"No, stupid. Something to do with this thing about the children, the investigation I've got involved in. Afterwards I was in shock and Lucio kissed me."

"Just a kiss then?"

"A kiss, a bit of a grope. He could have fucked me right there. But he had to keep driving the train."

"How irresponsible. This is how accidents happen. Guys taking their floozies into the cabin. And when you got to the station, did you say goodbye? Swap emails? What did you do?"

"He wanted to take me to a by-the-hour motel."

"Ah, this married man's a fast mover. And you didn't want to. Never on a first date."

"I don't know, I was a bit nervous. I don't know anything about the guy, apart from what I found out in the interview. Anyway, I hadn't waxed."

"As if it would be the first time you let that get in the way of hooking up with someone."

"I went to get material for a piece, not to get laid."

"A driver with wandering hands, a wanton journalist

caught up in a horror story. It definitely sounds bizarre, but I still don't see why it has to be a problem."

"I like the guy, a lot. He's so different from all the other jerks you see around. I mean, there's nobody in this bar remotely like him. I know that I'm going to get into trouble."

"What kind of trouble?"

"I don't know. It's as if he were behind some kind of veil."

"As if he's hiding something."

"No, as if there's something he can't tell me."

"You're inventing excuses. You like him because he's a bit of rough and that's catnip to girls like you."

"No, or at least not only that. There's something violent in him. Stop – don't misinterpret me. I'm not saying that he seems violent but that he's immersed in a universe of pain. And that's always violent. For the person suffering it and for the person who watches from the sidelines."

"Too much poetry and not enough realism. You're either seeing things or you're not seeing reality."

"I've got it bad."

"Did you arrange to see each other?"

"Monday night."

"I see. And you're going to a motel. And what if the guy's a perv or something worse, like a man who kills women in cheap hotels?"

"It's a possibility. Although beyond that dark aura which you say I'm imagining, he seems protective, in a gruff kind of way. He's not a caveman."

"Oh, Vero, I won't be able to rest easy on Monday, thinking that you might be lying drugged in a by-the-hour motel bathtub. I'm going to call you that night, just to be sure."

"Why don't you call the waitress over instead and ask for another caipiroska."

Verónica's username was Beija-Flor, as in the song "Codinome beija flor" by Cazuza. It means hummingbird – literally "flower-kisser" – but she preferred the erroneous translation "bella flor", "beautiful flower".

Nobody knew and perhaps nobody would ever know that she was Beija-Flor. That information belonged to a part of her life she would never allow anyone to describe as "secret". It was personal, that was all, one of those areas you keep in the shadows. It had started out as curiosity. An inquisitive spirit made her seek out things she was not supposed to see. The internet had turned out to be a repository of bizarre knowledge: she had seen people being decapitated, a cow mooing with two heads, a blonde woman moaning while simultaneously being penetrated by three black men. She had visited sites that spat racism, on which people were aroused by menstruation or promoted anorexia. Every now and then she indulged in decadent tourism of those places that provoked her curiosity, to a greater or lesser degree, as much as her revulsion.

She would visit a site, be startled or shocked by it, and leave. Rarely did she return to it. The only internet pages to which she kept returning with a curiosity that grew into excitement were the ones containing revelations of a sexual nature. Erotic, or even pornographic, stories. She didn't mind whether they were confessions or mere narrative exercises – invariably mediocre. She read them – and some of them she reread. They got her going.

At first she registered on the Todo Relatos page so that she could vote for the stories she liked best, but gradually she found herself wanting to write stories herself. In her case these would be purely literary exercises. While her colleagues dreamed of publishing novels or short-story collections, she was happy just to write pornographic stories under a pseudonym. She didn't know if it was her pornographic inclination that she was keeping quiet, or the fact that every night she turned into a fiction writer.

Verónica didn't try to analyse what she wrote. The stories were neither sexual fantasies nor autobiographical tales, even when she made use of things that had happened to her in real life. At the end of the day, she was creating literature, and everything was permitted.

The Marquis de Sade was probably largely to blame. She had been fifteen years old when she discovered on the bookshelves at home a copy of *Justine, or The Misfortunes of Virtue*. Rarely had the sight of a man's naked body induced in her the excitement and heat that she had experienced while secretly reading that book. Since then she had read most of the Marquis' work, but she had never rediscovered that primordial feeling of pleasure, fear, disgust, discomfort, chagrin (because she was not Justine) and joy (for the same reason).

Sade had opened in her brain a conduit for all her desires and anxieties. She began to search online for pornography linked to sadomasochistic practices. And her stories took the same direction – men and women united not only by desire but by pain. Or rather, by the desire for pain. She had only been bold enough to post two stories. Again, that had less to do with what she was telling than with how she was telling it. The question of style.

The night before her first date with Lucio, when she got home drunk from Martataka, she typed his name into a Word document but couldn't get as far as writing anything more. She surrendered before the evidence. She preferred to imagine nothing, not to presuppose any story. To let herself be carried like a *bella flor*, a beautiful flower on the current of a dangerous river.

6   *In the Labyrinth*

I

"Long Live The Sarmiento Toshibas", a colleague had written on a photo stuck up in the driver's cabin of the eight formation, a Toshiba train imported from Japan decades ago. The photograph was of a sunset and had been taken from the driver's cabin close to Haedo. The different hues of red had spread from the horizon over the landscape, creating the impression of a bucolic scene.

Less than a mile further on was the place where the largest percentage of suicides took place. There were various explanations for the popularity of this spot: the trains travelled faster at this point (at almost forty-five miles an hour) and the General Acute Interzonal Hospital was nearby. One theory was that many of the suicides were relatives of gravely ill patients. It wasn't hard to imagine somebody desperate leaving the white hulk that loomed up north of the railway, walking a short distance to the tracks and letting ten thousand tons of metal banish their problems forever.

That evening, however, even Lucio found a serene beauty in the reddish horizon he saw at Haedo. All he had to do was reach Moreno and return to Plaza Once, then his working day would be finished. He would have a shower at the station and then meet Verónica.

Some nights Lucio went to get a pizza with friends from work. Those get-togethers could go on very late. When he arrived home his wife was already asleep. Since she got up early to take the children to school, they would hardly see each other again until the following night. Lucio had told her that he was going to the pizzeria with his friends that night. A simple, credible excuse, allowing him quite a wide margin until he had to see his wife again.

"What's your wife called?"

That was the first thing Verónica asked him when they met in La Perla del Once. Lucio had arrived before her, his hair still wet from the shower he had taken at work. When she arrived, she had made him change tables, relocating to the smoking area, a small room at the entrance to the bar which stank of cigarette smoke. They had scarcely sat down when Verónica asked the question. He took a few seconds to answer.

"Mariana."

"And your children?"

"Patricio and Fabián. Is this still an interview?"

"No. I just like to put names to people. It's how they take shape for me."

"Do you dye your hair?"

"No. This is my natural colour. I used to lighten it, but now I stick to the colour I was born with. What else would you like to know about me?"

"What I want to know isn't something you can tell me here."

Lucio had never been unfaithful to Mariana. At least, not since they were married. When they were dating, he had had a fling with one of his neighbours. At the time Lucio had been living with his parents on Calle Fonrouge. A couple had moved in round the corner. She was about fifteen years older than Lucio. Their houses backed on to each other and, the first time they saw each other, he had been up on the roof, cutting back creepers. She had waved to him, and not long afterwards he had ended up in her bed. It had only been a couple of times. Neither of them had wanted to continue the relationship. He had never regarded this as true infidelity, because he had only recently started going out with Mariana. Once married, he had never wanted to have an affair, not seriously. Lucio was unfamiliar with the etiquette of an illicit relationship. He didn't know if there was anything like a code of conduct. And perhaps for that reason, to avoid any possible confusion, he suggested going to a love hotel after they had been together just a few minutes. This time Verónica agreed.

There was a hotel opposite and another on the corner of Mitre and Jean Jaurès. He asked her if she would mind walking there and she said no. The hotel opposite seemed too exposed and he didn't want anyone to see him, not even his friends from work, even though, if they did ever find out, they would admire him for the rest of their days. So they went to the other hotel. They walked diagonally across Plaza Miserere, barely speaking as they passed the shrine to the 194 victims of the 2004 República Cromañón nightclub fire and the remains of what once, before that tragedy, had been a venue for rock concerts. The hotel was on the corner of that street.

As the elevator made its brief ascent – just one floor – they kissed. They looked for their room without acknowledging the moans that could be heard coming from behind other doors. If the first kiss in the driver's cabin had been like a mutual mauling, now, too, they sought each other out with the same urgency. They fell onto the bed with half their clothes still on. Silently they went to war, Lucio gripping her wrists and she seeking his body with her teeth. When Verónica climbed on top of Lucio, her breasts free, trousers open, she grabbed hold of his wrists in the same way that he had held hers. She brought one breast close to his mouth and Lucio sucked on the nipple greedily. Silence gave way then to Verónica's moans as she let herself fall onto the bed. Lucio took off her trousers and removed the rest of his own clothes. He picked up the condom which was lying on the bedside table and put it on. She watched him, smiling. She was wearing only a white pair of pants now but he didn't take them off, just pushed the material aside and penetrated her, letting his full weight fall onto her as she clung to his back. She dug her nails into him as she reached orgasm. Only then did her body soften, and then Lucio pounded his hips harder against Verónica's pelvis until he came. They had not said anything to each other since leaving La Perla.

II

For three hours they had been in that room decorated to look like a wood cabin. A mirror on the ceiling returned the image of their bodies. They had not switched on the lights; there were just a few little yellow lamps bathing the room in golden hues. The silence was broken by the insistent ringing of Verónica's mobile phone. She didn't answer. A few minutes later a different sound alerted her to the arrival of a text message. She got up to read it, allowing Lucio a chance to study her body from a different perspective: the long legs and back, the round, firm backside of a girl who obviously worked out, the short hair that barely grazed her shoulders. Verónica wrote a quick text then came back to lie down beside him.

"A friend who sounds bored."

Verónica ran one of her hands along Lucio's body while he lay quietly looking into the mirror. He felt like the protagonist of a movie, or of a dream. The picture returned by the mirror seemed like something unconnected to him. An attractive girl, he himself lying beside her, his body darker than hers.

Just before they left, Verónica made a bit of a scene. She had been adamant that she wanted to pay half the cost of the hotel. That she was an independent woman and that nobody paid for her pleasure. Lucio was not prepared to submit to the humiliation of splitting the bill. He was a railwayman and perhaps he earned less than a journalist, but he would pay for the room. She accused him of being a low-rent chauvinist. She tried to put some notes in his pocket and only relented when she saw that he was genuinely annoyed. Verónica had to resign herself to letting him pay.

"Lucio, what shall I do with you?"

He looked her in the eye and stroked her cheek.

"You're going to be a good girl and you're going to miss me."

"I didn't say be, I said do. Never get involved with a married man."

"When can I see you again?"

"I don't know. Is there a time when I can call you, or send you a text message?"

"Text me, and I'll call you."

III

The hardest moment came the next day, when he got home from work. The night before, he had got back so late that his wife hadn't noticed him getting into bed and hadn't heard him when he left in the morning. So they didn't see

121

each other until dinner time the next day. Patricio insisted on showing him his schoolbook and Fabián wanted him to look at something he had made with the Playmobil in his room. He was always exhausted by his children's demands, but that night he felt as though they were protecting him and was grateful for the imposition. Mariana kept calling them to the table. She was already serving up a meat pie and wanted Lucio to take care of the drinks and bread.

Lucio was scared that what he had done the evening before would show on his face. It sounded absurd, but he had stared into the mirror searching for traces of his infidelity. As an adolescent he used to study his older sister's friends. He knew which ones were virgins and which not any more, and he used to try and discern the signs of their lost virginity in their features, their way of speaking or moving. In the same way he now found himself looking for telltale signs in his own face, or in what he might say that night.

Mariana didn't notice anything; she was too concerned about an episode of eczema that had suddenly afflicted Fabián. Afterwards, while Lucio washed the plates, Mariana put the children to bed and made coffee, which they drank in the kitchen the same as always. They talked about the children and Mariana told him about the problems experienced by a teacher who had asked to take some leave. They rarely spoke about Lucio's work. Mariana had known since before their marriage that Lucio didn't like talking about it, and she respected that. Just as she respected the silences into which he retreated after every accident. She settled for keeping him close, not leaving him too much time alone to think. She was always happy to welcome family, friends, anyone who might distract her husband and not let him dwell on the accidents. And when some nightmare woke him up in the early hours, she would go and fetch him a glass of water. Those were the only times when he talked; he told her in detail about that face that looked at him in horror, the sound of the body that broke into a thousand pieces, the smell of blood that impregnated the cabin and remained there.

In the bedroom they undressed by the light of the television set. A soap opera they usually watched together was about to start, though he often fell asleep and the next day would have to try to work out what had happened in the previous episode. He watched his wife in her underwear, putting on a nightdress, and thought that he liked her, that he found her attractive as a woman. That night he would have caressed her. He would have made her finish on top of him. But he couldn't bring himself to initiate sex. They settled into bed and this time he didn't fall asleep until he could hear his wife's breathing, slow and steady.

IV

Two days later he received a text that said *Can we see each other?* He had saved Verónica's mobile number under the name "Víctor R", in case his wife decided to look through his contacts. *Can do Fri am*, he texted back. Her next message said *Call me?* Lucio was driving a five formation and had just left Villa Luro. They spoke for a few minutes, until he was past Floresta and about to arrive at Flores. It was long enough to arrange to meet on Friday morning at half past ten. Lucio didn't like the idea of stepping out of a motel into the midday sun so, as a less risky option, she invited him to her apartment. Since he had nothing to write with, she sent him a text with the details.

On Friday Lucio left his house early. He walked along Calle Zuviría until he reached Avenida La Plata and looked for a bus stop for the number 15, a route he never usually took and which passed almost by Verónica's door. He was lucky and quickly got a seat, positioning himself opposite the window so that he could look out at the view. He felt as though he were on a day trip or on holiday, when there is more time to observe what's going on around you. When they passed the Parque Centenario, it was as though he were seeing it for the first time, even though he had taken his children there on various occasions. It was like stepping back in time twenty years. At that time he had taken driving lessons a few blocks away. When he got into the school's car and they told him to take the street leading to Hospital Naval to go around the park, he had felt as though he were discovering a new city. Why had he felt like that that morning? Was it that he was at the start of a new life? Or was it simply the excitement of discovery?

Since he was going to arrive at Verónica's earlier than agreed, he stayed on the bus for one more stop and got out at the junction of Avenida Córdoba and Scalabrini Ortiz. He spotted a bar and went in to have a coffee. The winter sunlight had a luminous, barely warm quality. There were a few locals in the bar reading the paper or slowly drinking coffee. Time seemed to have stood still in there, and Lucio liked that. He wanted to see Verónica, but this wait in the bar was as pleasurable as the thought of their encounter. He let a few minutes after their agreed meeting time pass, then he went straight to the address that she had given him. The building's doorman was standing at the entrance. Lucio rang the bell to her apartment. The doorman asked him where he was going just as Verónica answered, asking who it was. Lucio answered her; the doorman told him which apartment was hers. The doorman rang Verónica's bell twice and told her that he was letting Lucio in. Her voice could be heard saying "thank you", and the doorman ushered him in. Lucio went up in the elevator. Verónica was waiting for him, smiling, at the door to her apartment. She wore jeans with various patches that looked fake, a black pullover that was big on her and no shoes.

"Welcome to the Rosenthal abode."

They walked down a short corridor in which he noticed a painting and a couple of posters. Immediately on the left was a door leading to the kitchen. He followed Verónica through it.

"What would you like? Coffee, tea, maté?"

He watched her light the gas on the stove top. Standing behind her, he put his arms around her, kissed her neck and she turned around. They kissed and he stroked her ass, squeezing it towards him.

"I make a delicious espresso, or as good as. Or I can be your gaucho girl and brew you up a nice maté."

He kissed her again. Then she took his hand and led him into the living room. One of the walls was completely covered with bookshelves. On the others were photos and a poster of Marlon Brando in *On The Waterfront*.

"Let me introduce you to the man in my life," she said, pointing at Brando.

They fell onto the sofa, scattering magazines and newspapers onto the floor, along with Verónica's pullover. Under it she wore a white vest and, under that, a black bra. She unbuttoned his shirt and threw it on the floor.

"I like your hairy chest. It makes you look very virile." She tugged the hairs and Lucio felt a twinge of pain. They kissed each other on the mouth and Verónica bit his lip. He turned away.

"Did I hurt you?"

"No."

"I think I want to eat you."

"You're a cannibal."

"I'll show you how."

She pushed him back, kneeled down, undid his belt and trousers, lowered the zip and put one hand inside his boxers. She pulled out his erect penis and gave it the treatment he would like to give her nipples: kissing, licking and sucking it with increasing pressure. Lucio, leaning back into the sofa, watched her. She also looked up at him. She kept sucking and stroking until he came into her mouth. When she felt that he had finished ejaculating, she moved her mouth away, kissed him briefly around the pubis and lifted herself up to give him a peck on the lips. He held her and they stayed together like this for a few minutes before Verónica moved away to get her cigarettes and lighter, which were on a coffee table.

"How about now? Maté or coffee?"

"Coffee."

She picked her pullover up off the floor and put it on.

"I'm not shy – just cold."

Lucio looked around the living room, which seemed messy at first glance; in fact, it was just that there were books and magazines everywhere. Everything else was admirably well ordered. There was a plasma TV, a DVD player and a laptop lying on a desk made of dark wood. He imagined Verónica sitting at her computer screen writing her articles, or sitting in the armchair reading one of those books.

"Tell me something, have you read all the books on those shelves?"

Verónica came out of the kitchen and contemplated her shelves with pride.

"Not all of them, but a lot of them, yes." She walked over to the shelves and put some loose books back in their places. "A large part of my life could be told through the books I've read."

"Believe it or not, I was a great reader once."

"Seriously?"

"Because railway workers can't read, you mean?"

"I didn't say that."

Lucio told her that as a boy he had spent all the summer holidays in Santa Teresita, where his parents had a house a few blocks from the sea. His aunt and uncle also had a house there and Lucio had spent the days with his cousin Claudio, who was two years older than him. The rest of the year they barely saw each other, but for two weeks in January they were inseparable. And Claudio was a keen reader. He was reading all the books in the *Robin Hood* collection. Lucio, who imitated his cousin in everything he did, set out to read them too. And he discovered that he liked reading, and not only in the holidays. Throughout the year he steadily read books which he then discussed with Claudio. He took particular pride in reading something his cousin had not yet come across, which was difficult when his cousin had a two-year advantage.

"And which were your favourite books?"

"Emilio Salgari's. I loved the whole series about Sandokan and his faithful friend Yanez. Jesus, now that I think about it, Sandokan's love interest was called Mariana."

"How interesting. And you haven't come across any Verónicas in your reading? I don't know, in a book by Poldy Bird, for example?"

"No, not that I remember. On the other hand I do remember *The Prisoner of Zenda*, *Tom Sawyer*, a book by Verne that was called *Extraordinary Voyages* and *Twenty Thousand Leagues Under the Sea*."

Verónica went to the kitchen and returned moments later with two cups of coffee.

"Sugar, sweetener?"

"I prefer it bitter."

"Me too. I think you've read more books than I have. As a child I read the books in the Biblioteca Billiken red collection."

"Totally different. Those were shorter versions. Somebody once gave me the Billiken version of *One Thousand and One Nights* and there were only about three or four nights in it."

"So when did you give up reading – if you did give it up?"

"When I was twelve, my parents sold the house in Santa Teresita. I stopped seeing my cousin in the holidays. And after that I no longer had any interest in reading. I gradually got out of the habit."

Lucio put on his shirt without doing it up. He wasn't cold, but neither was he bold enough to walk naked onto the balcony, and he was curious to know what could be seen from there. He took his coffee out with him. The two houses opposite allowed a fairly unobstructed view of that part of the city. Rooftops and grey terraces.

"Have you always lived in Villa Crespo?"

"No. In fact for a large part of my life I lived at my parents' house on Avenida Callao where Juncal crosses it. So technically I'm a Recoleta girl. When I was old enough to choose, I came to Villa Crespo, my grandad's neighbourhood. And my father's, when he was a boy. Although my grandfather's house was on the other side of Avenida Corrientes, on Malabia and Camargo. And I like to say that I live in Villa Crespo. I'm even an Atlanta fan. Who do you support?"

"I like watching soccer and playing it, but I don't support any club. I support the national team."

"Ah, you've no blood in your veins! I bet deep down you support Argentinos Juniors or Vélez."

They drank their coffee and then she led him to the bedroom. She took off his shirt again and they collapsed onto the bed. She got up and took a condom out of the wardrobe, leaving it on the bedside table. She took off her trousers and socks and pullover and kept only her underwear on. Lucio watched as she climbed on top of him and felt her bury her face in his neck. He caressed her back.

V

On Saturday mornings Lucio played soccer in Parque Sarmiento. Drivers and signalmen against warehouse and administration colleagues. As they were getting changed, a co-worker teased him about the journalist he had taken on the train.

"Fucked her yet?" another one asked him.

"Like he'd get a chance."

"His wife would hang him by the balls from the Obelisk."

"Mind you, those girls can be right little whores. Show them who's boss and you'll have them eating out of your hand."

"Or eating your cock."

"She wouldn't give the time of day to a low life like Lucio, however slutty she is. With girls like that, you're lucky if you get close enough to smell their perfume. They're not for the likes of us."

Lucio would have loved to join in the chat. To tell them that, yes, he had fucked her and that her perfume smelled pretty good, but that the smell of her sweat-covered body after sex was even better. But he couldn't. His throat tightened and all he did was smile in a way that could be interpreted as inscrutable or modest, depending on which workmate happened to be looking. Lucio couldn't believe that that girl would sleep with him, either. It was like a prize, surely deserved, or perhaps it was just a part of that unreal life he led on the train. Because if one thing was true, both of the

129

deaths on the tracks and of his relationship with Verónica, it was that he couldn't tell anyone about them. They belonged to a dimension that ran parallel to his family life, his friendships at work and the routine which he had been following for two decades and which was interrupted only after an accident and, now, with Verónica's arrival.

On Saturday afternoon he went with Mariana and the boys to his sister's house in Liniers. That night, back at home, they ordered a pizza and he and his wife watched a movie on TV, one they had already seen, with Hugh Grant and Sarah Jessica Parker. The children had been asleep for more than an hour. Mariana hugged and kissed him. They took their clothes off and, as he caressed her, it struck Lucio that his wife's body reminded him of Verónica's. Not because they looked particularly alike, but because the texture of their skin and their way of moving was similar.

On Sunday he got up early, after Fabián had woken him. They went to buy bread and churros filled with dulce de leche, a weekly ritual. Patricio had woken up by the time they came back, although Mariana was still asleep. He poured out milk for the boys and made maté. He drank two gourds of maté himself, then sweetened one to take to Mariana in bed. She got up, still half asleep, and they drank more maté in the kitchen while eating the churros. Later Mariana took the boys out to play on the sidewalk with their bikes.

Lucio went up to the roof terrace to light the barbecue ready for the *asado*. A couple they knew were coming for lunch with their son, who was the same age as Patricio. As soon as the coals were burning, he went back down to the kitchen to salt the meat. Soon their guests arrived. The women started preparing salads. Lucio cut up a fontina cheese and some salami and put potato chips in a bowl. The adults drank Gancia vermouth with soda water, and the children Tang orange juice. Lucio cooked the *asado* in his usual order: first offal: chorizo, blood sausage, chitterlings – which had to be really crunchy – and kidneys. Then the meat: flank and short ribs. The adults swapped their aperitifs for red wine, a López, brought by the guests. For pudding they had crème caramel, which their friend had made herself.

After coffee, all seven of them went to the Carrefour hyper-market on Avenida La Plata. The other couple wanted to buy a mattress for their son's bed and so Lucio and Mariana took the opportunity to do their weekly shopping. Their friends didn't come back with them after that, but said goodbye at the store's exit. At home, Mariana made more coffee and tea for the boys. Very soon it was night. Having eaten too much at lunch, Lucio decided not to have supper. He watched television while Mariana bathed the boys. They went to bed early and fell asleep straightaway.

Lucio couldn't stop thinking about Verónica all weekend. On Monday, as soon as he had got up and was alone in the house, he wrote a text message saying that he wanted to see her again soon. She replied that she had just been think-ing of him. So it began. Verónica and Lucio stopped being occasional lovers – ending that casual arrangement he had dreamed of – and became a couple, with all the limitations imposed by his status as a married man. At that moment, Lucio had a foreboding of how Verónica would change his life irreversibly. From now onwards he would have to lie to his wife and arm himself with excuses, with alibis. Find times when he could meet Verónica, in the morning, afternoon, at night. She was available to him in a way that nobody had ever been before, but they never had long when they met. An hour and a half or two, never more than three. They holed themselves up in her apartment, drank coffee, a bottle of wine or shots, which she prepared, and they had sex. Afterwards he got dressed and returned to his normal routine, to the Sarmiento line or to his family life.

If their first kiss, in the train cabin, had been a response to terror, the kisses that followed it were not so very different. Their lips were charged with a rare violence: they bit each other, hurt each other. Lucio acquired bruises that would have been difficult to justify to his wife, if she had noticed them.

VI

Read the magazine. My article's in it, Verónica texted him. He had just finished work and was getting ready to go home. He went to a kiosk in the train station and bought the most recent copy of *Nuestro Tiempo*. On the front, a small coverline read THE DARK SIDE OF THE RAILWAYS: AVOIDABLE DEATHS AND MENTAL ILLNESS. WHAT THE RAILWAY COMPANIES ARE HIDING. He read the rest in the bus on the way home.

Inside, six pages had been given over to the subject, under the headline MADNESS AND DEATH ON THE TRACKS. There were text boxes quoting psychologists, railway users and even firefighters. The article began by saying:

"Anyone who thought the ghost train in Italpark offered a terrifying ride has never travelled on the suburban railways of Buenos Aires – a veritable nightmare for the hundreds of thousands of users who have to travel to the capital each day. But discomfort, poor maintenance and unreliable trains are just the problems we know about. There are other factors which contribute to making this old ghost train more ghoulish than a fairground ride. The suburban trains hide stories of suicides and accidents that could be avoided if there were a managerial policy in place to deal with them. As well as hiding or fudging the statistics, train companies gloss over another reality: the psychological problems endured by train drivers involved in serious accidents."

Lucio was presented as "one of the most experienced train drivers in Argentina" and "an authority on this profession, which can be both enthralling and terrifying". The article quoted a few things he had said, but she had only attributed the more positive observations to him. Everything that he had told her about the suicides and about the experience of train drivers appeared as information in the text, or was ascribed to "a source who prefers to remain anonymous". There was nothing in the article about his train-driving father and grandfather, or about the development plans that TBA had scheduled. Álvarez Carrizo isn't going to like this one bit, Lucio thought. He didn't care very much what the company's spokesperson might think. He knew that there was no way they would kick him out. But what did surprise him was that there was no mention of the children who played on the tracks. He had thought that that was what interested Verónica most, but it wasn't even mentioned. She was certainly unpredictable.

He thought of taking the magazine home and showing it to Mariana and to his friends, who would surely ask him about his experience of being interviewed. Instead, as soon as he got off the bus he looked for a garbage can and threw away the magazine he had bought only minutes before.

7   *Eyes Wide Open*

I

They look like a portrait. Or a photo. They are three people, unobserved by anyone, standing motionless on the paved area around a plaza. There are trees, children running and dogs sniffing about in the background of the image and, in the foreground, cars passing on the road. But everything apart from them is out of focus or drawn with a broad brush. And none of these three figures seems to register the square, or the people, or the dogs. The man looks about thirty-five years old. An anachronistic hippie. His unkempt clothes and beard would not inspire anyone's confidence. His arm is around a little girl of about ten or eleven. The girl is tense, as though keen to demonstrate her non-compliance in some matter, and she wears a white school smock. Beside her, a woman of about sixty holds a wheeled backpack of the kind used by schoolchildren. The young man strokes the girl's head and is smiling in an attempt to look cheerful, but if anyone looked at him (one of the passers-by, or a bored driver in the slow-moving traffic) they would discern a great sadness in his eyes. The little girl is fixated by a button, or a missing button, on the man's shirt. The older woman looks at the man with tenderness, but also with a fear of something going wrong, of some sadness befalling these two people whom she watches in silence.

The young man is called Rafael and he's clean. There is no cocaine or alcohol in his body. It's been hard. Years in hell and a few months in the purgatory of a self-help group. But there was a day when he woke up without thirst or anxiety. A morning when he felt, finally, that this was the first day of what he had been looking for: a body that he could manage.

The woman is his mother. She had taken responsibility for the granddaughter when Rafael and his partner entered the worst phase of their lives. She didn't want to leave the girl at the whim of destructive forces. When he left her, Rafael's wife, Andrea, had re-established her normal life. The separation had signified both Andrea's salvation and Rafael's continued decline. The mother opted to stay with her daughter-in-law and granddaughter, to help them. She had two other children, but neither of them caused her the worry and anguish that Rafael did. She looked after her granddaughter as though she were another part of her son's body.

The girl's name is Martina. It's likely that she has experienced fear at the sight of her father drunk, or high on coke, but she doesn't remember, or she has decided not to remember. On the other hand, she feels that her father doesn't love her. That's the only way she can understand how so much time has passed without him visiting her and why now they are only meeting in this square for a few minutes. Why isn't he coming back to live with them? If her mother refused, she herself would persuade her to let him come back. He strokes her hair, tells her that it won't be long before they can spend more time together. That they must be patient. He tells her that he has a job. He works in a bar, in a club where the boys play soccer. That as soon as he has somewhere nice to live, he is going to get a room ready for her.

Rafael had in fact tried before to see Martina again, but Andrea had not allowed it. She had made it clear that, now that she was clean, and for as long as he continued to destroy himself with alcohol and cocaine, she wasn't going to let him have anything to do with his daughter.

They didn't have much time. He offered to buy her something. She could choose: an ice cream, candied almonds, a Coca-Cola. She hugged him and said that she didn't want anything, she just wanted to be with him. So Rafael chose for her: a can of soda and some Sugus sweets.

I I

His pocket, his hands, his eyes burned. El Peque slept with the hundred-peso bill under his pillow. He had planned to wake up every hour to make sure that the note was still there, but when he awoke it was at the same time as usual. He looked for the note and there it was, as violet as the night before. He got dressed and put it back into his trouser pocket.

Dientes wasn't in the courtyard, so he went to look for him at home. Dientes' mother ushered him in and gave him a glass of milk, which was what his friend was having. El Peque ate a few cookies and said nothing. He didn't need to speak or to explain why he was there, because it wasn't unusual for him to have breakfast with Dientes. Together they went out to the street, and only there did El Peque tell him that he had something to show him. He reached into his pocket and pulled out the crumpled note.

"Where did you get that?"

"I can't tell you."

"You nicked it off your mum."

"No. I didn't nick it off anyone."

"Who gave it to you?"

"I earned it. But I can't tell you how."

"Don't be a dick, tell me."

"I'll tell you, but if you tell anyone else I'll bash your face in."

"Who am I going to tell? My idiot sister?"

"I won it in a game. Rivero gave it to me." And he told Dientes about the coach's proposal. He described what had happened that night, the tracks, the people, Cholito, the jumping, the running away and the note that he had won.

"And what if the train had knocked you down?"

"How's that gonna happen, moron, if I jump out of the way before it comes? It's the easiest thing in the world. Cholito got scared, the loser."

"Cholito is a loser."

El Peque had already decided what he was going to do with the money. He wanted soccer boots like some of his teammates at Breezes had. They went to a sports shop on Avenida Castañares, where a surly assistant told them that the cheapest boots were two hundred and twenty pesos. He didn't even show them to the boys. Dientes and El Peque came out looking at the ground.

"If I win two more times, I'll have three hundred."

"And if you win five, you'll have five hundred – so?"

But El Peque didn't want to save up. A note was nothing more than the promise of a future with shining boots, boots that would help him play better. And he didn't want a promise. He wanted to see and feel those hundred pesos converted into things. As if he were a wizard. I've got a note in my hand and suddenly – puff – I've got a ball, or a two-litre bottle of Coke, or whatever.

"He can stick his boots up his ass. I'm going to buy some fries."

"Just fries?"

"Plus whatever I want. Let's go to the shop on the corner."

"It's better to go to Coto."

137

They went to the hypermarket on Larrazábal. They got a shopping cart but this time they didn't play around like other times, hanging off it or having races between the shelves. They didn't secretly eat some of the products. Today they had a hundred pesos, more than most of the people around them.

They loaded up the shopping cart with two boxes of chocolate Oreos, a pack of dulce de leche *alfajor* cookies, two packets of sponge fingers, two caramel strips, two packets of gumdrops, some big, salted potato chips, more potato chips, this time smaller and prosciutto-flavoured (to try), and a six-pack of Coca-Cola.

"Ninety-four pesos and sixty centavos," said the cashier after scanning everything. "Would you like to donate forty centavos to the Favaloro Foundation?"

"Yes," said El Peque.

"No," Dientes said, louder.

"Well do you want to, or not?"

"No, we don't want to."

They put everything into four bags and left Coto, loaded down as never before.

III

The roof space was not very big and part of it was covered in rubble and bits of wood left over from some refurbishment or other. Nobody used that terrace – not even to hang up clothes – apart from the boys. Dientes and El Peque made themselves comfortable on one side and put the Coto bags down on the tiles. They had started eating the potato chips on the way back, and now they were thirsty. They opened a small Coke each and finished them almost in one gulp, then burped and sent the cans spinning over the side of the roof.

Someone down below (Martina's mum) shouted at them not to throw things. They opened a box of Oreos and divided up the individual snack packs, each containing two cookies. They didn't speak, savouring their confectionery.

They had already got through quite a lot of their haul when they heard footsteps coming up the stairs: it was Martina. When they were smaller the three of them often used to play together and had gone up and down the stairs to this terrace thousands of times, but in recent years they had begun to ignore each other and now didn't even say hello when their paths crossed in the courtyard.

"What are you doing?"

"Men's stuff."

"We're taking drugs."

"Yeah right. I believe you and everything."

"It's not anything that concerns you."

Martina shrugged and prepared to go back down the way she had come. El Peque called her by the nickname they used to mock her: Martota. Martina turned around and El Peque shouted "catch" and threw her an *alfajor*, which Martina caught in mid-air. She looked at it, looked at the boys and opened it. She left the wrapper on the roof and went down eating it.

"What do you say?"

"You say thank you, stupid."

"Thanks."

Dientes and El Peque decided to take the caramel strips to school. They found a hiding place for everything else and went back down around midday. El Peque took three *alfajores* with him. He went to his room and there were his brothers and Dientes' sister, who looked after them. He gave them an *alfajor* each. Soon afterwards, they all set off for school. El Peque chatted with Dientes as they walked.

"Man, this game is great. From now on I'm going to start saving for the boots."

"Yes, it's great," said Dientes with a certain sombre tone which could have been interpreted as worry, suspicion or envy.

IV

Rafael knew that one of his virtues – which, like all his virtues, was not often recognized by other people – was observation. He realized a lot of things simply by looking around him. He saw things to which others – so sure of themselves – remained blind. The best thing about that was that nobody saw what he saw. Especially not when he was behind the counter in the Breezes bar, almost invisible to everyone except the children, whom he liked to cheer up with the odd gift of a sandwich or some snack. As for the adults who met there to play cards, he never failed to recognize them: the failure, the grudge-holder, the thug, the whoremonger, the man who came to escape his unhappy home life, the man who was alone and found something like a family around those tables. He didn't like those people, he didn't like what he saw. But he wasn't there to deal in subtleties: his job was to serve. He was lucky to have found that job after such a long time of being unable to take control of his own life. Now he knew that, from there, from that invisible spot in the Breezes bar, he could set off on a path that would lead to Martina, and perhaps to Andrea.

"Rafa, can I have a large Coke?"

The children converged on the counter. The one asking for a drink was El Peque, the boy who lived in the same house as his mother and daughter. He took a five-peso note from his pocket and the others added coins to make up the nine pesos which the bottle cost. It was the first time he had seen El Peque with a note. He handed them the bottle and alongside it a generous portion of potato sticks, which the boys devoured in a matter of seconds, like termites. El Peque seemed to be on a winning streak: besides the note, Rafael had noticed how Rivero treated him. This disagreeable character, who mistreated the boys whenever possible, behaved differently with El Peque. He didn't insult him or berate him, in fact he was full of praise every time the boy touched the ball. Rafael was no soccer expert but he could tell that El Peque wasn't a star in the making. Why was it, then, that Rivero praised him so much? Because you could see – at least Rafael could see – that there was something servile in that encouragement, as if he felt obliged to be generous in what he said. Rivero didn't seem like a child abuser, but he would keep an eye on him all the same without letting anyone know. One of the advantages of being invisible.

V

El Peque was willing the month to fly by. He had just spoken to Rivero, who had told him that in a month there would be a courage contest. That's what the coach had called it: a courage contest.

Rivero had waited for all the other children to leave before approaching him. First he gave him a few tips on how to mark a striker going in for a header, and then he moved on to talk about the contest. He said that El Peque should get ready, that there would be another one in a few weeks. That he already knew he had faith in him.

"Well, not faith, that sounds too religious. What I have is trust. Because you're the toughest boy in this city."

El Peque told him that he didn't have any problem with competing more often. Every week if necessary. Rivero clarified that it was only ever once a month. El Peque thought that he was going to have to wait for about three months before he could buy the boots. He asked if he would be competing against Cholito again.

"Cholito's out of the game now. You snooze, you lose. Cholito can't compete again. Only the ones who win keep playing. So you know what to do…keep winning and you can carry on all year." And he added: "Don't think that this is going to be easy, by the way. You're going to be playing against someone who's already won twice, last year."

In less than a week, in less than three days, everything that he had bought in the hypermarket with Dientes was finished. El Peque didn't have a single peso left, and so he began to dream about the next courage contest. He pictured himself jumping after the other boy, winning again, carrying off a hundred pesos. He made a decision: he wouldn't save up for the boots. He would buy a load of stuff again. Every night he counted the days until the contest. During the last week he was as nervous as if he were going to play in the final of a soccer championship. And – though it took its time – eventually the night of the competition arrived.

VI

He said nothing to Dientes, and lied again to his mother. That night he walked to the corner where Rivero would come and pick him up. It was strange, but he thought more about what he would do the next day, going to the shop with Dientes, than about what would be happening in a few minutes. Rivero and the guy with the biker jacket arrived straightaway. El Peque got into the back. His opponent wasn't there yet, so he just pressed his face against the glass and looked out at the night-time city. The avenue they took out of his barrio was clogged by heavy traffic, slowing their progress. After a while they emerged into some dark streets. Rivero stopped the car, the man in the jacket got out, looked all around him and got back in again.

"Let's wait a few minutes. He'll be here soon."

Rivero had the radio on at a very low volume. He turned it up a little and El Peque could hear some sports commentators talking about a soccer match. The surrounding darkness was so dense that at first none of the three noticed that the other boy was a few yards away. Rivero turned the engine back on and flashed his lights at the boy, who ran over and climbed into the empty back seat. El Peque knew him. He was called Vicen and he played in an older division. Once they had shared a drink after a game. He was one of the boys El Peque liked. He didn't know why; perhaps because he never made fun of the others, or because he didn't talk all that much.

He didn't talk much in the car, either, but remained silent, looking out of his window, the same as El Peque. They drove back to the avenue and on towards the freeway. It was the first time that El Peque had been on a freeway at night and he was instantly fascinated by the lights of the cars circulating below, as though this were a crossroads and they had chosen to take the highest route. The cars looked like strange animals, or spaceships, something out of the ordinary. The ones below them seemed to be travelling slowly, but the ones beside them were silent and swift. He would have liked the car to stop so that he could spend a few hours watching those white and red lights moving around him.

Vicen was evidently not so engrossed by the spectacle of the cars, because he took something out of his pocket and turned his attention to that.

"What are those?" El Peque asked him.

"Cards. Do you collect them?"

"What kind?"

"Soccer players."

"Ah, no."

They left the freeway. After a little while they arrived at a dark street that ran across railway tracks, similar to the one they had gone to before. On all four corners of the junction there were industrial buildings with no lights on, and if it hadn't been for the parked cars, whose occupants could be seen in silhouette, anyone would have said they were in an abandoned part of the city.

"Have you done this before?" Vicen asked El Peque when they got out of the car.

"Uh-huh. I won."

"I've won twice," Vicen told him, playing down his victory.

Rivero gave them twenty pesos each.

As on the previous occasion, some of the people in the cars got out to inspect the boys up close. Some of them greeted El Peque with "How are you, champ" or "go for it, lad". El Peque smiled in response to the greetings. He liked being recognized.

After Rivero and the man in the jacket had taken bets from people standing outside and from those in the cars, and spoken to some others on the phone, the children took up their positions on the tracks. Seconds later, the man in the jacket called them back. A car was coming up the street and crossed the tracks before the barriers went down. There wasn't enough time for the boys to take their places again before the train passed, and they would have to wait for the next one. During those minutes they went back to Rivero's car and everyone sat in silence, even the man in the jacket, who was no longer talking on the phone and had lit a cigarette. Smoke filled the inside of the car. They didn't hear any noises; nobody else came down the road. Rivero looked at his watch and told them to get out. They went back to their places on the tracks and waited. Only then did Vicen break the silence, resuming the conversation that they had had when they arrived.

"How many times have you won?"

"Once."

"Against who?"

"Against Cholito."

"He plays soccer with me."

"He tried to scare me, telling me all kinds of shit."

"What a dick."

"Nothing scares me."

"Me neither. If we draw, will they give us half the money each?"

"No idea."

"I'm going to win anyway."

"Ha. Yeah, of course."

In the distance the train's yellow light appeared, weakly at first but steady and getting stronger all the time, dragging a shadowy mass behind it.

"Peque."

"What?"

"What if we both jump now?"

"No way."

The train was coming, preceded by the light, and in front of that a wind that struck the two boys' faces as they stared ahead, their eyes wide open. El Peque's body was as taut as a startled cat's.

It was coming closer.

In that moment he wasn't thinking about the hundred pesos. He was just looking at the train and, out of the corner of his eye, at Vicen.

He had to win. But Vicen wasn't jumping.

Too close.

How long to wait?

A bit longer.

"Come on, asshole, jump," El Peque shouted.

He heard Vicen's response.

"No."

And El Peque, without wanting to or thinking about it, jumped away from the line. The sound of the train came over him as though he were under the foot of an ogre. But it was only noise, and the sound of shouting, that kept him pinned to the ground close to the tracks. His eye or his body had registered something that lasted a millisecond, and it was Vicen, standing motionless on the track, not moving. Motionless at the moment El Peque had jumped and the train had come through, amid a terrifying noise of screeching and howling. El Peque looked at the train, which had come to a stop; the last compartment had ended up beside him. He looked down but he saw nothing. Everything was black. And above his head, shouting. More shouting.

El Peque got to his feet and started running alongside the tracks, away from the train. He ran in the darkness, leaving the screams behind him. He ran without seeing, because it was dark, or because he was crying or screaming as well. He saw a side street and dashed down it, to get away from the railway. At the next block he stopped abruptly, realizing that he had no idea where he was. Knowing that he was lost made him even more afraid and he sat down on the kerb to cry. He couldn't get his breath, he was choking, but he couldn't stop crying. He felt that he would never again see his mother, his little brothers and sisters. He wiped his nose and brushed away his tears on the sleeve of his jacket. A car drew up beside him. It was Rivero. The other guy ordered him to get in.

"What about Vicen?" he asked, hoping to hear that the boy had in fact jumped without him realizing. He didn't mind losing. Not getting the hundred pesos.

"Vicen beat you."

"He jumped?"

They didn't answer him. The car went faster than usual. Rivero said to him:

"Listen, Peque, not a word about this to anyone."

"If you say anything you'll go to prison."

"Prison?"

"Vicen didn't jump in time because you waited too long to jump. If you had jumped sooner, he would be alive."

"They could charge you with murder. So don't say anything to anyone, no matter who's asking."

"Not to your mother, to the police or to your friends. Not to anyone. Or the rest of your life in prison. Got it?"

"But I told him to jump."

"It doesn't matter. You'll still go to prison."

"Keep quiet and nothing will happen."

They left him in the same place as last time. He started running again, but this time he didn't have a hundred-peso note balled in his hand. He felt as though a fist were clenching around his chest and throat.

I

A journalistic investigation requires time, patience and reliable sources. The journalist must not rush even when she's racing against the clock to get a scoop. For that reason, perhaps, the best investigations are always into subjects that are not currently on the news agenda. When a journalist knows that she is the only one investigating a particular issue, she can take her time and wait to uncover the information she needs for the job.

Much harder to come by than time and patience, however, are good sources. Ones that can pass on information, open up new lines of enquiry, corroborate facts or dates, always off the record and under the protection of professional secrecy.

Verónica had been careful not to mention the railway boys in her piece about suburban trains. She didn't want to tip off any colleagues who would spot the potential exposé just as she had. Being the only one chasing the story would allow her more time to get the information she still needed.

Lucio had been a source in her article and, if it hadn't been for him, she would never have seen the boys on the Sarmiento tracks. There wasn't much more that he could contribute now. He didn't know more than what he had already told her and Verónica had no plan to go back on the train. She wanted to try a different tack. Smoking, lounging in the armchair in her apartment, she felt lost, with no clear idea of how to frame her investigation.

She was counting on her editor's approval to take the time she needed, so long as she kept turning in those regular space-fillers that could usually be wrapped up in a couple of hours on Tuesdays and Wednesdays. The rest of the time was for her and her investigation. It was one of Patricia's great virtues: ensuring that her writers had enough time to research their articles. She could be demanding, pedantic, liable to get annoyed by the excessive use of a gerund or the lack of precision in a piece of information, but she gave them all the time they needed.

That day Verónica decided not to go to the magazine. It was more relaxing to work at home, where she didn't have to go outside every time she wanted to smoke. She had to start at the beginning: work the archive. The chance of finding something interesting there was slim, but worthwhile if it provided the end of a thread which she could follow to find a way through the labyrinth.

While at university she had managed, thanks to a teacher who had recommended her, to get an internship at Editorial Atlántida, a publishing house that produced around ten different magazines. She had pictured herself spending six adrenaline-fuelled months at the heart of the journalistic world. As soon as she arrived, though, they had sent her to the archive to gather information for articles to be written by staff writers on the celebrity gossip magazine *Gente*. She wondered if getting stuck in a room with a lot of brown envelopes filled with newspaper and magazine cuttings was a way to pay her dues before she got any meaningful work. A week later they sent her back down there to catalogue photographic negatives. It was actually a very agreeable place: an old room that smelled of mahogany. But she wanted to be in the newsroom, among computers, printers and the cigarette smoke that still hung heavy in those spaces back then. She spent the third week looking through catalogues of children's illustrations for *Billiken* magazine, and seemed to be getting ever further from the day when she would find herself in a real live newsroom.

"It was a bit too old-fashioned for my liking," she said to her lecturer when she had to explain why she had given up the internship after a month.

If her lecturer was disappointed, he didn't show it, lamenting only that his favourite student had lost her chance of a career in an important publishing house.

Since then she had hated any activity related to archives. If it were up to her, she'd hire other people (interns!) to do the search for her. But luckily the internet had made this job much easier and it was no longer necessary to spend days poring over cuttings taken out of manila envelopes. For example, for this investigation she could count on the complete archives of at least three national newspapers (*Clarín*, *La Nación*, *Página/12*) dating back ten years.

She went to the kitchen, made maté, put hot water in a thermos and headed for her desk. Many hours in front of the computer lay ahead.

II

Verónica started searching by section – Society, Crime, City – using the key words "accident", "train", "children", "boys", "tracks", "mutilated", "dead", "Sarmiento railway", "accusation", "crime". She searched in time spans: starting with newspapers from ten years ago, she sorted the cases year by year until reaching the current day. She discovered, with surprise, that some incidents recorded in one newspaper did not exist for another. Or a news item appeared in one publication but was given space in another only two or three days later. In that ten-year span, what particularly drew her attention was the mention of some adolescents or preadolescents playing "chicken" on the tracks of the Roca railway. In fact, the article had appeared in the Psychology section and reflected on the way children deal with death. It had made reference to child bombers in the Middle East, to child addicts and then to children who played on railway lines. It said that the children came from a shanty town and were involved with a group of adults who gambled on their chances. The article added that these adults were as poor and as marginalized as the children playing "chicken". It concluded by saying that several deaths had been caused by this macabre game.

Verónica, who had a good eye for the way a piece had been constructed, noticed that her fellow journalist (who may in fact have been a psychologist or sociologist) had no firm evidence on which to base the story, but instead relied on assumptions and rumours. He did not state on which section of the Roca railway – which runs for some thirty miles between the Plaza de la Constitución and the city of La Plata – the game took place, or if there was more than one location. Nor did he give the name of the shanty town from which the children came or a figure for the number of deaths. That lack of information, far from annoying or frustrating her, made her happy.

Verónica was no fan of Excel spreadsheets, but in this case it would be a helpful way to collate all the dates, cases and places. She also created a new folder on the hard drive, where she kept all the articles relating to what she was looking for.

Continuing with the search, this time she discounted any cases of children who had been with a relative at the time of the accident and which had been subject to an inquest. Also those which had very clearly been accidents (kids who wanted to run across the lines and hadn't seen the train approaching). The easiest cases to rule out were the ones in which the dead or injured child had been seen by witnesses who explained how the tragedy had occurred: a child who was coming home from school and hadn't looked as he crossed the line; another who jumped down from the platform onto the tracks to pick up some coins he had dropped; kids who ran across and didn't get to the other side on time. Those cases were no use to her.

In all she found forty-eight cases of minors (adolescents and children) who had been killed or injured (usually mutilated) on railway tracks for ambiguous reasons, defined as "accident" or "reckless act", with no clarification of how the incident had occurred. The majority had taken place in Buenos Aires (both the capital and province), but there had also been four cases in the country's interior. One in Entre Rios, another in Rosario, a third in Salta and the most recent in Mendoza, two years ago. Of course, the interior had very few railways and newspapers tended to reflect what happened in the capital and its environs. In the other cases it seemed that nobody had thought to look for a pattern, even though there were some significant common factors: all the victims were poor children, mostly from deprived neighbourhoods or shanty towns. There were rarely any details about who had been on the tracks with the victims. There were generally no witnesses. If there was a witness statement, it came from the driver.

She ordered the cases by railway line and year, categorizing them as "not relevant", "suspicious", "very suspicious", and "something very strange going on here". She was basing her investigation on journalistic information, which was not always reliable, as she well knew. The pressure to fill space was enough to induce a reporter to make up a detail, or to leave one out. A paucity of details was also explained by the small space allocated by the editor to the news item. "You can always make something with what others have made," she told herself, very loosely paraphrasing Jean-Paul Sartre.

She discovered with some satisfaction that if she cross-referenced for time and location, the most suspicious cases were to be found on the Sarmiento railway in the last five years. She read her notes again and tried to find other connections. The Roca railway and a branch of the Mitre line returned some results that could raise eyebrows, but only from the last three years. She wondered if those incidents might be better documented in the local media – neighbourhood newspapers, small publications for locals worried about accidents in their area – but the thought of having to resort to a paper archive for these publications (because they had no internet archive) drained her enthusiasm for that line of enquiry. If necessary, she would ask Patricia to find a journalism student she could dispatch to these places.

The Sarmiento railway appeared with a regularity that led her to suspect the key was there. It accounted for seven documented cases in the last five years. Two fatal (one of which must have been the boy that Carranza knocked down, although the driver's name was recorded in neither case), four serious injuries (mutilations, according to the reporters) and one in which the child had miraculously escaped death but a passenger in one of the compartments had been seriously injured when the train braked abruptly. The seven incidents had all taken place in neighbourhoods between Caballito and Paso del Rey.

No place featured more than once in the reports: Floresta, Villa Luro, Morón, Ituzaingó, San Antonio de Padua. The chronological order did not coincide with the order in which the stations came, although Verónica didn't ascribe particular importance to that detail.

On the other hand, it frustrated her that there was no logic regarding the days and weeks. Two incidents had occurred on Tuesdays, three on Wednesdays, one on a Monday and the other on a Thursday. They hadn't been during specific weeks, either. Lucio had been so sure that they happened on Thursdays that she had assumed that the boys would always be on the tracks that day. It was impossible to establish a pattern of behaviour, except that the incidents didn't happen at weekends. But when she tried looking at the same information another way, she began to detect a logic that increasingly pointed to the existence of a criminal organization behind these incidents: the organizers might deliberately be changing the routine after every accident to escape detection.

She had seven cases. Now she needed to do something with them. But what if there was nothing there? What if these were, after all, unconnected incidents, or she couldn't even manage to work out enough about each one to move forward in the investigation? She felt as though she were throwing stones into the sea in the hope of hitting a dolphin. She had spent too much of the day trawling through cases. Better to leave it there. Not to think any more, at least for a few hours. She lit a joint and ran a bath. She thought of opening a bottle of wine, then decided she needed something stronger. For want of a Jim Beam, she poured herself a good measure of Jack Daniel's. The first swig of bourbon or Tennessee whisky always seemed horrible to her, much more horrible than any other whisky, but the more you had, the better it got, and it had a relaxing effect, like a massage inside your body. Tomorrow will be another day, she told herself.

III

At the age of twenty he had been offered two options: to enter a criminal court as an unpaid intern or to start working in a law practice, in both cases on the recommendation of his uncle, who was at that time a judge in a federal court. Federico opted for the law firm, and that decided his fate. Working with Dr Aarón Rosenthal meant much more than getting a good job. It could set him up for life. Very soon Dr Rosenthal discovered that his young employee was brilliant and responsible. More the latter than the former, according to at least one other member of the firm, who observed how Dr Rosenthal (none of his own three daughters having opted for a career in law) adopted Federico. In any case, Federico graduated as a lawyer at twenty-three, nearly three years after joining the firm, and grew within the practice until, nearly a decade after his arrival, he was made a junior partner.

Soon after he started work, he met Verónica. From time to time Dr Rosenthal's youngest daughter went to visit her father, and she was only a few months younger than him. Federico fell in love with her immediately, but two years went by before he plucked up the courage to ask her out, after learning that she had broken up with her boyfriend. That date was not a success and it was a long time – months – before Verónica agreed to go out with him again, one humid summer night. Without much hope of anything happening between them, Federico hoped to come across as agreeable, if not necessarily seductive. It was a surprise to him when the night ended with them renting a room in a love hotel. Even more surprising, she didn't take his calls the next day, or any of the days that followed. Federico replayed those hours of passion in his head and could find no sign that their romance had been destined to last only one night.

Three months later she turned up at the office. By then Federico had progressed from bewilderment to annoyance but, when he saw her, he fell in love again. He persuaded her to meet that weekend. This time she did not disappear after a night of sex, but neither did Federico get what, deep down, he really wanted: a stable and lasting relationship which he – and everyone else – could call official. When he tried to pressure her into a more formal liaison, her response was clear: there were other men and always would be.

Verónica was present at Federico's degree ceremony and he never left her side when Señora Rosenthal died. He met one of her boyfriends (an insufferable pedant who wrote books, or edited them, or copied them – he was never sure what exactly he did) and she had been happy when Federico showed up with a new girlfriend. They hadn't had sex again, but they maintained a bond which could be described as fraternal, if to fraternity we add a dash of incestuous desire. At the end of the day, for Dr Rosenthal, Federico was the son he had never had.

For that reason it didn't strike him as odd that Verónica should ask to meet him in a bar close to the practice, which was on Uruguay and Viamonte.

As usual, he arrived first. He didn't mind that, because it was a pleasure to see her arrive, weaving a path towards him between the tables. Verónica always seemed to him like the personification of wind; a small hurricane enveloped her, propelling her forward with the grace of a model. Now that hurricane was sweeping over him, covering him with her perfume as she sat down opposite him.

"I need your help," she said, getting straight to the point, as was her style. In that respect she was identical to her father.

"I was born to help you."

"I'm still on the case of the ex-Sarmiento Railway Company."

"Was the guy I passed on to you useful?"

"Quite useful."

Verónica passed him a folder and he leafed through it. Inside was a printed page and a few newspaper cuttings.

"All the information is on the first sheet. I've also made a note of where it all came from, in case you need anything else."

Federico studied the first page: there were dates, references to the Sarmiento train and to children who were not named but simply given a number. Verónica explained:

"I'm writing an article about children who have died or been injured on the Sarmiento line. I think that there could be a criminal organization behind these supposed accidents. But all I have are these pieces, which were published in newspapers."

"And you want me to find out more."

"See if you can get anything. Addresses, lawsuits, whatever there is."

"I don't know if I'll be able to turn up any very trustworthy information. I mean, nobody investigates an accident unless there are insurance companies behind them trying not to pay up. If you're lucky and there is something like that, you can even get the blood group of the man who puts the barrier up and down. But if not, be grateful if it says 'Boy, approximately ten years old, identity unknown'."

"Anything you can get me is going to be useful. I feel as if I've got absolutely nothing on this."

"I wouldn't mind if you had absolutely nothing on, to be honest."

"Come on, Fede, don't start flirting when I know that you're going out with the goody two shoes from reception."

"True. But she isn't a goody two shoes."

"She is. I know one when I see one."

I V

One day she was going to write an article on masculine susceptibility. You didn't need to be a psychologist to see that Lucio was annoyed about his low profile in the piece about trains. She explained that when the subject was controversial it was important to protect the source.

"Am I a source?"

"Sometimes yes, sometimes no. In this particular case you were a source, and a very useful one."

She explained, too, that she had decided, with great regret, not to include the story of his family, because it didn't chime with the tone of the piece. That that story would be wonderful for a family saga. She also told him that there was no mention of the children who played on the tracks because she planned to save that for another article. He didn't seem to believe her. But Verónica decided not to press the point: Lucio would realize that she wasn't lying when she went back to ask him for help again. And that happened just a few days later.

I need to see you for the trains/children article. Can I call you? Verónica texted him. They arranged to meet that evening in La Perla, where they had first had coffee together.

Verónica took a copy of her papers with the seven cases she had selected. She showed them to him.

"I'm working on something to do with what we saw that night. I compiled information on these other incidents that took place on the Sarmiento railway in the last five years. Were you there for any of them?"

Lucio looked through the folder carefully. He shook his head.

"Not for any of them, but I remember them all."

"I'd like to speak to the train drivers who were there."

Lucio thought for a long time, then finally said:

"No. I don't want to put you in touch with people from work. I want to keep what we have separate from the rest of my life."

"Lucio, I'm not asking you to introduce me to the guys you play soccer with on Saturdays. I just need information for my article, and it's very likely your co-workers have it."

"I know everything about these cases. Nobody knows more. They ran over a boy; that boy was always with someone else. Some were smashed to bits, others were mutilated. What do you want? A description of what it feels like to kill a kid?"

Did she know exactly what she was looking for? Perhaps he was right that the drivers would have nothing more to contribute to her investigation. She took the folder out of his hands.

"Whatever you think, Lucio, but don't act as though I'm meddling in your life."

Lucio said nothing. She lit another cigarette. She seemed annoyed as she blew out the smoke, looking at him. Finally Lucio said:

"The boy who wasn't injured."

Verónica opened the folder and showed him the case.

"Carlos, the one driving the train, said something. He works in maintenance now and he told me this once when we were in the workshop together. He said that the train made contact with the child. It hit him but by some amazing luck the impact threw him off the track. Carlos only managed to stop the train a few seconds later. Inside the compartments people were screaming because they were hurt, and some of them started panicking. Carlos got down out of the train without knowing what to do. He walked towards the back of

159

the train, where he thought the child would be lying, but
when he got there the boy had gone. One of the passengers
who had also got out shouted: 'To top it all off, the fucking
bastards drive off in a car.' It seemed that the boy had run
off and got into a car that was waiting for him."

"Did they manage to read the licence plate?"

"No. And Carlos didn't even see the car. It was just what
he heard the passenger say."

V

Damned coincidence. While she had been sitting sprawled
in the armchair, thinking of the conversation she had had
that night with Lucio in La Perla, the music system was playing Nina Simone's version of "The Other Woman". It made
her feel stupid.

She wasn't going to cry herself to sleep like the song's
protagonist. It had been a mistake to arrange that meeting
in the bar. What had she hoped to achieve? Why did she
insist on deluding herself like this? Lucio had stopped being
a useful source of information some time ago. Wanting to
put him back in his place was an adolescent way to deny what
was happening: she was feeling increasingly close to him.
She needed to see him, to spend time with him. She loathed
with a passion the moment when he went away and left her
behind. She knew the rules of the game. She wasn't going
to be so childish as to try to change them, but she couldn't
help feeling annoyed, anguished, beseeching. Even if her
way of beseeching was stupidly asking him to meet for a talk
about work. "You're losing the plot, Vero," she said aloud to
herself, and it sounded more like self-pity than self-criticism.

Worst of all, that night when she had asked him for facts,
contacts, memories, none of which he had been prepared

160

to give her (so what would he give her, then? His body? His married-man-father-of-two act?), they had abruptly finished the conversation, gone outside and said goodbye with a quick kiss on the cheek, as they always did in the street, then gone their own ways. He to eat home-made pasta with his little wife (because wives always cook from scratch) and she to the loneliness of her apartment. And she would have liked him to go home with her, they might have fucked or not, drunk beer or wine, they would have talked and looked silently at each other's bodies. True, afterwards he would have gone back to his wife, but at least…at least what?

VI

That morning there was an email from Paula reminding her that the following night they were getting together at her house, with the girls, "for an *asado*". She didn't give any more details – there was no need. It was to be a gathering of women, and for that reason they had chosen to eat *asado* – that ultimate symbol of masculinity, and one they were ready to sacrifice on the barbecue in Paula's patio. They didn't need men. At least not for grilling meat.

Patricia popped up in the chat and asked her how the investigation was going. She said that she had some good leads.

- I told Rodolfo Corso about your piece.
- Why did you do that?
- Because we've worked together on various newspapers, he's a good friend and he might have some ideas.
- I don't need ideas. I need facts.
- There's an art to fact-finding.
- Thanks. I'll bear that in mind.

- Rodolfo isn't going to steal your piece. Relax. I told him about your investigation and he said that he had some information that could be useful.
- That might be the fruit of his imagination.
- By their fruits shall ye know them. It says so in the Bible. Write to him. Have you got his email?
- I've got it somewhere.

She wrote to Corso immediately:

Dear Rodolfo,

How are you? The last time we saw each other was at that Edgar Morin press conference, wasn't it? Pato mentioned that she told you what I'm doing at the moment and that you might have some ideas. I've already got it pretty well tied up, but any extra help is always welcome. A thousand thanks, in advance. Warmly, Vero.

An hour later there was an email in the inbox which said:

Dear Vero,

Long time no see. Your memory must be worse than mine, though. We actually last saw each other at Patricia's birthday party. It's true that you were a bit tipsy, and perhaps you don't remember seeing me there. I was also drunk and performing erotic dances on the coffee table. I read the piece you wrote about suicides on the railways. I liked it, even if it was a bit overdramatic. I said as much to your boss when we had lunch yesterday and I told her this story, which might be useful to you.

Years ago, when you must have been in secondary school, I carried out an investigation for *Coloquial* on human trafficking in Misiones. Specifically in a little town called Capitán Pavone. I discovered that the mayor at the time, Juan García – a staunch supporter of President Menem, by the way – was involved in the trafficking organization. In the criminal underworld, this fine man was something like a wholesaler. Whatever you wanted, he could provide it: traffic in women, traffic in babies, slave labour for large estates. He also controlled the betting market and must have been involved in drugs, although I never managed to pin that one on him.

Around that time there had also been a very serious accident involving the only train that passed through the town each day. You're young, so you'll be surprised to hear that there was a time in Argentina when trains ran all over the country. It was precisely around that time that they stopped working. Do you remember our distinguished President Menem's promise, "if a branch line strikes, that branch line closes?" The thing is, that train ran over a little boy of eight or nine years old – I don't remember his exact age. Then somebody told me that it hadn't been a straightforward accident, but in fact a kind of competition in which people bet on boys as though they were horses. They told me that the person behind this scheme, once again, was Mayor García. I didn't look into it because I already had so much material against him that it was enough to put him inside for life three times over.

The trafficking story reached the national press (thanks to yours truly) and the mayor had to relinquish his post and leave the town. Obviously, the local courts absolved him of all charges, but his political career in Misiones was finished.

That's not the end of the story. A couple of years ago somebody told me that García was living in Buenos Aires and that he was still dabbling in politics. The person who told me that he had seen him said that he was "working" with drug dealers from the Comuna 8 district, right down in the south of the capital. He keeps a low profile, but it wouldn't surprise me if he's doing business with narcos and pimps. I'll leave you to discover which political party he's involved with.

I hope one day you'll take me drinking in one of those trendy clubs you and your friends go to (see – I know everything).

As soon as she had finished reading his email, Verónica wrote back:

Dear Rodo,

Thanks a million for this story, which provides a very useful background to my investigation. You're right about Pato's birthday. We shouldn't drink so much, so instead let's meet up for a lovely afternoon tea some time – more fitting for people like us. Warmly, Vero.

Verónica opened a blank document and called it "Juan García". Into it she copied the text of Corso's email. Her journalistic instinct told her that she was going to fill it with a lot more information than her colleague had provided.

VII

This time Federico and Verónica met in the Petit Colón, the bar where lawyers often went with their clients.

Verónica didn't like it because it reminded her of her teenage years, when either her mother or father would wait for her at the entrance to her school, which was a few yards down the same street. When she arrived, Federico was eating a toasted sandwich, which only served to reinforce the memory of herself eating the same kind of sandwich with her parents.

"Apologies – I didn't have time for lunch."

"If that's what you call lunch, no wonder you're so skinny."

"You seem on edge."

"I hate bars that have no smoking areas."

Federico opened his briefcase and took out the folder which Verónica had given to him the last time they met.

"It wasn't easy getting info, but I've got something for you."

"I expected nothing less."

"I've got something on six of the seven cases you gave me. The only case there's nothing for is the one where the boy got away unharmed; I found some information about the people inside the train who were hurt, but of course they've got no connection to the boy who caused the accident."

"I suspected as much. The boy escaped from the scene in a car."

"Here's the thing: that isn't mentioned in the case brought by one of the injured parties against the rail company. In the other cases the correct details regarding identity and addresses are given. One of the dead boys is still unnamed. Nobody ever came to claim his remains and he couldn't be identified. In that case, the most interesting witness statement is from the driver, who says that he saw people standing beside the tracks at the moment of impact, but that statement died along with the case. There wasn't much expert evidence to go on. Justice isn't only slow, it's also absent-minded and superficial."

"I need the name of the presiding judge in each case."

"It's all there in this folder which you gave to me and which I'm returning expanded and improved. In five of the cases, there are statements from the fathers, mothers and guardians. They all claimed not to have any knowledge about what their children were doing in those places. The boys said that they were playing. End of story."

"It's not the end."

"Sweetheart, I wouldn't arrange a meeting just to give you this information. I'd have sent it to you by email. There's something else I wanted to show you."

"Ah, I thought that the meeting was just an excuse to chat face-to-face."

"My girlfriend wouldn't let me do that." He searched in his briefcase and took out a map of Buenos Aires. "There's something very strange about the five cases for which we do have some information. If you look here, the alleged accidents all took place along a stretch of about twenty miles between the one that was closest to Once at one end and the one that was closest to Moreno at the other."

"To be more precise, they happened in Caballito and in Paso del Rey."

"Exactly, those are the end points. But look at the addresses given by the people responsible for these children. They all live in the capital. So I took the liberty of pinpointing on a map the places where they or their children lived, and to my surprise – and I'm guessing to yours, too – their homes aren't within a big radius. If we draw lines between all the addresses, as I've done on this map, you'll see that they fall within a radius no greater than two miles. They're not all on the same line, but there is a kind of zonal pattern which we could define as the neighbourhoods of Lugano, Oculta and Soldati."

Verónica felt a shiver that pricked all her senses. She had to confirm her hunch.

"OK, something else: do you have any idea which *comuna* those neighbourhoods belong to?"

"The *comunas*...those dear old Centres of Administration and Participation which for some absurd marketing reason they decided to rebrand as '*comunas*'."

"Do you know which one it is?"

"It's number 8, of course. The poorest one in Buenos Aires, the one with the highest rates of infant mortality, unemployment and illiteracy. I had to go there recently to renew my driver's licence."

"Fede, you're not only thinner and more handsome. You're cleverer than ever. I almost envy the receptionist."

VIII

García García García García. The name that Corso had given her was stuck in her head. It couldn't be a coincidence. Why had a boy from the Villa 15 shanty town been playing in Morón? Why had a boy from Soldati been in an accident in Caballito? How had a boy from Lugano ended up in Ituzaingó? Clearly somebody was taking them to these places. García, I'm going to grab you by the throat and I'm not going to let go, Verónica said to herself as she arrived back at her apartment.

She needed to think, to draw up a strategy. A text message arrived from Paula: *Bring good wine*. It was dinner with the girls that night. The feminist *asado*. She texted back: *I can't go, too much work*. Minutes later came an enigmatic message from Paula that read *Butch*. Then came another with the text corrected: *Bitch*.

She needed a double Jack Daniel's and two packets of cigarettes to help her think. She didn't believe she could have a decent idea before she had finished the first pack. She sat in the middle of the sofa and unfolded the map which Federico had so carefully marked up for her over the

167

coffee table. The lines crossed over each other, forming a slightly concave trapezoid. The centre, not very symmetrical or circular, but still quite clear, was at the point where the Dellepiane freeway crossed Calle Larrazábal.

For the moment, she decided to forget García. The guy couldn't be wandering about abducting children off the street. Those boys must have something in common: school, the soccer club they all supported, the hospital they went to. They were too small to be meeting in a bar. Perhaps they were street children, those ones you see begging at busy junctions. Or the ones who clean your windshield for a coin. She needed to see the area. Once there, she could get a better idea of what those boys had in common. If she could track down some of the ones who had survived, perhaps she could get them to tell her something. But how could she speak to them without arousing suspicion? If they found out that she was sniffing around, it could put her investigation at risk.

The first pack of cigarettes was nearly finished and she had already poured herself a second bourbon when her mobile started ringing. She thought that it was Paula or one of the girls, calling to give her a hard time. But it wasn't the girls. It was Lucio.

"I've just been told that there's been an accident. The seven formation knocked down a boy in Ciudadela."

"How's the boy?"

"He didn't survive. Jesus fucking Christ."

"And the driver's OK?"

"He's lost it, he's totally fucked-up. They've taken him to hospital."

Lucio's voice sounded grim.

As soon as they had ended the call, she rang Federico. It didn't cross her mind that it was nearly midnight and that he might be with his girlfriend, which could be awkward for him.

"A boy's been hit by a train at Ciudadela. The boy's dead. Please, I need you to find out which judge is going to be in charge of the case and make sure whoever it is pulls out all the stops and gets this boy's details. If necessary get my dad to pull strings to make the fucking judge work. Just tell me and I'll call him."

She drank what was left of the Jack Daniel's and looked at the map: she was sure that the boy was from Comuna 8. She lay back on the sofa and closed her eyes. She was tired, but it was still going to be hard to get to sleep that night.

IX

And she slept badly. She tossed and turned in bed, cursing herself for having no tranquillizers. Halfway through the night she got up to piss, to smoke a cigarette and drink some water.

Federico called her at eleven the next morning and gave her the information that had not yet come out in the press. The boy who had been run over by the Sarmiento train was called Vicente Garamona, known as Vicen, and had lived in Ciudad Oculta with his mother, Carmen Garamona, a cleaner who worked by the hour in two houses, one in San Telmo and the other in Belgrano. It was no thanks to the justice system that the boy's identity had been discovered, Federico said. His mother had reported him missing that same night, when he had supposedly gone to watch Vélez – the team he supported – play at their home ground. The Vélez stadium was not that far from Ciudadela.

"They're on the same railway line, one station apart," Federico told her. "But there's one detail which isn't in the police proceedings, perhaps because it seemed superfluous to them. Vélez weren't playing last night. Did Vicen get the wrong day and then decide to walk on along the tracks to Ciudadela? It doesn't sound very plausible."

Like everyone else, the boy's mother found out about the accident from the television. Maternal instinct told her that the dead boy could be her son. That day she happened to be working in the house of an architect, who went with her to the court. The mother identified the boy's clothes, which, though drenched in blood, were all that was recognizable.

The statement made in Tribunales did not include much information about Vicen. Nothing about his school or his friends. Neither did it say anything about the architect who had accompanied the mother to the judge's office. Federico had learned that detail from talking to the court secretary.

It was the first significant advance since Fede had shown her the map of Buenos Aires with all the places marked on it where the dead boys had lived. And that was something else she owed to him.

9   *Licking the Wounds*

A week before Lucio called Verónica to tell her about the most recent accident, they had been together in her apartment on Calle Lerma. He liked being somewhere that was so different from his home. He was fascinated by the quantity of books, CDs and magazines scattered all over the place which, nonetheless, obeyed some kind of order. As if this were a set, following a careful design. There was none of that chaos generated by his children at home. No toys chucked about, or bits of food that every so often appeared in the least expected places, no single socks lying in the corners.

What made this lovers' relationship pleasurable was the same thing that made a marriage of many years tolerable: routine. Verónica and Lucio had created their own habits and enjoyed repeating them. Her text message, his phone call, Lucio's arrival at the apartment, the music that would be playing low, like a soundtrack to their lives, the first kisses in the elevator, resumed in the kitchen while they opened a bottle of wine, or the caresses while she made coffee in the espresso maker, the removal of some clothes, if they were having sex on the sofa, the removal of all of them in the bedroom, Verónica's forays to change the music, or look for chocolates, or for imported cookies; the clothes that always went astray between the sheets, or under the bed, or got forgotten about in the living room; the last kisses in the elevator, the formal goodbye at the door. There wasn't time for much more in those two or three hours that they shared at least once a week and never more than three times.

Sometimes the routine was broken. Something would be said and not repeated.

"I like your back," she told him as she ran a long nail, painted red, along it. "It's like a wild animal. I like to imagine your back while you're fucking me, how it moves over me. If I found you fucking another girl I wouldn't react, I'd just stare at your back. But if you were underneath, with your back against the bed, then I would kill you."

Or that night of torrential rain, when Verónica insisted on opening the bedroom window that looked onto the street and he moulded himself to her body while she looked out of the window, giving herself to the rain more than to him.

And that time when there were no condoms and she offered to give him a blow job.

"And what about your ass?" Lucio asked her casually.

She told him to close his eyes and went to the bathroom. Soon she came back and began to massage his thighs, his cock and stomach with an oily substance. A scent of jasmine filled the room. Verónica's hands moved expertly.

"Do you like it?" she asked, and he nodded without opening his eyes.

Verónica lay, face down, beside him. Lucio opened his eyes. She offered him the little bottle containing the essence with which she had massaged him. He poured it on his hands and rubbed it over her back, down to her ass and deeply inside it. He left the bottle on the bedside table and penetrated her while she moaned with her mouth half-open and her eyes half-closed. He put his hand close to her mouth and she licked it first, then bit it, biting harder as he thrust into her. The pain shot from his hand up his arm, but he didn't try to take his hand out of her mouth. Instead he pushed harder against her and, only when he had come, did Verónica open her mouth and tightly close her eyes. A thread of blood trickled from the finger she had bitten. He wiped it against his own leg and rolled over to the other side of the bed. They lay like this, he facing up, her facing down, for a few minutes in silence, listening to the quickened pace of Lucio's breathing.

II

They hadn't met up in a bar again since starting to see each other regularly at the apartment. The arrangement to meet in a public place was therefore clearly a way for Verónica to signal that she wanted to separate this meeting from the time they spent together at hers. They settled on La Perla because it was close to where Lucio worked.

This time he picked a spot in the smoking section. She arrived almost at the same time as him. They greeted one another with a peck on the cheek, the kind of kiss they gave one another when saying goodbye at the door to Verónica's building. She took out a blue folder and passed it to him. Inside it were various newspaper reports. She wanted him to look at them and tell her if he had been involved in any of the cases. He couldn't focus on the articles; he could barely even read the headings. And yet each page reminded him of what had happened. The deaths, the colleagues who had stopped driving trains. Like Gringo Sosa, who spent a month as a patient in a psychiatric hospital after killing one of the boys; Marquitos Leme, who had quit and was never heard of again. No. He had not been directly involved in any of those accidents, but every one of them formed a part of his own story.

What Verónica was asking of him was absurd. There were doors that were closed and that Lucio wasn't prepared to open. If she started interviewing his co-workers, some bond between them would be broken. The silence that they sustained together, day after day, would be destroyed for something as trivial as a piece of journalism. Her insistence was absurd, almost idiotic. How could she understand so little, even now?

Because, if what she wanted to know was what it felt like to crush a person's body with the weight of a train, he could tell her about each one of his deaths. The faces, the sounds, the cries. The six of them were always with him. His six dead bodies. In this bar, in the haze of the cigarette smoke, in the tiles' dirty patina, on every one of those chairs that looked unoccupied.

III

Why had the boy asked for forgiveness with his eyes? His name was Pablo Muñoz, he was twenty-two years old, single and studying economics at the Universidad de Morón. Lucio found all that out afterwards, in the *Diario Popular*. The incident had merited a longer article than usual because it turned out that the boy was the son of a provincial congressman. Lucio had kept the page on which the article was printed. Pablo Muñoz had become a part of his life. He had locked onto Lucio's eyes and not let go until that image of the boy became noise beneath his feet.

A few days after the boy threw himself under the train, Lucio had gone to the Universidad de Morón. He had stood at the main door, watching the young people going in and out. He imagined that Pablo Muñoz must also have stood there, many times. If he had not jumped in front of the train, or if Lucio had managed to stop it in time, he might be there today, with his rucksack full of textbooks and notes.

Was it forgiveness that the boy had been asking for with that last look? He had wondered this every day, every hour since the accident. One morning, three weeks later, he thought that he had found the answer, that he knew what the boy had been trying to say.

That same morning he had gone to the city of La Plata. He had kept asking people for directions to the state legislature building until he found it. Once there, he had requested to speak to Congressman Muñoz. The receptionist had asked which party the congressman belonged to, because they had three gentlemen with that surname. Lucio didn't know, so he replied:

"The congressman whose son died under a train."

He was asked to wait in the entrance hall, together with a group of very disparate people all united by a look of needing a favour. After ten minutes a woman of about fifty appeared, asking who Lucio Valrossa was. This woman said that she was the congressman's assistant and asked him the reason for his visit.

"I was driving the train that knocked down his son."

The woman told him to wait and returned the way she had come. A few minutes later she was back with a short, fat, balding gentleman, who looked untidy despite his jacket and tie. The woman pointed at Lucio but did not approach him. Only the congressman came over to where the driver was waiting.

"I wanted to tell you that I am sorry about what happened to your son."

Congressman Muñoz nodded. He had nothing to say to him. He could perhaps have asked if the boy had suffered when the train struck him, or if he thought that it had been

175

an accident. But the congressman seemed not to want to talk about those things. He didn't want anyone coming to tell him what he wasn't ready to hear.

"There's something else. When your son appeared, there was no way to stop the train before it hit him. I saw your son clearly. He had a sad face. I'm sure that he was trying to tell me something with his expression: that he did not want to kill himself. That he no longer wanted to kill himself."

The congressman listened to him, studying the laces on his moccasins. When Lucio had finished speaking, Muñoz said to him:

"I'm grateful to you for coming all this way to tell me that."

He shook his hand, then turned away. Lucio waited for a few seconds longer in the hall. He thought of Pablo Muñoz's face, that sorrowful expression. The boy hadn't been asking forgiveness for jumping. He was begging him to say that he had not wanted to kill himself. Now Lucio had passed the message on and he felt that there was one less burden on his soul.

IV

"Does it hurt?"

"No."

"You're annoyed."

Lucio looked at her in the mirror. Verónica was standing behind him, both of them in the bath.

"Not at all."

Lucio looked again at his lip. It had stopped bleeding, but it was inflamed. He dabbed it with cold water. Verónica sat on the lid of the toilet, naked, her legs parted, like an object of artistic study. He was naked too, his hair tousled, his cheeks flushed. He washed his face. He would have liked to take a shower, but he suspected she wouldn't like it. When had he started to notice that there were things he did that irritated her? When had he started making efforts not to annoy her? Perhaps it was that time when they had both been lying naked on the bed. He had been stroking her stomach. He liked her navel, the beginning of the mons veneris, the taut, pale skin. He had said to her:

"I like imagining your belly pregnant. I'd like to make a baby with you so I could see your belly grow."

Verónica had tensed up and pushed his hand away.

"Don't be a cretin. Don't say something that you're not prepared to follow through on."

"I'll follow through on anything," he had said, not yet understanding what she was so annoyed about.

"No. Don't say that you'd like to see me with a pregnant belly, because it isn't true. Don't say that you'd like us to be partners, because that's also not true. Don't say anything that you don't want to, or can't, stand by."

Then she had got up and had stood behind him, putting her arms around him. Lucio liked the fact that she was as tall as him. Verónica's hands stroked his chest.

"Your wife is going to realize that somebody bit your lip."

Lucio said nothing. He went to the bedroom and started to get dressed. He couldn't find his boxers anywhere. Eventually he found them behind the bed, under a pillow that had fallen onto the floor.

Verónica threw herself onto the sheets, face down. Lucio contemplated the body that had, minutes before, been between his hands and felt a kind of vertigo, a sensation that sooner or later all this would end. He put on his trousers and kneeled on the bed. He wanted to caress her again, to touch her, feel her, possess her, all those things that made him feel that they were alive, they were together and that there was a quota of happiness in the world for them.

He stroked her back, moving down to her ass and her legs. Verónica had bruises on her thighs, her buttocks and the left side under her breast. He had caused those bruises. Some were violet coloured, others reddish or yellow. Now that it was over and he was getting dressed and going away, he could touch her with this tenderness. But when they were in the throes of desire they couldn't help but love each other harshly. They bit each other, pushed each other, gripped each other so hard their hands hurt. He had several cuts; his back was scratched. Her body was covered in bruises. And yet there were no complaints. Neither of them had asked the other to be more gentle. Lucio didn't know what was going on in her head, but he had been surprised by his own desires. He had never had sex like that with his wife.

Verónica didn't look at him. She kept her eyes closed as he lowered his hand to her sex and touched her. Later he moved his fingers away. Lucio wished then that life could stay like this. That something of her could stay with him, even if only on his hands: the dampness, the smell of her body. In a few minutes, everything would be gone.

He lay back down beside her and kissed her neck. She turned over and looked into his eyes.

"You know that I love you, right?"

Lucio couldn't find the words to reply. He kissed her and, when they parted, she said:

"Thank you."

"Thank you for what?"

"For your silence."

V

That Thursday he arrived home early. The boys were playing with a beach ball in their room and he joined them, rolling on the floor and fooling around with them until Mariana came in to say that she had made them maté. They went to the kitchen and spent a good half hour there, drinking maté and eating a cake Mariana's mother had baked. As there were still a couple of hours before dinner, Lucio decided finally to fix the blinds in the boys' room, which had been broken for a week. That meant changing various slats which had rotted and snapped. He had some spares he could use, left over from an old blind which some time ago he had refused to throw out. It made him happy that it had proved to be useful, as he had always suspected that it would. That job took more than an hour. Afterwards he started running a bath and, when there was enough water, went looking for Fabián and Patricio. Fabián had fallen asleep on the floor. Gently Lucio woke him up but, when told he had to have a bath, the little boy started to cry. He had to be promised a chocolate after dinner. He put the boys in the tub and let them enjoy a long bath time. Mariana had already put out towels and clean clothes for them both. The whole bathroom ended up wet, with the dirty clothes thrown on the floor. When they were ready, they went through to the living room. Dinner was already served up: spaghetti with braised chicken.

While Mariana took them off to bed, Lucio cleared the table and washed the dishes and pans. He still hadn't finished by the time she came back so she took the opportunity to go on the computer, because she needed to download some practice exercises for the fifth-grade class. Lucio never used the internet. It bored him. He had an email account which Mariana had created for him, but he never checked it. She, on the other hand, spent quite a lot of time on the computer. He preferred to watch television or listen to the radio while he got small jobs done around the house.

In fact he was watching the television when his mobile

rang. For a moment he feared that it was Verónica. An absurd fear, because she never called him; she only ever sent text messages. It was a colleague from work.

"Plate Number 7 smashed into some kid. Malvino was in the cabin."

"Fucking kids."

"It's a mess."

"Where is he now?"

"They took him to the Central in Haedo, because he had a panic attack. Pierini and Saúl have gone over there."

"And the kid?"

"He didn't jump out of the way in time. It caught him full on."

He hung up, swearing. Mariana looked at him, but she didn't need any explanations. Nor did she need Lucio to explain why he was going out: he wanted to be alone. He walked along the sidewalk, turned a corner and decided to call Verónica, although it made no sense to do that. He wasn't calling her because he wanted to pass on information for her piece but because he needed to hear her voice, share this moment with her. If he could, he would have got on a bus and gone straight to her apartment. But he didn't feel he could do that.

Nor did he feel any better after the call. He had hoped that her voice would be like a balm for his pain, but it hadn't worked that way. There he was, in the dead of night, in a lonely street, and yet he felt as though he were standing on a train track. He could hear the screams, see the boy's face, feel the sensation of reducing a body to dust.

VI

Four days passed with no news of Verónica. He had not sent her any texts or called her, either. But every time he got an

SMS he thought that it was from her. And eventually, one Monday morning, it was. She texted him: *I need to ask you a favour.*

"I need to ask you a favour," she repeated when he called her on the phone. "Could you go somewhere with me?"

"Go with you?"

"It's really hard to explain. Actually, it's simple."

"Is it hard, or simple?"

"I need you to come with me to Lugano. I would go alone, but I think it's better if I go with someone. And I thought you'd be the right person."

They arranged to meet the following morning at the junction of Avenida Rivadavia and Avenida La Plata. She would collect him, in a white Volkswagen Gol, and drive with him to Villa Lugano. She didn't give him any more details.

This time she arrived punctually, at eleven o'clock in the morning. Lucio was surprised to see a baby's car seat in the back.

"It's my sister's car," Verónica quickly explained. "It even smells of baby food."

"I can't smell anything," he said and added, looking back at the car seat, "Chicco – my children had a high chair the same brand."

They took the freeway towards Ezeiza and left it after a few minutes at the exit on to Calle Larrazábal. They drove down a series of streets that were unfamiliar to Lucio but which Verónica had marked on a map.

"I'm going to give my sister a GPS for her birthday."

"Where are we going?"

"To visit some houses."

"Your family?"

"No, no need to panic. The corner of Larrazábal and Zelarrayán is, for want of a better term, the geographical

181

centre of the area where all the boys came from who've been run over on the Sarmiento line in the last five years. I have the addresses for six of the cases. I even have the address for the boy who was killed last week."

Verónica stopped the car at an intersection and looked around her.

"Those boys would definitely have hung out around here. What do you think they'd be doing? Cleaning windshields? Look at those kids in smocks. Shouldn't they be in school? Any one of them could be next, but how do we find out?"

She started the car again and drove further into the neighbourhood.

"Are they all from round here?" Lucio asked. "What is this? Mataderos?"

"I think Mataderos is over to the left. This is Lugano, Villa Soldati is to my right and also on the left is the Villa 15 shanty town, better known as the Ciudad Oculta, the 'hidden city'. Two cases come from there, the last one and one other. But today I want to look at the other four. We've arrived: this is our first stop."

Verónica parked the car and asked Lucio to wait inside. She got out and walked towards a stuccoed house with broken glass stuck along the top of the dividing wall for protection. She knocked on the metal door. Presently a woman of about seventy came out. They spoke for a few minutes then said goodbye. Verónica returned to the car.

"Not a good start. The family moved out soon after the accident. Let's move on."

Verónica drove back through the streets by which they had already come, continuing on, very slowly, through a district of high-rise blocks, as though she could find what she was looking for just by circling the area. She looked for the address and, after various wrong turns, located the right building. She got out of the car then came back a few minutes later, got back in and slammed the door. Clearly something had made her angry.

"The people in the apartment don't know anything. According to a neighbour, the parents and the kid lived there, but he was still pretty much a baby when they moved out. Obviously they never officially updated their domicile and the idiots in the courthouse didn't bother to check the address."

She looked up the address of the third child. Ten minutes later they arrived at a block of low houses outside which rubbish had accumulated on the sidewalk. Verónica checked the number she had written down and went to the corresponding house. The door was open and she called "hello". A girl appeared with a baby in her arms. From the car Lucio watched as Verónica talked and the girl shook her head.

"Let's go. Nobody knows anything here."

The fourth address was a run-down house partitioned into apartments. A fat, dark-skinned man was sitting in the doorway, looking rather friendless. This time Lucio offered to get out instead of her. Verónica hesitated, then agreed that they could go together.

"Good morning," Verónica said.

The man must have been about forty and was sweating despite the cool weather. Or perhaps it was a layer of grease that covered him. He looked at them without smiling.

"Does the Palmieri family live here?"

The man looked at her as though he didn't speak Spanish. Verónica tried again: "The Palmieri family. Carlos and Elvira Palmieri. One of the children was called Luis and he lost an arm in a train accident. Do you remember them?"

"I remember." He let a few seconds pass before adding: "That family doesn't live here any more. I think they went back to Paraguay."

"You don't happen to know if there's any way I can find them? Any relatives you know of?"

"Didn't I just tell you that they've gone? I don't know anyone from their family."

Verónica was about to return to the car when Lucio asked: "And the lad who lost his arm. Do you remember him?"

"Of course. How could I forget?"

"Do you know how the accident happened?"

"That boy was always hanging around in the street. Plus… with parents like that."

"They never said anything to you about the accident?"

"The mother went crazy afterwards. But then she hadn't looked after him."

"And what did the boy do all day? Did he go to school?"

"You must be joking. He never went."

"Did he ask for money or collect cardboard to sell?"

"He was too slow-witted to make money. He spent all day playing soccer."

"Was he good at soccer?"

"So they said. Until the poor bastard lost his arm."

"Did he play here, in the street?"

"Here, all over the place. He played in a club, I think."

"In Deportivo Español? In Yupanqui?"

"No, I think it was on this side of the freeway. A five-a-side club, not one with a full-sized ground."

"Do you know which club?"

"Why would I know something like that?"

They returned to the car. Verónica sat and looked at Lucio with eyes wide open. Then she kissed him on the mouth. The fat man, still watching them, would have had no idea why.

That Saturday they had played against the maintenance team from Moreno. One of those games that it would have been better to miss. The opposition seemed to think they were playing in a World Cup final, the way they acted. Worse still, a few of them had been wearing proper soccer boots and one of them had raked his soles down Lucio's calf. He didn't break it, thank God, but those cuts would take time to heal.

Verónica came across his injured leg after they had sex. She brought her face close to the wounds and studied them with fascination, as though contemplating precious jewels. She placed a finger on one of them. Lucio moved his leg away.

"Don't be a baby," she said, looking at him.

Lucio said nothing, but he moved his leg back. She stroked it, circling each of the wounds. They were the shape of rubies. Again, she placed a fingertip on the one that was still raw. She barely touched it. It was such a light caress that she seemed barely to be touching Lucio's leg at all. Very gently, she pressed it. Lucio felt a burning sensation.

Lucio smiled at her and she must have taken that as an invitation to press harder. She pushed her finger into the wound until she felt Lucio trembling. It was too much for him and she drew back a little. Now she looked at her finger, with his blood on it. She licked her finger and then sucked the trickle of blood that had started to run down Lucio's calf. Verónica dug her long nails into him, near his knee. Lucio moved to touch her nipple and she smacked his hand away, while still sucking his leg. That slap surprised him; she should watch herself. He pulled her hair, hard, in a quick motion. Verónica screamed. In that moment Lucio manoeuvred himself beside her and tried to lie on top of her back, but she quickly turned over, so that she was face up. Lucio grabbed her wrists and held them with one hand. One strong, big hand. Hers were like two trapped swallows. It was clear that he was hurting her, but she didn't complain. Lucio beat his hips against her pelvis and still she said nothing. Each time he thrust harder against her, as roughly as he could, his body going in and out of her body.

Verónica looked straight into his eyes.

"That's it, murderer, fuck me like that."

He thrust into her even harder, while the word *murderer* covered him like sticky saliva. He came, and didn't collapse onto her but rolled over to lie beside her. Verónica looked at him with an indecipherable smile.

10   *Clean*

I

It was a small gripe but one that he couldn't get out of his head. Who should name a soft toy – the person giving it or the person who receives it? Because it's one thing to give an impersonal, average, any old toy, and it's another thing entirely to give a toy with personality. He decided to baptize it. It was a furry dog with its tongue hanging out. Bushy struck him as a good name.

Rafael was going to meet Martina in the square that morning. His daughter would come with her grandmother and they would spend some time together. Rafael was feeling happy because he had got his wages from the club. He would be able to pay for the room he was renting, buy a present for Martina and even get himself a pay-as-you-go phone. He put twenty pesos on it and wrote the number down on a piece of paper to give to his mother. So that she would have it, but also so that she could pass it on to Andrea. He wanted to talk to his ex-wife.

For the first time in a long while, he had shaved. He had got rid of the beard that had been with him all those years. Now, looking at his clean-shaven reflection in the mirror, he saw himself as he was ten years ago, barely out of adolescence, when he had just finished secondary education at night school and dreamed of studying art. Back then he had imagined that, with time, he could become a sculptor like Henry Moore, famous and garlanded. A decade later he was merely a survivor. It could have been worse.

He had long hair. He put it in a ponytail, making his face look even fresher, his forehead broad and his small brown eyes (which looked fearful, to his dismay) more visible. He had always had that rather timid expression, although he was not, in fact, timid. His expression confused people. It wasn't one of fear, but indifference, rejection, incomprehension. Anything but fear. He stroked his cheek. His skin felt smooth. He liked seeing himself once again as that adolescent who had got lost so many years before. As if he had skipped those years of hell to reappear now.

He walked the blocks between his hostel and the plaza at an unhurried pace. It was early, and he wanted to enjoy every moment of that Saturday. When he arrived at the meeting point his daughter and mother were not yet there. He sat on a free bench and contemplated the chilly spring morning. It would be hotter next month. If it had still been winter he would have had to get a warmer jacket than the one he had, which was only good for days like these.

He caught sight of his mother and daughter before they saw him. They were holding hands, distracted by the children who were running around, some of them playing with a ball. Martina wore a pink padded jacket with a fake-fur-lined hood. He knew the lengths Andrea would have gone to to make sure that her daughter was well nourished, went to school and wore good clothes. Four years in which he had been absent, making trouble, harassing his own family. He also thought about his mother, who had sacrificed her life to help Andrea and Martina – to help him in other words – to the detriment of his siblings. These days they treated Rafael with contempt or indifference as a way of expressing the jealousy they felt about the love shown him by their mother. When his mother and daughter finally saw him, Rafael stood up to greet them.

"Daddy, you look different, like someone much less old."

"I'm not old."

His mother stroked his cheeks, as though feeling for traces of his lost beard. Then she went off to stroll around the square. She preferred to leave them alone. To give them that short time to get to know each other. Martina must have a clear recollection of her father's presence in their home. She had lived through the chaos that he generated, and had suffered more than anyone when he left the house. She had kept asking for him, though, demanding to see him. She had asked her mother and got nowhere. So she had tried with her grandmother, who had promised her that, when her father was well, she would take Martina to see him, even if her mother was against it. And the grandmother had kept her promise, because here was Martina, with Bushy in one hand and the other holding her father's, on the way to the drinks stand.

Martina told him everything; each time they met, her aim was to provide her father with a second-by-second reconstruction of her life. What the house she lived in was like, what school was like. She told him about her teacher, her classmates, her best friend. She explained, in detail, what a greatest common divisor and a minimum common divisor were. She repeated, from memory, a lesson on San Martín, the liberator of Argentina, Chile and Peru, and she challenged him to ask her the capital cities of all the Argentine provinces. Chubut was the only one she was unsure about. She told him that she didn't like playing with the boys at school because they were all rough, but that she did like playing soccer. That she had two friends in the house: El Peque and Dientes. Rafael told her that he remembered the two boys. That he hadn't seen Dientes for a long time, but that he often saw El Peque at the club where he worked, because he played soccer there.

"Poor Peque," Martina said. "He hasn't been out of his room for more than a week. His mum says that he's ill."

Then it dawned on Rafael that he hadn't seen El Peque at the club for days. He hadn't paid much attention to his absence because all of them had been so upset by the news that Vicen had been killed by a train in Ciudadela. They had found out about this at the club the same way as everyone else: first through a news item on television which didn't name the victim. Then a few days later somebody brought in a copy of *Tiempo Argentino*, in which there was a piece naming the boy who had been run over by a train as Vicente Garamona, Vicen, the boy who came from Ciudad Oculta to play soccer at the club. Rafael couldn't believe that a life might be cut short by something as stupid and dangerous as playing on train tracks. Somebody, one of the regulars who idled away their afternoons between card games and moscato wine, remembered that another boy who used to come to the club had lost an arm in similar circumstances.

Everyone wondered what Vicen could have been doing in Ciudadela, so far from where he lived. Somebody said that boys from the shanty town ran all over the city looking for cardboard to sell or stealing stereos from cars. Rafael didn't say anything as he poured out the glasses of wine, but for him it was obvious that, if the boy was larking around on the tracks, he hadn't gone to Ciudadela to steal things. Even so, he couldn't understand what he had been doing so far away, what he had been up to. Thinking of Vicen had briefly taken his mind away from his daughter. For a moment he was terrified to think that something could happen to her, a child as small and fragile as that boy was. Hearing Martina's voice reassured him.

"But his mum doesn't know the truth."

"What doesn't she know?"

"That he isn't ill."

"He's pretending to be ill so that he doesn't have to go to school?"

"No. He's mad. He's gone mad."

"Come on, it can't be as bad as that."

"Dientes told me. He said that El Peque had seen something that made him go mad."

"Something?"

"He saw someone die. Dientes says that El Peque told him not to tell anyone that he saw another boy die."

"And how did he see this?"

"I don't know. But Dientes says that the boy exploded into a thousand pieces, like in a horror movie."

"Dientes said that to scare you. It must be made up."

"Nothing scares me."

I I

In the last few months, Rafael had become friends with Julián – you could almost say he was his only friend, not counting the people he had met on the rehabilitation programme. Julián was not his real name, though he had one that was a little bit similar: Xian. He was Chinese and ran a convenience store a few yards from the hostel where Rafael lived. Xian had decided to call himself Julián, his wife called herself Elsa and they had called their daughter, who was born in Argentina, Juliana.

It had started as a simple business relationship. Rafael often went to Julián's store to buy what he needed for the day: ham, bread, spaghetti, rice, sachets of Tang powder for juice, hamburgers, toilet paper, soap, crackers, yerba maté. Not much else. Gradually, Julián started showing his curious side. Not so much in relation to Rafael's life, but to Argentine customs. He might ask him what he should do if his van was involved in an accident, or where he should go to get vaccinated against measles, or why, when preparing maté, the water must not be boiled. Rafael gave brief answers to start with, but soon he discovered that Julián was not only willing to learn about life in Argentina but keen to talk about himself, too. Then Rafael took his cue to start asking the questions. That way he found out that Julián had arrived in the country five years previously, that he had lived in London for two years before that. That he had been born in Beijing and that Elsa, his wife, was from a little town three hundred miles from the Chinese capital.

"Me, city man. She, country woman."

Julián was a teacher of martial arts and a writer. He had published a book on kung fu techniques.

"I sold many thousands of copies. I earned nothing. Everything for the state. That's why I left."

In London he had taught kung fu and tried to translate the book, but he couldn't get used to the city. Since he already had a lot of relatives in Buenos Aires, they suggested he move there. It wouldn't be difficult to start a business if he could count on the support of his fellow countrymen.

"I paid for everything. No debts and no enemies. Everyone happy," he said and laughed because that was the name of the convenience store: *Todos Contentos.*

Their friendship would not have progressed from that of a shopkeeper and his customer (like the kind Rafael remembered from his childhood in Bernal, when his father used to spend the evenings chatting to the owner of the local store while they ate little pieces of provolone cheese) if it hadn't

192

been for Julián telling him one day that he wanted to support a soccer club. Could he recommend one? Rafael told him that he was an Independiente fan.

"Red make me think my country flag. Another team."

"Let me think. You could support Boca, River, Huracán, Chacarita. Any of them apart from Racing."

"Chacarita. I like this name: Chacarita."

"I should warn you that they're about to be relegated."

"It doesn't matter. The love for the shirt is stronger. I, from today, fan of Chacarita."

A few weeks later Chacarita were playing against Independiente in San Martín and Julián invited him to go and watch. They went together to the Chacarita terraces. Julián didn't get to celebrate much because the Reds won two–nil, but he had already familiarized himself with his team's line-up and even insulted the coach with impressively accurate cheek. As they travelled home on the 114 (Julián not wanting to talk or ask questions, too depressed by the defeat), Rafael told him about his history of addiction, about his daughter and Andrea. When they got off the bus, Julián said to him:

"You are strong. I like strong people. In kung fu, I taught people to use their spirit. You are a fighter and you have already won some battles. That is very good."

Perhaps because of those words, when Andrea did finally call him on the mobile, Julián was the one Rafael told. Julián nodded as he heard the news, gave his wife and employees a couple of instructions in Chinese and said to him:

"Let's go to the cafe."

That was the first time that they sat down together at one of the tables in the old bar, Por La Vuelta, on the corner of Zambroni and Obligado. The waitress, who looked to be in her late teens, brought them two strong espressos.

"She sounded very serious. I said that I'd like us to see each other, speak to each other. She wasn't at all sure about us meeting, but eventually she agreed."

"She is scared to imagine that you are well and to see you looking bad. But she's going to see you well. You don't need to worry."

Since he didn't have to go to work until the afternoon, the hours passed unhurriedly for Rafael that morning. He wished he could stay there, in the bar, a cup of coffee on the table in front of him, listening to Julián's slightly shrill voice. Going to Spring Breezes made him feel uncomfortable. He couldn't pretend to be blind. Invisible to others, yes. Blind himself, no.

III

Because Rafael knew that something was going on and that Rivero was responsible. He could tell that simply from observing the coach, who walked around the club as though he owned it. In fact, he was the one who took decisions that ought to have been made by the club's president, an old man who smoked Toscano cigars and spent his time playing cards with the other pensioners.

But if there was one thing Rafael had not expected, it was that Rivero himself would approach him and open the door to a place that he did not know if he was willing to go. It was one afternoon when the conversation he had had with Martina about El Peque was still very fresh in his mind and when the memory of the boy who had been killed on the tracks had not yet faded among the club's regular patrons.

Rivero had installed himself at one of the tables in the bar. He had ordered a Fernet with cola and, when Rafael took it over to him, he asked him to stay, to sit down, because he wanted to talk to him. Rafael had not spoken to anyone about his doubts. Rivero could not know about them, unless he was a mind reader. Or unless he was cannier, more observant than him.

"I hear you have a daughter. How old is she?"

"Ten years old."

"Ah, that's a nice stage. No messing around with boyfriends yet."

Rafael didn't want to offer him anything of himself, not even a fake smile. So he merely nodded and waited for Rivero to get to the point.

"What you earn here can barely be enough for a pot to piss in, am I right? Especially if you're separated – because you are separated, aren't you? What with giving money to the witch, and the kid who needs books and pens, and some girlfriend you want to take out. Do you have a girlfriend?"

"Not right now."

"And forget it if you want to go to a strip club. Those chicks get more expensive all the time. Bah, that's life. Listen, my friend, would you like to earn a bit extra?"

"Yes, I'm interested in any kind of paying work."

"OK, let me explain. First, a question: do you like soccer, do you go to games?"

"Yes, quite a bit."

A lion, that was what Rivero seemed to him. A lion, well fed, powerful, not frightened of anything. Who could afford to be generous even with the prey he was about to eat.

"Look, I need someone I can trust. Someone on the ball, who knows how to pay attention. This club is a seedbed. The kids come here and we nurture them. We bring in urchins off the street and turn them into fine players. And from here they go on to Argentina Juniors, to Vélez, to River. We can be proud of the quality of our kids' game. If it weren't for the fact that the club's such a shithole, we could be playing in the best junior leagues, but what can you do? The president prefers to have these old farts in here playing cards. Don't you think we should get shot of all these oldsters?"

"I've never really thought about it."

Or perhaps one of those circus lions. Who seem tame but can suddenly pounce and deliver a fatal mauling.

"What I want is to keep supplying the youth academies of the big clubs with good players. And for that I need people. Because most of the lads playing here we find kicking balls about in the streets, in the squares. I've got people on the lookout in those areas, I myself go out every weekend to scout for boys. I probably look like an old paedo eyeing up the children. But the truth is that that's the way to find the best players." Rivero took a long drink of his Fernet and cola. He wiped his mouth with his hand and went on: "I won't beat about the bush. I need someone to go looking for boys in the areas on the other side of the Dellepiane freeway. Do you know where I mean?"

"Yes, I know the area."

"Even better. You need to go, watch the boys who are play-ing soccer, have a chat with them and bring the ones who are worthwhile back to the club. Notice that I said 'worthwhile', and not 'best'. Because one thing is not always the same as the other. I'm not interested in the skilled-up little shit who wants to be a star. Don't get me wrong; if you find a Tevez then grab him and bring him over. But what I'm after is a boy with a bit of spirit, someone who's ahead of the game. And for that I need you to know about psychology as much as soccer. Talk to the boys. If they seem like delicate flowers who'll get their dads onto you for the slightest thing, I'm not interested. The best ones are the lads who can look after themselves. Do you follow me?"

"I think so. Boys with the spirit of men."

"Exactly. You said it. I can see we understand each other. It's the kind of work you'll have to do at the weekend or whenever you can fit it in. I'm not going to be hovering over you to make sure you do the right hours. There's a hundred pesos a week in it for the work, but for every boy you bring who's worthwhile, there's another five hundred pesos. A nice figure, right? And I'll pay you in cash, the moment the kid signs his club membership card. The hundred pesos you'll get every Monday, whatever happens. Are we in business?"

Rafael felt that he was putting his head in the lion's mouth. A lion that was at that moment showing its teeth in a smile that looked paternal, affectionate but which opened all the same into the maw of a wild beast.

"Yes, absolutely. This Saturday I'll go and watch some kids play."

"Excellent. The best ones are the boys of about ten years old. What a shame you don't have a son. If you did, you could bring him here and I'd turn him into a Maradona for you."

IV

Two years ago he had also been clean. That was when he had joined a group of recovering addicts. It was at a Pentecostal church in Aldo Bonzi, run by a North American family. The process had been much easier than he was expecting. He hadn't abandoned his previous friendships, though, and when his old associates saw that he was clean they had offered him a quick and simple job: to go to Bolivia and bring back a packet containing a kilo of cocaine. The most tedious part of the job was the twenty-two hours it took to get there and back by coach. When he arrived back in Buenos Aires with his delivery he got paid the agreed amount and decided to call Andrea to show her how well he was. Grudgingly, she had agreed to meet him in a bar on Avenida Eva Perón. He had thought of proposing that they get back together.

But nothing turned out as Rafael had expected. Andrea had arrived and started talking without leaving him any space to show himself to be a reformed man ready to start a new life. She said that she had been going out with someone for a few months, that he and she couldn't go back to being a couple. That she was very happy to see him well, recovered and working but that he should forget any idea of getting back together with her. Their only bond was Martina, nothing else.

Rafael left that meeting with confusion in his head and hopelessness in his heart. For hours he walked aimlessly until he felt a thirst in his throat that grew until it took over his whole body. He went into a seedy bar near Liniers station and asked for a whisky. They brought him a rough Criadores which scoured the walls of his stomach. He had never been sure about what happened after that – it was one of many moments of amnesia that he experienced in those years. All he could remember was that days later he found himself drinking beer and snorting coke in a drugs den some distance from the capital, that somebody had a revolver on the table and that he didn't have a single peso left from the money he had made from his trip to Bolivia.

So began a precipitous fall that took him ever further from Andrea. That was why, now that they were meeting again, he knew that he was walking a tightrope, twenty yards above the ground and with no safety net.

This time they met in a bar on Zelarrayán, one that they had been to several times in the past, on the way home from a concert, back when they were still together. He got there before Andrea. He saw her cross the road and come towards him with a cautious smile. She was dressed the same as always:

hair caught up in a ponytail; padded jacket similar to the one Martina wore, and underneath it a black polo neck. As far as Rafael was concerned, she hadn't changed in all these years, but doubtless she thought she was fatter, because she had dressed in black. And in fact, almost the first thing she said was:

"We've both put on weight."

They spent half an hour together. Rafael tried not to overwhelm her with details of his new life. He told her only that he was living in a hostel in Soldati, that he was working at a soccer club, that he was clean and intended to stay that way. He didn't ask, he didn't want to know, if she still had a boyfriend. He found out only that she was working on the till in a superstore. The rest of the time they talked about Martina, her school, her lessons, her friends. Rafael was on firm ground with these, since his daughter had told him the details herself. Andrea expressed some anxiety about Martina's thinness; she told him that she had taken her to see the doctor, who hadn't found anything wrong.

"She takes after me – I was a skinny boy."

There weren't many people in the bar: at one table was another couple, quite a bit older than them. Where would Andrea and he meet one another in twenty years' time? Would they have a coffee together, like today? Would they talk about their thirty-something daughter? Would they be together again? Better not to wonder about such things, to have the last, cold gulp of coffee, to call the waiter, pay – insist on paying and do it. Let Andrea see that things were going well for him, that he wasn't obsessed with knowing if she had a partner or not. That he wasn't even going to moot the idea of getting back together. He was happy just to see her without fighting, and to be spending increasingly more time with his daughter.

"And don't think that I didn't know you've been seeing Martina. Your mother ended up spilling the beans one night."

They said goodbye inside the bar. He told her that he would like to stay there a bit longer. He watched her leave, crossing back over the street the way she had come. Then, without thinking about it too much, he stood up and went out after her. Andrea walked at a steady pace and Rafael followed about twenty yards behind. At no point did she look back; if she had she would have seen Rafael straightaway, since he made no attempt to hide but simply matched his pace to the rhythm of her gait. He didn't have any particular intention. Nor did he think about whether what he was doing was right or wrong; he just wanted to accompany her, at a distance, as she walked home, thinking perhaps of the meeting they had had a few minutes before. Rafael watched her and saw a different Andrea – Andrea on her own. Her body emanated the solitude of someone who doesn't have to account for anything around her. She moved in a world of strangers, people who were there but might just as well not exist. Who, in fact, did not exist for her. She wasn't the Andrea of the bar, the one who had watched him, who weighed up what he said, who was on the defensive. Nor was she the Andrea her daughter knew, or her mother, her workmates or bedmates. That Andrea walking ahead of him was an Andrea covered in loneliness. He saw her as fragile, defenceless. And Rafael, who was already juggling various feelings about his ex-wife, added one more: compassion.

Andrea arrived at the tenement house. Rafael saw her disappear inside it. He turned round and began to retrace his steps.

V

Dientes spent a large part of that morning on the terrace, alone. He had found a place to sit against the wall and was languidly torturing a line of ants carrying scraps of leaves. The sun was beginning to bother him, though, and boredom crept over him, from feet and hands to head. He was about to get up and go down to the courtyard when he saw El Peque emerge from the stairway. He hadn't seen him for a week, not since El Peque had told him about Vicen.

"What are you doing here?"

"What are *you* doing here?"

Neither of them answered. El Peque sat down beside him without saying anything. Dientes was hot from spending so much time in the sun. He felt as though he were sweating even though it was quite a cold day. He slapped his hand down, squashing some ants.

El Peque looked for something in his trouser pocket. He pulled out some balled-up paper. In fact it was a twenty-peso note, which he smoothed out over his legs.

"Shall we go and buy some Coke?"

They walked to the newsagent on the next block in silence. As well as the litre-and-a-half bottle of Coke, El Peque bought a big packet of Don Satur salted crackers. They walked on to the Plaza España and sat down under a tree. El Peque opened the packet while Dientes unscrewed the bottle top. He took a long drink and passed the bottle to El Peque, who drank about half a litre without pausing for breath. He put down the bottle and burped. Dientes crammed crackers into his mouth.

"I'm going to school today," El Peque said, reaching into the Don Satur packet.

"What about the club?"

"I'm not going back to the club any more."

VI

Rivero was in the habit of leaving his mobile on a table in the bar, or sometimes on the bar counter. If it started ringing, Rafael would leave whatever he was doing and quickly take it to him at the pitch, where he was training the boys. So this wasn't the first time it had happened, but it was the first time Rafael had tried to remember who the caller was. The mobile was ringing right in front of him, on the bar top. He saw that on the screen it simply said GARCÍA. Six letters which, for him, still had no significance.

He picked up the mobile and went over to where Rivero was. Training was just finishing; in fact, the coach was coming back towards the bar. Gesturing thank you, he took the call. Since they were both now walking in the same direction, Rafael could hear what Rivero was saying. "Complicated...I still haven't got anything...we'll get there...the woman and the kids don't want to budge...no, it's a headache...OK, whatever you think."

Rivero went to one of the tables in the bar and sat down. Rafael went his own way and couldn't hear any more. Quickly he mixed a Fernet with cola and brought it to the table just as the conversation ended. You could tell from Rivero's face that he was angry.

"Che, have you started looking for boys?"

"This Saturday I'm going to Plaza Calabria."

"Look sharp, then."

"We'll see what's out there."

"Make sure you find something. The shit's hitting the fan. And when that happens, everyone gets covered in shit. You too."

Impelled by the joy of their release, expelled by an educational system that didn't want them there a minute longer, the children poured out of school like a plague of termites. Scuffing their feet until they started running, walking quietly until the insults started flying, looking angelic until four of them decided to set upon a little classmate. Somewhere in the middle of that throng were Dientes and El Peque. They were late because, while everyone was lining up to leave, a promising fight had begun to develop between two classmates, only to lose heat once they had reached the door. The would-be combatants had gone off in different directions. Disappointed, Dientes and El Peque had set off for home.

Then, as if from nowhere, Rivero appeared. Dientes noticed that El Peque seemed to take a small step back, an imperceptible gesture to anyone who wasn't a close friend.

"Peque, old friend, you've turned your back on the team."

Rivero was standing, smiling a yard away from them, stopping them in their tracks. All around them the other children walked and shoved their way past, indifferent to the scene. Dientes remembered the dog they had poisoned and how, when it discovered them stealing cables, it had stood watching them at the entrance to the garage.

"Come with me, I need to talk to you."

El Peque walked forwards while Dientes stayed where he was. It was obvious that Rivero didn't want him to join in the chat. Rivero and El Peque started walking, Dientes following a few yards behind. They didn't go very far, stopping when they came to the corner of the block. Rivero was the one doing most of the talking. El Peque seemed cowed, and every so often he moved his head gently from one side to the other.

The coach patted him on the shoulder and walked away. Dientes caught up with El Peque.

"What did he want?"

"He wants me to go back to playing the train game."

"What did you tell him?"

"That I won't."

"Did he get angry?"

"I don't know. I told him that my mum won't let me out at night on my own any more. And then he went."

Dientes turned and ran in the direction that the coach had taken, shouting:

"Rivero! Rivero!"

Rivero turned round and looked at him with a puzzled expression, as if he didn't recognize the boy who had been standing beside El Peque minutes before or who had accompanied his friend the first time he went to Spring Breezes. Dientes introduced himself.

"I'm a friend of El Peque. We went to the club together, do you remember?"

"I think so."

"El Peque told me that you run a competition to see how long someone can last on the railway."

"El Peque talks too much."

"I'd like to take part."

Rivero fell quiet for a few seconds, weighing him up, as though he could look into his brain and read everything that he was thinking.

"How old are you?"

"Twelve."

"And your parents let you go out at night?"

"I live with just my mum. She lets me do whatever I want," Dientes exaggerated.

Rivero said nothing for a while, then:

"You also play soccer, right?"

"Yes, nearly every day."

"OK, come to the club on Tuesday. I'm not promising anything. But don't be cocky like your friend. Don't go blabbering all over the place about what El Peque said, or about what you said to me. Real men speak little and do much."

Dientes turned round and ran to where El Peque was waiting for him. As he ran, dodging around several friends from school, he thought that he too was going to earn a hundred pesos. He could last longer than anyone.

11   *The Hidden City*

I

Verónica had gone to the "smoking room", a small space with a window into the building's interior courtyard that also served as a repository for all the things no longer required in the newsroom of *Nuestro Tiempo*: CPUs that didn't work, old monitors, old copies of rival publications, broken chairs and posters left over from a publicity campaign for the magazine. The window was open, despite the cold, so the only advantage of being in there rather than out on the street was proximity to the rest of the newsroom. Verónica was smoking while trying to piece together the different elements of her investigation, but her mind kept drifting to the trip to Villa Lugano which she had made with Lucio the day before.

Before calling him and asking him to go with her, she had organized the information that she had so far: the map modified by Federico and the details of Vicente Garamona. Four boys were from neighbourhoods in the south of the city and two from a shanty town known as Ciudad Oculta, the "hidden city". She had decided to start with the easiest, the boys from Lugano and Soldati, but there was a problem: Verónica couldn't remember ever having been to that part of Buenos Aires. She knew that it existed, that there was an abandoned fairground there, and she had once been to see a Davis Cup game at the Parque Rosa stadium. But she certainly hadn't paid much attention to the places she passed through on the way. In fact, she tended to mix up all those neighbourhoods in the south: Mataderos with Lugano, Soldati with Pompeya, Ciudad Oculta with the shanty town known as Villa 1-14-21. That disorientation alone had momentarily overwhelmed her. After all, she had discovered many new places in the course of her investigations. The ability to progress quickly from ignorance to detailed understanding was a vital journalistic skill. That weekend she spent hours studying the map, swearing that she would learn those streets with funny names by heart.

On Sunday she reached the conclusion that it wasn't enough to familiarize herself with the area's layout: she needed to go there with someone. She thought of asking Patricia to send a photographer with her, with the excuse of getting a few shots from the neighbourhoods, but it struck her that this could be counterproductive for the investigation. Doubtless Federico would be wiling to go with her. But Fede – who had studied at the Pontifical Catholic University of Argentina – was even less streetwise than she was. He was more likely to be a hindrance than a help.

But why was she agonizing over this so much if what she really wanted was for Lucio to go with her? Did she really feel so insecure and scared, or was it simply that she wanted to share part of the investigation with him? Sunday evening wasn't the right time to make this kind of decision. She would try to contain herself, wait until Monday morning and only then send him a text.

If she had been hoping to indulge some fantasy of couple-dom, he had been very quick to put his cards on the table, making some stupid remark about his children as soon as he got into the car. As if she was going to forget that she was with a married man. Lucio could be so blindingly obvious sometimes and it confused her; it tore her up.

They had covered Lugano and Soldati together, from the exit off the Dellepiane freeway to Avenida Eva Perón. They had skirted Ciudad Oculta in the west and gone as far as Villa Soldati in the east. The expedition could best be described as a failure. Verónica hadn't expected all the victims' families to be lined up waiting for her, but neither did she expect the number of useful encounters to be zero. If she had learned anything from working with more experienced journalists, it was that there's no such thing as coincidence. Absence on this scale could only be interpreted as flight, a disappearance prompted by something that she could scarcely begin to articulate as a hypothesis of investigation.

That day the only clear piece of information she had managed to obtain was that one of the boys played indoor soccer at a local club. And Lucio had been the one who got that piece of information. On one hand, that made her feel proud of choosing him to accompany her on the trip. On the other, she felt a combination of annoyance and despair to think that she had so nearly missed that crucial detail, and that there might be many others right under her nose that would escape her, too.

There were still the two dead boys from Ciudad Oculta to consider. She had better get a move on, in the last case at least, because if there was a repetition of what had happened with the other victims, it wasn't a wild theory to imagine that the family might soon move. How could it be that whole families disappeared from the system, leaving no trace?

But getting access to the *villa* wasn't going to be easy. There were no streets, apart from one avenue that ran across the shanty town from east to west, and the houses were chaotically numbered with an internal logic that only made sense to the people who lived there. It wouldn't help her to have Lucio along this time.

She explained the problem to Patricia as they drank coffee in front of the vending machine. Her boss recommended that she speak to Álex Vilna, the magazine's deputy editor, who was in charge of the Domestic Politics section. Verónica didn't much like the idea of talking to Álex. He had a much more important position than her, and was two years younger. A couple of times he had made a pass at her, but she had played the innocent and now she feared that any request for help could be turned into a debt for future payment. She found him disagreeable: too neat and tidy, smelling of some perfume he'd picked up in duty-free, professionally nice, vain, with a manner that oscillated between smug and obsequious depending on who he was talking to. Also, the last time that he had made advances (at a launch party hosted by the Industrial Union), she had hit him where it most hurt: in his pride. He had studied at the highly traditional and highly competitive Colegio Nacional de Buenos Aires.

"I don't go out with guys who went to elite schools," she told him.

But if Patricia was telling her to speak to him, she must have her reasons, so Verónica took a deep breath and went to his office. She felt like an exotic dancer limbering up for a pole dance.

"Álex, can I borrow you for a minute?"

"For as long as you want. I've got two hours to finish this column, but I've always got time for you."

"I'm writing a piece about children who get involved in accidents, and there are two cases in Ciudad Oculta."

"Only two in the whole *villa*? You must be missing some."

"These are very specific cases. The other figures aren't relevant. The thing is that I should go into Ciudad Oculta, but I don't know how to go about it."

"Especially if you go with your Gucci handbag."

"I don't have a Gucci handbag."

Álex looked at her and smiled. The client was happy with his striptease. She should really lean forward so he could slip a bill between her tits.

"You know why I prefer Catholic journalists to Jewish ones?"

"Because they're sluttier?"

"No, because faced with a problem like this, the Catholic journalist immediately knows what to do."

What a jerk, Verónica thought, but she made an effort to return his smile.

"Well, clearly my education in the Torah and all those kilos of knishes I ate are preventing me from seeing the light. Illuminate me."

"The priest, my love. There's always a priest in a *villa* who can act as a link. They're the ones who keep close ties with the whole community. It's the famous 'option for the poor'. Meanwhile, rabbis run around cutting off dicks."

"Rabbis don't do circumcisions, you resentful goy."

"Listen, in Ciudad Oculta there is in fact a church with quite a lot of history. Nuestra Señora del Carmen. During the dictatorship various social militants were disappeared in the area. Years ago I covered a Mass that Bergoglio gave in the street, in that parish."

"Don't tell me that the Archbishop of Buenos Aires takes Mass in Ciudad Oculta?"

"No, obviously not. It was for a fiesta of the Peruvian community, which is quite important in Oculta, although less so than in the Villa 1-11-14. I interviewed the parish priest at the time. They have a soup kitchen for single mothers and their children."

"I happen to be looking for exactly that: single mothers with children."

Álex scrolled through the contacts on his phone.

"Make a note. The priest is called Pedro, like the first ever pope. Say I told you to call. Look out, though: as far as I know he's taken a vote of poverty and obedience. I don't know if he took the celibacy one."

I I

It was true that she didn't have any Gucci handbags, but she still didn't know how best to dress for a shanty town. Verónica had spoken to the priest and Pedro had invited her to visit that same afternoon, even though she hadn't told him what it was she wanted to talk to him about.

She settled on a fairly discreet pair of black trousers, some low shoes that seemed horrible to her and a dark crimson sweater which she hadn't worn since the days when she used to like punishing herself by wearing clothes that made her feel ridiculous. She asked her sister Leticia if she could borrow the car again; her sister had got so used to lending it to her that she didn't even ask where she was going.

This journey to the capital's southern neighbourhoods was more congenial second time round, even though Verónica took a different route. This time she didn't go by the freeway but took Avenida Eva Perón and circled Ciudad Oculta before turning onto Avenida Piedrabuena. She looked around for a paid parking lot, before deciding to leave the car in the street.

The priest was waiting for her at the entrance to the *villa*, at the intersection of Piedrabuena and Argentina. He was easily recognizable by his clothes: a greyish-blue shirt with a mandarin collar and a space for that white strip usually worn by priests. He also wore tight petrol blue jeans like the kind favoured by a 1960s rockabilly. His belt, with its rectangular buckle, seemed designed to go with the collar and its rectangular insert.

On top of that he was wearing an unbuttoned black coat, which gave him a certain air of Neo, Keanu Reeves' character in *The Matrix*, only ten years further down the line. Her eye was particularly drawn to one detail: the priest was bald. Or rather, he shaved his head. You could tell that his baldness was the result of a lot of time spent in front of the mirror with a razor. For some reason, and without knowing why (she was Jewish, after all, and oblivious to the precepts of Rome), she found this evidence of narcissism shocking.

He seemed to recognize her too. Was she also dressed in a uniform that could be decoded? The uniform of a journalist? Or of a middle-class girl about to plunge into a shanty town?

"You're Father Pedro, right?" she asked, by way of greeting. As a seasoned journalist she could have done better than that.

"Verónica?" He kissed her on the cheek as she was awkwardly extending her hand for a handshake. "Let's not be formal. Please just call me Pedro, like everyone else here." He gestured at the *villa* as though it were his domain. "If it's all right with you, I suggest we go to the church and we can talk about what you need without interruptions."

That part of the *villa*, at least, seemed not at all frightening. Verónica watched people going past, mothers and children, teenagers in school smocks, just like in any other neighbourhood of Buenos Aires. True, the houses looked more precarious, but there was nothing to suggest that she needed the company of a priest to keep her safe. If she had come on her own, she would have had no problem.

"I must seem like a rubbish journalist, asking someone dressed as a priest if he's the priest I've come to meet."

"I imagined you asked because you thought I could be a different priest. There's a few of us here, you know."

The light-hearted exchange emboldened her to say:

"I've always wondered about the white strip you all wear in your collar. What's it called?"

They had arrived at the church, a humble brick building that rose sturdily from among the ramshackle homes surrounding it. The priest unlocked a door and ushered her into a kind of office.

"This," he said, taking it off, "is a dog collar."

He put it on a bookcase at one side of the room and hung the coat on a hanger, then motioned her towards a chair while he sat down on the other side of the desk. Pedro undid two buttons on his shirt and rolled up his shirtsleeves as he explained.

"The dog collar replaced the soutane. The truth is we don't use it much. I walk around here without it. It's not an essential part of being seen as a priest."

"They don't oblige you to wear the dog collar?"

"We Salesians take a very broad view of life. Are you Catholic? Normally I wouldn't ask someone who comes here what religion they are, but I can see you're interested in questions of sacerdotal etiquette."

"That must be because I'm Jewish. I'm curious about all things Christian."

"Well, interestingly, non-Orthodox rabbis tend to dress much more informally than us Catholics. Would you like a coffee or some water?"

The offer seemed more like a way of ending the conversation about religion. Verónica declined it and told him about what she had come to look for in Ciudad Oculta. She

213

explained that she was carrying out a journalistic investigation into children who had been knocked down by trains. That two of the boys were from that *villa* and she wanted to speak to their families.

"I know about those two cases," said Father Pedro.

He had lost the breezy tone of their first exchanges and seemed to be looking into her eyes as though trying to read her mind. It would be better not to hide the truth from him.

"Some of the information I have found and some of the conclusions I've reached are making me think that these weren't mere accidents, that there's something behind them. Something and someone, obviously."

"And you think that the family knows."

"The truth, Pedro, is that I'm quite lost in all of this. I have some clues, very few concrete facts and too many vanishing lines. No. I don't necessarily believe that the family knows, but perhaps they can help me onto firmer ground, as far as the investigation is concerned."

The priest drummed his fingers on the desk. He seemed to be sizing her up.

"The first case was three years ago."

"Agustín Ramírez, son of Luciana Ramírez, eleven years old," Verónica recited from memory.

"I knew them both well." Pedro had let his hand rest; his expression had softened. "They came to our soup kitchen. Luciana left soon after Agustín's death. She went to Santiago de Estero. She had family there. I don't know how you'd find her."

"And Vicen? Did you know him?"

The priest nodded. "Carmen and her other children live near here."

"Vicen had brothers and sisters?"

"Four. He was the second. The youngest is a baby, just a few months old. Carmen has always taken immense care of her children. She doesn't just bring them here to eat, she makes sure they have their vaccinations, she brings them to the infirmary we have here, and she does everything she can to make sure that the older ones go to school. Vicen was a loner and got into trouble sometimes, but all the kids from round here are like that. He was a good lad."

"I'd like to speak to her."

"She generally works in the mornings. We can see if she happens to be home."

They walked about three hundred yards down the avenue that ran across the *villa*, before taking a turning to the right. The houses seemed more higgledy-piggledy in this part of the town, as if they had been jammed in and squashed down, one next to the other. Pedro stopped in front of a rusty metal door which barely fit into the unplastered wall.

The door was opened by a slight woman of indefinite age, with very black short hair, dressed in a faded dressing gown with a black woollen jacket on top. Her sleeves were rolled up despite the cold. Pedro introduced them to each other and explained that Verónica was a journalist who was interested in knowing more about Vicen.

"I don't want to talk about that."

Verónica had remained a couple of feet behind the priest. Now she came forward a little and glanced into the house through the space left by the woman in the doorway. She was surprised to see that someone was looking back at her from inside. She was young and had a baby in her arms. Verónica stepped back again.

Pedro urged the woman to reconsider; it was always good, he said, to try to establish how things had happened. Vicen's mother stood her ground. The face of the younger woman with the baby in her arms appeared behind her. She was a teenager, really. These must be Vicen's siblings.

"Get back inside," the woman admonished her. The teenager shrugged her shoulders and turned away.

Verónica thought of saying something then, but she realized there was no point. If the priest could not convince Vicen's mother, she would be hard-pressed to come up with a better argument. She wanted to leave, to put a distance between herself and this woman who looked at her with such suspicion. She pictured herself as a roving reporter, probing the pain of victims in order to display it on air. But no, she didn't want that. She wasn't on the hunt for pain that could be turned into articles. She was looking for facts, leads. To shine a light on the murky circumstances of that boy's death.

The woman closed the door and left the two of them standing there. Verónica was the one who said, "Let's go". The priest seemed more confused and frustrated than she was. They walked in silence back to the church. She saw the only firm lead she had crumbling and without it all her suspicions about the boys' deaths appeared baseless. For a moment she felt that she had nothing, that she would have to abandon the investigation.

"This isn't the time to give up, Verónica," the priest said, as if reading her mind. "Let me speak to Carmen. Perhaps if I talk to her alone she'll have a chance to reflect and tell us something that might be useful to you."

They had stopped at the door of the church. Pedro's words had moved her, and she had an urge to cry. She felt stupid for getting emotional over something said by a priest. It would be best to leave quickly. She asked him to call her if he heard about anything. He offered to accompany her out of the *villa*, but Verónica said no. When the priest insisted, she didn't know if that was because it really was dangerous for her to walk on her own or if he just wanted to be nice. Either way, they reached Avenida Argentina without either of them having spoken a word.

She said goodbye to Pedro, crossed the avenue and walked towards her car. She was searching in her bag for the keys when she heard:

"Hey, Señora."

On the other side of the car, standing on the sidewalk, was Vicen's sister. She was alone this time, without the baby which had been in her arms minutes before.

"My brother was murdered, wasn't he?"

She spoke in an almost-whisper that Verónica could barely hear. She was not entirely sure that those had been her words. Verónica walked around the car and towards the teenager. She glanced back towards the *villa*. It crossed her mind that at any minute the girl's mother might appear and tell her to go back home. She thought of bundling her into the car and taking her further away, so that they could talk.

"When you left with the priest, I followed you. I wanted to speak to you."

"What's your name?"

"Milagros. Mili for short."

On the next block there was a bar sign. Lightly she took the girl by the shoulder and said:

"Come."

Mili followed her and they went into the bar. Verónica asked for a Coca-Cola for the girl and a coffee for herself. Mili seemed serious, but not uncomfortable. She was wearing a blue jumpsuit and a denim jacket, which she didn't take off.

"Your brother was run over by a train, but I think he was on the tracks because somebody had taken him there."

"Vicen was always getting into scrapes."

She must have been fifteen or sixteen years old. Verónica thought her beautiful. She was attractive in that way that other women find aggressive and men find intimidating. Verónica would have liked to have been like that at her age.

"Did Vicen go to school?"

"Yes, he went. He had to take fourth grade again. My mum practically killed him."

"Which school did he go to?"

"To 24, same as me."

"Are you still studying?"

"I left in the second year."

Verónica couldn't bring herself to ask what Mili was doing now. She didn't want to put herself in the position of an adult giving advice to an adolescent who might be taking drugs, or selling sex, or waiting for something to happen in her life that would take her out of the *villa*. She hadn't come here for that. In a few years this girl would look like a thirty-year-old, and when she got to thirty she'd look fifty. In the best-case scenario, she'd have loads of children – that was if she didn't die young at the hands of a drunk and violent husband.

"Outside school, who did your brother hang out with?"

"With kids from the barrio."

"Kids his own age?"

Mili shrugged her shoulders, just as she had done when her mother had sent her back inside their shack.

"His age, or older, or younger." Mili took a quick sip of her Coca-Cola and added: "He liked playing ball. He wanted to be a soccer player."

"Did he go to any club?"

"Yes, he used to play at Spring Breezes. Once I heard him say that the coach was going to take him to River or Vélez to play there."

"Can you remember what the coach was called?"

"No." She took another sip and fell silent.

Verónica was about to ask another question, but something stopped her. Years ago, a photographer had given her a lesson in journalism. She had been twenty then and writing her first articles for a general interest magazine which, on this occasion, entailed interviewing a woman who had been the victim of medical malpractice. The woman had been wrongly diagnosed as suffering from a particular illness, and the medication she had been prescribed had left her sterile. Verónica's questions, neatly written in a notebook, addressed the role of doctors, the hospital, the type of treatment the woman had received and the way in which the mistake had been discovered. At one point the woman had been talking about how her husband had convinced her that she should sue the clinic and the doctors, then she had fallen silent. Verónica had been about to use that silence to jump in with a question about the legal challenge when the photographer (a surly and cynical type of about forty, whom she still regarded as one of her best journalism teachers) put his hand on her knee. He had bent down to take a photo and from that position touched her leg. Verónica looked at him, puzzled. She thought that the photographer must be steadying himself, but he made a gesture with his mouth, a barely perceptible indication that she should keep quiet. When Verónica looked back at the patient, the woman started talking about how frustrating her life had been since the medical disaster, knowing that she would never have children; how this tragedy had been the catalyst for her marriage unravelling, because she and her husband had now separated. After the interview, the photographer had lit his umpteenth cigarette of the day and, as though in passing, said, "Sometimes saying nothing is the best question you could ask." "If I don't speak there's no interview," she had retorted, thinking she knew everything. "It's like a song, sweetheart, like music," he had responded. "You have to learn to hear that internal call for quiet, so that you can let the other person say the thing you've been wanting to hear since the interview began. If you were a man I'd explain it with a soccer metaphor that you're not going to understand. You have to know how to leave gaps. And stop writing down your questions – it makes you look like a journalism student."

And now that moment of silence had arrived with Mili. The girl took another sip of Coca-Cola, and retrieving from her memory something that had been seeking expression for a long time, she said:

"A few months ago the coach took him to a game at night. Vicen got back at like one o'clock in the morning. I ran into him on the avenue. He told me a load of bullshit. I mean, Vicen and I used to cuss each other a lot. We were always fighting. I told him that that was no time for an idiot like him to be out in the street. He said something similar back to me. To mock him, I took out a hundred-peso note that I'd been saving, and he took another hundred-peso note out of his own trouser pocket. I was stunned. I thought that he must have fallen in with one of those degenerates. I totally lost it. I grabbed him by the neck and slapped him a couple of times, asking where he had got that money. Any other time he would have slapped me back twice as hard, but this time he looked scared and he said, 'I won it in a contest against another guy.' I didn't believe him, but I didn't want to say anything to my mum, either. The day that he got run over by the train he had said he was going to watch a match, but I think he went back to the same place where he got that money."

"Did he tell you what kind of game it was?"

"Yes, but I didn't understand. It sounded like something he made up to get me to stop hitting him. It was against another kid. That's all I remember."

12   *Light Years*

I

"Do you know what time it is?"

"No."

"Half past five."

Verónica was talking to him from bed. He had got up a few minutes earlier with a dry mouth and gone quietly to the kitchen to pour himself a glass of tap water. Then he had returned to the bedroom, taking care not to bump into anything, trying to remember where each thing was: the desk, the armchairs, the coffee table, the bedroom door, the wardrobe. In the bedroom he could hear Verónica's steady breathing. Light from the street filtered in between the slats of the lowered venetian blind. He walked to the window and looked out. There were no cars or pedestrians. That was when Verónica woke up and spoke to him.

No, he didn't know what time it was, just that there was still some time to go before dawn. He went back to the bed and lay down, not so much because he wanted to keep sleeping as because he felt a bit ridiculous standing there in his underwear.

It was the first time that they had spent the night together. Mariana and the boys had gone to visit an aunt in San Pedro for the weekend. He would have gone with them, but that Saturday he had to work. He had hesitated to tell Verónica that he had a free night, that they could meet each other for longer than the few hours they usually had together each week. He wondered if it might perhaps be better to go straight home from work and spend the evening alone, watching a soccer game or some movie on cable while drinking a really cold beer and eating a hamburger. All day he mulled over his options. He liked the thought of spending a whole night with Verónica, but he didn't know if it was a good idea as well as a tempting one. Finally, tired of his own doubts and knowing that if he didn't tell Verónica he would spend the whole time thinking about her, he had sent her a text to let her know about this development.

He went to her apartment after his last shift on the railway that day. Verónica had ordered in sushi for supper. Lucio ate it, despite a certain aversion. He didn't much like fish anyway, and much less the idea of it raw. The combination of cream cheese with avocado and rice didn't appeal to him either. On the other hand, picking up the rolls with chopsticks was fun. He found them easy to use. So he dexterously picked up the portions of sushi before submerging them in a very salty soy sauce which had the virtue of masking the taste of fish. At least the white wine they drank made up for the onslaught on his taste buds that evening.

"Today I'm your geisha," she said to him at some point that night (which seemed very distant now, six hours later).

After taking off her clothes, Verónica had made him lie down on the bed. He wanted to touch her, but she didn't let him. She pushed his hands out to the sides, as though he were being crucified or had his wrists tied to the edges of the bed. She put a condom on him and climbed on top. Then she moved slowly, going up and down with a straight back, not letting any other part of their bodies, apart from their sexes, make contact. Lucio liked looking at her naked. He liked the rounded shape of her hips, her white skin sprinkled with moles, her firm breasts, moving as she raised and lowered herself on his cock. He would have liked to bite her waist, to roughly handle her nipples, but any attempt to raise his arms was met with a brusque response.

Verónica came without changing the rhythm of her movements up and down, just by making them more intense.

"They say that geishas know how to make a shogun come without moving their bodies, just by contracting their vaginal muscles. But I'm a fake geisha. I don't know how to do that."

She bent forward to kiss him, then took Lucio's hands and placed them on her breasts. She started to move faster and faster, while Lucio's hands squeezed her body roughly.

Six hours later, Lucio was trying to go back to sleep in that unfamiliar bed. It wasn't that he felt uncomfortable; he didn't actually know if he liked being there or not. The only certainty was that he was in Verónica's bedroom, lying beside her, waiting for Sunday to dawn. Would they have breakfast together like a married couple? Would they read the newspaper in silence? Would they play at being the spouses they weren't, at a routine they didn't share, at that placid love they didn't have to fall back on?

He thought about all this for another hour, and with each passing minute something inside him told him that it was a mistake to stay there any longer. He got up again and started to get dressed. Verónica sat up in bed.

"I see that you're an early riser, Sundays included."

"It's just that I remembered I —"

"No, Lucio, please. Don't make up excuses. Just to torment you a bit, let me say you're not original. Guys often get seized by the Cinderella syndrome – not at midnight, but a few hours later."

Verónica looked for her bra, which was lying on the floor, then collapsed back onto the bed as though the effort of putting it on had used up all her remaining energy. Lucio came over and sat beside her. He stroked her face and neck.

"I'm not Cinderella," he said.

"But would you be Cinderella if I asked you to? Would you be whatever I wanted you to be?"

"Of course."

"Would you wear a mask for me?"

"A mask?"

"Not the face of a lover, but another kind of love. A mask, nothing more."

Lucio didn't understand exactly what she was asking of him, but he suspected that it involved some kind of need that he would not be able to satisfy, not then, not ever. Even so, he repeated:

"Of course. For you I would."

I I

Her friends kept pestering her with emails and text messages. They weren't unreasonable. In contrast to men (who prioritize soccer sessions or lads' nights out over meeting up with a lover), women understand perfectly that a friend may abandon them temporarily for a pair of well-filled boxers. But there were limits, and Verónica had gone too far. Her relationship with the one they had dubbed "the General" (in tribute to the Buster Keaton train caper of the same name) was absorbing her completely. At the same time, they knew that what really prevented her from seeing them was her work, not her love life. Nobody really knew what she was up to, but whatever it was was getting in the way of get-togethers, nights out, drinking sessions and gossip. Worst of all, that night there was a hen party and none of their negotiations, threats and bargaining had succeeded in prising her out of her apartment. Verónica had replied to the first messages with promises to make up for lost time as soon as she could finish the article she was working on. When she wrote to Paula to say that she wasn't going but that she needed to see her to get some advice on the married man, her friend had answered with a stream of insults, finally suggesting that she go to confession in a church, a temple or wherever it was that Jews went to do that kind of thing.

The texts kept coming, so Verónica decided to switch off her mobile until the girls calmed down a bit. That way she could concentrate better on her own stuff. Her desk was covered with newspaper cuttings and index cards. She knew that those pages contained the key to many things she had not yet managed to piece together. Thanks to Vicen's sister, she now had the name of the soccer club and the firm suspicion that some kind of sinister game was being organized from there. If she could establish that one of the other dead boys had gone to that same club, she'd have a stronger lead. Could Juan García have been a member of the club? She didn't think that was possible. It seemed unlikely that he would limit himself to that kind of activity here if in Misiones he had been trafficking women and drugs. How could a supposed political leader cover his tracks so well? In the newspaper archive she had found the same information that Rodolfo Corso had given her. Afterwards his profile completely disappeared.

The only clue she had was an article that had appeared less than a year ago in *Página/12*. It reported that there had been a meeting in Comuna 8 with leaders from all the parties and that the ruling party had boycotted the approval of the operating statute. The report added that an opposition politician had left shouting, "González is sending his thugs to intimidate us. He thinks he's still in his Misiones fiefdom." Verónica was struck by that specific reference to Misiones. The erroneous reference to González instead of García might not be the politician's but the reporter's, to whom it would have sounded similar. Verónica detested sloppy journalists.

She called Federico, even though it was now eleven o'clock and he was probably with his girlfriend. That wasn't something that bothered Verónica. From the way he answered, her friend seemed to be alone and keen to talk. So she made some small talk before getting to what really interested her.

"Fede, my love, I've got a new lead in my investigation into the boys and the trains."

"I guessed as much."

"That I had a new lead?"

"That you were calling me about something related to work."

"Don't be silly."

"I'm sensitive."

"OK, Señor Sensitive, I need your help. You aren't going to find many women who'll say that to you."

"That's true."

"There's this guy called Juan García who's very difficult to locate."

"Hardly surprising with that name."

"Exactly. There are millions of Juan Garcías in the world. I even found some beefcake who's a model or Mr America or something. But I'm not interested in him at the moment."

"I'm glad to hear it."

"This García was mayor of Capitán Pavone in Misiones until 1998. He had to resign because he was implicated in a scandal that included the trafficking of women. A journalist based in Buenos Aires denounced him. The guy was completely exonerated in the case brought against him by the Misiones justice system."

"Which we do not hold in the highest esteem."

"Exactly. We don't rate it highly. But at least the case took place, so it must be traceable. What I'm after is very simple. That you retrieve his ID number and find out everything you can about the Juan García we're after."

"A complete audit."

"More even than that. More than you can find in a standard database. I want to know everything about this guy. If he has property, outstanding warrants, traffic infractions, credit cards, electoral roll, hospital admissions. Whatever you can find."

"And what do I get in exchange?"

"The same as always: my eternal love – and my dad's, too."

III

There were times when Lucio would have liked to have had a friend he could talk to about Verónica. More than once he had felt tempted (after a game, or in the changing room at work) to ask El Gordo Denegri or Lombardo to go for a drink, so that he could talk about her. It wasn't that he wanted to boast about having a lover (although the idea that his co-workers would admire his powers of conquest wasn't unappealing) but so that he could get some clarity on what was happening. He wasn't very adept in these matters. He wasn't like El Gordo, who had slept with half the female lottery ticket sellers at the Plaza Once railway station and was still married and happy to talk about the missus and the kids as if these occasional lovers didn't exist beyond the moment of bedding them. Surely Denegri or Lombardo – who was single and had a different girlfriend every month – would have some illuminating advice to offer on his relationship with Verónica.

But he couldn't bring himself to say anything to them. After work, or the Saturday game, he walked away alone, ruminating on the last encounter with his lover or fantasizing about the next one. If there was one thing he dare not think about it was breaking up. That idea seemed a greater betrayal to him than the infidelity to his wife. It was as if he and Verónica had started something that couldn't come to a clean and simple end. Finishing with her didn't even enter into the realm of possibility.

And yet he knew that sooner or later it would happen. A malaise had grown between them. It had been silent and subtle to start with, then become more evident. Verónica needed something from him that he wasn't able to define, much less satisfy. The days that Lucio left her apartment to go back to his house were the worst. As he got dressed, Verónica would fall into a kind of mutism from which she would not emerge until the next time they met, or spoke on the phone.

Neither of them spoke about this. Lucio suspected that Verónica was simply getting tired of having a lover, a married man who always returned to his wife. He could have talked to her, explained that there were two different universes. And that she occupied one of them, a universe marked by things that were incredible and mysterious as well as by the horror of the trains. In the same way that he wished to expel from his head the image of the bodies crushed by trains, he wished he could stay forever between Verónica's legs, or simply stay watching her while she put a CD on her computer and half-closed her eyes to listen better to the song. They were songs that he hadn't known before then and which now formed a part of that universe where happiness and madness could lift him high or plunge him into the depths, like a wild roller coaster. He could have explained all this to her, told her that he needed and wanted her, but at those times he also remembered how she had deliberately brought death and pain to the bed. How she had taken pleasure in putting her fingers in his wounds. He thought of Verónica's agitated expression, how she had called him a murderer while they had sex; he remembered her ambiguous and gloating smile. She had given him bruises and he had responded in kind, with marks that still showed on her skin. And if Verónica found pleasure in messing with his head, he reacted a different way: by showing indifference to her anguish.

To make things worse, Lucio began to suffer cramps in his legs when they were having sex. This wasn't an occasional discomfort but something systemic. All he had to do was tense his body to feel as though his legs were being crushed under a rock and then run through with a knife. He limited his movements, kept his legs still until the pain passed. This strong discomfort continued until they separated in the bed, and then his body would slowly return to its natural state. He said nothing about this to her, either, but Verónica must surely have found his behaviour strange. He with his painful legs and her falling into an unresponsive silence – they were light years away from that kiss on the phantom train ride, even though it had taken place only a few months ago.

IV

He didn't say anything to his friends, but El Gordo Denegri did say something to him. He asked Lucio to go with him to visit Carlos Malvino, who had not been back to work since running over the boy in Ciudadela. He was still signed off work on doctor's orders. El Gordo Denegri was Malvino's greatest friend; even their families knew one another because every so often they got together for a meal. In fact, it was through his wife that he had found out that Malvino was still in a bad way. Every day Malvino went as a day patient to a psychiatric clinic. He spent the morning and afternoon there, then went back home. His wife also mentioned that the psychiatrist had recommended that Malvino meet up with his colleagues, that he needed to face up to the reality of his job on the railways. El Gordo Denegri didn't want to go on his own, so he asked Lucio to go with him.

The psychiatric clinic was in Ramos Mejía, in a location that was, for various reasons, ill-chosen. First, it was on the seventeenth floor, which seemed highly inadvisable for people with mental health problems. What if someone jumped off the balcony? Or one of the patients decided to go to a different floor? What would the building's other residents think if they found out that they had run into a psycho with murderous tendencies? Second, the entrance to the clinic was on Avenida Rivadavia. From the seventeenth floor there was a perfect view of the Sarmiento railway line, which passed only fifty yards from the front door. It didn't seem like the best idea to treat someone who had had a disturbing experience so close to the scene of their trauma.

El Gordo and Lucio talked about all this on their train journey from Plaza Miserere. They had chosen a compartment in the middle, to be far from the drivers. It was strange to be travelling on this route as passengers, sitting in places not usually reserved for them. Perhaps that was why they talked so freely about the clinic, and even laughed when El Gordo said that having it on the seventeenth floor seemed crazy to him.

In the elevator, when they pressed button number 17, they felt as though the others gave them strange looks. They may have thought that the two men were going there for treatment. From outside the clinic looked like a perfectly average apartment, or a doctor's office. There was nothing to suggest that psychiatric patients were on the other side of the door. They rang the bell and the door opened.

The receptionist asked them to wait for a few minutes until a doctor appeared. She must have been about fifty and wore her white coat open. In fact, she was the only person wearing any kind of uniform, so it was hard to tell if the people who periodically walked across the waiting room were patients or doctors. The psychiatrist asked them a couple of questions but didn't seem that interested in chatting with them. It was as if this kind of visit were part of a routine that she had repeated countless times. She emphasized the importance of their friend re-establishing contact with his daily life before the accident. The doctor called someone over (a nurse? another patient?) to take them to where Carlos Malvino was. The clinic occupied the entire seventeenth floor and they crossed various rooms in which there were people chatting or writing. It seemed like a school for adults, with men and women of very different ages moving around silently. Malvino was sitting at a table with three others. When he saw El Gordo and Lucio he came over to them with his customary serious expression. He gave them each a hug and they all sat down in a kind of living-room area that was in the same room. At first, the other patients kept looking over at them, but then they went back to their activities without paying the men any attention.

"Not a bad life, eh?" said El Gordo, sprawling in the armchair.

"They make me draw, they make me write crap. I'm sick of this loony bin."

He was badly shaven and wearing a shirt that didn't look too clean. Apart from that he didn't seem very different from the old Malvino, a rather sullen character they had known for the best part of a decade. They talked about soccer and the Argentine team, which was playing that week. Lucio told them about the match that the drivers had played against maintenance the previous Saturday. El Gordo hadn't gone because he had more hernias than ribs. One of the drivers, El Negro Pernía, had fucked up his ligaments and wasn't going to be able to return to work until after the operation. The company was going to have to take on more drivers because they were short of staff at rush hour. El Gordo asked Malvino if he had long to go and Malvino shrugged. Then he added that doctors didn't know anything, and his friends agreed. They had told him that he was suffering from post-traumatic stress syndrome. Doctors talked claptrap and solved nothing.

After a silence during which they could hear the whispering of the people sitting at the table, Malvino confessed that he was considering never driving a train again. El Gordo almost said something, but instead only murmured some platitude. Lucio found himself struggling to concentrate on what his friends were saying because the continuous murmur around seemed to be drilling into his head. Without thinking he told Malvino that he was making the right choice. "What a nightmare," El Gordo lamented without any need to clarify to what he was referring. Malvino said that he was going to ask to be transferred to train dispatch. El Gordo remembered that, when the train he was driving crashed into a car, he had spent months terrified that at every railway crossing a car might try to get across as he was approaching. Malvino said that he didn't feel fear, just hatred.

"I hate that miserable son of a bitch who was on the line. If I ever come across the other one, I swear I'll smash his head against the wall as if he were a cat."

"What a nightmare," El Gordo repeated, like a mantra.

"When I remember how I smashed into that kid I'm happy. Because he deserved it. They're bastards. Those shit-bags fuck your life up. All the people who throw themselves under trains are shitbags. And the idiots who fall over, who didn't realize that a train was coming down the track, what are those bastards doing on the line? I never want to drive a train again, but if I did I'd mow them all down. I wouldn't sound the horn and press the brake for that scum. They deserve to be crushed. No other solution."

They spent less than an hour with Malvino. Afterwards, in the elevator, El Gordo Denegri said:

"He's fucked."

Lucio didn't answer. He felt too shaken by his own thoughts. Malvino had woken in him something he hadn't known before: hatred. Because Lucio also hated the people he had run over. He wasn't even going to exempt that young man who had given him the apologetic look. They were all scum. Malvino was right. He hated them and he hated that job and the kids who played at seeing who was more macho. And he hated the bastard who had jumped too late and burst beneath the compartments. The hatred burned in his chest and buzzed in his ears like the murmur of those other crazies in that shithole that he had no intention of ever visiting again.

V

She had managed to persuade Paula to meet for a chat. She needed to tell someone about what had been happening with Lucio. Paula's only condition was that they not go to Martataka but somewhere quieter, and that the only alcohol be white wine. She had a hangover from a party she had been to the night before.

They arranged to meet in Barman y Robin, a small bar in Las Cañitas that was still not very popular. Paula give her a rundown of the party she had been to. Neither of them was all that interested in the details, so it was a quick recap, over before they had finished the first round of wine.

It took Verónica longer to recount the twists and turns of her relationship with Lucio.

"It goes with the territory, I know that. But, well, there was a connection between us and, I admit it, I wanted to be with him. We looked for each other and we found each other. Then he started with this silent act, this married-with-kids hysteria. You'd think I'd know all about that kind of thing by now, but apparently not. I can't tell you how surprised – no, furious – I feel when he gives me the silent treatment."

"Vero, if you just listened to yourself you'd find all the answers."

"Don't go all Dalai Lama on me and start speaking in aphorisms."

"Let me explain. Have you read Lorrie Moore?"

"A bit."

"OK. She has a story you have to read. It's called 'How to Be an Other Woman' and it's in her book *Self-Help*. It's about a girl like you who gets involved with a guy like him. Although it has to be said that your guy sounds more interesting."

"Thanks."

"There's no leeway with married men. They're like library books. However much you like them, one day you have to take them back."

"The thing is, I don't even want to keep the book. I just want the print to be clear."

"Deep down you want to keep it."

"Ah, well, now you're getting Freudian."

"The married man is always a hysteric. He demands that you hang on every detail of his life, his wife, his children. If the youngest has got a temperature, he can't see you. If it's the wife's birthday, ditto. You end up even knowing when his mother-in-law's birthday is."

"October the eighth."

"Seriously?"

"No, silly, it's a joke."

"But the married man game is so perverse that even if you know about the mother-in-law's birthday, that the dog has fleas and the cleaning lady didn't turn up, you still know nothing about his life. Nothing essential."

"I understand that I don't know about his life. In our relationship there are certain key filters that prevent me knowing or evaluating how complicated he can be, or probably it's simply that he doesn't want to be with me. I can't know those things unless he tells me."

"And he doesn't tell you."

"He just sits there, silent."

"You see? I hope that at least you're having good sex, because a married man is only good for screwing if nothing better comes to hand. It's madness to expect anything else."

"Pau, I think I hate you."

"It's not advice I'm giving you, but a diagnosis: leave him before you feel you've wasted a big chunk of your life."

That same night Verónica wrote a long letter to Lucio. An email, if Lucio had an account. She kept it in a file of drafts and felt relieved, even though she knew that she would never send it. She went to sleep imagining Lucio's body illustrated by her with a tattoo needle. She saw herself writing a love letter on his skin, while her man's body became inflamed and bleeding with the pain.

Federico was quick and efficient. He called her on Monday at lunchtime to say that he had investigated Juan García, that he had got hold of the Misiones case details and that he had his ID card number. But that was where the trail went cold: Juan García had disappeared from the face of the earth.

"He sold some properties that were in his name and didn't keep anything. From then onwards he didn't buy cars, or property, or take out credit cards, or open a bank account, or make any social security payments, or pay any taxes. He has no driving licence, or any kind of insurance. Anyone would say he's dead."

"But he's not dead."

"Unless the dead vote. Which also wouldn't be unheard of. The only place in which he appears is the electoral roll. The address given there is Avenida Julio Roca 3874."

"You're a genius, Fede."

"Unfortunately, I'm better than a genius, I'm a practical man. Since the office boy spends most of the day twiddling his thumbs, I sent him to that address to get a clearer picture of how García lives. The office boy's just got back and he says that the address doesn't exist. That stretch of the avenue is the Parque Roca. And unless he lives inside the park as a forest ranger, it appears to be a fake address."

"There are no rangers in the Parque Roca. It's fake. The address is in Comuna 8, right?"

"Like all the kids who died under trains."

When she hung up, Verónica was furious. She felt as though Juan García were mocking her. They had to make that son of a bitch squirm. Verónica didn't yet know how, but she would think of something. For now, she had to go into enemy territory. She had to go to Spring Breezes.

13 *Who Doesn't Know Juan García?*

I

Men who love soccer take particular pleasure in seeing a good kick-about and they may not even watch the whole encounter, because ten or twenty minutes are enough to know that those games, arranged informally, not respecting certain basic laws such as the offside rule, played without the benefit of a referee and depending for their success on a gentlemen's agreement to recognize fouls, throw-ins, the legality of goals – something not always honoured – those games can be much more engrossing than a professional fixture in a stadium, not to mention on TV, which represents the absolute adulteration of the sport of soccer converted into a mere game for multitudes who, in the majority of cases, will never know the joy of pulling off a rabona or a gambeta or getting thumped for trying to dribble a ball between two hulking defenders with a licence to kill, as often happens in a kick-about.

There were no more than ten people watching those boys in the Plaza Calabria. Some of them must have been fathers or friends, because they were shouting out to the players using their names and giving directions. That small group spread out over the improvised field followed the action with a certain rhythm. The boys – meeting one another in teams of six or seven players – were between ten and fifteen years old. There was a striking variation in physique between the biggest and the smallest, as if the different ages or sizes had not been considered important when the teams were formed.

Among those who stayed longer than usual watching the game was Rafael. He had spent much of the morning observing different games on various patches of land in the old neighbourhood of Parque Almirante Brown, and had continued on as far as Plaza Calabria. He was on the look-out for boys who seemed to be around the age Rivero had stipulated. He would watch for a few minutes and, once he had reached the conclusion that no special talent was hiding there, he moved on to a different part of the park, looking like a soccer lover who had all the time in the world on that springlike Saturday morning.

For the last few minutes he had been watching those boys in the square; they moved quickly, with no tactical discipline, but with an astounding clarity when it came to knowing where to stop and where to go and look for the ball. As always, the defenders were shaky, hoofing the ball forward, terrorizing anyone who tried to cross them, especially because they were all at least a head taller than the rest of the boys. On one of the teams there was a dark-skinned boy, quite small, skinny, pure nerve, who played with the seriousness of an adult. In fact all of them played like that, as though they were in a cup final. The dark boy ran fast, closely controlling the ball, and had a mean left foot. He wasn't afraid of being tackled and he knew how to place his body to mitigate the effects of the blow and at the same time hit back. The boy knew how to play soccer and was brave to boot.

Rafael had arrived when the game was already under way, so he didn't know what the score was, but while he was there the brave boy's team scored four goals against two from the other side. When they finished playing there was hardly any celebration, as though the result were the least of it. The boys separated into groups and the one with the skills started walking with three others towards Avenida España. Rafael approached them. He congratulated them on how they had played and the boys, who must be used to praise, didn't pay him much attention. He told the skilled one that he was from the Spring Breezes club and that they were looking for new players. He asked his age. The boy was eleven. Being small, he looked younger. He was called Jonathan. The others wanted to know which division Breezes played in. He explained to them that it was a five-a-side soccer club but that they often took boys to try out at Vélez and River, just as Rivero had briefed him. The four boys liked the sound of that. One asked if they could all go for a trial and Rafael told him that for now they were only looking to fill one position, but in the future, why not? Jonathan asked what the club colours were and if they would give him a shirt and shorts to play in. Violet and orange. Yes, they would give him the kit for official games, and the club would pay for it. That seemed enough to convince Jonathan, who said that he was definitely going to go. Rafael explained how to get to the club from the park. The boy knew the area very well and understood perfectly. Rafael gave the boys ten pesos to go and buy a Coke, and they went off happy.

Rafael had his suspicions that Rivero wasn't only looking for boys to put together a good soccer team. And while he entertained such suspicions, he ought not to bring any child to the club. But he also thought that, if he took no one, Rivero would make his life impossible. The best compromise was to bring a boy back while simultaneously trying to discover Rivero's secret.

"So, old man?" García's voice sounded imperious. And he, who was used to being the one who gave the orders, who said what could and couldn't be done, was obliged to hang his head (even if the gesture couldn't be seen, since this was a telephone conversation) and to use a tone of voice that García would accept as submissive. Rivero didn't have to make an effort for his voice to come out that way. There had been years of working for García, of blind obedience. After all, it was only for a few minutes every day. The rest of the time he could do whatever he wanted, take it out on whoever he felt like. But he would have preferred to be like García, the man who never had to measure his tone. That was true power: not having to watch what you said.

"So, old man?"

"All done, boss, it's all arranged."

"You're screwing me around."

"It's not easy, boss."

"What d'you mean?"

"You have to be careful when it comes to kids."

"I'm losing money, old man. Do you know what that's called? Lost profits."

"This new lad I've got looking —"

"What new lad?"

"The one who looks after the bar for me. He's found one that could work."

"Could or will?"

"Will."

"Don't screw me around any more."

"And I've got another one."

"Watch out for the family."

"That's what I'm saying, boss, you have to be careful."

"And the other little kid, the one who was good?"

"He doesn't want to know. I went to see him. I didn't want to lean on him too hard. He's got a mother."

"It's going to be on Tuesdays now."

"Yes, boss."

"Two Tuesdays from now."

"That's not very long."

"Are you fucking kidding me?"

"No, no. But the thing is, you have to find a way to sell it to the kids."

"Sell it however you want, but I've already got a load of guys interested. It's on the twenty-seventh."

"Yes, of course. No problem."

"Let's see if you can wake up a bit."

"Yes. Just one question, boss."

"…"

"Is everything sorted with the boy – Vicen's – family?"

"The mother cut up rough. Iriarte convinced her, and they're leaving in a couple of days."

Rivero hung up with a bitter taste in his mouth. He was used to García's orders, but he didn't like lying to him. The boy Rafael had brought in was still green. He hadn't had enough time to observe him. In any other circumstances he would have taken another couple of weeks to be sure that the kid could work. Plus, there was that other boy, the one called Dientes. He didn't like it one bit that the boy had put himself forward for the tracks. It was the first time that had happened, and he considered it a bad omen. The fact that Dientes had found out and that he had approached him showed that anyone could get wind of it. He didn't like the fact that El Peque had talked about it, or that these things were left to chance.

He sat down at the table and Rafael appeared with the Fernet. He poured him out a generous measure, which was how he liked it.

"Che, that kid you brought in…"

"Jonathan."

"Are you sure that he was on his own in the park?"

"He was with some friends."

"No family, I mean."

"Yes, he was on his own."

"And the other kids, none of them was a brother or an uncle?"

"They were all more or less the same age as Jonathan. I don't think they were relatives."

Could he trust Rafael? The guy didn't seem very switched-on. That could be good, or bad, depending on the circumstances. He took a long drink from his glass. There wasn't much room for manoeuvre. Just two weeks. He'd have to pay a bit more attention than usual.

III

He had a two-peso note, a fifty-centavo coin, another of twenty-five, three tens and a five-centavo piece. Altogether, three pesos and ten centavos. El Peque stared at the money laid out on a step as if it were an oracle that could tell him the future. He didn't know what an oracle was, but he had an aunt who could look at coffee grounds and tell the person who had drunk the coffee whether they would die or win the lottery. Without knowing what his lot would be, he carefully folded the note and put it in his trouser pocket with the coins. In the other pocket he had a piece of chewing gum. His mother would soon call him for dinner, but he put the gum in his mouth anyway.

If his mother found out, she'd make him spit it out with a sharp blow on the neck.

El Peque was sitting on the stairs that led to the terrace. From there he could see the courtyard and main door. He neither wanted to go up to the terrace nor down to the courtyard. Dientes must be doing his homework or getting washed. He chewed the gum with indifference and boredom.

It was getting dark, but he still recognized him. Rafael had come in, the man who worked in the club bar. He was carrying some shopping bags, and after stepping over the threshold he paused for a few seconds, as though unsure what to do next. He must have been sent by Rivero to persuade El Peque to go back and play at the club, or to take part in the competition on the railway again. Or perhaps he had come to kill him because it was his fault that Vicen wasn't around any more. He didn't have time either to hide on the terrace or to run down to the room where his mother was. All he could do was make himself small and hope that Rafael didn't see him. He kept quiet, without breathing, but that didn't help: Rafael had seen him and was coming his way.

"Hi Peque, what are you doing here on your own?"

El Peque shrugged. If his mother appeared at that moment, he could take his chance to get away and go inside. But there was no one in the courtyard.

"You haven't been to the club for ages."

"My mum won't let me. She wants me to study more because I'm doing badly at school."

"That sounds like a good plan. School first, fun later. That's what I always say to Martina."

"Martina?"

"Yes, to your friend Martina. She's my daughter."

"For real?"

"Do you remember I told you that I'd lived here? I used to live here with Martina and her mum. I've known you since you were tiny."

"No, really?"

So Rafael hadn't come looking for him? He had come to visit Martina?

"Everyone at the club misses you. Well, not everyone. The ones you used to stick the boot into don't miss you."

"Everyone sticks the boot in at Breezes."

"True enough. Anyway, I'm going to see if I can find Martina, her mum and my mother, who's Martina's grandmother."

"Doña Esther is your mum?"

"Yup."

Rafael started to walk away towards Martina's house. Then, as if he had forgotten to say something, he came back to the stairs. He rummaged in one of the bags and took out a packet of Rumba cookies. He offered it to El Peque.

"Here, have this."

Wasn't he going to say anything about going back to the club? About competing on the railway track?

"Thanks."

Now Rafael did go to Martina's. He knocked on the door and Andrea appeared. She gave him a kiss on the cheek and ushered him in. El Peque seized his chance to run back home to his mum. He was shaking as he came into the kitchen, where his mother was making a tomato sauce for the spaghetti.

"Hey, who's after you? And the cookies?"

"Martina's dad gave them to me. He's come to visit her."

"Martina's dad? Rafael?"

El Peque nodded, but his mother made the opposite gesture.

IV

He washed the glasses, the snack bowls, the piece holders from Triolet, the game that had accompanied the beer and the aperitifs. He put the sodas back in the fridge. He made a mental note to buy more olives and potato chips. This was Rafael's daily work. Every now and then he looked over towards the pitch where the boys were training, among them Jonathan, the new player he had brought to the club, which had earned him a bit extra. Thanks to that money he had been able to do a big supermarket shop for his mother and his daughter; he hadn't chosen any basic items, only ones which could be considered a luxury. He had managed to surprise Andrea, and he was proud of that. And also of having left after coffee without even suggesting that he might stay. He would have loved to touch her, to spend the night with her, to feel her breath close to him, like when they were young. But it wasn't the right moment. There were various tests he would have to pass if he wanted to get his wife back.

The thrill of having money didn't blind him to the realization that something strange was happening at the club and that Rivero must be the one responsible. A boy had died. He had seen the look of terror on El Peque's face when he had bumped into him in the internal courtyard at the boarding house. He had thought for a moment that he was going to run away. He had always got on really well with El Peque, who normally made a point of coming to say hello. He used to like treating him to some fries or a few slices of cured ham. In normal circumstances, El Peque should have been happy to see him. And that confirmed his suspicion that there was something fishy about El Peque's absence from the club.

He would have carried on mulling over these worries if someone hadn't interrupted him. He didn't see her arrive because his eyes were fixed on the boys playing soccer, so he jumped when she spoke. The woman had leaned her elbows on the bar, just like the shorter boys, who had to lever themselves up against the bar to be seen. But size wasn't a problem for her. She was a tall woman and quite young, young enough not to be the mother of any of the boys at the training session.

"Can I have a word with you?"

In the days that followed, whenever Rafael thought about Verónica this was the image that would come to mind, of a woman whose manner fell somewhere between childish and seductive, whose voice was low, barely above a whisper, whose expression invited confidences. He had the sensation that the woman speaking to him somehow stood apart from her surroundings, not only from the club bar, but from the rest of life too.

"My name is Verónica Rosenthal, I'm a journalist on the magazine *Nuestro Tiempo*. Could I bother you for a few seconds?"

She could, and for as long as she wanted.

"I'm writing an article on youth soccer in neighbourhood clubs. Have you been working at Breezes for long?"

"For a few months."

"Always in the bar?"

As a barman – always. But how could he tell her that he now also looked for boys to bring back to Breezes? How to explain that he had a hunch something strange was going on at the club? What could interest a journalist who was hoping to discover the next ten-year-old Messi?

"This club is surrounded by very poor neighbourhoods. Do children from those barrios come to play here?"

"Yes, quite a few."

"I imagine that they must be dealing with a lot of problems, right?"

"Problems?"

"Yes, neglected children who perhaps don't go to school or have parents who can feed them adequately, for example."

"There's some of that. Really the person to speak to is Rivero, who manages the youth soccer teams."

He pointed at the pitch, where the coach was giving directions. Verónica asked him how long it would be until the game ended. Rafael explained that training finished in twenty minutes. Then she said that she would wait. She asked for a coffee and sat down at one of the tables. The few regulars who were there stared at her as though observing an exotic bird at the zoo. Verónica got out her cigarettes, then, realizing that smoking wasn't allowed inside the bar, she left her things and went towards the door. From there she kept an eye on her bag and waited for her coffee. She hadn't finished her cigarette when Rafael took the order over to her table, but she threw the butt away and came back in to sit down.

"I imagine you know the stories of all the boys who come through here."

"Children are very transparent. You know right away if they've got problems."

"And what sort of problems have you seen?"

"A lot of children who need an adult to care about them."

"And the club steps in."

"Up to a point, yes."

"The coach is like a father, right?"

"The coach is very important to them. That's why it's better if you speak to Rivero."

Verónica opened her bag and looked in it for something. She took out her card and gave it to Rafael.

"Here are my contact details. I want to write a piece with lots of personal stories. If you remember any and you want to tell me, give me a call or send me an email."

Rafael barely glanced at the card before putting it into his trouser pocket. He wasn't mad enough to start confiding his worries in a journalist who wanted to write a paean to community clubs.

V

If he had learned anything in the twenty years that he had been working for García, it was how to solve problems. Ever since his brother had taken him to work with him in Misiones, Rivero had dedicated himself to doing whatever they asked him to do without thinking twice. And to think that he had had his doubts about going to Misiones. He had been thirty then, and had played for Tiro Federal, which in those days was in the second division, and he wasn't even a first-team player. He couldn't get to the end of the month on what he earned. He had already lived his moment of glory a few years before, when he had played in the Platense first team and had scored a goal against Independiente one hour in. He could have continued to play a few more years for a provincial team in some club vying for the Argentino A, but that wasn't the soccer-playing life he had dreamed of. So he had hung up his boots and joined his brother in Misiones, where García had won the mayorship of Capitán Pavone and money seemed to come easy. And so it did.

He didn't become a millionaire, though – far from it. Money that comes easy goes easy, too. And Rivero liked getting stuck into all García's businesses: gambling, drugs, whores. He gambled hard, took a lot of drugs, paid for expensive women. He needed an outlet for the adrenaline his work produced, that excitement of having power, of getting the things García wanted done. In a world without corruption, Rivero would have been the perfect police-man. He liked the law to be obeyed. Except that the law in this case was García's. And doing his boss's bidding entailed no shortage of blood, deception, abduction and death. When García felt that Rivero was going too far, that he obeyed too much, he put him somewhere quieter, though no less important for that. He became responsible for moving women to brothels in the rest of the country. Girls from Misiones, from Chaco, a few Paraguayans, who were destined for faraway places in Patagonia or Mendoza; some would even end up in Chile or Brazil. That was good work. There was less gambling, not so many drugs and you could screw the girls for free.

Then came the break-up. The work fell off significantly; everyone did what they could, and García promised that he would not forget those who had been loyal to him. Rivero could be all kinds of things, but first and foremost he was García's faithful dog. So, when the boss relocated to Buenos Aires, he called Rivero again. This time there weren't any women to abuse with impunity, but García had found him a job that connected him with his childhood passion: soccer. Even so, he couldn't recapture that excitement that had gripped him when he was a soccer player. He barely felt that his life was still connected to soccer. At the end of the day he wasn't there to create a winning team. He was there for something else, and he did it very well.

That day, for example, he had managed to convince the new boy, Jonathan, to take part with Dientes in the railway competition. Dientes hadn't been at the club in the last few days, but he knew he wasn't going to have any problem with him, that his participation in the soccer team was a formality. He just wanted a shot at the tracks. He had to keep look-ing for boys like Dientes or Jonathan. Tough kids, and not those jerks who dream of being Maradona and never get to be anyone.

He went to the bar room for his Fernet. Rafael brought it to him and told him that there was someone waiting to interview him. Only then did Rivero glance over at the table where the woman was. The person looking back at him was more like a girl. Rivero made a gesture inviting her over and, at the same time, Rafael went away. She stood up, picked up her bag and jacket and came towards his table. A very nice-looking girl. Rivero felt a shiver run over his body. The feeling of a predator spotting its prey.

The woman in question was called Verónica something or other and she was writing an article on children who play soccer in neighbourhood clubs. She was from *Nuestro Tiempo* magazine. Rivero had a vague familiarity with the publication in question. He didn't like the sound of it. It was a campaigning magazine or something, one of those ones that defend human rights and love slinging mud at the police. But, as he said to her himself, he couldn't say no to such a beautiful lady. Let her go ahead and tape an interview with him.

She asked him about the importance of developing the players from a very young age, about how community clubs act as feeders for academies at the big clubs. She asked questions with a confidence that Rivero found irksome. He answered in a way that exaggerated his achievements, his triumphs as the head of the Spring Breezes youth teams. The journalist had to see him as a successful coach. As he listened to her talking so confidently, he was thinking that it would be good to come across a girl like that in a bar, a few whiskies under his belt. He would whisper in her ear the kind of thing that class of woman wants to hear from a man.

"I imagine that, as coach of the team he played in, you must have been devastated by the death of Vicente Garamona."

It was like suddenly braking, hitting something and feeling the airbag blow up in your face. For a second, or longer, he couldn't breathe.

"I don't understand the question."

"Vicen, the little eleven-year-old who was knocked down and killed by a train about ten days ago."

"Yes, that was very hard for everyone."

"How did you find out?"

"How did I find out about what?"

"About his death. Did someone tell you, did you see it on TV?"

"I can't remember now. It was very hard. I think one of the boys who was friends with him told me."

"It must have been difficult talking to his mother. Did you speak to her?"

"Yes. It was a tragedy. Listen, Señora —"

"Verónica, please call me Verónica."

"Listen, Verónica, this is all still too terrible. I don't see that it's particularly relevant to your article."

"It's true. You're right. But, as you say, it's so awful that I couldn't not mention it. If you'd rather, we'll leave Vicen to one side and talk about nicer things."

The journalist asked him a couple of questions and he answered automatically. He was trying to work out who this woman was, what she was looking for, how she knew that Vicen had played at this club if that information had not been published in any article and hadn't even been mentioned in court. Something was going very wrong. It was a relief when, with a smile, she told him that she had enough material for her article. She stopped recording and took out a packet of cigarettes and a lighter from her pocket. She shook hands

251

with him and, as she was leaving, as though remembering some inconsequential question that had slipped her mind before, she said:

"Ah – I'm so sorry to take up more of your time, but do you know Juan García?"

"I don't know any Juan García."

The journalist laughed, as though he had made a very good joke.

"Come on, Rivero, we all know at least one Juan García. The same goes for Juan Pérez."

"I don't know any."

"No worries. He's the coach of another team. I thought perhaps you might have worked together or played in the same team."

She turned round and went. Rivero was left staring at her ass, a purely instinctive reaction, because he wasn't thinking about that ass as it moved towards the door. In fact, he wasn't thinking of anything. He was simply repeating to himself: that girl is crazy. And finally he added to the mantra: and she's dangerous.

VI

Four days after the journalist had come to the club, Dientes turned up to train with the team. Rafael was surprised to see him make his way to the pitch and report to Rivero. What was El Peque's friend doing at the club? Or, come to think of it, why hadn't he come while El Peque was still playing for Breezes? He would have liked to go up to him, have a chat, but he was afraid that such a move would be frowned on by Rivero. Especially as it was clear that emotions were running high. Rivero had asked him about the journalist and he had answered that he had barely spoken to her. Whether Rivero believed him or not wasn't important. The atmosphere in the club had changed and Rafael didn't want to call attention to himself.

That afternoon he saw Dientes running in with the other soccer players. He came up to the bar with his friends to get a Coca-Cola but Rafael didn't say anything to him. He decided that the next morning he would go to the boys' house.

It was strange going over there without a plan to see Martina. He reached the door of the house then waited for a few minutes, hoping that Dientes or El Peque might come out or walk past. Finally he gathered the courage to open the door onto the street, which was never locked. He walked into the courtyard and didn't see anyone there either. He went over to the stairway and up to the terrace. There was El Peque. This time the boy didn't look terrified to see him, as he had last time. That was in his favour, at least.

"Peque, would you come with me to the shop on the corner? I want to buy some desserts for Martina and I've no idea what to get."

They went out together without seeing anyone and walked as far as the shop, where Julián was at the till and greeted Rafael with great warmth. El Peque picked out desserts, jellies, crème caramel, madeleines and filled cookies. In every case, Rafael separated one item off and put it in a bag for El Peque. Seeing his bag fill up made El Peque jump for joy. Not until they were back outside did Rafael bring up the subject of Breezes.

"Your friends at the club miss you."

"I've already told Rivero I'm not going back. Has he sent you to get me?"

"No, he didn't send me. Nothing like that."

"I don't want to play any more."

"Dientes has started coming."

El Peque didn't answer. He walked along concentrating on the paving stones, as though his life depended on keeping count or not stepping on any cracks. Rafael decided to be more direct.

"Peque, I don't know why you decided to stop going to the club. I also don't know why you're so afraid. You stopped coming right at the time that Vicen died, and the truth is, I don't know if one thing is connected with the other. But I'm worried that Dientes is going now and that he'll end up as terrified as you. Or that something bad could happen to another boy in the club."

"That's nothing to do with me."

He was so little, so vulnerable in this adult world, so in need of protection. Rafael felt the urge to give him a hug. To make him feel that he was safe. He shouldn't have to live with that fear.

"Peque, you're too young to understand these things, but with every passing day I feel more responsible for Martina's well-being. And I also don't want anything bad to happen to you two. You can trust me as though I were your father."

Without looking up from the paving stones, El Peque said:

"The thing is, if I tell someone, they're going to kill me, or I'll go to prison."

Rafael kneeled down to be on the same level as El Peque. Gently he lifted the boy's face so that he could look into his eyes.

"Peque, nobody will do anything bad to you. I promise. It's better if you tell me."

"I just wanted to make a hundred pesos."

VII

He felt dizzy, like in the first days after he had stopped using coke and the world seemed like somewhere alien, not able to contain him. He walked El Peque home, then gave him a hug and promised that nobody was going to hurt him or Dientes or anyone. Rafael knocked at the door of his wife's apartment and Martina opened it. He told her that he had been passing and had bought her a few things. Martina's grandmother, his own mother, invited him in, but he decided against it. He left the house and continued in a daze just as he had been a few minutes earlier, when all his suspicions had been converted into certainties.

Rivero was using the boys for a criminal game.

Rivero was a murderer.

Rivero had accomplices.

Dientes was in danger, as was every boy who played soccer at Breezes.

It was time for him to go to work, but Rafael didn't go to the club. He couldn't go back and keep serving in the bar as if nothing had happened. He had worked his last day there. He would never go back to Breezes.

Instead he went to his friend Julián's shop. Even though there were a lot of people there, he told him that he needed to talk. It must have been clear from his face that something terrible was happening, because Julián quickly called his wife over to mind the till and went with him to the bar on the corner.

"Has something happened to Martina, or to your ex-wife?" Julián asked as soon as they had stepped outside.

By the time they got to the bar, Rafael had told him almost everything: his suspicions, what El Peque had said, Vicen's death, El Peque's terror, the danger that now faced Dientes and perhaps also the boy that he himself had brought to the club.

"And what are you going to do?" Julián asked him as they sat down at a table some distance from the other patrons.

Rafael answered him immediately, as though he had already taken a definitive and irrevocable decision.

"Report them. That man and whoever he's working with need to be locked up."

"I don't know all the Argentine customs, but isn't it dangerous to do that?"

"Somebody has to do it."

And that somebody was him.

He walked as far as the police station. There were a few people in front of him. When it was his turn to be served, he said that he had come to file a complaint. The policeman at the counter asked him if it was regarding theft, a missing person, or threats from a third party. Rafael said that he wanted to report a person who was responsible for the death of at least one child. The policeman looked at him for a few seconds and nodded as though wondering what to say to him. He asked (or ordered) him to wait, saying that they would call him. After half an hour in which several people who had arrived after Raphael were seen, an official called him over to a desk. He had to hand over his identity document and give details of his address, job and marital status to a policeman who noted down the details on a form. Showing the same indifference with which he had asked about his home address, the officer asked the reason for his complaint. Rafael told him that he worked at Spring Breezes and that he had discovered that the coach there was using children in a competition on the tracks of the Sarmiento line, and that this had been the cause of at least one boy's death, a few days ago. The policeman nodded again as though he were thinking, and then asked him in a friendly way to wait for a few seconds. Some minutes later he returned and asked Rafael to accompany him. They walked across the police station to an office. The officer passed the papers from his file to a man dressed in civilian clothes who was sitting behind a desk and got to his feet to shake hands with Rafael.

"I'm Superintendent Carabel. Please take a seat."

Rafael repeated, again, what he had said to the police officer, adding everything he knew about Rivero and the next competition. Then he fell silent. There was nothing more to say. Now the superintendent knew everything about Rivero's criminal activity.

"You do realize that you're making an allegation against a criminal gang that sounds very dangerous?"

"Yes, I imagine that they are very dangerous."

"I'd like to thank you for the courage you have shown. Most people prefer to look the other way, feign ignorance. The famous 'don't get involved'."

There was a silence that seemed to underscore the admiration in the superintendent's words. Then he continued:

"What I really don't want is to put your life in any danger. Look, you have provided some excellent information for us to take this forward. I would prefer, for safety's sake, that the report remain anonymous. So what would you say if I tear up this document with your details and we act off the record? The consequences for this criminal gang will be the same."

Rafael agreed and the superintendent tore up the document. He threw the pieces in the wastepaper basket and shook Rafael's hand, all the while thanking him again for his sense of social responsibility. Those were his exact words.

Rafael left the police station with a feeling of having done something important. Now he had to go back to the boarding house and speak to Dientes' mother.

VIII

He arrived back at the house about three hours after talking to El Peque and went straight to the apartment where Dientes lived with his family. He was knocking on the door for some time, but there was no sign of anybody until his mother appeared from another apartment, the one in which he had lived so long ago. Rafael went over to her trying to look natural and not at all agitated, apparently without success, because her expression was full of anxiety. He told her that he was looking for Dientes' mother because he needed to tell her something about the club where the boy played.

"Well then, it's going to have to wait for quite a while. Dientes' grandmother fell sick and they've taken her to hospital. I imagine Rosa won't be back before dinner time."

His mother watched him carefully as she spoke. It was the second time he had been at the house in one day and that didn't seem at all normal to her, but she didn't want to probe into his reasons. Rafael asked after Martina. She had already gone to school.

"Well, tell Andrea that…"

Tell her what, though? That he loved her, that she should take care of Martina, that he wanted to get back together with her? Which of these things could he communicate to her with his mother as intermediary?

"Actually, don't say anything. It's better if I call her."

He walked aimlessly for a couple of hours. He thought of going back to the house to see if Dientes' mother had returned, but the idea of worrying his own mother, or having to give her any more explanations, put him off. He would go that night. Besides, Andrea would be there then, and he could tell her what was happening.

By now they would have registered his absence at the club. He couldn't even go and pretend to have got his times mixed up. He felt exhausted. He went to the hostel where he was staying. The route took him past Julián's shop, but Rafael didn't have the energy to tell him about the developments of the last few hours. He shut himself in his room and threw himself on the bed. He wondered what the police would be doing with the information he had given them. If there would be arrests. How should he act if there were no developments in the next few days? He was so tired that he couldn't help falling asleep.

When he woke up it was starting to get dark. He left his room and went to the communal bathroom to have a piss and wash his face. He needed to wake himself right up. He felt anxious, his nerves frayed. He needed something to drink. A beer, even if it was not a beer. He would buy two, one without alcohol and another normal one. He would drink the alcohol-free one first and, if it proved enough to trick his body, he'd leave the normal one at his neighbour's door. An unexpected present.

It was already dark by the time he headed down to the shop. Rafael walked a few steps towards it. He didn't see them coming. He was distracted, calculating that it was now too late to go to Dientes' house. That he would need to be quick about drinking the alcohol-free beer – or both beers – then hurrying off to the house. He didn't see them coming and so he couldn't defend himself. He felt the first blow in the pit of his stomach. In an instant he was surrounded by several men. One of them kneed him in the thigh and the other aimed a blow at his face that he just managed to dodge. He was winded though; that and the pain in his leg floored him. He couldn't see who was hitting him. They were just arms, legs and a mouth that said:

"Try reporting this to the police, son of a bitch."

Kicks rained down on every part of his body. He felt that he was drowning in his own blood and he could only see out of one eye. It was at that moment that he seemed to hear the sound of a revolver's firing pin. He didn't even manage to close the eye that was still all right. But the noise of the shot never came. Feet were still kicking him, but fewer than before. Somebody else had entered the fray and he wasn't against Rafael but seemed to be defending him, hitting the others. Perhaps he was dreaming this, but before losing consciousness he caught sight of Julián meting out kicks to all the other guys. And he seemed to be winning.

I X

His testicles, lower abdomen and left leg hurt. His face burned, he was nauseous and breathing with difficulty. There was a taste of blood in his mouth. He was thirsty. He spoke and his voice sounded very weak.

"I'm thirsty."

Somebody lifted his head, and that was when he discovered that his back and neck felt as though they had splintered. They gave him a glass of water. He must be able to open his eyes, but he didn't want to. The taste of blood was still there. At least his mouth was moist now. He would have liked to wipe his lips with his hand. He tried to move his arm and couldn't.

He heard Julián's voice telling him to open his mouth and felt his friend's fingers on his face. He was putting some tablets onto his tongue. He told him to swallow. He brought the glass of water back to his lips.

He was sweating. He opened his eyes – the right one only barely – and everything around him was dark. There was nobody there. He could just make out a few shelves with merchandise on them. He closed his eyes again.

He felt the presence of someone beside him.

"Do you feel better?"

He said that he did. Julián was sitting beside him.

"Am I in the shop?"

"In the storeroom. I wanted to take you further in, but my wife said I should leave you here. I was annoyed, but she's right. More quiet here. Nobody to disturb you."

"What time is it?"

"Eight o'clock in the morning. I'm opening in an hour."

"They nearly killed me."

"My fault, I was careless. I was threatened by Chinese gang. Put cameras everywhere. I just look up and I see car. Very suspicious. I watched two hours. I had to take money from customer who paid for bottle of beer with one hundred pesos. He did not want to pay deposit. When I looked again, four men getting out of car. I saw you on camera. I shouted to Víctor to look after till and I ran out."

"You saved my life."

"My fault. If I seen before, they don't hit you so much. I haven't practised kung fu for long time. The four men very soft. They run off straightaway."

"They knew about the report I filed at the police station."

"So they police. Or friends of police."

Rafael sat up. He was on an improvised bed assembled from a mattress on top of some drinks bottle boxes. He needed to go to the bathroom. He had abdominal cramps and a cold sweat had settled in his head. Julián took him to the bathroom at the back of the premises. That was where he lived with his wife and the three other Chinese men who worked for him and did not yet speak Spanish.

Rafael stayed in the bathroom for a long time. He looked at himself in the mirror. One of his eyes was swollen and half-closed. There was a dramatic scratch across his face, as though he had dragged himself along the asphalt. He put his head under the running water and felt better. The cold water was helping him to recover his composure.

When he returned to the storeroom, Julián had brought him some charcoal tablets and some painkillers.

"Take it all."

Rafael obeyed. It had been a mistake to report them. If Julián hadn't turned up they would have beaten him to death, or finished him off with a bullet. He couldn't go back to the hostel, or go to his family's house without putting them in danger. He couldn't stay at Julián's either.

"Very dangerous people. You have to think carefully or they kill you."

Julián was right. He was done for. Suddenly he had an idea. He reached into the back pocket of his trousers. There it was. He took out the card and read: VERÓNICA ROSENTHAL, JOURNALIST, *NUESTRO TIEMPO* MAGAZINE. There was an address, an email, a landline and a mobile.

Miraculously, his own telephone had survived the beating. He decided to call her. She was going to be able to help him. He only hoped she didn't think he was a madman inventing a fantastical story.

14 *Cuyes, Gazelles and Jackals*

I

When Verónica arrived at Spring Breezes, she stood on the sidewalk opposite for a few seconds, studying the building. At first glance this seemed no different from any neighbourhood club, not that she had much experience in this area. She crossed the road and went inside.

She didn't have any particular plan in mind, except to say that she was planning a piece on neighbourhood youth soccer. After that, she would improvise. A good journalist should be like a good free jazz musician.

In the bar there were a few bored-looking regulars who paid her no attention. She went to the bar, behind which there was a young guy whose gaze was fixed on the pitch. He was observing how the boys played. That gave Verónica the opportunity to spend a few seconds observing him. He was skinny and looked weak, dressed modestly but neatly. He reminded her of some kind of animal, perhaps a cuy, a type of guinea pig she used to see in Córdoba as a child. She mustn't frighten him. So she made an effort to channel the most friendly version of Verónica. She leaned on the bar, which was clean, called him and, smiling, said:

"Can I have a word with you?"

Afterwards, whenever Verónica remembered Rafael,

that was the image that would come to mind, of a fragile young man anxious to flee the story in which he was trapped.

She needed only to ask a few questions to realize two things: that Rafael was not a member of the criminal gang, and that he was hiding something. She imagined that he might recently have come out of prison or be an ex-addict still in the process of recovery. Something that made him feel guilty in the midst of a society all too willing to hurt him. Verónica would have liked to say, "Don't worry, you're innocent; it's the others who are bastards." But she didn't feel able to go that far.

She pressed on with her questions and he evaded them by pointing her in the direction of Rivero, who was on the pitch coaching the children. He was on the short side, overweight, wearing an Adidas tracksuit. He wore his mobile phone in a holster, like a cowboy's gun. She thought: if the Atlanta coach trained his boys with a mobile phone in one hand we'd kick his ass hard enough to send him flying over to the Chacarita home ground.

She asked Rafael for a coffee and sat down at one of the tables. Now she was aware of the other men in the bar looking at her. She took out her cigarettes, then, realizing that she couldn't smoke there, left her bag on the table and went to stand in the doorway. When she saw Rafael taking her coffee over to the table, she threw her cigarette away and came back to continue the conversation but, once again, he referred her to Rivero. He repeated his name for the second time and his tone betrayed him. Poor Rafael, he must not know how to lie, or even how to feign ignorance. The best thing was to make it possible for him to get in touch with her. To tell her whatever it was that fear was making him hide. She gave him one of her business cards and Rafael quickly put it in his pocket, as though she had passed him a wrap of cocaine or an advert for a brothel.

I I

The guy sat down at a table a few yards from Verónica without registering her presence. Rafael went to his table and told him that she was waiting for him. Rivero looked over at her with a certain suspicion and motioned her over to his table. Verónica picked up her bag and jacket and went to join him. You didn't need to be a particularly shrewd observer to see that the guy was a stereotype, a collection of clichés: untidy appearance, lecherous manner, flabby body, a bald spot crossed by a few greasy strands of hair. To infer criminality from these characteristics would have been pandering to prejudice, but then there was his expression: those eyes didn't lie. Verónica was experienced in many different kinds of male gaze, and this wasn't the expression of an old creep leering at a pretty girl. She would have put up with that as being par for the course. There was something aggressive, intimidating, emanating from the pupils. Those eyes inspired fear.

The guy shook her hand and introduced himself. Verónica took a seat and told him that she was preparing an article on neighbourhood clubs. She put the questions to him that you would expect a journalist to ask in these cases. Several times she even consulted a notebook she carried with her, as though reading her own notes on the subject. That was to avoid looking at him, not so much because she found him disagreeable but because she believed that the eyes can be a weapon that one should know how to deploy at the right time. So it was a deliberate ploy to seem lost in her notes until she looked up and said:

"I imagine that, as coach of the team he played in, you must have been devastated by the death of Vicente Garamona."

Rivero was a nasty piece of work, no doubt about it. He obviously wanted to dissemble, to pretend that he didn't understand the question, but he couldn't prevent his face from going through all the states of guilt: surprise, fear, confusion and finally anger. His eyes, when they met Verónica's cool, intransigent gaze, were full of hatred.

It was clear that the guy had something to do with Vicen's death and that he was the one supplying the boys for the railway game. She wasn't going to be able to prove it in this interview. It wasn't her intention that he should incriminate himself during their conversation. But if she left him sufficiently rattled, she knew that he would make a false step. And she needed to be ready to recognize that moment when it came.

But there was something else. Or, rather, someone else: Juan García. Verónica had arrived at the club with various aims: to find clues, to see the face of one of the men responsible for the crimes and to get a message to Juan García that, no matter how hard he tried to hide, she was going to find him. So she stood up, said goodbye as agreeably as possible and employed a gambit that she had learned as a child, from watching *Columbo*.

"Ah – I'm so sorry to take up more of your time, but do you know Juan García?"

Now these bastards know that I know; they won't be able to carry on without looking over their shoulders, she said to herself as she left the club. And, much as she liked animal metaphors, it didn't occur to her to think that she was a gazelle stalking two jackals.

Verónica had stopped talking to Lucio about her investigation. He didn't tell her anything about visiting his friend at the psychiatric hospital either, much less about their conversation there. He was sorry not to be able to share these experiences with her any more. Right from the start he had felt that Verónica was somebody he could trust. And he hadn't changed his mind about that. The interest had simply evaporated.

Bed was still a place where they understood each other. Or, at least, a place where their bodies reinstated the communication that had been lost by words. Even pain was an element in that language in which they needed to take refuge so as not to become distant to one another.

That night they had drunk too much. It was still early – dusk had scarcely fallen by the time Lucio arrived at Verónica's. That week he was finishing early, but he had claimed to be working overtime so that he could go to the apartment without his wife suspecting anything. Verónica welcomed him with a bottle of cold white wine that she had already started drinking before his arrival. There were also some little cheese crackers and familiar music drifting from the computer.

By the time they finished the bottle of wine they had taken off almost all their clothes. The cushions of the two-seater sofa had also fallen onto the floor and they were sinking into the hard base of the seat. Verónica led him to the bedroom, trying not to stumble over the cushions or knock over the glasses. Lucio collapsed onto the bed face down and Verónica threw herself on top of him. He liked feeling her as a dead weight on top of him, her breasts squashed against his back, her soft pubis on his waist. Lucio wanted to kiss her. He tried to turn over but she wouldn't let him.

"What's wrong, little boy, are you scared of me?"

He could have switched places – pushed her off and got on top of her – but he let her have her way. There was a wonderful pleasure in giving up control, letting someone else take the lead.

Verónica placed one hand on Lucio's crotch, caressed his testicles, reaching for the erect cock which was sticking into the mattress. Then she took her hand away and stroked around his anus. She pushed a finger into him, penetrating him. Then she did the same with another finger. Using the pressure of her groin against his ass she angled her fingers deeper into him. With her free hand she took his shoulder and made him lie on his side while she propped herself up so that she could reach over with her other hand to masturbate him slowly.

"You like this, don't you?" Verónica whispered in the voice of a huntress moving in for the kill. And Lucio kept as still as a hare, startled in the darkness by sudden light.

His body was too big for Verónica, for her to do all the things she seemed to want to do. She had to stretch her arms to maintain pressure in one hand, rhythm in the other. She leaned her jaw on his arm the moment before he ejaculated. Lucio felt how she increased the pressure a little more with both hands just as he was finishing. The semen fell onto the sheet. Verónica ran her fingers over the tip of his cock, slowly extracted her fingers from his anus and hugged him. She pressed her ear against his back, like a doctor about to ask him to take a deep breath. Her hands left a damp trail on Lucio's body.

The music in the other room had stopped playing. Lucio's mouth was dry. He wanted to drink. He got up from the bed.

"Are you going?"

"I'm thirsty."

He went to the living room to fetch the wine, but the bottle was empty. Verónica also stood up and went to the kitchen, returning with another bottle of white wine and a corkscrew. She gave them both to Lucio and collapsed onto one of the armchairs. Lucio poured out two glasses and passed one to her.

"The silence is killing me. I'd better put on some music." Verónica went over to the computer and scrolled through the songs to find the ones she wanted to hear. She was completely naked, but she moved with the elegance of someone at a social gathering who knows that she is beautiful. She could just as easily be naked as wearing a short skirt or tight jeans. She always seemed somewhat indifferent to the reactions she provoked.

A grave voice came on, singing some melodic song. Verónica liked that slightly sad, slightly monotonous style of music.

She went back to sit in the chair and drank from the glass. Lucio had stretched out on the two-seater, still stripped of its cushions. He felt too tired to get up and put them back in place. His face rested on the armrest and he looked at Verónica. It was getting dangerously close to the time he needed to leave. Perhaps she would want them to go back to bed, but he knew that that wasn't an option; the next step was for him to put on his clothes and go. He tried to think of something else, even if only for a moment. He remembered what he had talked about with Malvino, the previous afternoon.

"Do you think it's possible to hate someone you don't know?"

"You mean without knowing them personally?"

"Without having had any direct contact."

"Well, one can hate Hitler, or General Videla, without having to have shared anything with them."

"People you don't know."

"If we're talking about Martians, who may not even exist, I think the answer is no. To feel hatred, you need to feel a profound contempt for what that person does or thinks. I'd even say that the thing they do or think must directly influence our lives. That's why I can understand the stupidity of a soccer fan who hates a supporter from another club. It's idiotic, but there's a kind of logic to it."

"You're the only woman I know who talks about soccer."

Verónica drank deeply from her glass, then placed it on the coffee table. She looked at him with shining eyes, as if she enjoyed finding the weak spot in her prey so that she could choose that place to bite.

"And what does your wife talk to you about?"

Lucio said nothing. It was time to get dressed and leave. His body felt heavy.

"Your wife doesn't talk about soccer. She talks about that night's soap opera. Your wife doesn't listen to Mick Harvey. She emotes over Arjona. Your wife fucks like a wife and never tries out new ways to bring you pleasure."

He had to get out of there. Get dressed in silence and leave. But he decided to play her at her own game.

"You're wrong. My wife is much better than you are in bed."

She could have said something to insult him, or started crying or laughing, but instead she stretched out her hand, picked up the glass of wine and threw it at his face. Lucio raised his hand to try to protect himself and the glass shattered, cutting his cheek and his right palm. Verónica shut herself in the bathroom and shouted at him from there, ordering him out of the apartment. Lucio got dressed, took some paper napkins to clean the blood off his face and went. He had to wait in the front hall of the building until the doorman came to let him out. During those minutes he was scared that Verónica would come down, say that she was sorry and beg him to come upstairs again. Or that she would shout at him through the entry system. But Lucio left without hearing anything more from her.

I V

Angrily she banged down the toilet seat, which he had left up, and sat down to piss. A long stream that seemed to go on forever. She sat there for a good while, her elbows propped on her legs, her hands covering her face. She didn't want to hear anything that was happening outside the bathroom. A few seconds earlier she had shouted:

"Get out of here, I never want to see you again."

Her own voice echoed in her head and even the sound of her piss couldn't cover it. On the other side of the door, Lucio was moving around silently. She didn't know if the glass had hurt him much or not at all. She wanted nothing more than for him to get dressed and leave.

She heard the apartment door close. Lucio was leaving and did even that almost noiselessly, given the circumstances. Anyone else would have slammed the door. And his consideration annoyed her even more than if he had left shouting and swearing.

She sat there for a few minutes more until her legs began to cramp and she got cold. Coming out of the bathroom she felt dizzy, thanks to all the wine they had drunk. She thought of going to clear up the broken glass that was scattered around the living room, but she felt ill, as though she might vomit. Instead she sat down on the bed. Despite the effects of the alcohol, she couldn't stop thinking. About Lucio, about how little he had put into the relationship, about the ease with which he left his house for hers, his wife's cunt for hers. She should have thrown the whole wine bottle at him, not just the glass.

If this had happened five years ago, Verónica would have got dressed, put on make-up and set off for a nightclub or some new bar frequented by lots of interesting guys. She was getting old. Her thirties seemed to have come on very quickly and she had given in too easily. That night, at any rate, she didn't have enough energy to take a shower or even change her underwear.

In spite of her anger, which burned in her guts, she began to fall asleep and it was a while before she noticed that her mobile was ringing. By the time she did realize, it had stopped ringing. A few seconds later it started ringing again, and this time she got up to answer. Could it be Lucio, finally having something to say for himself? She made her way towards her mobile, which was in the living room, threading her way through the broken glass. The screen read CALLER UNKNOWN, so it couldn't be Lucio. She picked up and the voice at the other end sounded faraway and unfamiliar.

"It's Pedro."

She didn't remember any Pedro among her acquaintances.

"Who?"

"Father Pedro."

Of course. How could she have forgotten the priest from Villa Oculta?

"I need to speak to you," the priest told her. The line was very bad; even so, Verónica could tell that he was worried or scared about something.

"Go ahead – I'm listening."

"In person and in private – it's very important."

"I can come to your church right now."

"No, it would be dangerous for you to come alone at this time of night."

So Verónica offered her own apartment as a place to meet. They arranged to convene there in just over half an hour. She glanced around the living room in its chaotic state and caught a glimpse of herself in the mirror, looking like the archetypal broken woman. Broken and naked. Quickly she put on her jeans, underwear, a clean T-shirt and some sneakers, then got to work clearing up the broken glass. That job took about fifteen minutes. She arranged the armchairs, picked up the bottles and glasses, cleaned the ashtrays and aired out the room. Verónica was just opening a window when the intercom buzzed. As she went downstairs to open the door it occurred to her that she hadn't brushed her hair or washed her face. But she consoled herself with the thought that she was going to meet a priest. This wasn't the moment to be worrying about her looks.

The priest was waiting for her with his hands in his jacket pockets. It wasn't cold, so this seemed more like the stance of a troubled man. She was reminded of that old Italian movie she had seen once in a cinema club: *Fists in the Pocket*. She kissed him on the cheek and they went upstairs together. They didn't exchange a word until they were in the apartment and she asked him to ignore the chaos. She invited him to sit down in the armchair and asked if he would like a coffee.

"I'd prefer something stronger, if you don't mind."

So much the better; it meant that she didn't have to focus attention on preparing a hot drink. Verónica went to the little bar and brought out a bottle of bourbon and two glasses. She sat on the two-seater sofa and poured out two double measures of whisky.

"Do you know what the sacrament of silence is?" Father Pedro asked Verónica, who didn't even know what a sacrament was.

She shook her head.

"When a priest takes confession from a penitent, he has an obligation not to tell anyone what was revealed to him as part of the confession. It can't be discussed, even with the parishioner, outside the confessional."

"In no circumstances?"

"None. Breaking the sacrament of silence would signify the automatic excommunication of the priest concerned, even if he's a bishop, or the Pope himself."

The priest took a long drink of Jim Beam and Verónica did the same. Then he went on:

"Confession is a sacrament and to violate it is to go against God's laws."

Verónica began to realize that Pedro had not come to the apartment expressly to give her a theology lesson.

"Today Vicen's mother came to the church. And she asked to take confession. I could have refused, I could have called on another priest to fulfil the sacrament. I should have done that, because I already knew that I was prepared to undergo excommunication if necessary."

"Vicen's mother told you something connected to the case?"

"A few days after Vicen died, a man with the surname Iriarte came to the *villa*. He told her that he knew her son had been in an accident and that he had been killed. This man offered her and her other children somewhere to live. In El Chaco. Vicen's mother is from there, but she didn't want to know. Here she had work, but the prospect of owning her own home was tempting. Obviously she was suspicious. She thought that there was something odd about the offer and she didn't immediately accept it. So, to convince her, Iriarte told her that the proposal was part of a housing plan developed by a sub-secretariat of the city government."

"Hang on, the alleged accident took place in Haedo, which is in Greater Buenos Aires, and they offer her a house in El Chaco. And the offer comes from a sub-secretariat of the City of Buenos Aires, which has no jurisdiction either in the province of Buenos Aires or in El Chaco."

"She was still unconvinced, so on top of that they offered her a cheque to cover her relocation costs. Seven thousand pesos in exchange for moving straightaway. She showed me the cheque. It was issued by the Undersecretary of Housing and Environmental Management, within the Ministry of Social Development."

There was another silence. Dense, viscous. One part of Verónica had calmly taken note of Pedro's revelation. Another part, though, had been engulfed by an anguish comparable to that felt by someone present at a deathbed. Like in those movies where someone decides to give their life for the sake of truth or justice and accomplishes this with their dying breath. Verónica was watching a priest die in front of her eyes. She couldn't be unmoved – regardless of faith or its absence – by the fact that someone who had devoted his life to an ideal should decide to relinquish it. And that this offering was made in the names of both justice and her own investigation. Quietly, Verónica said, "Thank you."

"Faith is a gift from God. For a Christian it means more than life itself. A religious vocation is absurd and incomprehensible without faith. I have always wanted to be a holy man, but I've never managed it. I have sinned and repented more than once during my ministry. I know that I am a weak and sinful human, but faith has sustained me. When I felt that it was beginning to get lost or diluted in other feelings such as solidarity, empathy or support for fellow beings, I resolved not to sin again. To commit myself to a life of holiness. But I didn't manage it. Here I am…"

"Here you are…"

"Getting drunk. At least I hope that it hasn't been in vain."

"It won't have been, I promise you."

"It's strange. The first time I saw you, crossing Avenida Argentina, you seemed like an angel to me. Afterwards I was honest with myself and recognized that I simply found you attractive. That my attempt to neutralize that desire was another sign of my discomfort with this role that I've been playing."

Verónica poured herself another Jim Beam. Then she saw that Pedro's glass was empty too and refilled it. She would have liked to talk, to help him with a psychoanalytic interpretation or something similar, but she felt inadequate to the task.

"And if I desired you in the same way as any other man, I should recognize it. And if I wanted to help you achieve what you were looking for, I should do everything possible to help you achieve it. Now I don't know who I am. But I do know what I'm not."

Verónica was going to say "thank you" again, but the words stuck in her throat. This was madness. But what wasn't? She got up from the sofa as best she could, making an effort to keep her balance, and walked towards Pedro. Sitting astride him, she started to kiss his eyes, his cheeks and finally his mouth. She felt Pedro's hands running over her back and buttocks. She couldn't speak, nor was she sure whether this was another way to say thank you, or to push him, once and for all, into the abyss.

V

She had put on a tailored suit. It wasn't her favourite form of dress, but every now and then she enjoyed playing the part of a young professional, a secretary or a promising executive. She had managed to get an interview with the lawyer Roberto Palma, Undersecretary of Housing and Planning for the Buenos Aires city government.

It hadn't been hard to establish that the Iriarte who was said to have negotiated with Vicen's mother was an advisor to Palma. She had written an email to Rodolfo Corso asking him if the names Rivero, Iriarte and Palma rang a bell from his journalistic investigation into the trafficking of women in Misiones. Rodolfo replied:

Dear Vero,

I see that you are still on the trail of Juan García. It's a shame that we're talking about a journalistic investigation and not a game of bingo, because this would be the moment to shout "Full house!" All three men are connected to our friend. Rivero was a second-rate bully with an impressive criminal record (although it's been cleaned up in the courts – you don't need me to tell you about Argentine justice). In reality, I don't know which Rivero you're referring to, because there were two of them – brothers. That said, both of them were García's thugs.

Iriarte was practically a kid in those days. A promising mobster. He had one defect: he liked hitting women, and there had been a charge against him that I didn't manage to check at the time.

The distinguished Dr Palma didn't work in the municipality but in provincial government. He had some bureaucratic post, I can't remember what it was. But his main activity was something else. He was García's defence lawyer in the trial that was brought against him for trafficking women. It went so well for him that he moved part of his operation to Buenos Aires. Now he's secretary of something or other in the city government.

I hope to see my name in the Acknowledgements when you publish your first collection of reportage.

She had requested an interview with Undersecretary Palma from his press office. When asked to give a reason, she said that she wanted to write a piece on the plan to eradicate the *villas*. For some time the city government had wanted to be rid of these shanty towns which were occupying land that was worth a fortune. Their intention was to evict the people who lived there and build offices and expensive apartment blocks on those sites. That part of the plan wasn't being publicized, but it was enough to see who was backing the proposal, and which lobbyists were pressing for it, to guess at the real strategy for that land. Palma had appeared giving interviews in which he boasted about offering the residents of the *villa* a better quality of life outside it. He was happy to speak to any newspaper or broadcaster. And Verónica, on the pretext of a fast-approaching deadline at *Nuestro Tiempo*, had managed to get an appointment that same afternoon.

Palma showed her into his enormous office, with views onto the Plaza Mayor and the Casa Rosada, the presidential palace, beyond it. He offered her coffee and Verónica asked instead for a glass of water.

"How are things at *Nuestro Tiempo*?"

Palma made a couple of observations about the magazine to show that he read it. He was very careful to say that he didn't share the publication's ideological line. Verónica began by asking him about his plan to demolish the *villas*. The undersecretary gave answers that seemed to have been written for a publicity pamphlet. Verónica could have collared him for abuse of cliches, if nothing else. You didn't have to be a great journalist to spot the flaws in Palma's plan. It would be enough to be a curious one. But she wasn't there for that. When she saw that Palma was running out of things to say, she decided to get to the nub of the issue that had brought her to his office.

"Tell me, Dr Palma, what position does Ernesto Iriarte hold in the sub-secretariat?"

The official blinked a few times before answering:

"He's an advisor to this portfolio."

"Your advisor."

"To the sub-secretariat, yes, and to me too. I am the undersecretary."

Verónica made as if to consult her notes, although she had every figure and name memorized.

"Iriarte offers homes to people in emergency situations."

"Well, he often acts as a mediator between the families and the sub-secretariat."

"I understand. But I have a piece of information here that I don't altogether understand. Apparently he offered a house to Carmen Garamona, from the Villa Oculta."

"I don't know about that particular case, but it is part of his foundation. We take people out of the *villas* and offer them decent homes to live in with their families."

"Aha. Help me with this, Dr Palma: what seems strange to me is that Señora Gramona would be offered a house in El Chaco as compensation for her son being run over by a train in Haedo."

"As I said, Verónica, what we do is offer people homes. We have arrangements with different provinces for people who want to go back to their place of origin."

"A good way of reducing immigration from the interior."

"It could be taken that way. I don't see the problem."

"And, along with homes, you offer cash payments. Because you yourself authorized a payment of seven thousand pesos to this woman."

"Look, if we take this case by case I think you'll see that we help people in many ways."

"I'm sure you've helped many families who lost their children under the wheels of trains. I'd almost say that the city government should open an office exclusively for that."

"I don't understand what you mean, or what you're trying to prove. I'm giving serious answers to your questions, even though they seem inconsistent and out of place. Let's finish this here."

"Please don't be annoyed. A couple more questions, and then I promise we're done."

Palma's cheeks were flushed and he had started nervously tapping on the table. He was ready to throw her out of his office, but she thought that she could risk a couple more questions.

"Are you still in touch with the Rivero brothers?"

"I don't know anybody called Rivero. Your last question, please."

"No, it's better if I don't ask it. I was going to ask if you still see Juan García, but you're going to tell me that you don't know him. Have a good day, Dr Palma."

VI

Those were not the best days of Verónica's life. She had asked for some days off from the magazine so as not to have to go to the newsroom. Patricia gave her them without asking why. Verónica could have said that she was working day and night on the investigation about children on the railways, but she didn't even want her boss to call and ask her how it was all going. She had come a long way since first suspecting that the train driver's suicide concealed something more than a personal drama. She had the name of the chief suspect in running that criminal operation, she had interviewed the man who must be responsible for selecting the children and the man responsible for making witnesses' and victims' families "disappear" by removing them from Buenos Aires. If she wanted, she could stop now and write the article. With the wind in her favour she could even have criminal proceedings brought. There was always some investigating judge with an appetite for trouble. But it was unlikely that the justice would go the full distance and condemn these men for the earlier deaths. At most they would be prevented from playing their bloody game. And she wanted to see the murderers and their accomplices behind bars.

There was another reason, however, why Verónica wouldn't settle for what she had got so far. That was the risk that her discoveries to date were only the tip of the iceberg, that another journalist might come along to put the metaphorical cherry on the investigation. She herself had sometimes jumped on investigations published in other media and managed to find out more. She wasn't going to let that happen to her.

She had reached an important point in her story, but she didn't know how to go further. Juan García couldn't be found anywhere, nor did she have concrete proof of anyone's involvement, not even Rivero's, and he seemed the most compromised. Palma had alibis which, however wild they seemed, would lead any judge towards a presumption of innocence rather than guilt.

She wanted to concentrate on the investigation, but she couldn't. She was still brooding on what had happened a few nights back. The fight with Lucio, Pedro's appearance, and, finally, the priest in her bed. Lucio was the one most on her mind. Perhaps because what had happened with Pedro had surely been more unsettling for him than it was for her. As for Lucio – she thought of him continually. The best thing to do was take the bull by the horns. She sent him a text asking him to call. It was exasperating, this business of having to wait to talk until he wasn't with his wife. She wouldn't be the one to break the agreement, although she felt like calling him, even calling him at home. She had had his telephone number since before they became lovers, since Carina, the sister of his dead co-worker, had given it to him. At that time, when she had called the house and his wife had answered, Verónica hadn't felt able to speak to her. If she rang again, would she dare to ask for Lucio? This time, she didn't even get as far as dialling the number.

After several failed attempts at communication, they managed to speak and arranged to meet the next morning in a cafe. A change of scene was called for. When she arrived at the bar, Lucio was already there. Seeing him calmly standing there, without the phantom of sex, or the desire for it lurking around them, stirred a tenderness in her that she had not felt in their previous encounters. She couldn't forget, though, how Lucio had destroyed any chance of their happiness as a couple. It sickened her.

VII

Call me when you can. Lucio received the text on the way home. At first he thought that it would be better not to answer, but he was curious and wanted to speak to her. He got off the bus a few stops earlier than usual, to be able to talk to her without being overheard. The call went to voicemail. She must be using the line. He rang her back a couple of times more and each time the call went straight to voicemail. He didn't know what to do. If he got home and she rang him then, he wouldn't be able to take the call. But he also didn't like the idea of switching his mobile off until the next day. He decided to wait on a street corner until his phone rang. Ten minutes later he got another text: *Can I call you?* He dialled her number and she answered.

"How are you?" Verónica's voice sounded relaxed, warm. Very far from the tone of their last exchange. Perhaps she was ashamed, or just tired.

"I'm OK – and you?"

"Hurting."

"Is that good or bad?"

"It's bad. Lucio, I need to see you. I think that, after what happened, we should talk."

They arranged to meet in a bar on the block where Calle Boulogne Sur Mer crossed Avenida Corrientes, not in La Perla, their usual meeting place. They needed somewhere neutral, free of memories that might intrude on the conversation. A meeting over coffee, not alcohol, alternately watching or ignoring the people who walked past on the avenue, with the only background music an espresso machine and the glare of a television screen as decoration.

Verónica drank her coffee unsweetened, but she still picked up a spoon and stirred it. He had noticed this habit in her soon after they first met, but for some reason he had never felt able to ask her why she did it.

"I can't bear to carry on being hurt by you," Verónica said, staring at the circles made by her spoon in the cup.

Lucio was taken aback.

"I'm hurting you? Look" – he pointed to his cut cheekbone and showed her his fingers with the lacerations still visible from the last night they had spent together. Verónica considered them dispassionately.

"That's nothing compared to the injury done to me by our relationship."

Was there any point in going over the details? In saying that she had started this? In reminding her of all the times she had seemed like someone carrying a branding iron with which to mark his body or mind? In recognizing that he also took pleasure in her suffering, that he wasn't prepared to be generous to her? All those words were superfluous, and yet they were still talking.

"I don't know, Lucio, I'm tired of this. The other night ended up a bit of a disaster. I don't know any more what I can tell you and what I can't – but I'll tell you anyway. That night I ended up sleeping with another guy."

Lucio felt a void open in his stomach, like an implosion of his organs. He didn't want to pick up his coffee cup for fear that his fury would make his hand shake and that she would notice. With as neutral a voice as he could manage, he said:

"You're a big girl. Do whatever you like. Just don't tell me."

Verónica was doubtless trying to find ways to hurt him. She couldn't resist the pleasure of causing him pain.

"This seriously was a disaster. The guy was a priest. Or is a priest. I don't know if he's already cast off his robes by now."

Lucio laughed. Verónica was mocking him. What would she invent next?

"All that's missing now is for you to tell me that your period's late."

"Don't be an idiot. If it was late I'd never tell you." Verónica checked the time on her phone and got up. "It's probably best if we don't see each other any more."

She picked up her phone and her bag and left. Lucio asked the waiter for another coffee.

VIII

For three days she stayed locked in her apartment. She didn't even go out to buy food but made do with what she found in the fridge, the freezer or the cupboard, which was never much, because she didn't like doing a weekly shop. She had decided not to take calls even from her friends. But when Pedro called she did answer, thinking that perhaps he had found out something new about Vicen. Very quickly she discovered that Pedro wanted to talk about his problems, about the challenges he faced. Verónica kept up her side of the conversation and tried to be encouraging, but she didn't invite him to the apartment, nor did he suggest they see each other. Pedro called twice more. The third time she told him that she too was going through a difficult time, personally and professionally, and that she felt unable to help him. That his problem was too much for her and that she couldn't do anything except urge him to live the life he wanted.

During those days, Marcelo, the building's doorman, had cause to worry about her again. He had knocked on her door a couple of times and offered to do some shopping for her or any other job she needed. He was so kind and unconditional that he was the only person to whom she gave any kind of explanation.

"I've got a few problems, but nothing so serious that you won't see me out and about again in a few days, back to my usual bouncy self. If I need something I swear I'll call you."

Later, when the phone rang and she saw that it said CALLER UNKNOWN, she thought it would be Pedro again, coming to park his theological hell at her door. Better not to answer. The telephone rang again, a second and third time. What if it wasn't Pedro?

"Hello, I'm Rafael. You interviewed me at Spring Breezes."

Verónica, who had been sitting at her computer, stood up when she heard Rafael's voice.

"I need help. The club coach, Rivero, is bad news. I reported him and nearly got killed. I've got nowhere to go."

"Where are you, so I can come and get you?"

Rafael gave her the address. In less than five minutes Verónica was in the street trying to hail a taxi. In half an hour she had arrived at the destination. The address corresponded to a Chinese supermarket. She asked the taxi driver to wait – they would be returning to Villa Crespo in a few minutes. She went into the supermarket and walked up to the till, where a Chinese woman was standing. With some incredulity she said:

"I'm looking for Rafael. Is he here?"

The Chinese woman shouted to someone in her language. A man peered around a door at the back of the supermarket. Then the same man appeared, this time accompanied by Rafael. His face was badly bruised and he walked with difficulty. It was no exaggeration to say that they had almost killed him.

"Julián is my friend," Rafael told her, indicating the Chinese man standing next to him. "But I can't put him at risk by staying here any longer. And I can't go back to the hostel because that was where they went looking for me."

As far as Verónica could see, Rafael didn't even have a bag with some things in it. It was just him, and no luggage. She gently squeezed his arm.

"I'm going to take you somewhere safe. You're coming with me to my apartment."

15   *Leaving my Heart*

I

Rafael really didn't look good. Without even asking him, Verónica made the decision to call a doctor while they were still in the taxi. A female doctor, in fact: her sister Daniela. She told her that it was a long story that would take time to explain, but that she had someone at home who had been badly beaten up. Could she come and see him? Daniela agreed somewhat grudgingly, saying that three o'clock that afternoon was the earliest she could come.

When they arrived at the apartment, Verónica told Rafael the truth about her investigation: that the article about neighbourhood clubs was a ruse to get to people like Rivero.

"As soon as I saw you, I could tell you had nothing to do with it. That's why I gave you my card, because I was hoping that at some point you would get in touch."

Rafael told her that he had found out that Rivero was organizing the contests on the railway tracks. That he had suspected something strange was going on for a long time, that he had only recently been able to confirm his suspicions when one of the boys told him what was happening. That he was sure Vicen had died in the contest, because the boy who had told him had been with Vicen on the Sarmiento line that night.

Verónica made him repeat everything several times. She didn't want to subject his claims to a police-style interrogation, but she needed to be sure Rafael had not misconstrued something or forgotten an important detail.

Rafael also told her about what had happened in the police station when he went to report a crime and how Julián had saved him that night.

"How did Julián know they were beating you up?"

"He's got security cameras. They point in every direction from the supermarket. He put them up after he was threatened by the Chinese mafia."

"If there's a recording, then the faces of the people who attacked you will be on it."

Verónica made Rafael call Julián, who confirmed that there was indeed a recording of the attack. She called Federico and asked him if there was anyone in the office available to remove a recording from a security camera.

"And since when are you a client of this firm?"

"I am the heiress apparent of sixty-five per cent of the firm."

"Divided among three sisters."

"My twenty per cent is still more than the ten per cent my father gave you, which was given with our consent – and in the secret hope that you'd end up married to me."

"OK, you've convinced me. Give me the details and I'll get someone to go and pick it up. What's the danger that someone will want to steal that recording?"

"Medium, perhaps high."

"I won't send the office boy on his own, then. He'll go in the company of a gentleman we find can be very persuasive in these situations. I'll send you the bill afterwards."

After the call, she went on with the questions. There was one crucial detail of which Rafael knew nothing: when the next contest would be. He couldn't go and talk to the boys; he couldn't risk returning to the neighbourhood without endangering his life. But she could.

"If I understood correctly, your family lives in that house. Could someone put me in touch with the boy who took part in the competition and with the one they're lining up to do it next?"

"My daughter is friends with them. She's in school at the moment, but I'll call my mother later and talk to Martina."

Verónica put a frozen pizza into the oven and they ate it together for lunch. Neither of them seemed to be hungry and more than half was left over. At three o'clock on the dot Daniela arrived. Verónica withdrew to her room, so that her sister could examine Rafael in peace.

11

Martina was going to wait for her at the door to the boarding house. Rafael had talked to his daughter from Verónica's mobile; he had told her that he was fine but that he wouldn't be able to visit her for a few days, that his friend would be arriving shortly because she wanted to have a chat with Dientes and El Peque. That she should introduce them. Afterwards, Rafael spoke to his mother; he told her that he had a special job on and that it would be a few days before he could get over to see her.

A few hours earlier, Daniela had told her sister that to the naked eye, there didn't seem to be anything seriously wrong with Rafael. Bruises, the odd cut, but no compromised organs or anything like that. All the same, she recommended that he have a scan to rule out internal injuries, that he have a tetanus injection and take some ibuprofen for the pain.

Downstairs, as she was leaving, Daniela warned her:

"I don't know what you're involved in, Vero, but you're on thin ice. It takes several people to hurt a man that badly.

If they hit you even half as hard they'd leave you dead or brain-damaged."

Verónica tried to allay her fears with some excuses invented for the occasion, but her sister saw right through them. They had been brought up together, after all.

When Rafael and Verónica were alone again they started planning their next steps. For her, the most important thing was to find out the date of the children's next assignation on the tracks. For him, the priority was to let Dientes' mother know this date, so that she would keep him at home. He insisted, too, that they find out who the other contestant would be. Verónica didn't agree: she argued that if Dientes didn't take part they would simply replace him with someone else and the problem would be the same, the difference being that they wouldn't be able to do anything to intervene. However, if Rivero still thought that Dientes was going to jump, there was a chance of trapping them. Him and his accomplices. Accomplices whom Rafael did not know and who would go unpunished if the contest were interrupted at this point.

It was after six o'clock in the evening when Verónica arrived at the tenement house. A young girl was waiting in the doorway. It was Martina.

"I told them that a friend of my dad wanted to talk to them. They're up on the terrace."

Martina led her to the foot of the stairway. Luckily they didn't come across anyone else. Verónica was uneasy. She didn't like dealing with children. It was a different story with her nieces and nephews. She had known them since they were born and had watched them growing up. Even then, there were lots of times when she found her patience tested. Children seemed to her like aliens who spoke their own language and had feelings she didn't understand. That was her conviction as she climbed the stairs up to the terrace. There she found Dientes and El Peque sitting on the rooftop, looking serious, as if they had been sent to see the teacher or, worse, the principal. She wasn't sure whether to give them a kiss on the cheek, as she had done with Martina, or let a scarcely audible "hello" suffice as a greeting. She decided on the latter option. The children remained sitting where they were.

"You're Dientes, you're Peque, right?" Her intuition was spot on. "Rafael has told me a lot about you and I want you to know something straight off. I've come to help and protect you. You mustn't be scared. And whatever you say won't go any further than me. And Rafael, of course. But if necessary, not even your mothers will hear about it."

Verónica felt like smoking but repressed the urge, not wanting to set a bad example. Remembering that she had some Cherry-Lyptus lozenges somewhere in her bag, she located the packet and offered them one each. They accepted and Verónica said that they could keep the packet. Dientes put it into his trouser pocket.

Better get straight to the point.

"Do you two love Rivero?"

The boys' eyes widened. They didn't know what to say.

"Seriously. Do you love him? Do you wish he was a member of your family?"

"Rivero is very demanding," said El Peque.

"Boys, will you let me get away with swearing? I think Rivero is a bastard."

El Peque laughed and Dientes shook his head, as though disapproving of his friend's reaction. But they both seemed to soften in response to what Verónica had said.

"I know what Rivero did to you. I also know what he did to lots of children before you. He's been doing this for years.

You boys weren't the first. And Vicen isn't the only boy who's died."

El Peque hugged his knees tighter.

"I know you did it because you wanted to make money. But Rivero is a bad person who hates children like you, who doesn't care if they get killed or lose their legs because a train ran over them."

"But it's fine if you jump quickly," said El Peque.

"When I was your age, my dad wanted to teach me to fish. You know those rods that have a hook on the end? I don't know if you've ever seen how sharp they are. Anyway, my dad told me that, however careful you are, everyone who goes fishing gets jabbed by the hook at least once. And because I'm a scaredy-cat and I hate injections or any kind of jab, that was enough to stop me. I never, ever went fishing. Not even that one time."

"What a cissy," Dientes observed.

"Yes, too right. But I never got jabbed by a fishing hook. Now, imagine that a train, that enormous train coming towards you, is going to hit you at least once. But this time there's no second chance. You're not going to get a few stitches because a fishing hook sliced open your finger. Sooner or later, you're going to be killed by a train."

"Did your dad get cross when you didn't want to go fishing?"

"A bit. He got over it, though. It's true that if you don't compete, Rivero will be cross, but I've already told you he's a bad person and that he only wants to make money out of you. And what I want is to make Rivero pay for all those children who died and for the suffering of people like you, Peque, who had to see some horrible things."

"And if he gets hold of us afterwards?"

"I'm not going to let him get hold of anyone."

"Are we going to kill him?" El Peque asked.

"We could tie him to the rails and let a train run him over," Dientes suggested.

"I'd love to do that, but we can't. We have to settle for seeing him go to prison. And for that I need your help. I need us to be like a superteam. Are you on board?"

They both nodded.

"The first thing I need to know is when you have to go to the railway track with Rivero."

There was a silence. Verónica didn't say anything more. It was just a matter of waiting.

"Tuesday night."

"And on Monday you have training at the club."

"Yes, tomorrow – Friday – as well."

"And how's he going to transport you to the tracks? Do you know yet where it'll be?"

"He didn't tell me the place. They're coming to pick me up on the corner of Zelarrayán and Gordillo."

"They picked me up on that corner too, and they brought me back again afterwards. But the second time I got scared and I ran off."

"So how did you get home?"

"I ran like a thousand blocks, I ran past the whole train with everyone looking out at me and, when I got to a corner, I stopped for a breather. And Rivero turned up there with another guy."

"Do you know what the other guy was called?"

"No."

"I'll tell you what we're going to do. You're going to go to training tomorrow and on Monday as if nothing's happened. And on Tuesday you're going to go with Rivero to the tracks. You're not going to see us, but I promise you that that day we're going to be there the whole time watching to make sure nothing happens to you. And before you get onto the tracks, when all the bad guys are there together, Rivero and his friends, that's when we'll appear."

"Are you in the police?"

"No, I'm a journalist."

"And are you going to come with other journalists?"

"No, people who work in the justice system will go with me. Don't you worry. Do everything he tells you to do. We're going to be taking care of you. Do you know who the other boy will be?"

"No, he didn't tell me."

"And how much does Rivero pay you?"

"Twenty if you lose and a hundred if you win."

Verónica looked for her wallet and took out two fifty-peso notes. She gave them one each.

"This is for helping me put the superteam together. Don't tell anyone you've spoken to me."

Verónica left the boys on the terrace. Martina was at the door, as though acting as lookout should any adult arrive.

"Your dad told me that you're very pretty, and he's right."

"I look like my mum."

Verónica leaned forward to give her a kiss on the cheek and went towards the taxi, which was waiting for her a few yards from the boarding house.

III

As she was on the way home, her mobile rang. It was Lucio.

"Why don't we meet?" Verónica suggested spontaneously, adding that it couldn't be at her apartment because somebody was staying with her.

"The priest?"

"No, no priests."

"Your sister, a boyfriend?"

"It's hard to explain. It's to do with work."

"A colleague from work?"

"Stop trying to guess. It's someone connected with the investigation."

"I thought you'd given that up."

"I'm deeper in than ever, Lucio. You wouldn't believe how far I've come since that time you came with me to Lugano. I think I'm about to nail some really nasty sons of bitches."

"And you've got someone living with you."

"Come on, let's meet somewhere close to a hotel."

IV

During the time they were lovers, there were times when she didn't exist. Lucio completely forgot about her existence. As if he were experiencing selective memory lapses, he could go for days without thinking of her, without anything bringing her to mind. Then she would suddenly pop up in some absurd context: while he was playing soccer, in the queue to pay a bill, while ordering a pizza. For no particular reason, she would start to be on his mind all the time. He wouldn't be able to concentrate on anything but the prospect of seeing her again. And that state could last for hours or days, until an exchange of text messages confirmed a new date. But on the days when he didn't think about her, Verónica simply formed no part of his life. If anyone had been able to read his mind at those times, they would never have found out that he had a lover.

Since walking out of the bar, however, Verónica had taken up a more permanent place in his brain. It wasn't that he thought about her all the time, but she was always present, like a malaise, a muscular ache, a low fever, present enough to stop him acting naturally in any situation. He kept repeating her name to himself, or whispering it. At night when he went to sleep he tried to think consciously of her, he wanted to take her out of that dark place in his head. The next day he would wake up with the same sense of disquiet.

He couldn't go on like this. He decided to call her. She seemed not surprised, but perhaps a little distracted. He would have preferred open rejection, or anger, to the feeling that she was thinking of something else while they talked. He was beginning to think that it had been a mistake to call, when she said:

"Why don't we meet?"

They met the next day in La Perla. Lucio still wanted to know who was staying in Verónica's apartment, but she wasn't prepared to tell him. They didn't stay long in the bar. Instead they went to the hotel on the corner of Cromañón, where they had gone that first time. As though entering a time warp, they were allocated that same bedroom designed to look like a wood cabin. Lucio watched Verónica's body in the mirrors. Verónica's body penetrated, moved by the force of his hips. Verónica's body marked with bites and bruises. Verónica's mouth around his cock. Little by little he felt himself drifting away, as though these scenes belonged to a pornographic movie he was watching without desire. Or perhaps it was just a dream and he wasn't really there. Suddenly the cramps came back, those stabbing pains in his legs that forced him to tense his body and keep still. Exhausted more from effort than pleasure, they lay staring at the ceiling, watching each other in the mirror. Lucio was in a movie and had to get out of it. When they left the hotel he walked with her, like the first time, as far as Avenida Rivadavia. That biting cold was in the past, but now they had the exasperating spring wind to contend with. Verónica got in a taxi and he decided to continue walking along the avenue. He was happy to walk as far as Río de Janeiro and take a number 112 bus from there. He needed to walk and think. He must not see Verónica again. He had been certain of that since the moment in the hotel room when they had looked at themselves in the mirror. That wasn't the reason he felt the need to clear his head while listening to the rhythm of his feet on the sidewalk, though. Seeing Verónica again, repeating their first encounter, had brought starkly to mind the other element in that parallel life: the death trains, the children baiting his futile attempts to brake. Those children whom – as he had discovered when he visited Malvino – he hated, just as he hated all the people who had thrown themselves under his train. And he could not escape his destiny. His instinct or fear knew it: one day next week the boys were going to be there waiting, standing unflinching in the path of the train. He could pretend not to know, ask for the shift that ended mid-afternoon. Or he could follow the current schedule and work the night shift all week. And if nothing happened next week, then he would work nights the week after, until he saw them appear in front of his train. He would keep his senses, his intuition, his reflexes, his hatred alert. It might not be his turn. Or it might. At the end of the day, he too was playing Russian roulette.

16   *Supergirl*

Verónica looked at herself and Lucio in the ceiling mirror and saw two jaded bodies, mercilessly exposed. She was even moved to pull the sheet over herself. She had had worse nights with other men, and at this stage in her life she knew that they happened sometimes, that it was better to move on. If it had been some other guy – even Lucio himself a few weeks earlier – they would have got dressed, had a beer, listened to some music and hoped that next time desire would prove a better catalyst to physical pleasure. But that was the problem. She didn't want another night. Perhaps he didn't, either. They had been like two dead bodies, from the first kiss exchanged in the motel room (the first kiss used to take place in the elevator). And those bodies that had once been so quick to warm up were broken; nothing got them going. The caresses were perfunctory, kisses gelatinous, arms and legs as heavy as lead.

Lucio had been considerate enough to walk her to Rivadavia so that she could get a taxi. They said goodbye awkwardly, with a cursory kiss. She was quite sure, as she settled into the back seat of the taxi, that this was the last time they would meet. It had been a mistake to suggest meeting up to go to a motel. She had let herself be fooled by his call, which was so unusual. And that tone of confusion, or remorse – it amounted to the same thing – had in turn confused her and made her feel guilty about what she had been thinking over the last few days. There would be no more confusion or remorse.

She arrived at her apartment and was about to put on all the lights while kicking off her shoes and starting to take her clothes off (she was used to getting to the bedroom or bathroom in only her underwear) when she remembered that Rafael was sleeping on the living-room floor. Her usual routine would have been quite a shock for him. So instead she came in silently, went to the kitchen, opened the fridge without putting on the light and got out a bottle of water. From the living room came the sound of Rafael's steady breathing. Given all the other problems having him in the house entailed, it was lucky that he didn't snore.

First she went to the bathroom, pissed, brushed her teeth and took off the rest of her make-up, then cleaned her face with cream and went to her room. She closed the door and turned on the television. She found a subtitled movie that she could watch without turning up the volume.

II

Verónica had decided that it would be most practical for Rafael to stay in the apartment until Rivero and company were safely locked up. She asked the doorman to lend her a mattress. Marcelo brought one down from his apartment and insisted on manoeuvring it into place himself. Knowing Marcelo, Verónica realized that his real intention was to scrutinize Rafael, who evidently didn't make a good impression because, when Verónica showed the doorman out, he asked:

"Are you sure you know what you're doing?"

She resolved the clothes problem, too, by going to Avenida Córdoba, where the outlets were, and buying him jeans, two

T-shirts, three pairs of boxers and three pairs of socks. Next she went to the supermarket and, overcoming her phobia of bulk-buying, bought a consignment of non-alcoholic drinks, some beers, bread, potato chips, various kinds of ham, hamburgers, water crackers, yoghurts, apples, mandarins, rice and some TV dinners. She also picked up shaving cream, disposable razors and a toothbrush.

Verónica was worried that Rafael would feel uncomfortable about everything she had bought, especially the clothes. So when she got to the apartment she discreetly put the food away in the kitchen and left the clothes in a bag on one side of the living room. In passing, she told Rafael that there were some clothes for him there, but she didn't mention that they were new. Then, quickly moving on, she gave him a set of spare keys. She told him not to go anywhere near the south of the city, even by accident. He should try not to see anyone. If he needed anything else, she would get it for him.

Rafael had managed to recharge his mobile with the cable she had. Verónica, making coffee, heard him call someone who must be his wife. She tried not to listen in, but couldn't help overhearing Rafael tell his wife that he loved her. The coffee maker started bubbling at that moment, and Verónica tried to focus on what she was meant to be doing.

Federico called to say that he had got hold of the recording from the security cameras at the Chinese supermarket.

"You can see four guys, first of all in the car and then hitting someone. The Chinese man really knows how to fight. He was like something out of *Kill Bill.*"

"Is it possible to identify the thugs?"

"You can see them quite well. I've got screenshots of their faces, but all the same, I wouldn't get your hopes up. It's going to be difficult to find them. I don't want to go stirring up a hornet's nest. It wouldn't be helpful for them to know we're looking for four hoodlums when we still don't know who's pulling the strings."

"Fede, I need your help with the most complicated bit of all this."

"Go on."

"On Tuesday they're taking some boys to the tracks again. We know that it'll be on some part of the Sarmiento route and that it'll be at night."

"So our window is four hours and twenty-five miles. You really know how to make things easy."

"Let's say three hours and fifteen miles, bearing in mind that it's not going to be in the vicinity of Once station. There's something else. These guys need to be caught in the act. That's the only way we can be sure they'll go to prison. I've got witnesses like Rafael and, if necessary, the two boys he made take part. In fact, one of them's supposed to be jumping on Tuesday."

"So is he not going to?"

"That's the point. We need to give him protection."

"We should give him a fucking medal. He's infiltrated a criminal organization. I'll call you when I have everything."

Late that Friday night, Verónica went to the magazine newsroom. She talked to Patricia, explaining that the investigation into the trains was now very advanced. That she couldn't tell her the details, but that she had some very good info. That she should fight the editor for the cover of the next edition.

Federico called her when she had left the newsroom and was on her way back home.

"Done, Vero, it's all settled."

"I expected nothing less."

"Bearing in mind what happened to your lodger, going to the federal police doesn't seem like a great idea."

"And so of course you didn't."

"There are police chief friends of your father who could give us a hand. But I'm young and creative, so I decided to give your father's contacts a miss and go with my own. Since this García character operates in the city, I went to national organizations where it's harder for him to exert any kind of influence. There's a Council of Childhood that does great work and can count on some police assistance. I spoke to one of the people who run it. He's a lawyer who taught me at university. We came up with a strategy that would consist in discreetly placing police at some of the points along the route that's being used for this activity. It shouldn't take one of their patrol cars more than six minutes to reach any part of the railway."

"And the boy?"

"I need to know where he lives, and on Tuesday we'll assign a bodyguard to follow him. It would be very helpful to have a photo, but if there isn't one we'll get one by the weekend. Are there other boys his age living there?"

"One other."

"We'll get photographs of them both tomorrow and I'll send you the picture so you can tell me which one he is."

"Is there anything else you need?"

"It would make life easier if we knew where the competition's going to be."

III

Lucio no longer suffered from cramping in his legs, at least not when he was having sex with his wife. Now, though, he felt as though his arms were going to sleep and a stitch were being pulled from below his neck up to his head. This happened every time he had to drive a train. At the end of a shift, he felt exhausted, as though his work had entailed an enormous physical effort, and he arrived home bone-tired. Sometimes Mariana was waiting up for him and they chatted while he had dinner.

On Saturday night he had a nightmare. One of those dreams that sometimes tormented him. He was driving a train. Not a current model, but one of those Fiats that looked like a camel. In the dream, it was daytime when he started driving, but night fell quickly. He could see very little – and then nothing at all. Suddenly a flowery dress flew into the windshield. It wasn't a woman – just a piece of clothing. It flapped against the glass and blocked his view. All he could see were the blue and red flowers on the material. He realized, in the dream, that the dress was Verónica's. In that case, he concluded, Verónica must be dead. She had been hit by the train. Why had nobody said anything? Verónica had died. He started crying, then felt a hand on his face. It was Mariana beside him, as she was every time he awoke from a nightmare. Gradually he calmed down. He got up and went to the kitchen to get a glass of water, Mariana following behind him. She stood beside him, keeping him company until Lucio decided to go back to bed and try to sleep for a few hours. Then it would be his turn to get up, give the children breakfast, buy the Sunday croissants, prepare the maté. Everything as usual.

IV

Dientes and El Peque had made a pact. They weren't going to spend the money given them by Supergirl (their name for Verónica) until Tuesday was over. Only afterwards, on Wednesday, would they live it up in the barrio, frittering away their money. By then Rivero would be in prison and perhaps they would have been awarded more money. Or a medal that they could sell to the guy who bought metal.

El Peque didn't want to be left out of the superteam they had formed and which, as far as they knew, comprised Supergirl, Rafael and the two of them. El Peque knew that he wouldn't be able to contribute much from home, so he decided to go back to soccer training at Breezes. Rivero was surprised to see him arrive with Dientes that Friday. But he didn't mind him joining in with the other boys, who were delighted to have him back. When the others were out of earshot, Rivero asked him:

"Are you up for jumping against Dientes? Because if Dientes wins, he goes on to the next round and then he could compete against you."

"I'm up for anything," El Peque replied, and Rivero gave him a cheerful slap on the back.

The truth was that there was no way El Peque was going to put himself in front of a train again. He didn't plan to get that far. He was there to see what was happening at the club, like a spy in enemy territory. He needed to watch, listen and retain everything in his memory so that he could relay it to Supergirl. She would be happy if he brought her good information and would congratulate him on how well he did his job. He didn't care about the money she had given him. It was enough that Supergirl let him be in the group.

V

Verónica spent the whole weekend in her apartment. She started writing some of the article, partly as a way to organize the information she had so far. Rafael went out a few times to walk around the barrio. Doubtless he wanted to leave her alone to write without distractions. All the same, they had lunch and dinner together on Saturday and Sunday and two of those meals he prepared himself: spaghetti with a tomato and tuna sauce and risotto with saffron, little bits of salami and peas.

She wasn't used to sharing her home with anyone, especially not a stranger. But Rafael had a manner that made her feel comfortable. She didn't mind his presence and she liked having an excuse to interrupt her writing for a coffee and chat with him. In those two days Rafael told her the story of his life. His relationship with Andrea, his descent into cocaine and alcohol, his battle to recover, his mother's resilience, his work at Spring Breezes, his love for Martina. Verónica remembered overhearing him on the phone to his wife.

"Do you still love Andrea, then?"

"I never stopped loving her. The further I fell, the more I felt that I still loved her. And now I'm well, all I want is to get back together with her."

Verónica felt envious of Andrea.

She didn't want to think about Lucio. She had to get used to the idea that what had happened the other night had marked the end of their relationship. That there was no longer any bond, whether physical, romantic or emotional. She shouldn't waste even half a neuron on the General. Her friends would be very happy when they found out that she was once again single – although arguably a woman with a married lover is always single. It was ironic that the first weekend she was spending with a man in a long time should be in the company of someone with whom she had no sexual bond. But she felt so vulnerable that, if Rafael was to encourage her even a little, she wouldn't be able to trust herself to keep strictly to her role of protector. And there had already been that disaster with Father Pedro. She'd better have a cold shower. And not leave the bathroom door ajar.

They ate like a chaste married couple, at the table in the living room with the TV on. There was never much to watch on Sundays, so they had settled on *Dirty Dancing*, dubbed into Spanish. She had seen the movie so many times that it surprised her when Rafael claimed not to have heard of it. They were interrupted by the ringtone on Verónica's mobile. She couldn't imagine who would be calling her at that time on a Sunday night. Even more puzzling, the telephone number didn't come up, just the message CALLER UNKNOWN.

"Verónica Rosenthal?"

It was a man's voice that was not in any way familiar.

"Speaking."

"It's García, Verónica. Juan García. I think you and I need to get together and talk."

His tone was that of a loving friend who's been neglected, calling to reproach someone.

VI

There are certain things you never ask your father: if he's ever had sex, if he's ever loved anyone else apart from your mother, if he's been a coward or a swindler. To all these questions that Lucio had never asked he could add another: if his father had ever hit someone while driving a train. He did not know, either, if his grandfather, in his old steam locomotive, had ever heard the sound of bones being crushed beneath the weight of metal. Nor would he ever talk about this to his own children. He wasn't going to let Fabián and Patricio work on the railways, anyway. There had been a moment in his life when he too could have said "no" and refused to follow in the family tradition. That moment was lost in the fog of youth. Life may not have been generous to him, but it had been fair. He knew that he was never going to be an engineer, but neither would he be short of work. He would never be rolling in money, but he would have enough to make sure that there was always food on the table and good-quality sneakers for his children. But that strange contract with life had hidden the train accidents in the small print. And Verónica too. So, had it been worth the pain? Every image, every sound, every physical sensation associated with those six lifeless bodies? Had Verónica been worth it? His only certainty was the one that had struck him after the last time they met. If it weren't for Verónica, he wouldn't be here now, driving the night train on the Sarmiento line.

VII

The odds of one driver or another having to operate the train that would become an involuntary protagonist of that macabre game on the tracks were hard to calculate. Countless times, his gaze fixed on the rails, Lucio had tried to work out a mathematical formula that would reveal the pattern of these hellish events. He factored in the frequency of trains, the quantity of night services and the number of operators driving at that time. But the experienced drivers knew that it didn't work that way. Anyone who had driven these trains for at least five or six years knew simply that the probabilities increased the later it got and the further the train was from its buffers. It was the second time that Lucio had gone against the regulations and requested to drive one of the trains that nobody wanted to operate. The first time had been on that cold winter night when he invited Verónica to come with him in the cabin to see for herself what was happening on the line. None of his friends had made any reference to the competition with the children, preferring to focus on the fact that he was inviting a girl to travel with him in the cabin. It was easier to deny reality.

Now Lucio was, of his own volition, going back to drive one of those trains. But this time there was no woman and no obvious reason for him to swap shifts. The subject was so taboo that his co-workers would rather not broach it than satisfy their curiosity about why Lucio was volunteering for the shift they all dreaded. They let him do as he pleased. They could rest easy, knowing that they would not have to work any nights this week or next.

VIII

They arranged to meet on Monday at half past twelve in the Trattoria della Zia Rosina, a fairly new restaurant on Honduras and Bonpland suggested by him. Verónica asked how she would recognize him, and Juan García's only response was to laugh. He said, "See you tomorrow," and hung up. Obviously García wouldn't invite her to his office, much less to his house. She needed to know his movements, though, to get him to incriminate himself. It was the only way of trapping him. She called Federico again, who made a weak attempt at remonstration.

"Your father's going to ask if I should be invoicing you or the magazine for my hours."

"Say that this work is pro bono, as the Yanks call it."

Verónica brought him up to speed on developments and asked if he could get her a device to record the conversation with Juan García.

"Brilliant idea," said Federico. "It'll never occur to him that you might be taping him."

"Can you think of something better, then?"

"Somebody comes into the restaurant a few minutes after you. He or she sees who's sitting at your table and marks that person for our men. We follow him discreetly, very discreetly. We track him down to his bunker and pass the info on to you."

"Do I have to do anything?"

"Not particularly. You can act offended when they check you to see if you're wearing a recording device."

She arrived punctually. She wasn't nervous. On the contrary, she felt that she had scored a victory in coaxing García out of his lair. If she hadn't put pressure on Rivero and Palma, she would never have seen his face. And he had called her himself. To intimidate her? To make her believe that he was innocent?

Entering the restaurant, she noticed that various tables were occupied, which struck her as surprising, because it was still early for lunch. She looked around the room and saw that she was being hailed from a table where a couple was sitting. Verónica addressed herself to the male:

"Juan García?"

"Apologies for any confusion," said the woman, who was about fifty. "Would you come with me to the ladies' room?"

Verónica didn't raise an objection. Nor did she protest when the woman patted her down and passed a strange apparatus over her body.

"Don't be alarmed. It's a scanner. It's for your security."

"Mine?"

"Of course. If you recorded Señor García, there would be terrible consequences for you."

They came out of the bathroom and the woman accompanied her to another table, where a man was sitting on his own, reading the menu. He looked up at her arrival.

"Verónica Rosenthal, what a pleasure to meet you," said García and, motioning her to sit down, he continued: "How is your father? The Rosenthal practice has handled various cases in which we were involved."

"Do you know my father?"

"Let's say that my lawyers know him. And they admire him. Dr Rosenthal is a great jurist."

The waiter brought her a menu. García asked if she would like wine, but she opted for still water. García acted like a wonderful host.

"From the menu I would recommend one of the house pasta specialities, *malfatti all'uso nostro* – absolutely delicious."

"I'd rather have a Caesar salad."

García made an observation that was supposed to be funny about watching one's figure and how hard he found it to resist the temptation of good food. The man was sturdy, but nobody would have called him fat. When he had stood up to greet her, Verónica noticed that he was a little taller than her and wore an expensive suit, possibly Armani or Hugo Boss. He must be nearly sixty years old, but his dark skin and hair made him seem younger. García asked for asparagus with Parmesan, and a little prosciutto and provolone cheese to share. He also decided against alcohol. He poured her a glass of water from the bottle that was on the table.

"Rivero and Palma are very worried after those visits you paid them."

"So they should be."

García shook his head as he selected a slice of prosciutto.

"They're responsible for a perverse and deadly game," Verónica continued.

"You need evidence to say that sort of thing."

"And I have it. Enough to put them both inside. And their accomplices too."

Her lunch companion sighed deeply, as though he were tired of endlessly delivering the same lesson.

"Circumstantial evidence. Nothing that a good lawyer couldn't disprove before an easily influenced judge. And most of them are easily influenced. Just ask your father. Look, there are three justice systems. The courts, which take years to pass sentence. Journalism, which decides what is good or bad and hands down condemnation from its newspapers or broadcasters with total impunity. How often have allegations made in a magazine later not been corroborated in the courts? But by then the magazines have sold their copies, their advertising space, and they move on to the next thing."

"Journalists simply place the facts before readers, for their consideration."

"That's a lie. But we haven't come here to talk about your profession, which of course is a very worthy and respectable one."

"You said that there are three kinds of justice, and you named only two. I don't think that the last one is taking the law into your own hands."

"Ah, no, of course not. If all of us decided to settle our own scores we'd live in a constant state of war. There is a third kind of justice, which involves acting discreetly in order to allow the other two kinds – the courts and media, that is – to do their job."

"I don't quite understand."

"It's easy. That's why I've invited you here. To negotiate." He picked up a folder from the chair beside him and put it on one side of the table.

"I haven't come to negotiate."

"Wait until you see what's on offer. Palma. I can give you Palma. This folder, which is for you, contains all the evidence of how the Undersecretary of Housing and Planning for the Buenos Aires city government manages his funds irregularly. How properties and money are given in exchange for all kinds of services, some, needless to say, absolutely illegal."

"You're handing over one of your men to me?"

"Ah no, I don't have any men – or women – nor do I hand anyone over. I have proof of a crime and I turn to a young but brave journalist so that she can write a brilliant article and start a process that must surely end in the courts. We all win: citizens, the state, journalism, and you."

"Palma is not the only person responsible. You and Rivero are too."

"Verónica, you are very innocent. Apart from anything else, Rivero couldn't even be responsible for a bottom-division soccer team. And I am just one small link in the chain. Do you appreciate the metaphor? There is a chain made up of links. You cut out a link, but the chain simply attaches to the next link and continues being a chain. It never breaks. It may get smaller, but it won't break."

Verónica didn't feel like arguing any more. Without speaking, she waited to see if Juan García had anything more to say. He also seemed to be waiting for her to speak. Eventually, he was the one who broke the silence.

"Look, you think that you know, but you're wrong. Nothing that you envisage is going to play out as you hope. That's why I am being very generous with you. This is my proposal. You get Palma on a silver platter and you forget about everything else. You could get a great article out of it."

"As I said, García, I didn't come to negotiate."

Verónica stood up and picked up her bag.

"I'm very sorry that you've hardly touched your salad. And I'm sorry, too, that you failed to grasp how important it was for you to accept my offer. Ah, one other thing. Tell the boys who are waiting outside not to waste their time by following me."

Verónica came out of the restaurant much more confused than she was prepared to admit. She had tried to remain dignified but felt her arguments foundering against García's certainty. After walking a few blocks towards the underground station, she stopped and called Fede.

"The guy knows that we're planning to follow him. Cancel everything that isn't strictly necessary."

"Vero, stick to the writing and keep out of my work. I'll call you in a few hours."

Even Federico seemed more confident than she was. Something wasn't right. A lot of things weren't right. Unfortunately, she couldn't identify them or, for that matter, act on them.

She went to the newsroom. Her boss had shown commendable patience all this time, letting her take off as many days as she needed. She understood that Verónica needed that time to push forward with the investigation. From time to time Patricia asked how it was all going, or Verónica herself brought her up to date with some new development.

She decided not to tell Patricia about what had just happened in the trattoria, but insisted again that they reserve the next edition's cover story for her.

That Monday should have been a quiet day at work: reheat a couple of wire stories, write some short pieces and spend the rest of the time pinning down details of her investigation. Patricia was tearing her hair out because nobody was available to cover something for a last-minute piece. She asked the Politics editor if he could spare her the section's intern. The editor said that was fine, so long as she bore in mind that the intern couldn't write to save her life. What Patricia needed was someone to bring back the information.

"If you weren't busy on your story," she told Verónica, "I'd have sent you."

"It must be a twisted story, if I'm the one who springs to mind."

"No, it's the usual stuff. Another attack by the Chinese mafia."

"It's always difficult to find anything out in those cases."

"But you would have written me a nice colour piece. A neighbourhood convulsed by the death of their Chinese shopkeeper, who they bought milk and cookies from every day. Actually, two shopkeepers. The wire says that two of them died. In Villa Lugano."

Something inside Verónica signalled alarm. She looked on the wire for crime news. Under the keywords "murder" and "mafia" was the story about what had happened in the south of the city. The wire said that two Chinese men had been shot dead in a supermarket on Zuviría and Albariño. That the suspects had burst in and started firing. Police sources pointed to an attack by the so-called Chinese mafia because nothing had been stolen apart from the security camera recordings, meaning that the assailants could not be recognized. Witnesses at the scene said that there were four men in the gang and that at least two of them did not appear to be Asian, leading police to speculate that the Chinese mafia was contracting local hitmen. The dead men were named as Xian Lusin, known in the neighbourhood as Julián, and Luo Binyuan, whom locals called Víctor.

"Julián," Verónica said to herself. "Julián," she repeated. She read the wire story again and the only word she saw was *Julián*. She made her way to the bathroom as quickly as she could. She washed her face to cover up her crying. Luciana, one of the designers, came into the lavatories and saw her looking so distressed that she asked how she could help.

"I had an argument with my boyfriend," Verónica explained, hoping to be left alone. Luciana said something innocuous but soothing and went into one of the toilet cubicles.

After she had composed herself she returned to her desk. They had killed Julián and another Chinese man. She must tell Rafael. No, she couldn't tell him. Rafael would go running over there and there was no doubt that, if they had gone there, they must also be looking for him and for that compromising recording. But Federico had the recording and had already seen the murderers' faces. They were too late to do anything about that. All they had achieved was vengeance on Julián for having defended Rafael. They had failed to intercept the video evidence. She shouldn't tell Rafael. At least not today. It was a relief, at least, to think that Federico had the recording they were looking for.

Juan García is a predator out for blood, Verónica thought. I have to keep calm, she told herself. Julián's death was a body blow, so shocking that she couldn't think clearly. She wasn't being lucid – she had not even said anything to Patricia, who would surely have come to some conclusion that Verónica could not yet see. She was committing some grave error of judgement that could cost her her life, or Rafael's, and perhaps both.

X

On Mondays, Rivero limited soccer practice to a few informal games, with minimal direction from him. The boys simply formed teams and played. Rivero had decided to make two combined teams, mixing the boys from Dientes' division with the ones from El Peque's. The friends had ended up playing against one another, as was often the case when they played soccer in a square or a park. Jonathan, the new boy, was in El Peque's team. He played well, he knew how to control the ball and he was a good tackler.

Dientes was thinking that whoever was going to compete against him on the tracks was not in the match. They must be keeping him focussed, like with soccer players before an important game. He, being new, got thrown in at the deep end. He didn't mind – he knew that he could have won anyway. Everything Supergirl had said about Rafael was right, but he still would have liked a chance to compete and beat his rival. Now that he knew that Supergirl had his back, though, he preferred the idea of being a hero, of seeing Rivero punished for the deaths of the other boys.

When they had finished training, they all went to the bar to buy a big Coca-Cola. They put their money in and asked the new guy working there to sell them a bottle. Nobody liked Rafael's replacement. He wouldn't give them so much as a potato chip, even if he saw them wilting from hunger. And he always looked miserable.

Dientes took a long drink from the Coke. He was in the middle of burping when he saw Rivero calling him to one side. He went over to him.

"Champ, there's a change of plan. The competition is going to be today."

"Wasn't it tomorrow?"

"That's what I'm saying. We've changed the day. It's supposed to rain tomorrow, and we don't want you to catch a cold. Is your mum at home?"

"No, she's in the hospital with my sick grandmother."

"Has she got a mobile?"

"Yes."

"Call her and tell her that a chance came up to play a game at River's home ground. That afterwards someone from the club will drive you back home."

Rivero offered the boy his mobile and Dientes had no option but to call his mother and repeat the excuse that Rivero had fabricated. He spoke to his mother, but he was thinking of Supergirl. She wasn't coming until the next day to look after him. Even though he had been wanting to go track-jumping all this time, he didn't want to any more. No, he didn't want to jump. But he couldn't go back, either. Supergirl wouldn't forgive him for being a coward. He had to go anyway, however scared he was.

To make matters worse, Rivero wouldn't leave him on his own for a minute. He had called one of the boys from the opposing team, Jonathan, and had said the same thing to him about the change of date. So Jonathan must be the one Dientes would be competing against. He was taller and he seemed faster. In the distance he spotted El Peque, who was waiting so that they could walk home together.

"Rivero, can I go to the bathroom?"

"OK, but be quick."

Dientes walked towards the bathroom and on the way gestured to El Peque to go with him.

"Change of plan. The competition is today. I'm playing against Jonathan."

"I reckoned it would be Jonathan. But why today? Supergirl is waiting for us tomorrow. There won't be anyone there to trap Rivero today."

"That's why, Peque, the success of the superteam depends on you. You have to let Supergirl know that I'm going to be on the tracks today."

"And how can I let her know?"

"Oh – no idea."

The days had started getting longer. Spring gave way to the first bouts of heat, tempered by an annoying afternoon wind. A thread of diurnal light stretched across the horizon. Lucio saw the sunset – on every night shift that he was driving the train – as signalling the start of his participation in a crazed game of *Jeopardy*: one in which he had to travel from a point in Buenos Aires to the city of Moreno with the certainty that at some moment in the journey two boys would appear in front of him, defying fate. He would have to brake hard, doing everything in his power not to hit them while knowing that that was futile, that he was completely at the mercy of the children and whether or not they took pity on him and jumped to the sides of the track before the train crushed them. "Fucking little bastards," he snarled while he fixed his gaze on the furthest possible point of those empty tracks. Still empty.

The hours passed without incident. Perhaps it won't be today, he thought, engulfed by a darkness that was illuminated only by light from the train. Perhaps it would be the next day, or Wednesday, or Friday. Or perhaps Lucio was inching closer to the inevitable. It was a new moon tonight, dark and starless thanks to the clouds that covered the sky. He had just one full circuit to do before that day's shift finished. The few passengers who had alighted at Castelar were replaced by others who would continue on to Morón, Liniers or Plaza Once. The train pulled away, over the crossing, then advancing towards Ituzaingó at maximum speed. In thirty-five minutes they should arrive at Once. Lucio didn't like moonless nights.

17   *Full Speed Ahead*

I

He got angrily into the car. Neither the chauffeur, nor the bodyguard, nor his assistant spoke a single word on the way home. He was in a foul mood, after having to negotiate a route through the kitchen, a service corridor and then a courtyard, so that he could leave by the back door of the Trattoria della Zia Rosina. The conversation with the journalist had annoyed him too. The tone of that woman who thought that she had everything under control would be irritating to anyone and much more so to him, who was not used to sparring with journalists or women. He had offered a fair deal and she had refused to accept it. He didn't like wasting time, and however many minutes he had spent in that place had been too many.

The problem was that she wasn't a woman but a girl, reacting like a rebellious teenager to a strict father. A misguided girl. The trains were a small part of his operation. She imagined that he was anxious to resolve this problem and thought the trains and the kids kept him awake at night. What a deluded idiot. If he had learned anything over the last twenty years, it was that the smallest business in a person's portfolio should concern him as much as the biggest. That was why he wanted to be done with this journalist and her suspicions. She wouldn't stop him doing anything. If he felt like it, he could get together a gang of kids tomorrow and make them jump with parachutes. If he wanted, he could immediately erase all trace of what had been happening over the last few years on the railway in the western zone. But the journalist had stuck her nose in where she shouldn't, Rivero had chosen the wrong guy as an employee and Palma had kept money that wasn't for him. The three of them together were less dangerous than a boil on the butt, but they were still an irritant. Like a boil, they needed lancing.

He made a call from the car, giving the order for them to go to the Chinese supermarket immediately and liquidate the person who had tried to report them to the police.

Had news that the competition was going to be on Tuesday somehow got out? That fool Rivero wouldn't be able to give him a straight answer. He was incapable of arriving at any conclusions on his own. He must not know. And if one of the two kids had mentioned it to his parents or to someone else who had tipped off the journalist? It was almost impossible, but that "almost" was enough to make him uncomfortable. He went by his instincts, which had so often got him out of trouble.

"Rivero, change the day. It's today."

"But, boss —"

"Just shut up. That journalist must have found out about tomorrow. So it's today. Let everybody know. Take the kids there."

"Whatever you say, boss."

"And don't let the kids go home first or anything like that. There mustn't be a single leak. Understand?"

Two out of three. There was still Palma. He'd get to that. No need to spill blood if there was another way to sort it out. There was something worse than death for Palma, and that was to see an end to his political career, to his swanky life in the gated community in Canning. Prison and poverty. That was what Palma was getting. Pity the journalist hadn't accepted his deal. He and she could have saved themselves a lot of unpleasantness.

He decided not to spend another minute on the matter that day. A couple of hours later, though, he received a phone call that got him worrying again.

"The lads are back. Negative. The hippie wasn't there. The lads got payback with the Chinese."

"That's their business."

"But there's some good news. They brought back the recording from the security cameras. I think we know where the hippie is."

"You think, or you know?"

"On the recording from Friday you can see him come out of the building with the journalist."

"What do you mean with the journalist?"

"The one who went to see Rivero. They got into a taxi and went off together like two little lovebirds."

"She must have him hidden in her apartment. So that was the important witness. She thinks she's got the ace of spades. We'll change it for the four of clubs."

"OK. And if she's with him in the apartment?"

"Then we kill two birds with one stone."

"She's a journalist, though."

"I don't give a fuck."

11

Their names don't deserve to be remembered: 1 and 2 were sitting in the front. 3 and 4 were behind. The car was an Audi A4 1.9, a bit old (2003) but in perfectly good order. The colour was metallic black and there were 75,000 miles on the clock. The wheel rims were original with Dunlop SP Sport Maxx GT tyres, changed a thousand miles back, multitronic automatic gearbox, sequential with shift paddles on the wheel, turbo diesel. Electric sunroof, dual-zone climate control, ABS, six airbags, cruise control, automatic headlight activation, onboard computer with automatic sensor and instrument check. It also had an up-to-date safety certificate of the kind required by all vehicles licensed in the province of Buenos Aires. Their car was the best thing about these men.

1, 2, 3 and 4 were small-time hoodlums, exclusively dedicated to causing damage by injury, intimidation or murder. That was their core business. Robbery was a sideline for them, never the main event. Their actions were well defined.

All four knew how to use weapons and pulverize an opponent. At some point they had dreamed of being karate masters or kick-boxing champions. They started out as bouncers in a nightclub in some corner of the capital and they were recruited by Dr 0 to form a task force. Dr 0 had a good eye, as good as a soccer talent scout. He knew how to spot the obedient savage beneath the mountain of muscles.

The four men spent much of the day in the gym, leaving it only to work – in other words to maim, intimidate, kill. When Dr 0 told them to go to the Villa Soldati neighbourhood and execute someone who had betrayed them, they didn't need further instruction: traitors get beaten to a pulp, and then killed.

They didn't like failure, they demanded a lot of themselves. Rather than leave a job half-done, they would beg Dr 0 to let them finish it. This time, they didn't just want it wrapped up, they wanted revenge. Along with the traitor they would take out the karate master, the Chinese *karateka* (even though two of them had studied karate, they didn't differentiate between a karate kick and a kung fu one).

Dr 0 asked for patience, a few days, until the boss decided to act. On Monday at half past one in the afternoon the authorization came, and at four o'clock they climbed gratefully into the Audi and sped towards the south of the city. It was no hardship to leave uneaten some sweetbreads that they had ordered from the grill on the corner near their gym.

This time they parked the car at the door to the supermarket. 3 and 4 shot the Chinese *karateka* who was standing at the till. A Chinese woman ran towards his prostrate body. Amid shouting and wailing, 1 and 2 headed towards the back of the shop. After entering the storeroom, they checked all the rooms leading off it without finding the traitor. Another Chinese man appeared, with a knife, and pounced on 3, who shot him in the face while 2 fired three times to finish him off. They went back into the shop, where everyone had disappeared apart from the woman, who was clinging to the *karateka*, crying. It never even crossed their minds to ask where the traitor was. Nobody had suggested that they do that. They simply removed the CPU from where the recordings from the security cameras were stored. Dr 0 had asked them to take it to him. Not three minutes passed between the time they parked the car and the time they got back into it and drove off towards Dr 0's office. Afterwards they would go back to the grill to order a few more portions of tender sweetbreads, freshly made.

III

If anybody had asked her what she had done between the moment that she had heard about Julián's death and the time of Federico's call, two hours later, Verónica would not have been sure what to answer. She might have finished writing the piece Patricia had asked her for; or perhaps she had gone into loop mode, obsessively rereading the news item about the attack on the Chinese supermarket. Two hours passed this way. And so it might have continued, into the evening, until there was no other journalist in the newsroom, if her mobile hadn't rung. It was Federico. He was upset. He had just heard about the deaths in the supermarket.

"I was going to call you to say that we managed to follow García and had some information, but this news about the murders is terrible. Where are you?"

"In the newsroom."

"Are you planning to stay there? Is Rafael with you?"

"Why would he be? He's at the apartment."

"Verónica, the gang has got the recording from the supermarket."

"So? We have the copy that shows them beating up Rafael."

"They've got you on tape, you taking Rafael back with you. These guys were looking for your witness. They must be on their way to your place."

How could she have been such an idiot?

Rafael.

"Get the police over there right now," she shouted at Federico.

"I don't know who's in charge of that district."

"Speak to my dad, get him onto the Minister for the Interior. We need a patrol car at the entrance to the building right away."

"That's not easy to arrange. You call Rafael and tell him to get out of the apartment."

"Now, Fede, a patrol car, it's urgent."

"Stay right where you are."

Verónica hung up without answering. There was silence in the newsroom and everyone was looking at her. She asked:

"Who's got a car here?"

Álex Vilna had brought his. He offered to take her wherever she needed to go. Verónica's response left no room for any negotiation.

"Give me the keys."

Álex told her which parking lot he had left the car in and she ran out of the newsroom, leaving her colleagues to look at each other with consternation.

She called Rafael's mobile. No answer.

She ran along the sidewalk, dodging pedestrians and slowing down only to repeat the call. Rafael still wasn't answering.

She tried again, two, three, four times. She called her own landline to see if he would pick up, but it went straight to the answering machine.

Verónica drove out of the parking lot without asking if there was anything to pay. Given the traffic at that time of day, she could get to the apartment in twenty minutes. Ignoring traffic regulations, she might get it down to fifteen or sixteen.

She also had to keep calling him. But Rafael didn't answer. Where could he be? She imagined the worst, that the gang had arrived and murdered him. No, it couldn't be that. She would have found out. The doorman would have called her. Marcelo. She searched for him in Contacts and called him.

"Marcelo, it's urgent. Rafael, the guy who lives with me, is in danger. Some hitmen are on their way there to kill him. I can't reach him. Please go in with the key I gave you to my apartment and make sure, if he's there, that he leaves, that he goes anywhere but that he gets out. It's urgent."

"I'll call you when I've got him out of there."

Verónica hung up, threw the phone onto the passenger seat and accelerated past another car. She swung into the cycle lane then crossed over the avenue after the lights had gone red, paying no attention to the honking of drivers around her. Thirteen minutes after leaving the parking lot she was only three blocks from her building.

IV

None of the four knew Juan García. They didn't even know that they worked for him. They belonged to Dr 0's team. They were professionals, and never asked why they had to do this or that job. They carried out orders. To perfection. That day they had already done a job, but the results had not been as expected. It was true that they had managed to take revenge on the Chinese *karateka*, but the traitor had escaped. Now they had simply to remain vigilant and wait for a call from Dr 0. That happened a few hours later. He gave them an address in the neighbourhood of Villa Crespo. It was an apartment block. They had to break the lock as silently as possible and go up to apartment A on the second floor. There they should find the traitor and a woman. They had to liquidate them both and return to base as quickly as possible. They must not kill anyone else they came across, unless that person was trying to impede their mission. Dr 0 recommended that they avoid a bloodbath. That they finish off the traitor and the woman and then come straight back.

The checked that their weapons were in order. Number 3 put the address into the GPS and 2 climbed into the passenger seat. Numbers 1 and 4 sat behind. Number 3 liked listening to the radio as he drove. The other three said nothing when the voice of a Cordoban reporter blared out of the speakers. They liked to travel in silence, focussing on the task ahead.

"I'll call you when I've got him out of there."

That was the last thing Marcelo said before Verónica rang off. He had recently woken up from a siesta when she called. He was on his own, and had been about to make himself a maté. After listening to Verónica's instruction, for a moment he stared at the phone in his hand. When he stood up he discovered that his legs were shaking. He thought that he would immediately go downstairs to warn the young man who was in Verónica's apartment, but for that he would need the keys. He had those in a box that he kept with his tools. Verónica had mentioned something about murderers. In other words, when he went down there, his life would also be at risk. He went to the bedroom. On top of the wardrobe was an unlocked safe. Inside that safe were papers, a box of ammunition and a gun. It was a revolver that used .22 calibre bullets and which he had bought while still working as the doorman in another building. He had never used it. For four years he hadn't touched or even thought about it. He loaded the gun and bullets fell onto the floor; he had to grope for them under the bed. He couldn't go out with a gun in his hand and he wasn't brave enough to tuck it into his waistband, like plain-clothes police officers or criminals. He put it into one of the pockets of the first jacket that came to hand.

Out on the landing, Marcelo pressed the elevator call button and saw that it was on the first floor. He wouldn't get down to Verónica's any quicker by taking the stairs, so he waited for the elevator to come up. It occurred to him that he could go straight down to the ground floor and call on the intercom while monitoring the people going in and out of the building, but if Verónica had called him it must be because the guy was not responding to calls. Perhaps he was asleep, as he himself had been a minute ago, or had gone out for a stroll. If that was the case, he would go down to the lobby and wait for him at the door.

He decided to stop the elevator on the third floor and walk down one flight of stairs. He didn't want any surprises when the doors opened. There was no sound to be heard on the landing. He walked down, listening intently for any noises. He went to Verónica's apartment. He didn't ring the bell but just opened the door with the key and went straight in. There was nobody in the living room. He could hear some kind of noise coming from the bathroom.

"Young man!" he called, because he couldn't remember the name of Verónica's house guest.

The lad came out of the bathroom with just a towel wrapped around him. He had shaving foam on his face and a razor in his hand.

"What are you doing here?" he asked, surprised and suspicious.

"Verónica sent me. There's no time to lose. Some men are coming here to kill you."

"What? Kill me?"

Marcelo gestured at to him to be quiet. He had heard the sound of the elevator coming up and stopping at the second floor. Several people must have got out, because they took a while to close the door. Without saying anything, he walked towards the young man and took his arm, still wet from the shower. They couldn't lock themselves inside the bedroom or the bathroom. Silently he led him over towards the balcony. The young man looked at him, terrified.

Marcelo opened the balcony door and pushed him outside, without taking his eyes off the front door. He took out his gun and pointed it at the door.

"Jump," he said, through gritted teeth.

"I'm naked," protested the young man, who still had the towel wrapped around his waist.

"Hang from the balcony. It's them."

It was the last thing he said before the lock broke and a man appeared at the door, followed by several others. The young man climbed over the railing and just let go. His scream coincided with the sound of Marcelo's gun firing at the man who had been coming in but then, surprised, took a step back. The second man reached past the first and fired his gun. Marcelo felt his left shoulder burning. He dropped his weapon and clutched his arm. Now the men were coming towards him. With no time to think, he followed Verónica's friend, throwing himself heavily over the balcony and onto the sidewalk. He landed beside the young man, who was still lying on the ground screaming in pain. So much screaming should have brought people running, but there seemed to be nobody around. The few passing cars accelerated so as not to have to stop. They were the only two there.

"Call the police! Help us!" Marcelo cried, even though he could see nobody who might hear him.

One of the thugs had now appeared on the balcony. The young man had dragged himself to the edge of the sidewalk and was protected underneath the same balcony. Above him, the hitman took aim, but from there he could only see Marcelo. The doorman thought then that he was about to be shot, but nothing happened: the hitman disappeared off the balcony. Marcelo tried to take his chance to stand up, but he couldn't. The young man was dragging himself with an exasperating slowness. Marcelo couldn't even do that and, anyway, he felt as though he might faint at any moment. He almost wanted to. He could see that the men were already on the ground floor in the hall and that they were coming towards the door. They were coming for him and the young man. Marcelo no longer had the energy to keep his eyes open and he fell into a deep sleep.

VI

She was only three blocks away. Miraculously, Álex Vilna's car had made it this far without a single scratch. Her mobile had not rung, from which she deduced that Marcelo had still not managed to get Rafael out of the apartment. When she was, by her calculation, only thirty seconds away from her building, she ran into a crowd of children coming out of school at the end of the day. Parents were double-parked and children were recklessly crossing the road so that cars had to stop and reverse. Verónica leaned on her horn like one possessed. As soon as she had managed to pass the human tide, she made a turn and stopped the car a block and a half from her home. Something strange must be happening at the street entrance because, just as he was about to turn in, a driver in front changed his mind, backed up and drove straight on. That added a few seconds' delay to Verónica, who leaned on her horn again. She swerved into the street, making Álex Vilna's tyres screech. Her building was fifty yards ahead, on the left. Ten yards before she reached it, she slammed on the brakes. The scene in front of her was like something from a nightmare. The first sight that met her eyes was Marcelo's body stretched out on the sidewalk, unconscious or dead. Further on was Rafael, who was slowly moving away from the building, dragging himself along like a wounded animal. Verónica tried to open the door to jump out and help him, but her seat belt held her back. Sometimes, inanimate objects seem to have our own best interests at heart. The belt held her back and, in those seconds that she was trying to extricate herself from it, she saw some men (three? four?) come out of the building with all the calm of people who know themselves to be in full control of a situation.

Paying no attention to the injured doorman, the four men made straight for Rafael. The scene in front of Verónica showed Marcelo lying nearly at the edge of the sidewalk and the men walking towards Rafael, who had almost dragged himself as far as the next building.

And no police anywhere to be seen. And nobody on the streets or on the sidewalks.

Verónica closed the door again, put the car in first gear and accelerated.

She didn't think about what she was going to do. At that moment all she wanted was to get the men away from Rafael.

As she drew level with the hitmen, Verónica turned the car in towards the sidewalk, skirted Marcelo with surgical precision and crashed into the men with Álex Vilna's car. When she felt contact with the first bodies (the two who were closest to her) she didn't brake. Those two men fell onto their accomplices. The car and the gang smashed into the glazed entrance of Verónica's building, glass shattering on contact with the bodies and the car as it drove over them. Only then did she brake, or think she must have braked. The engine cut out.

Verónica didn't close her eyes. Just as she hadn't when she had seen the boys standing on the tracks of the Sarmiento line. She heard shouts, she had the impression of hitting something more solid than a body, perhaps a rock or a wall. But they were the bodies of the people she had already run over and who no longer screamed or, if they did, she no longer heard them. The car had come to rest at an angle, as though there was something solid and heavy under one of its tyres. Then came the sound of police sirens. Verónica undid her seat belt and turned the key again in the ignition.

Despite everything that had happened, the engine started. In the rear-view mirror she saw patrol cars surrounding the area while uniformed officers positioned themselves behind the vehicles with their guns drawn. Somebody shouted at her to stop. She put the car in reverse and went back a couple of yards, crushing, for a second time, the bodies under the car, while the building's frontage collapsed entirely and glass rained down. It was like reversing in a storm, down a street made of irregular stones. The police shouted louder at her to stop and get out of the car. Only then did she turn off the engine and get out with her hands in the air. She thought of shouting "journalist" or something to identify herself, but instead she said loudly:

"Call an ambulance, idiots."

18   *The Death Train*

I

Her eyes were closed but she wasn't sleeping, or even dozing. She just wanted to see black. Somebody opened the door but must have thought that she was asleep.

"Upstairs, señora, they've come to get you."

Verónica had arrived at the police station an hour previously. They had led her into a small office, where a police officer took her statement about what had happened. During this procedure various people came in and out, looking for the officer. She supposed that Federico had arrived, but she didn't see him. She asked after Rafael and Marcelo. At first they had no news for her, but then a policewoman came in and told her that both men had been admitted to the Hospital Álvarez. That one had a bullet wound in his arm and that the other had broken the tibia and fibula in his right leg. Nothing too serious.

The officer taking her statement made her sign a series of papers and left her in the office until someone came to pick her up. To her surprise, her father was outside, with Federico a respectful few feet behind him.

"I spoke to the public prosecutor and you have to go and provide a longer version of your statement on Thursday. How are you feeling?"

"I've got a splitting headache."

"Darling —"

"No sermons, Dad."

"I just want to know how you are."

"I've had better days."

She needed to be more careful with her father. While his concern was genuine and she had a duty to allay his worry, there was also no reason for her to drag herself down the road of guilt and explanations.

"Thanks, Dad. Thanks for coming and sorting all this out."

"I have to get back to the office. Federico is going to take you back to your apartment. You need to rest. What happened was terrible, but you must be strong."

"I'll try."

"Let's have lunch tomorrow."

"Wednesday or Thursday would be better. I'll call you."

The three of them left the police station together and said goodbye at the door. Verónica walked with Federico to the parking lot. She said:

"I have to go to the Hospital Álvarez."

Federico nodded without saying anything. They got into the car and Verónica felt her body flooded with the sensations of a few hours earlier. A combination of hatred for the people who had killed Julián and who wanted to kill Rafael, revulsion at what she herself had done, a mixture of disgust and relief. In the police station they had told her that two of the men were dead and that the other two had been seriously injured. She felt no remorse, guilt or regret. Just a physical disgust. A desire to be someone else, or for someone else to have done what she had dared to do. Federico's voice took her out of these thoughts.

"When I called you, I said that I had some news about Juan García."

A few weeks ago, Federico had meant nothing more to her than an episode from her distant past. A boy she had seen grow up but who would always remain for her a delayed adolescent, affectionate in his manner but clumsy in bed. She had thought of him as a kind of brother. A younger brother (even though he was a few months older than her), with whom she had once had an incestuous fling best forgotten. Now she was seeing him as he really was: somebody you could count on.

"Basically, García did know that we were there when you met him. And we didn't know that the restaurant had a back door opening onto another street. Now it just so happens that one of our guys wanted to go to the bathroom and walked to a bar that was round the corner and halfway down the block. When he came out of the bar he saw a Mercedes driving down the street parallel to the one where our people were waiting. Instinctively he walked to the next corner and saw the car stop more or less level with the restaurant. He told us and, just in case, we sent someone on a bike to keep a lookout and to start following the car, if necessary."

"And it was necessary."

"The guy came out of there, with a woman and a couple of goons. It wasn't easy to keep up with him. He had anti-follow techniques that our people hadn't seen before. But we managed to stay on his trail. The guy went into the carport of a building on Avenida República Árabe Siria and Cabello. A building built less than ten years ago. And here's the kicker: it's a place well known to the Rosenthal law firm."

"To my dad?"

"To the firm. Two years ago we were the local representatives for the state of Bavaria in an investigation into money laundering which involved Bavarian civil servants and businessmen from Germany, Russia, Israel and Argentina. There was a German company that was working directly with funds based here. The company was called Unmittelbare Zukunft. The local connection was difficult to uncover because a lot of the information we had came camouflaged with false addresses and names of people who didn't exist. But one of the accused parties was a company that imported agricultural machinery, based in that building. And another important point: that company has its headquarters in Posadas, the capital of Misiones. We'll be at the hospital soon so, to cut a long story short, our investigation almost came to nothing. We found some fall guys who had been used as frontmen, but we never got to the bottom of the story. For example, we couldn't establish the nexus between Misiones and Buenos Aires."

"The link."

"The link. I think if we dig through the dirt and look deeper into the Capitán Pavone case, and the Undersecretary for Housing's contacts, we might discover that Juan García is a money launderer – as well a pimp, a drug trafficker and child abuser."

"And money laundering tends to be the chief activity of that kind of person."

"And therefore the place it hurts him the most if you start interfering. You'll find everything I've told you in the glovebox. There isn't enough yet to put him behind bars, but it's a good start."

In the hospital they looked for Rafael and Marcelo's rooms. The doorman was on a high-dependency unit, because he had needed an operation to extract the bullet from his arm. Rafael, on the other hand, was on the ward, in a room shared with one other person. Visiting hours had finished, but Verónica went in anyway, while Federico distracted the nurse with random questions. She knocked on the door to his room and Rafael's quiet voice told her to come in.

He was lying with his plastered leg outside the sheets, watching some sports show on TV. Or perhaps it was his room mate who was watching it. Verónica walked up to the bed. She asked him how he felt and he said that nothing hurt any more, which was extraordinary considering all the injuries he had sustained over the last few days.

He thanked her for saving him.

She apologized for not having arrived earlier.

Neither would accept the other's courtesies. At that moment Verónica's phone started ringing. She didn't recognize the number but answered anyway.

"Are you my daddy's girlfriend?"

"Who's speaking?"

"Martina, Rafael's daughter. Are you his girlfriend?"

"Martina, what a coincidence. I'm with your daddy right now. How did you get my number?"

"It was stored in my grandmother's phone from when he called the other day…Wait a moment." She said something to another person who was with her. "Tell me, then. Are you his girlfriend?"

"No, of course not. Wait and I'll pass you on to your dad."

"No, you wait. Before you pass me on there's someone here who wants to speak to you."

Verónica stared, unblinking, at Rafael.

11

He ran, ran like the wind, like Bullseye in *Toy Story*, a movie he had seen at Dientes' house. They were a superteam but he had no superpower, not even that of flying very low. He needed to get home quickly and he could only use his skill at dodging people as though they were troublesome defenders. Besides, after running five blocks without pause he began to feel tired. He walked one block briskly, had a breather and started running again, but the second spurt only lasted three blocks. He slowed down for a few hundred yards then accelerated again. His legs began to feel very heavy.

He arrived home with his tongue sticking out and his heart pounding like the supporters' drum at a Nueva Chicago match. He desperately needed water but there was no time to lose. He went straight to Martina's apartment and banged on the door. Her grandmother opened it, saying that Martina was doing her homework and couldn't come out.

"I need to speak to her."

"It'll have to be later. She's got to finish her language homework because she got a bad mark last time."

"It's urgent."

"Not now, Peque."

"I need to tell her that I'm in love with her."

The grandmother looked at him as one might look at a Martian asking for a glass of wine.

"I'll call her."

Shortly afterwards Martina appeared.

"What's wrong with you?"

"Come." He grabbed her arm and pulled her some distance from the door. Between gasps for breath, he told her that she had to get in touch with the woman who had come to see them.

"Ah, her."

"Or with your dad."

"She told me I was very pretty. I don't trust her one bit."

"Martina, listen, I need to talk to your dad. Can you call him?"

Martina stood, thinking.

"Wait here." She went into the apartment and returned in less than a minute. "I stole my grandmother's mobile. Let's go up to the terrace."

El Peque climbed the stairs two at a time, while Martina calmly scrolled through the contacts, looking for her father's number. They settled into that corner of the roof that no adult ever came to – apart from Supergirl – and Martina dialled Rafael's number. There was no answer. She tried a few times and got the same result. El Peque started to panic. He had to let Supergirl know that the contest was that night, not the next day.

"It's a matter of life or death," he said.

"I've got an idea," Martina said, while she navigated the mobile's keypad. "When my dad called on Thursday, my grandmother said he'd done it from someone else's number. I bet it was that woman's."

"You think?"

"They must be going out or something, because otherwise you don't use someone else's phone. Wait, here in Accepted Calls there's a number that doesn't come up with anyone's name. Yes, it's a call from Thursday afternoon. I'll try it."

After listening to it ring for a few seconds, El Peque heard a voice at the other end of the line.

"Are you my daddy's girlfriend?"

What was Martina doing? Had she gone mad?

"Martina, Rafael's daughter. Are you his girlfriend?"

If she wasn't careful Supergirl would cut her off.

"It was stored in my grandmother's phone from when he called the other day."

"Martina, put me on, I need to speak to her," said El Peque, both pleading and angry at the same time.

"Wait," Martina brushed him away and listened to the voice at the other end before saying, "No, you wait. Before you pass me on there's someone here who wants to speak to you."

She gave the mobile to El Peque and made a gesture to him that he neither understood nor cared about, since it presumably had something to do with her father's romantic life.

"Hello, it's me, El Peque."

"Peque, how are you, is everything OK?"

"Everything's terrible. The contest has been moved to today. They took Dientes there straight from the club. You can still save him, right?"

III

It seemed very, very long ago, that morning when she had eaten breakfast absently flicking through the newspaper and thinking every so often that she was finally going to meet Juan García. It could have been a year ago, the lunch with the mafioso politician might have taken place a few months ago, the afternoon at the magazine was more like the fruit of a fitful dream, one of those of which you remember only a fragment, nothing more. And this day had been filled with stories that would take a lifetime to assimilate: her escapade in Álex Vilna's car, crossing the city with no respect for traffic lights or speed limits, or other road users; that dramatic encounter on the sidewalk outside her apartment with Marcelo – whom she had thought dead – and Rafael, who had seemed to be about to die; and the assassins who had never suspected that ten seconds later they would meet their own deaths. How long until this long day was over?

And now she had sent an eleven-year-old boy on a suicide mission with no protection. Federico's first response had been to make various phone calls consisting of brief but intense exchanges. While he spoke, he gestured to Verónica to walk with him. They returned to the parking lot. Federico looked in the boot for his briefcase and took some papers out of it; they were screenshots from Google Earth. The night was already very dark and it was hard to see in the weak light of the parking lot. They walked back to the hospital entrance and sat on one of the benches where patients waited for emergency treatment. Verónica watched her friend, feeling helplessly unable to resolve anything herself. Federico had dismissed her suggestion that they warn the Sarmiento railway authority. He told her that they wouldn't pay her any attention, even if the Minister of the Interior were to make a special intervention. Only when Federico had finished the last of his calls did he turn to Verónica, who had picked up fragments of the conversations. He stood up and spread the Google Earth printouts over the bench.

"What you can see reproduced here is the entire trajectory of the Sarmiento line, from Plaza Miserere to the city of Moreno. Along twenty-six miles of track, there are 175 places, in total, where the line crosses streets. It sounds like too many to watch. But that's not necessarily the case. Ramiro – our new intern from Ituzaingó – and I did some intelligence work on this. There are some crossings in areas where it would be impossible to hold the competition because there are bridges over the line, for example, or railway crossings, or very well-lit avenues, or busy streets. Then there are the places where a child has already died or been injured. They never return to those places. For some reason they don't use them again. So, if we eliminate all those, there are only eight remaining where the competition could be held."

"Just eight?"

"Eight, in a twenty-two-mile stretch. Three in the capital and five in Greater Buenos Aires. If the contest is held in the capital it won't be too difficult to find out when they arrive at the designated place with the children. I've just spoken to the security people we work with at the practice, and we can put those three places under surveillance."

"There are still five others."

"Those are crossings located in Padua, Castelar, Ituzaingó, Morón and Haedo. It would seem that these guys have exhausted all the possible sites between Haedo and Ciudadela and that the only crossings left are well to the west. I spoke to people from the National Child Protection Service and also with an appellate judge from Morón. It's possible they may be able to send specialist police teams to Padua, Castelar and Ituzaingó."

"Can we trust them?"

"The cops? It's all we have."

Verónica looked at him, asking for more precision.

"'All we have' isn't enough."

"Look, if this ends badly I can assure you that no cop from that team will be able to continue working in the police force. They'll be cleaning out the animals at the zoo."

"The other day you said that a patrol car could get anywhere in six minutes."

"With some advance planning, yes. It's harder in a hurry. There are two places which the police in those districts would struggle to reach quickly: Morón and Haedo. Strangely, they're the two most central crossings. You'd think that if one of the other three points could be ruled out, a patrol car could get just as easily to Haedo as to Morón, but it would take fifteen minutes."

"Come on, then."

"Where to?"

"To Haedo and Morón. How long will it take to reach them from here?"

"However long it takes us to get to the freeway – then we go down Calle Dolores Prats as far as Avenida Rivadavia, then either turn back towards Haedo or continue towards Morón. Reckon on a bit more than half an hour, if we put our foot down."

"Let's go right now, then. On the way I'm going to call one of my sources to see if he can warn the drivers who are on duty tonight."

IV

Sometimes he believed that it wouldn't be the boys who appeared in front of him on the tracks, but Verónica. Verónica and the flowery dress he had seen in that dream on Saturday. Would she reappear in his dreams? Would he see Verónica's dress fly through the air? Would he see her step towards the edge of the platform before jumping, just at the moment his train passed? Was she capable of something like that? He remembered the story of something that had happened ten years ago. There was a young driver who was shortly to be married but, at the last moment, changed his mind. The fiancée didn't take this at all well and one day they came to tell the driver that she had tried to commit suicide by taking an overdose, but that she had survived. He went to visit her in hospital. She spoke harshly to him and told him two things: that she was pregnant, and that the next time he saw her she would be standing in front of the train. And she was as good as her word. One day the girl appeared on the crossing at Caballito station and threw herself onto the tracks under the train he was driving towards Plaza Miserere. The poor fellow didn't come back to work and was never heard of again.

Verónica was not one of those girls. Who *was* Verónica? As if his thoughts had the power of invocation, his mobile

343

began to ring. The screen said VÍCTOR R, which was how he had saved Verónica's number. The coincidence of her calling just as he was thinking about her meant he must be dreaming after all. Besides, she never called him.

"I'm sorry to call you, but it's urgent."

"I can speak and drive at the same time."

"Are you on the train?"

He stopped the train at Castelar, opened the doors and made sure the platform was clear before closing the doors again and pulling away.

"I'm on a shift. I've nearly finished."

"Lucio, what I have to tell you is very important: the competition with the boys on the tracks is today."

"How do you know?"

"I found out. It's vital that you warn the other drivers and, better still, get them to stop the trains."

"That's impossible. So those fucking kids are going to be in front of my train today."

"It's a mafia, Lucio. There are politicians, businessmen, important people involved in this. I know who's finding the kids and how they get them there."

"Whereabouts are they going to be, Verónica?"

"I haven't been able to find that out."

Verónica, Verónica, Verónica, Verónica, Verónica. Speaking her name, he felt desire all over again. He heard her speak and all he wanted was to have her in his arms.

"You were the one who put me on to this."

"For good, or bad?"

"For good. Knowing you has been for good, Lucio. Call me when you get to Plaza Once."

"Vero, I want to see you."

"Lucio."

"Seriously. I mean it."

"Call me when you get to the terminal. And be on your guard."

They ended their conversation as the train reached Morón. So the death trains and Verónica had been brought together again. That secret life where Verónica's body coexisted with the bodies crushed on the line presented itself to Lucio once more as what it was: reality. His dreamworld was somewhere else. The dream was his wife, his children, the routines he loved, his friends, playing soccer with people from work. The dream was believing that life could bring peace. The reality was an intense, unique and unrepeatable moment, as each encounter with Verónica and as every collision with a person he knocked down had been. By contrast, dreams evaporated, became intermingled. Mariana, his children, the house where they lived were intangible and became shapeless in his life. What remained was Verónica, desiring Verónica, having her here with him. What remained were the trains from which he could never step down, the accidents which never ended.

He thought of calling his co-workers on other trains to warn them about what was going to happen that night, but he didn't get the chance. As always, he saw them too late – perhaps this time even a little later than usual. Two boys staring at him, their bodies rigid as they prepared to wait until the last possible moment.

He didn't sound the horn. Instinctively he braked, clenching his teeth as if that could help the train to stop. For the first time that night, he closed his eyes, something that he had never done before any other accident. The train screeched like a pig being slaughtered. Shouts and cries could be heard coming from the compartments in response to the sudden application of brakes. Nothing else. There was no sound of bodies hitting iron. He didn't feel bones grinding underneath his driver's cabin. The two boys had managed to jump in time.

Terror gave way to hatred. Lucio climbed blindly down from the cabin. Through the night's darkness, slightly illuminated by light coming from the compartments, he saw a boy get to his feet and run away. Without thinking or caring that he was leaving his passengers stranded there, he went after the boy. All he could see was that small body jumping nimbly over the sleepers between the rails. The boy was fast, but Lucio's fury gave him extra energy. The train was behind them and Lucio began to close the distance between him and the boy. Finally, the kid's legs gave out, he stumbled, and Lucio grabbed him by the shoulder. The effort sent both of them falling onto the tracks. The boy tried to wriggle away.

"Stop moving, you little bastard."

"Please, señor, don't kill me."

He must have been about ten or eleven, just a few years older than Lucio's boys. But when he chased them it was for fun – he'd throw himself on top of them, all three of them laughing. Just as when you wake up from a pleasant dream and try to return to it by squeezing your eyes closed, Lucio wished he could be at home playing with his children. But the dream didn't come back. He was still there, looking at a child who was staring at him, terrified.

"I didn't want to do it. Supergirl was going to get here in time so I didn't have to jump."

"Super who?"

"Verónica."

Was the kid mocking him?

And what if this thing happening to him really was a nightmare? He was about to ask which Verónica – although he already knew the answer – when two figures stepped out of the shadows. One was dressed in sportswear and the other, absurdly, in a jacket and tie.

346

"Let go of the boy," the one wearing the Adidas kit ordered.

Lucio looked at them. Immediately he understood everything.

"You're the pieces of shit who make these boys jump, right?"

The boy had taken his chance to free himself and move further away, but he was still sitting on the ground. Lucio was kneeling.

"You're scum."

He wanted to stand up. He didn't know what he would do next, beat up the men or look for a stone to throw at their heads. He did know that he wasn't going back to the train, that he wouldn't be driving it any further.

Now the boy ran off, far away from them.

"Get rid of him," the man in the Adidas kit said to the other one.

The other man took out a gun and pointed it at his face.

Lucio closed his eyes. Something exploded.

V

Verónica hung up just as they were reaching the tollbooth at the Dolores Prats exit. She had been unsure about whether to call him for two reasons: the possibility that Lucio was at the moment contentedly eating dinner with his wife, and the fact that Federico would hear their conversation. Finally, she had decided to dial his number. Her hands were shaking and she no longer knew if that was because of all that had happened that day or simply because she was a foolish girl calling an ex-lover. Lucio wasn't with his wife, but Federico had listened attentively to everything she had said, and perhaps he had also caught some of what Lucio said.

"Do you always speak to your sources that way?"

"Don't be a moron."

She was being unfair to Federico. She should be nicer. Besides, he was right: it wasn't the right way to treat a journalistic source.

"I had a thing with him, but it's over."

They were making slow progress along the narrow and congested avenue. Federico was doing what he could and had even crossed Avenida Gaona on a red light, just avoiding a collision with a van travelling away from the capital. They took the underpass, over which the Sarmiento railway ran, and reached Avenida Rivadavia, at which point they had to decide what direction to take.

"Haedo or Morón?"

"Haedo," Verónica whispered. Her body was tense and she had an urge to piss; she was clenching her toes, something she did when she was hyper-alert.

As they drove along beside the railway line, Verónica kept her gaze fixed out of that side of the car, watchful for a passing train or a crowd of people: the former would have been a sign that, at least for the moment, everything was under control. Since she was looking sideways, Federico was the one to sound the alarm.

"Something's happening up ahead."

The traffic was heavier here, and in the distance they could see a stalled train. Federico inched forward until he had drawn level with the first compartment, but on the other side of Avenida Rivadavia. The crossing was blocked because the train had come to a stop across it. From where they were, they could see that the driver's cabin was empty. Federico made a dangerous manoeuvre, a U-turn that nearly caused him to crash into some of the cars going towards Morón. The people they could see standing in front of the first compartment looked confused, but this wasn't a scene of panic.

Verónica got out of the car and walked towards the tracks. There was no injured child to be seen; no train driver, either.

She remembered what El Peque had told her: that when he was scared he ran away, that he ran along beside the train until he had left it behind him and that he met Rivero all the same. Verónica thought it probable that the boys had run back towards the station. And if Rivero and his men were waiting for them, the meeting place would be at the next railway crossing. She ran back to the car.

"Put your foot down, Fede, we're going to the next crossing."

They drove on to the next barrier, then parked the car on Avenida Rivadavia. They got out and walked towards the poorly lit tracks. Even in the dark, they saw him coming. A boy. Dientes. Verónica ran towards him without even calling to him. She grabbed him and hugged him, feeling her eyes fill with tears.

"Are you all right?"

"I knew that you would come."

"And the other kid?" Federico asked.

"He jumped. I didn't see him after that."

"And Rivero?"

"Rivero's over there." He pointed back towards the tracks, a dark area within which it was impossible to make out anything from where they stood. "He turned up with another guy when the man grabbed me."

"Which man?"

"The driver, he was mad. He wanted to kill me. He grabbed me and threw me on the ground. Then Rivero and the other one turned up and I managed to escape. I got a fright when I heard the noises. They sounded like gunshots, but I don't know. I thought that I was going to get killed, like my dad got killed."

"Take Dientes to the car and make sure Rivero doesn't show up, because he'll try to get him," Verónica ordered Federico, and started walking towards the darkness. He took her by the arm.

"You stay with the boy and I'll go."

Verónica shook him off angrily. "I told you to go to the car and wait there!" she shouted, then ran towards the tracks.

She didn't need Dientes to know his name. Verónica was certain: the driver was Lucio. She was terrified that something had happened to him. She wanted to get somewhere and find Lucio there and for him to speak, to say anything. To feel that the most important thing was that they were there, that the worst was over, that the boys were safe and that he too, however furious and scared he was by what he had been through, was alive. He hadn't run over anyone. He wasn't going to see the children playing on the tracks any more. Lucio.

She saw him on the ground. Lucio. He was lying across the tracks. He didn't move, just as Marcelo had not moved earlier that same afternoon, and yet Marcelo was alive. Lucio was stretched out on the ground just like Rafael, who was now recuperating in hospital. Verónica put her arms around Lucio's body and sat him up. She couldn't look at his face, all covered in blood, but she hugged him tightly. She felt his body's warmth, his blood, still wet, on her, and she spoke to him and cried and murmured unconnected phrases. Finally she looked at him, she looked at the destroyed face that was barely recognizable.

"Don't leave me. Don't be an idiot. Don't leave me."

It was a reproach she might have made on any other day when he was returning to his house, to the warmth of a home and a family. Lucio, don't leave me. She would be naked, sitting on the bed. She would watch him get dressed.

Lucio, don't leave me. I love you. You know that I love you. Don't leave me. And he would turn round, smiling, and kiss her. He would stay with her. Please don't leave me. And they would listen to music or watch a movie together. In the end, happiness was that. The moment when a person decided not to leave. To stay with you.

19   *The Journalist's Violent Calling*

I

She stayed in the shower for at least twenty minutes, the water running over her neck, her glazed eyes, the foamless sponge in her hand. Stepping out of the bathtub, she wrapped her hair in a towel and dried her face. She rubbed her eyes and cheekbones hard. She didn't have the energy to dry herself any more than that, but sheathed her wet body in a dressing gown and went to her bedroom. Robotically, she took the clothes she planned to wear from the wardrobe. She thought of heating up water for a coffee, but wanted to do as little as possible. Once she had dressed, she slid into her bag the envelope from Federico containing all that he knew about Juan García. She picked up her keys and left the apartment. It was ten to seven in the morning.

In less than fourteen hours she had mown down four henchmen (two dead, two seriously injured), she had been in a police station and then a hospital, travelled to Haedo, had spoken to Lucio on the phone and had held his dead body on the tracks of the Sarmiento line. At that point she had lost all notion of time, but she did remember the police arriving soon afterwards along with Federico, who had left Dientes with a social worker from the child protection department.

She had screamed at Federico when he tried to remove her from the scene. He had kept a firm hold on her and dragged her to the car. He even had to push her into it. They drove along the freeway without speaking, Verónica turning her back on him. She was sitting sideways in the seat, almost squatting, her head against the window.

He went with her to her apartment. The building's shattered frontage had been boarded up and a police officer was standing guard. Her father had already sent a locksmith to repair the door to the apartment and close off the balcony. Federico made her tea. They still didn't speak. He made and received various phone calls. Dientes had been taken home and Jonathan located. They still knew nothing about the whereabouts of Rivero and his people.

He insisted that she rest and try to sleep. He stayed until two o'clock in the morning, leaving only when she had promised that she would go to bed but that she wanted to be alone. Once Federico had gone, she turned on the computer and tried to put her material into some kind of order. Despite the involvement of official bodies, such as the police and a government agency, everything indicated that there had been no arrests. It was possible that those men would wait a long time before playing their sordid game again, or that they would simply move to a different railway. She had evidence that could implicate Rivero, including in Lucio's death. But the guy could just spend the rest of his days as a fugitive, living under a different name in some far corner of the country – or even in Buenos Aires itself.

From the balcony came the sound of birdsong announcing dawn. At first light, she began to feel cold. She decided to have a shower and start a new day.

Outside the building, she stopped a taxi and gave the driver Juan García's address in Palermo. Mentally she rehearsed what she had decided to do and say.

The building had been constructed along modern lines. In place of a doorman, there were security men at the entrance whose appearance seemed to suggest the missing link between monkey and man. She asked for Juan García.

"There's no Juan García here."

"Don't waste my time. I'm going to stand outside and smoke a cigarette on the sidewalk. You tell him that Verónica Rosenthal has come to talk to him about the German company Unmittelbare Zukunft. I'd better write it down for you. You can read, right?"

She hadn't finished the first cigarette when Missing Link called her. In the lobby was an older lady, over sixty, who proffered a professional smile. She invited Verónica to go with her.

"I apologize for the security measures."

"There's no need to apologize."

"All the same, Señor García has asked me not to take any particular precautions with you. That is why we didn't ask for your ID at the entrance to the building. Nor are we going to check to see if you are wearing recording equipment."

"I feel I should be thanking you."

"Señor García will see you in a few minutes," said the older lady, impervious to irony.

She had to wait longer, this time, than she had waited outside. She wanted to smoke. The older lady reappeared and led her into an office. Behind the desk was Juan García.

"My dear Rosenthal. I didn't expect to see you so soon, or so early. You must be an early riser, like me."

He gestured at her to take a seat opposite him.

"Here I am."

"I didn't think that you would find this place, either. Your boys must be good. Congratulate them on my behalf."

"I've come to negotiate."

"I'm afraid that the time for negotiating has passed."

"Whereas I feel that it's only just beginning." She threw the envelope with the material Federico had given her down on the desk. Here is everything that links your business to the German firm Unmittelbare Zukunft. And the contacts with the agricultural machinery company in Misiones. And the relationship to people in Israel, Italy and Uruguay. There are also all the requests made by the Bavarian authorities as part of their investigation into money laundering. Up until now they haven't managed to locate the local ringleader. Have a look, if you want."

Juan García gently pushed the envelope towards Verónica.

"I don't need to see it. There's no denying you're a good sniffer dog. I was going to say 'bitch', but it doesn't sound right."

Verónica gave no reaction. García continued:

"As a politician, I'm accustomed to rewarding people who make an effort. If we based our working and political relations on the level of effort made, we'd live in a better country. But I can see from your face that you're not in the mood for a long chat, so tell me what you want."

"I want Palma, Rivero and the people who take part in the track-jumping contest."

"Oof, you're asking for a lot. If you include everyone who places a bet as participants, that would mean implicating hundreds of people. It's like soccer games, you see. Thousands go to the match and millions more watch on television. Something similar happens here. A few dozen people go along, and hundreds more follow on the internet."

"You record the contests?"

"I'm not saying yes or no. But I'm surprised that a young girl like you wouldn't think about how new technologies can be used. Right, so now I know what you're asking for, but you haven't said what you'll give me in exchange."

"You won't be mentioned in my article, not even as a suspect, not even in connection to the cases that took place in Misiones when you were mayor. I won't do anything with the material that I have from Unmittelbare Zukunft. You and I won't cross paths again, from the moment you give me what I want."

"Aren't you scared you might have an accident? I don't say it as a threat, mind you, but I'm intrigued that you would choose to stop where you have."

"A dead journalist is always the worst outcome for a politician and his associates."

"I'll tell you what I can give you. Palma you already had before, and he's still on the table. Rivero is like a Muscovy duck – he shits himself at every step. A spell in prison would toughen him up. I can also give you the guy who shot the driver. You've already finished off various men who were implicated in all this. That's six or seven altogether. Not a bad number."

"I also want your promise that this competition won't continue, either on the Sarmiento line or any other railway in Argentina. If I so much as suspect that the competitions are starting again, in any part of the the country, your name will be on all the front pages."

"Even if I wanted to, it's impossible without Rivero." García looked for something in one of his desk drawers and took out an envelope. "Here's everything you need for Palma." He pushed the intercom button. "Marcela, could you come in here for a moment?"

Five seconds later, the secretary appeared.

"When the señorita leaves, could you give her a copy of the video titled *Muscovy Duck*? Oh, and make a note for her of the address where Señor Rivero lives with his partner."

When they were alone again, García continued speaking: "A couple of the contests are recorded on that tape. I'll be sensitive enough to give you the ones where everything ended well. Let's not have any more blood, even if it's on tape. And there's a bonus track for you, if you know how to use it. Along with Rivero and the man who fired the shot, you see other men, gamblers, and there's the odd licence plate. I imagine that you'll know how to make use of that material."

I I

When she came out of Juan García's building, Verónica walked towards Avenida Las Heras and called Federico. She told him what she had and who had given it to her. She didn't mention what she had offered in return. Federico agreed to send over the office boy in an hour. She would give him the material and the address where Rivero and his accomplice were hiding, so that they could be arrested.

"Just one thing," Verónica asked him in a voice that, even to her, sounded serious and tired. "Please keep everything under wraps for twenty-four hours. The magazine comes out on Thursday and I don't want us to be bringing this information out a day later than the newspapers."

"But what if they escape?"

"They won't escape. García will make sure of it."

When she got back to the apartment, Verónica called Patricia, who had left various messages on her answerphone, worrying about her sudden departure from the newsroom. She also had a few missed calls from the night before.

Patricia answered immediately, as though she had been waiting for the call. She wanted to know how Verónica was. She had heard about the accident at the door of the building but didn't know what had really happened. Verónica offered up a brief and sketchy version of events. She didn't feel like describing all that she had been through. She would rather talk about the forthcoming article. She told her boss that she now had all the material to write it and that she would hand it in that very afternoon, at the close of day.

"Listen, the magazine goes to press on Wednesday. It's fine if you hand it in tomorrow."

"I'd rather get it done today. Tomorrow I won't be able to."

She asked for two photographers for the next day. One to record the arrest of the gang leader and his accomplice and the other to cover the moment when an undersecretary of the City of Buenos Aires was arrested and taken away.

"The grass doesn't grow under your feet," said Patricia, admiringly.

Verónica made a cafetière of coffee and filled up her thermos. She took two strong aspirin and got to work. She saved a copy of the video García had given her onto her computer and opened it. Rivero and the other man were shown arriving with two boys. The camera recorded a few people milling around, in the same way that the activity in a paddock is filmed before a horse race. There were greetings, laughter; the only people who seemed tense were those two boys. Who might they be? What had become of them? Had one of them died the next time this game was played? The boys took their positions on the tracks and stood waiting, their bodies braced. Verónica couldn't help feeling nervous. She pressed Pause and asked herself if there was any point in continuing to watch. García had told her that there was no blood and, at least in this matter, there was no reason not to believe him. She decided to skip forward a few seconds. The boys were still in their positions. She pressed Forward again. Now the train had stopped and one of the boys could be seen lying on the ground. The other one, she wanted to believe, had jumped to the other side. The film stopped there and another similar one began, centring once more on Rivero and his inevitable sidekick. The boys were not the same. One of them was El Peque. Verónica felt a jolt of indignation and fear. She didn't want to see any more, didn't want to see El Peque jump. What she had seen already was enough. She made various screenshots of images where Rivero's face could be seen clearly, along with the other man and some of those who had come to place bets. She made a few more of cars with licence plates that were perfectly decipherable. There was nothing casual about those shots: García must have used them to blackmail people. He must have dozens of recordings showing the faces and cars of the people who attended the contests. If the need arose, he would use them against anyone implicated. Verónica felt no pity at all for those idiots who were so easy to trick. She saved all the material on her computer. Later she would make a backup.

The office boy arrived to pick up the envelope she had promised to Federico. That was the only interruption to her work. By midday she had written more than half her article. The most important thing was to organize what material she had, to avoid using García's name and to keep herself out of the story. She didn't like first-person journalism: it seemed to her the recourse of egocentric journalists, mediocre investigative reporters or frustrated writers. And she was none of those things. Even so, she found it hard not to convey her contempt, her hatred, her fear and the desolation she now felt. She couldn't include anything about her relationship with Lucio, of course, but every time she typed his name, in the course of explaining the driver's role in her investigation, she choked up and couldn't continue.

She made herself an instant tomato soup and heated up a few slices of pizza left over from Rafael's stay. Perhaps it was because of her current state of mind that she missed him. During the few days they had spent together she had felt at ease in his company, something which had not happened with another person for years.

She went down to buy cigarettes, feeling Marcelo's absence at the door. She walked to the news kiosk, mentally composing her article with every step. Along with the cigarettes she bought chewing gum and a packet of Halls Cherry-Lyptus. She owed El Peque and Dientes a present. What could she give them? A soccer ball? Sports shoes, boots? If they didn't live so far away she would have made them members of Atlanta soccer club.

Federico called her in the afternoon to say that the public prosecutor had decided that the two operations would be carried out simultaneously at three o'clock in the afternoon. That as a courtesy, since she had provided this information, they would not tip off any other media organization until the men were in custody. She had the photo exclusive. He also asked her how she was feeling.

"I've had better days. And, to be honest, I haven't had many worse. But I have a hunch that the sun is going to keep rising around six every morning."

She finished writing the article at about eight o'clock that night. She called Patricia again, who was stressed because the writers were all running late and she wasn't going to be able to leave until ten o'clock. Verónica told her that everything was ready. She gave her the details the photographers would need for the following afternoon and promised her that, as well as the article, she would send the video screenshots which showed the men who had organized the competitions. Verónica didn't plan to hand over for publication any images showing the gamblers' faces or their cars. First she wanted to find out who they were and how they had become involved. She had enough material for another article, and she wasn't going to waste it for the sake of an image.

Patricia had given her a 4,500-word space for her investigation. She could arrange the content as she wished. After making calculations, she found that she had already written about 6,000, which meant that she needed to cut down, a task she hated but one she wasn't prepared to leave in Patricia's hands, not because her boss would do it badly – generally she improved a piece – but because this time she felt that to relinquish control over so much as a full stop or comma would be to betray all that she had lived through in the last few weeks. Finally, she wrote a lead piece of 3,000 words. She thought of dedicating a long inset box to Lucio, but the idea of him having his own article upset her even more. So she decided to include him in the main body of the article, explaining how he had come to be her main source. She did the same with Rafael, except that in this case she used an invented name: Roberto. None of the children's names were included, with the exception of those who had been killed or injured. With luck, some reader would recognize one of those children and get in touch with the newsroom or the authorities with more information.

Five hundred words went on a box dedicated to Julián, detailing how he had become an unintended victim of the investigation. She described him through Rafael's eyes: his interest in Chacarita, his enthusiasm to know more about local customs, to take his place among people in the neighbourhood. Without meaning to, Rafael had given her enough material to write a profile of Julián which was both a piece of journalism and a tribute.

The thousand remaining words went on a second article. A double-page spread, complementary to the investigation, which accused Palma exclusively. The folder Juan García had given her showed him to be much more than just the money man using public funds to run this atrocious game. Money from the same funds had also been diverted to companies of which Palma had part-ownership. And there were unjustified expenses, trips abroad, payments to people who didn't exist. Palma was a true wizard of financial fraud, which had undoubtedly made him rich. It was more than likely that a considerable portion of that money had ended up with García, or someone like him. Palma could take the blame for them all.

Even though she had never done it before – and it always struck her as silly when she came across it in print – she decided to use poetic licence and dedicate her article to El Peque and Dientes, "founder members of the Superteam". The only people whose actions stood out and who were not mentioned in any part of the article were Father Pedro and Marcelo. She felt that not including the priest was a protective gesture on her part. He would certainly prefer not to be mentioned. She left Marcelo out because to relate what had happened in the building would involve her in the story.

Here it is, said the email she sent to Patricia with the articles attached. *Great if you can read it and let me have any comments now. Tomorrow, as I said, I'm not going to be available. I'll send you the video screenshots I promised in another email.*

Forty minutes later, Patricia called.

"Verónica, this is the most superb piece of writing I have read or edited in all my professional life. I'm calling you just to say thank you for doing this work and for reminding me what it is to be a journalist."

"The piece is good. But you need your head examining."

"Listen to this. Our editor has asked that we also run an opinion piece by a psychologist explaining the trauma that this kind of experience could cause the children who took part."

"And what did you say to him?"

"I told him to shove it up his ass. That if he touched so much as a fucking comma, tomorrow he'd have my resignation and yours plus a lawsuit for journalistic malpractice, if there is such a thing."

"Thanks, Pato, you're like a mother to me."

"And you can fuck off too."

It was already nine o'clock at night. She hadn't slept for thirty-eight hours. Tomorrow she would surely be at Lucio's funeral or cremation. She should go – or should she? Approach his wife, talk to her. See his children who in her mind were like little ghosts, uncomfortable presences in her story, like a pain in the ovaries. To mourn among his co-workers and his family. At the end of the day, she had been part of his life. But she didn't have the strength. She no longer had the energy to do what was necessary. She wanted a glass of whisky but decided against it: finding a glass and pouring it out felt like too much of an effort. And despite her tiredness, she feared that thinking about Lucio was going to keep her from sleeping. So she took a Valium, silenced the telephones, took off her clothes and fell down onto the bed, a dead weight.

III

She woke up with a thunderous need to piss and staggered to the bathroom. Then she returned to her room and got back into bed. What time must it be? It was hard to tell with the window shuttered. Plus, it was raining. She had no desire to get up. She groped for her mobile and checked the time: five past seven in the evening. She had been asleep for almost an entire day, only getting up to go to the bathroom. She had missed a couple of calls from Federico and one from her father. There was also a text message from Fede: *All OK?*

Can I come and C U? She replied: *I'm fine, I want to rest. I'll call you tomorrow. Big kiss.*

She decided to get up, if only for a bit. She was quite hungry. There was a bit of coffee left in the thermos and she reheated it in the microwave. In the fridge she found liverwurst and in the cupboard some mini toasts. She sat down in the kitchen to eat, and to drink her coffee. Then she went into the living room and poured a glass of Jim Beam. Verónica opened the balcony doors, turned off the light and sat watching the rain. She stayed there for a couple of hours, with the bottle of Jim Beam to hand.

It seemed as though the rain would never stop. It fell heavily and slowly. She tried to think of nothing, but that wasn't easy. Every so often images that she had hoped not to remember popped into her mind. She didn't switch on her computer or check her email. Somewhat drunk, she settled on the sofa and put on the big television. *Scarface* had just started and she watched it for a while. She had seen it many times before, but it never lost its appeal. She went to the kitchen and found a box of Ferrero Rocher which she had been given some time ago and not eaten, for fear of putting on weight. She poured herself another whisky and settled down to watch the movie.

That was when her mobile rang. She had intended to switch it off at some point but must have forgotten to do so. With some effort she got up and went to look for the phone. The screen showed a number she didn't recognize. She answered and a woman's voice spoke at the other end of the line.

"It's Andrea, Rafael's wife."

The voice seemed to be coming from somewhere faraway. In fact, everything seemed strange and remote to Verónica: the rain, the sound and lights of the television, the shadows in the living room. And especially Andrea's voice, telling her that Rafael had disappeared. They had returned home after he was discharged from the hospital and Rafael had found out only then that Julián was dead. He had retreated into a silence that worried them. He had gone to bed, to rest, but then left the house without anyone realizing. He had now been away from home for more than six hours. Andrea had called his mobile but it kept ringing before going to voicemail. She didn't know what else to do, how to look for him. She didn't want to go to the police after what had happened to him. She was scared that somebody would hurt him. Or that he would hurt himself.

Verónica struggled to take in what Andrea was telling her but, just as a shock can counteract the effects of alcohol and promote lucidity, she began to understand what Andrea was asking of her.

"Andrea, keep calm. Rafael will be fine. We're going to look for him and we're going to find him. I'll call you on this number later."

She thought of calling on Federico yet again. But something told her that she was better placed than anyone to find Rafael.

Verónica put on tracksuit bottoms, sneakers and the light, hooded raincoat that she wore on the few occasions she went out jogging. She put her cigarettes, lighter, wallet and phone in the pockets of her raincoat. The rain was getting heavier all the time. There were no cars in the street, let alone taxis. She had to walk all the way to Avenida Córdoba to find one, and by then she was already soaked. She gave the driver the address of Julián's supermarket. If she was going to embark on a search, that was the place to start.

"You're going to Soldati at this time of night?" the driver asked.

Verónica confirmed that she was and left no room for further conversation. Instead she took out her phone and looked for Rafael's number. She called him several times without answer. Seen through the rain-streaked window, Buenos Aires looked like an empty and phantasmagoric city.

"Do you live there, or are you just visiting?"

The driver looked at her in the rear-view mirror. Verónica hated chatty taxi drivers, but this one wasn't talking about the weather or politics. He wanted to know about her, and that felt dangerous as well as irritating.

"Just visiting," she said and looked back at her phone to discourage any further conversation. The driver kept quiet for a long time. But after a few minutes he said:

"Why don't you come and sit in the front, so we can talk more comfortably?"

Verónica didn't answer. She waited for the first red traffic light, then got out without warning him. The driver shouted "Crazy bitch" and she started walking against the flow of traffic, hoping to find another taxi. For a moment she was scared that the guy was going to get out and follow her, but he didn't. When the light turned green the taxi pulled away and she stopped walking. She had no idea where she was. Just before the taxi driver started talking, she had thought she had seen a hospital on the right-hand side. She walked to the corner. It was Avenida Juan B. Justo. She took refuge from the rain in a bus shelter and hoped another taxi would appear. Five minutes later she saw one slowly approaching and flagged it down. Verónica got in, repeated the address and this time, without saying a word, the taxi driver started the meter and began to drive.

When they reached the supermarket, she paid and got out. She found herself alone outside the shop. It was closed and she couldn't see anyone inside the premises. Rafael wasn't there, anyway. He could be anywhere – in a bar, in the hostel where he had lived, in a drugs den scoring coke. Verónica remembered Rafael telling her about the little bar he used to go to with Julián, but she had no address for it. It must not be far away from here. Although it was very likely to be one of those daytime bars that only opened during business hours. Rafael had also told her about meeting his daughter in a plaza. Which plaza? She tried Rafael's number again, without luck. On her telephone, she had a map of Buenos Aires. She located the supermarket on it and moved the screen in search of a plaza somewhere between her current location and the house where Rafael's family lived. There was one seven blocks away. She set off in that direction, this time with very little hope of a taxi passing. She wasn't scared of walking in this neighbourhood, which could be described as dangerous for a woman, or for a yuppie obsessed with personal safety. Her clothes were soaked through and the brisk walk made her sweat. She arrived at the badly lit plaza and scanned it. In the distance she could see a shadowy figure sitting on one of the further-flung benches. It wasn't possible to tell from where she stood whether it was Rafael or not, but she had no doubts: she was sure that it was.

Verónica hurried, almost running, towards him. Rafael turned to look at her. There was nothing in his eyes to say how he was feeling. One of his legs was in plaster and there were crutches flung down beside the bench.

"You knew they'd killed Julián."

Verónica bent down and took his hands in hers. Rafael was even more drenched than she was.

"He had a wife, a little girl…"

It felt like the start of a longer observation, but as Rafael opened his mouth, it seemed as though no words would come out of it. She hugged him as best she could and, crying, he

367

repeated "a wife, a little girl". What were they both doing there, in the middle of the square, at midnight, in this interminable rain? The darkness that came over them was no greater than the solitude each felt enveloping them at that moment. Only they knew all that they had been through, what it had taken to arrive there, at that plaza, that night. She knew why Rafael was crying. And he had some concept of her pain, but he didn't know the reason for her uncontrollable weeping, the tears that mingled with their soaked, exhausted, fragile bodies.

Verónica helped him to his feet and Rafael said, more to himself than to her:

"I went to the shop, but I couldn't bring myself to speak to Elsa."

Verónica's phone started ringing. It was Andrea. She answered and told her where they were. Andrea wanted to come over. She said that her taxi-driving neighbour could bring her in five minutes. Rafael and Verónica walked slowly to the corner, she staying close by him all the time. She was scared that, even with a leg in plaster, he could still escape. Andrea arrived a few minutes later, hugged Rafael and kissed Verónica. It didn't make sense for her to go with them. She told them that she would pick up a taxi on the next avenue. They left her there. Andrea made a gesture of thanks and said something to her before she got into the car but Verónica neither heard what she said nor saw the gesture. She wasn't there any more. She wasn't anywhere.

She walked blindly until she reached a bus stop. A number 46 bus appeared almost straightaway and she put out her arm to stop it. She had no idea where the bus was going, but she didn't care. There was hardly anyone on board. She sat on the last single seat, her body frozen even though it wasn't cold. At the same time, she was still sweating. She would have liked to light a cigarette. She rested her head against the window and closed her eyes, but didn't sleep. The bus had taken Avenida Rivadavia and was running parallel to the Sarmiento railway line. They passed Villa Luro station and she got off when they arrived at Liniers. It was now scarcely raining any more, but her clothes were still wet. She climbed up the footbridge linking one side of the train station to the other. Halfway across she stopped and looked down at the tracks. There were no trains at this time of night. Lucio had died a few miles from here. Both times they had been together on the train, they had passed under this bridge. A few stations further down the line he had kissed her for the first time. Nothing of that past reality remained. All that endured were those rusty tracks and the trains, endlessly repeating their routine, indifferent to broken bodies. This bridge remained, along with the people who walked across it, the buildings that lined the railway, the passengers getting on with their lives. The only ones who were not there were Lucio and her. Lucio's kiss. Lucio's body and his face, disfigured by bullets. Nothing remained.

She wanted to close her eyes and reappear in any place other than this. She took the steps down to the north side of the station. On the opposite sidewalk, on Calle Viedma, she spotted an open bar. She went in and sat at a table in the middle of the room. There were a few guys, all staring at her. An old man at the back of the room was smoking, so she took out her own packet of cigarettes and lit one. She asked for a beer. She needed some alcohol, even though she knew that it couldn't help her.

The waiter brought her a Chopp beer and a bowl of peanuts. She drank a long draught. A young man who had been leaning on the bar approached her table. He said something to her and she answered automatically. The man sat down.

He was slight and seemed shy. It must have been hard for him to come and speak to her. He told her his name but she didn't register it. He talked about the storm, about the summer which was taking its time in coming, something else that she didn't catch. Verónica called the waiter over and paid for her beer. She asked the young man if he knew of any nearby motels. They left together.

The boy took her to a by-the-hour hotel two blocks away. At the vigil for her mother, Federico had never left Verónica's side. Whatever she had needed, he was there to get it for her – a glass of water, to call a friend, making her toast or getting her coffee. During the funeral he had continually hugged her and held her. Close friends and family, Federico included, were invited to Verónica's father's house after the burial. She had taken advantage of a lapse in Federico's attention to get into a car with her sister Leticia's family. When they reached Avenida del Libertador, she had asked to be let out there, saying that she would go to her father's later on. Verónica had called a friend who lived a few blocks away, on the top floor of a building on that avenue. You could see the coast of Uruguay from his windows. They had had sex a few times, but they had never been anything more than casual lovers. He had been in his apartment and waited for her there. They had fucked. She had stayed a little while, looking out across the River Plate, then she had gone to her father's house.

Now she was looking at the young man's body on top of her, in the ceiling mirror. She closed her eyes and tried to coax some reaction from her body, to let it be carried away by her senses, to get it to react like a normal body, but she couldn't manage it. Half an hour later, as they were getting dressed, the boy discreetly left a fifty-peso note on top of her jacket. He must have thought that she was a prostitute.

Verónica took the money without saying anything and put it in her bag with her cigarettes. They separated at the door of the hotel and she walked back to Calle Viedma, where she had seen taxis passing earlier. She stopped one and went back to her apartment.

She had left the television on, the glass of Jim Beam and the chocolates out on the coffee table. Tony Montana was no longer on the screen. A movie had started that she didn't know and wasn't interested in. Verónica took off her raincoat, sneakers, her socks, her still-wet tracksuit bottoms and her sweatshirt, and was left in her underwear. She covered herself up with the bath towel she had used to dry herself off, took a sip of whisky and went to sleep on the sofa.

IV

She woke up in the morning, very early. The television was still on and showing one of those commercial programmes that sell gizmos for losing weight or lifting sagging buttocks. Her mouth felt sticky and she had a slight headache. It was Thursday, and no longer raining. She still had various things to resolve.

At ten o'clock she had to be at the Tribunales courthouse to make a statement in front of the investigating judge about the events outside her building on Monday afternoon. Her father called her to arrange a meeting beforehand. When push came to shove her father didn't delegate a job to anyone, not even to Federico.

Once they were together, he repeated to her what she had to say: how, fearing for her friends' lives, she had borrowed a car and driven to her apartment. How, when she arrived and saw the scene, with her friends apparently lifeless on the ground, she had lost control of the car and mounted

371

the sidewalk with such bad luck that she had knocked over four people who, as fate would have it, were the killers of a supermarket owner in Villa Soldati and who had gone to the building with the express aim of killing a witness in the case. She had been involved in an accident – a misfortune with happy consequences.

The judge seemed willing to accept whatever she said. The only objection he raised was that the insurance company would surely want to carry out its own investigation so as to avoid paying for the car repairs. Her father told the judge not to worry, that his law practice was negotiating an agreement with the company and that there would be no problem. The judge seemed more like her father's assistant than anything else. Verónica was reassured by that, but nonetheless uncomfortable being the witness (or protagonist) of the scene.

Verónica and her father had lunch in Tomo 1, not a restaurant she liked, but she wasn't going to put up any resistance that day. She ate *bocconcini de pâte a choux* with spinach and crispy dry-cured ham; he asked for classic spinach ravioli with a tomato ragout. They talked about her sisters, the children in the family, some lost uncle who lived in Tel Aviv and had recently made contact again, via the law firm's web page. They avoided talking about the events of the last few days. He asked her nothing about work, not even about all the use she had made of his law firm in the last few weeks. As they were leaving, Verónica hugged him.

"Thanks, Dad, thanks for all your help."

"It's all down to Federico. That boy is still in love with you."

"Oh, Dad, don't stir things up. Anyway, he's got a girlfriend."

Her father shook his head and walked off quickly towards the parking lot. She walked a few blocks in the opposite direction. She needed to get some air.

Federico himself rang her later on. It crossed her mind not to answer, but that would be mean and he deserved better. They talked for a while. Federico told her that Rivero, his sidekick and Palma had been arrested the previous afternoon. That day the newspapers had published this information, but they hadn't been able to say much, nor draw any conclusions, much less link the death of the train driver with the boys or Julián's murder. Everyone would wake up the next day to her scoop in *Nuestro Tiempo*.

Federico also told her that he had talked to Álex Vilna about his car. That the question of insurance would be resolved and that he had offered to rent a car for Vilna until his own one was repaired, but that the Politics editor of *Nuestro Tiempo* had rejected his offer with such insufferable pedantry that he had felt like telling him to get lost.

She could tell that he was worried about her. Federico offered himself as a dinner companion, to go to a movie, to chat, to do whatever she wanted. Verónica politely turned down each of these suggestions. She would have liked to spend some time with Federico, but she feared that afterwards she would have to say no to sleeping with him and she didn't have the stomach for the kind of lopsided relationship they might be left with.

The first copies of *Nuestro Tiempo* would be arriving in the newsroom at midday, but she didn't plan to go there. She phoned Patricia and asked if she could delay her return until Monday. The editor put up no objection. She told her that the photos had come out very well.

Verónica decided to go to visit Marcelo in hospital. She bought him a box of sweets and wrote him a brief note that was intended to be funny, as well as a way to say thank you. The doorman's wife was with him, along with some other relations she didn't know. He seemed to be much better, and eager to get back to work. They would probably discharge him on Saturday morning. There were some problems claiming on his workplace insurance, Marcelo's wife told Verónica under his reproving gaze, because what had happened to him wasn't recognized as a work-related accident.

"My friends in the union will sort it out," said Marcelo, playing this down.

The distribution of *Nuestro Tiempo* began at news kiosks in the centre of town, so Verónica walked to the underground station and took a train to Calle Florida. She killed time in a bar until she saw the vans that delivered newspapers and magazines going past. She bought a copy of *Nuestro Tiempo*, which had photographs on the cover of Rivero and Palma in handcuffs. The heading above made clear that this was "Thanks to an exclusive investigation by *Nuestro Tiempo*." The main headline, in the catastrophic typeface favoured by the magazine, was FALL OF THE TRAIN MAFIA, then, in slightly smaller print: THEY FORCED CHILDREN TO RISK THEIR LIVES. She didn't reread the article, but focussed on the pictures. They had used all the screenshots that she had taken from the video. There was also a photo of Palma at some public event, standing next to the chief of the city government and with an ex-governor of Misiones. García's not going to like that one bit, she thought, but she didn't care what García might think. She had done enough to honour their agreement. There was no mention of him in person, nothing that could link him to the case. He could congratulate himself on the way he had managed to avoid punishment.

That night she followed the repercussions of her investigation on the internet and television. Even TV channels that were unfriendly to the magazine had been obliged to talk about her article. Her mobile started to ring. Producers were calling to invite her on to radio and television programmes.

She accepted the requests for radio interviews which could be done by phone and, of the television offers, only agreed to those which could be recorded from Monday of the following week. She didn't feel like showing off the dark circles under her eyes to the whole nation.

Her friends also called her, asking for detailed descriptions of what she had been through. She gave them a brief, lighter version of the adventure, enough for them to coin a new nickname for her: Wonder Woman. At some point the intercom buzzed. She definitely wasn't going to answer it: she was afraid. Whoever it was kept buzzing, though, and she was about to call Federico when her mobile rang. It was Paula.

"Can you open the door, honey? I'm downstairs."

Paula had made some pork and chicken tacos and brought tortilla wraps, a bottle of Nieto Senetiner Malbec and a two-pound tub of ice cream from Freddo.

"I guessed that you were going to stay closeted in your apartment on your night of journalistic glory and that, if I called you, you'd try to boot me into next week."

They ate, drank and bitched about all their mutual friends. While Verónica made coffee and they talked about inanities, Paula took her hands and said:

"This will pass. The world around you has shattered into a thousand pieces. But it will pass. I promise you."

Verónica nodded and couldn't hold back her tears. Paula hugged her and they both cried. They sat together in the living room until three o'clock in the morning.

On Friday Verónica took part in various radio interviews. Obviously, she had nothing to add to what was in the article, but that didn't stop her colleagues pushing for more. She was used to the pointless reverberation that can accompany a news story, and stoically endured her interviewers' limitations, their pushiness and lack of understanding.

She had also received numerous congratulatory emails. One was from the magazine's editor, saying, *I see that the* Nuestro Tiempo *school of journalism has found its most outstanding student in you.* She thought of giving him the answer he deserved, making the most of the protection afforded by her five minutes of fame, but she opted for a dignified silence.

The email that most got her attention was the one she received from Rodolfo Corso. It said simply: *And Juan García?* Rodolfo had good instincts, and he had figured out the truth. She wrote him a long reply, with all the details of what had happened, then deleted it. She didn't answer him, either.

Father Pedro called her. He said that he had read the piece and that he felt happy knowing she had been able to pass all the tests of forbearance that were necessary to achieve justice. He didn't mention whether he had decided to abandon his vocation or if he was still leading the church in Villa Oculta.

On Saturday morning she received a text message from Rafael reminding her that Andrea had invited her to have lunch with them. That they were waiting for her. Verónica had no memory of arranging anything, but it didn't seem like a bad idea, especially as it meant that she could see Dientes and El Peque at the same time.

Once more she borrowed the car from her sister Leticia, who was now past complaining. When she dropped by the apartment to pick up the keys, her sister Daniela was also there and the two of them subjected her to an interrogation, centred especially on the man who had been staying at her apartment. She reassured them by telling them the truth: that her guest was back with his family now, that there was nothing between them, that, in fact, she needed the car to go to his house, since they had invited her to have lunch there.

On the way there she bought some chocolate-covered dulce de leche *alfajores*. She parked the car outside the entrance to the tenement house and saw Dientes, who was walking down the block. When he recognized her, he smiled and ran over.

"Tell El Peque that I'll drop by to say hi later on," she said.

As well as the cookies, Verónica had with her a bag containing the clothes she had bought for Rafael and which he had left in her apartment. Rafael seemed quiet, but he made an effort to look pleased to see her. She was also happy to see him safe and sound and surrounded by the three females in his life. For lunch Rafael served up his mother's home-made gnocchi. Martina eyed her with suspicion. She must still be thinking that Verónica was her father's girlfriend. You'll get older and understand, Verónica thought. Andrea and her mother, on the other hand, treated her kindly, but she couldn't help thinking that both mother and ex- (or current) wife shared some of Martina's mistrust, and so she didn't feel entirely comfortable during the lunch.

Afterwards, Rafael offered to take her over to see Dientes and El Peque. First they went to see Dientes. His mother wanted to invite her in, but she declined the offer. The mother treated Verónica formally, deferring to her as though she were in a position of authority. She thanked her for all she had done and for getting the police and the prosecutor to rescue her son. Verónica asked her permission to take him, with El Peque, to do some shopping. She was happy to agree, as was El Peque's mother.

"Where are we going?" Dientes asked when Verónica opened the back door of the car for them.

"To find a sports shop."

"I know where there's one," El Peque shouted.

Once inside the shop she got them to choose some soccer boots and, since it was there, she gave each of them an Argentina shirt.

"Boys, I promise you that next time I'm going to bring you each a shirt from the best team in the world: Atlanta."

She took them back home and dropped in on Rafael's family to say goodbye to them all. The boys walked her back to the car and, as she drove away, they stood waving until she could no longer see them in the rear-view mirror. She felt strange – not happy, but satisfied. She was tying up some loose ends in her life. That was no bad thing.

Sunday was a day of reflection and inner turmoil. If she had done everything correctly the day before, why didn't she feel like continuing in the same vein? She set to scanning all the material Federico had given her on Juan García. In a Word document she wrote a brief summary of their conversation and of her thoughts regarding these documents. Then she attached them to an email for Rodolfo Corso. She wrote:

Dear Rodo,

I hope that you're well. You were asking about García, and here he is. I can't do anything else because I've made certain promises. But I imagine that you'd be delighted to see that bastard's face again. Good luck and take care. Love, Verónica.

On Monday morning the first thing she did was take out a bottle of Rutini from the cupboard and go down to the front hall. As she had guessed, Marcelo was there. He wasn't sweeping because he couldn't use his right arm, but he was still overseeing the final stage of the repairs to the entrance. Verónica gave him the bottle of wine.

"Today isn't our anniversary."

"It doesn't matter, I owe you a whole cellar full."

And finally that day she returned to the newsroom, before the others, because she didn't want to arrive when everyone

378

else was already there. She was afraid that they would burst into applause, like in one of those Hollywood movies when someone returns from waging battle. Gradually her colleagues appeared, greeting her with affection. The only one who seemed less than effusive was Álex Vilna. He must be resentful because she had wrecked his car and didn't have the slightest intention of paying for the damage with sex. Patricia arrived and greeted her as though she had never been away. She reminded her that at two o'clock that afternoon there would be an editorial meeting with all the writers from the section. Verónica realized that she had nothing prepared, and no ideas for a piece. She checked the time. It was a quarter to two. She had fifteen minutes to put together a pitch. Like any journalist worth her salt, that meant she had ten minutes left over to invent three or four proposals that would convince any editor.

V

They got on the 114v bus on Zelarrayán and Albariño and didn't get off until they had crossed the Sarmiento railway on Avenida Segurola. They retraced their steps for a few yards and got into the space between the walls of the buildings and the tracks. It was hot. The midday sun hit hard and, even though summer hadn't arrived, you could feel it coming. Dientes and El Peque were wearing the Atlanta shirts that Supergirl had sent them. Martina was wearing a Los Piojos T shirt from their album *Civilización*. It had a strange illustration on it, like a devilish face.

They walked along beside the line, scuffing their feet or kicking the loose stones. The tracks, like the sky, were clear and the rails shone with the reflection of the sun's rays.

"I don't know why you're wearing Atlanta shirts."

"They're a present from Supergirl."

"Ah, her. She only gave me some chocolates."

"You're not in the superteam, just your dad and us."

"What am I in, then?"

They walked a few more yards then stopped to rest in the shade supplied by some trees.

"Right," said Martina, taking a deep breath and reprising, apparently, an earlier conversation. "So how did it work exactly?"

Dientes and El Peque stepped out of the shade and stood on the tracks.

"It was like this, see? We stood beside one another."

The boys adopted the stance of goalkeepers before a free kick.

"Both at the same point. You couldn't go in front or behind."

"And you could see the train coming from far away because it's got a light on the front."

"An enormous headlight."

"No, it was two lights."

"And you had to wait."

"As long as you could. Without shitting yourself."

"Then, when the train was really, really close, you jumped to the side. Like this."

At which Dientes leaped off the rail and rolled onto the ground. El Peque then did the same, but he fell onto some sleepers on the other line. They got up and looked at Martina, as though waiting for her approval or admiration.

"What a stupid game."

"You're saying that because you never did it. There's a reason why they never ask girls to jump."

"It was just for men, not girls."

"Ah, just for brave men like you. Supergirl, save me, Supergirl!"

"That was Dientes."

"I didn't shout like that. She just turned up when I was running back."

Far away, in the direction of Plaza Miserere, they could see a train. Dientes and El Peque walked over to where Martina was and stood there. The train came closer and the boys watched it wordlessly. When it drew level with them it made a deafening noise and the ground shook underneath all three of them. They could hardly see the people sitting behind the windows in the compartments. The train rushed by, creating a warm breeze. Dientes grabbed a stone and threw it after the train. Then El Peque did the same.

"I won. I threw it further."

"Shall we go?" Martina said.

They walked back along the gravel path. El Peque played in the middle of the track, jumping over the sleepers. Dientes and Martina paid him no attention. They reached the railway crossing and turned right. Somebody, seeing where they were coming from, shouted:

"You shouldn't go on the tracks, it's dangerous."

They agreed, to escape a lecture, and kept on walking. On Calle Yerbal the cars and pedestrians sloped by at a weary pace befitting the hot afternoon.

"I've got ten pesos," said Dientes, taking a crumpled note out of his pocket. "We can buy a Coke or three ice creams."

"Coke."

"Coke."

"Here or back home?"

"Let's go home," said Martina.

They walked to the bus stop, counting out coins for the journey home. Dientes on one side, El Peque on the other and Martina in the middle. Scuffing their feet and contemplating the city and the people with indifference.